THE TEMPLE
OF THE
THREE WHISPERS

BOOK SIX:

THE CITY BEYOND MEMORY

BRIAN HARMON

The Temple of the Three Whispers
Book Six: The City Beyond Memory

ISBN: 978-1-945559-32-7

Don't miss these other great books by Brian Harmon!

The Temple of the Blind series:

The Box (Book I)
Gilbert House (Book II)
The Temple of the Blind (Book III)
Road Beneath The Wood (Book IV)
Secret of the Labyrinth (Book V)
The Judgment of the Sentinels (Book VI)

The Temple of the Three Whispers series:

The Lady of Cedric's Cove (Book I)
Circles in Hermes' Footsteps (Book II)
Misplaced in Mysteria (Book III)
The Denselands (Book IV)
The Impassible Wall (Book V)
The City Beyond Memory (Book VI)
The Keeper's Dollhouse (Book VII)
Priestess of Ruin (Book VIII)
The Temple of the Three Whispers (Book IX)
Whispers in the Murk (Book X)

The Rushed series:

Rushed (Book 1)
Rushed: The Unseen (Book 2)
Rushed: Something Wicked (Book 3)
Rushed: Hedge Lake (Book 4)
Rushed: A Matter of Time (Book 5)
Rushed: All Fun and Games (Book 6)
Rushed: Something Wickeder (Book 7)
Rushed: Evancurt (Book 8)
Rushed: Relic (Book 9)

Hands of the Architects trilogy:

Spirit Ears and Prophet Sight (Book 1)
Pretty Faces and Peculiar Places (Book 2)
Broken Clocks and Amber Threads (Book 3)

For Aunt Reva – thanks for being a fan!

Chapter 1

"Vampires," insisted Corey. He was standing there, his pudgy hand stuffed into a full-size bag of barbeque potato chips, the afternoon sunlight filtering down through the summer leaves around him.

"Why would vampires control the *internet?*" asked Violet. She was sitting on a tree limb, twelve feet above the ground, staring down at him in her dirty dress, her sneaker-clad feet kicking back and forth, her long, raven hair blowing in the breeze. "What do those two things even have to do with each other?"

"Gotta keep up with changin' times," he replied with his mouth full.

"But they're *vampires*," she pressed. "They're, like, magical and stuff."

"It's a twenty-four-hour world now," he insisted, nodding as if he simply knew these sorts of things at only ten years old. "Can't just sneak around at night anymore. People'll notice. Too dangerous."

"So their solution was to take over the internet?"

"Maybe. Or maybe it was them who *invented it.*"

She was amazed at how his brain worked. He was always coming up with crazy ideas she'd never heard of before. Yesterday he was trying to convince her that aliens were behind all the world's biggest fast-food chains. And earlier this week he was going on about how all the most famous monuments were actually storehouses for weapons of mass destruction and how the government used major sporting events to brainwash people.

He stuffed another handful of chips into his mouth, seemingly having made his point about vampires being the internet overlords, and she turned her attention out over the forest.

This was her father's recreational property, deep in the hills and forests of Southern Missouri. There was a beautiful vacation home on a private lake big enough to ski on, which was pretty cool, but what she and Corey liked best was the hundreds of acres of hunting land that they still hadn't come close to exploring all of.

It was one of her favorite places. She loved the woods. There were hills and gullies and a little creek trickling through the middle of it all. She'd found bluffs to climb on and sand bars to play in. And depending on the time of year there were wild blackberries and raspberries and strawberries and mulberries to find.

Her father's vacations were always worth every skinned knee, sharp thorn and sunburn, as far as she was concerned.

"Someone's over there," said Corey with his mouth full.

She looked down at him, confused. He was staring off into the trees, his pudgy features scrunched together as he crunched on his chips. The only other people here were her parents and they were both out on the lake right now. This was private property. No one else should be here. But when she squinted off in the same direction, she saw something disappearing through the foliage. "Deer?" she guessed.

But he shook his head. "Person."

"You sure?"

"Mm-hm. Upright."

She sat there on the limb, staring out into the leafy forest, trying to catch another glimpse, but it had moved too far away. "Should we follow them?" she whispered loudly.

"Mm-hm," he replied without having to think about it. He was already moving, his hand still rummaging in his chip bag.

She dropped down through the branches the same way she went up, her every movement quick and graceful, as always, without a hint of fear.

There shouldn't be anyone out here in these woods. There was a groundskeeper who maintained the place, but he usually wasn't around when they were staying here. And there were security fences and active cameras encircling the entire perimeter of the property, making it impossible for anyone to just wander in by mistake. The very idea of someone lurking around despite all that should've sent them running to tell someone.

But Violet and Corey weren't like other kids, not in a great many ways.

They set off through the underbrush, Corey in the lead, ever-careful not to let any branches snap back and hit her. (He'd always looked out for her, for as long as she could remember.) Deeper into the shadowy forest they ventured, down a sloping valley between two low hills and under a dead tree that had fallen across it.

She was starting to wonder if it might only be an ordinary deer after all, that his imagination was running wild on him, but then she caught sight of the figure they were pursuing, visible for only a second or two through a gap in the brush. It did, in fact, look like a person, tall and thin, with no shirt and pale skin.

Something about the sight seemed wrong, but she couldn't quite put her finger on it.

Corey pushed on ahead of her for a moment longer, catching up to where she glimpsed it, then stopped and looked up at the trees above them.

"Where'd the guy go?" she whispered.

"Not a guy."

"What?" She frowned up at him, confused. Were they following a woman? Because what kind of woman would be wandering around with no shirt on?

"Not *human*. Too tall."

"What're you talking about?"

He pointed up at a branch ten feet off the ground. "Head was almost as high as that," he explained. "Nobody's that tall."

"You're seeing things," she informed him.

"Know what I saw," he muttered and pushed onward.

She trailed after him, her face scrunched up. Corey had a very active imagination, but he didn't tell lies. What if he was right? Just what were they following? And why was it here in these woods?

"Went this way."

The path ahead of them was growing narrow, the hills on either side becoming steeper and rockier with each step they took, until they were walking between two stone bluffs. He pushed through the brush and ducked under more fallen trees. She was having trouble keeping up with him. She was about to tell him to slow down when he abruptly stopped.

"Cool…" he sighed.

She caught up to him again and peered around him. The bluffs came together at the base of the gully up ahead. At the point where the two met, there was a gaping cave entrance almost as big as a garage door.

"In there?" she whispered, uncertain. "You sure?"

He nodded. "Saw 'em."

She didn't care much for the idea of following some mysterious, naked, *giant* stranger into a creepy hole in the middle of this wilderness, but Corey was already making his way toward it. "Hold on!" she hissed. "It could be dangerous."

But it was too late. He was already heading for the cave, determined to explore. Before she knew it, they were descending into darkness...

Violet blinked and stared down the stone corridor spread out before her, confused. Did everything just change? Where was she? What was this place? And did she fall asleep for a minute there? It felt like she was dreaming...

It all came rushing back to her. The phone call out of the blue from Gina. All Trails Crossing. January Street. The Lucianna Mysteria. And then that bizarre carriage ride into the Denselands. Albert and Brandy. Getting separated from everyone. And then Andrea and Everett and that enormous wall...

The lake road gate. She remembered standing in front of it while Andrea reached out with the golden spear.

But then everything went wonky. She didn't see her turn the key. She never heard any locks opening. There was no clicking or clanking or grinding, no brilliant light or whoosh of stale air. There were no dramatics whatsoever. The moment the key was all the way inside the lock, she felt a jarring lurch deep in her belly and then she was face down on the stone floor of this shadowy stone passage, her head spinning, feeling a little bit like she'd just stepped off an intense amusement park ride.

"That never gets old!" exclaimed Everett.

She lifted her head and squinted at him. "You're a little *different*, aren't you?"

He flashed her a very unashamed grin. "Seems like it, yeah."

She pushed herself off the ground with a soft huff of a laugh. The kid reminded her of Corey. He had the same sort of endless enthusiasm for all the strange things in the world. Even way back when they were children, he was always up for any adventure she suggested.

Like exploring the forest around her dad's vacation home...

She frowned as she recalled that cave. It was such a vivid dream. And it felt so strangely *familiar*... And yet, she didn't recall ever finding any such cave back then.

Wouldn't she have remembered something like that? It seemed like the sort of thing that would've absolutely enthralled them both.

For some reason, it made her think of that mysterious voice in her head in that bizarre dream beneath the strangely colorful sky that shouldn't have been colorful at all because she had no eyes to see any kind of color with.

(Did...she maybe hit her head at some point?)

12

"Are you two okay?" she asked as she stood up.

"I'm fine," chirped Everett. He was already on his feet, shining his flashlight down the passage ahead of them, clearly eager to see what came next.

She turned to check on Andrea, only to find that she wasn't there. The two of them were standing alone at the end of the stone tunnel. "Andrea?"

"Where'd she go?" wondered Everett.

"Andrea?" she tried again, raising her voice. What happened? Why wasn't she here? The three of them were all standing together when she reached out with the key.

She looked down to see that their feet were still wet from the flooded gouging station. She could see wet footprints on the floor, but only hers and Everett's. There was no sign of Andrea anywhere.

"We couldn't have left her behind," insisted Everett. "She was the one with the key."

She turned and shined her light down the dark passageway laid out ahead of them. It was the only way to go from here. "Aw shit," she groaned.

Chapter 2

"Don't cry..." whispered Andrea through clenched teeth. "Don't cry... Crying won't help..." But she wasn't sure how long she could hold it back. She was standing alone in an unsettlingly familiar corridor of smooth, gray stone, shining her light one way, then the other. Tears kept welling up in her eyes, blurring her vision. How did she even get here? She slid the spear—or leaf or key or Whisper or whatever the heck the thing was supposed to be—into the slot in the wall and felt a sort of roller coaster-like lurch in her belly. It was just like it happened back in the Lady of the Stage Theatre. Except unlike then, she immediately found herself utterly alone. And she was suddenly back in the Temple of the Blind again.

It looked exactly like it did back then. The same smooth stone walls, the same empty darkness, the same unsettling silence. Except that she was never alone in the temple. She was only alone after she landed in that spirit highway thing. She didn't think she could handle being alone inside the temple. It was *way* too scary in there!

Worse still, she'd lost the spear. She didn't remember letting go of it, but when she arrived here, her hand was empty and it was nowhere to be seen. Did she drop it? Did someone steal it?

"Don't cry," she breathed, her voice cracking in spite of her best efforts. "Just don't cry." If she started crying, she didn't know when she might stop. And she couldn't just sit down in this horrible stone passageway and bawl. There were monsters in places like this. Terrible, mean, *murderous* monsters.

She chose a direction and started walking. Within a few minutes, she discovered an intersecting passageway and shined her light both ways. It all looked the same. Same width and height. Same smooth stone. Same shade of gray. It was exactly like that scary labyrinth five years ago. But she *couldn't* be there. The temple was gone. She saw it fall apart with her own eyes. Its pieces rained down around her as she held that freaky portal open for her friends. Was this some kind of hallucination? Like what she went through back in that ghostly cemetery? That felt just as real as this at the time.

A great, wet sob escaped her before she could stifle it. She clasped her free hand over her mouth, half-convinced that the sound would attract one of those hound monsters.

She needed to get ahold of herself. She couldn't let her emotions overwhelm her. This wasn't the place. But she was rapidly losing the battle. Her eyes blurred. She blinked and felt tears streak down her cheeks.

Why did she have to be alone? She didn't want to be alone again.

She took a deep breath and held it as she tried to calm her pounding heart. Nicole would tell her she could handle this. She just had to work through this fresh wave of fear and reset herself. She'd survived being alone like this before. She was braver than she knew.

But it was so frustrating. Why did this keep happening to her?

She closed her eyes and exhaled slowly, releasing the air in a long, quiet breath.

Voices drifted through the unsettling silence.

Her eyes flashed open and she shined her light down each corridor again. She couldn't make out the words, but she was quite sure she could hear people talking somewhere down one of these tunnels. Were Everett and Violet still nearby?

She turned her head and held her breath, listening. It was still there. Little more than muffled syllables echoing through empty corridors, but she couldn't tell which direction it was coming from.

Then it fell silent again.

She stood there a moment, hesitating. Then she steeled herself and called out into the darkness: "Hello?"

Her voice was shockingly loud in the eerie silence. It made her cringe. She couldn't help imagining horrible things turning toward the sound of it, salivating in hungry anticipation. But she had to risk it. What if whoever was there was moving away from her? What if this was her only chance to be found?

"Anybody there?"

Somewhere behind her, someone laughed. The sound startled her, making her twirl around and jab her light in that direction. It wasn't merely that it was unexpected and made her jump. There was something *awful* about the sound of that laugh, something that made the hair stand up on her arms. It wasn't a kind laugh in any way. It was short and hard, practically a bark. It sounded strangely wild. It sounded *cruel*.

"...lost..." whispered the gruff voice of an unseen man from the passage on her right.

Again, her heart was pounding. She could barely catch her breath. That was a bad idea. She shouldn't have drawn attention to herself. She should've kept her mouth shut. These weren't hounds or Caggos or any other manner of temple creature. These were spirits. Like back in that awful hospital.

"…so scared…" whispered the strangely mocking voice of an old woman from somewhere in the darkness ahead of her.

"…all alone…" croaked a terrible growl of a voice that sounded as if it came from the floor at her very feet.

From somewhere behind her came a chillingly unconvincing child's laugh.

And somewhere much farther away, she thought she heard the echoes of a distant scream.

She squeezed her eyes shut again and forced herself to breathe. She was panicking. She was starting to hyperventilate. She needed to get a grip. She wouldn't do herself any favors by getting so worked up that she passed out and hit her head. She wasn't sure if that was a real danger or not, but it was where her terrified brain had led her, as if she needed another thing to worry about.

Still, those voices wouldn't stop. There were so many of them. She could hear muttering and mumbling and crying from every direction, all muddled together so that she could make out no individual words. It was like standing in the middle of a crowded street. There were dozens of them. Hundreds. In every direction. She was surrounded.

What was she supposed to do? Which way did she even start running?

Something touched the back of her bare leg. It was a dreadful sensation, cold and fleshy against the back of her thigh and sliding down the back of her knee.

Her body seemed to react on its own. She screamed and bolted. In an instant she was running down the black passageway in a blind panic, her skin crawling. She turned a corner, then another, with no thoughts of whether it was the right way or the wrong way. She only wanted to be away from whatever horrible thing left that slithery feeling on the back of her knee.

As she ran past an opening in the wall on one side, she glimpsed a shadowy, emaciated form darting past in the next passageway, seeming to keep pace with her. The sight made her scream again.

This wasn't good. She couldn't control her fear. She couldn't get away from these things if she couldn't even keep her mouth shut. But she couldn't help herself. What *was* that thing? It looked like something straight out of a horror movie, all twisted and skeletal.

From somewhere far too close behind her came a chilling wail. The sound made the hair on her arms and neck stand up and she had to clasp her free hand against her mouth in an effort to force back more screams.

So much for not crying, she supposed. She could feel the tears streaming down her face and over her trembling fingers.

Ahead of her, her jolting light flashed across a strange, shadowy shape on the floor and she stumbled to a stop, her hand doing nothing to hold back the scream that boiled up next.

Something horrible was crawling there. It was moving away from her, not toward her. It disappeared back into the gloom before she could fully make out the crumpled shape of broken-looking arms and legs scurrying out of sight, which was good. But it also meant she couldn't go that way, not if she wanted to keep from seeing what the rest of the thing looked like.

She turned and shined her light back behind her. But that was where that awful scream came from…

"…poor child…" purred an eerie growl of a voice that sounded like it came from just over her left shoulder.

Again, she screamed. She couldn't *stop* screaming. These things wouldn't give her a single second to collect herself.

"Run…" sighed a whisper of a voice that seemed to come from directly above her, sending her fleeing again.

"…so young…" purred a voice like rusty nails and broken glass.

Another passage broke away to the right up ahead. She didn't remember seeing that before, but she was fairly sure she was running straight most of that time, so maybe it was the way out. She ran toward it, desperate. And as she turned the corner, she heard the sound of someone sobbing in the passage that continued straight ahead.

She wasn't sure how much more of this she could take. She needed to get out of here. She needed to find her friends.

But she turned another corner and stumbled to a stop.

The passage in front of her was different from those behind her. In spite of the fact that it appeared to be the same stone walls, illuminated by the same flashlight in her hand, it was somehow *darker*, almost like shadows cast by flickering candles, yet she couldn't say precisely why since she could see no actual shadows moving on those surfaces. She blinked back her tears and looked closer, trying to understand exactly what it was she was seeing, but there was nothing there.

"…sweet…" whispered a voice that made her body feel as cold as ice. "…flesh…"

She shivered hard and twirled around, convinced that something terrible was right behind her.

"...bone and blood..."

"Leave me alone!" she whimpered, squeezing her eyes shut.

A strange and sinister sound—half laugh and half growl—sent goosebumps up and down her body and she twirled around again, another startled scream escaping her.

There was nothing there. And yet there *was*. It wasn't something she could see with her eyes. It was something she *felt*.

That passage was all wrong. She was sure of it. That was where all these horrible voices were coming from. And they were trying to herd her there. They *wanted* her to go there. If she tried going that way, there was no telling what might happen to her.

She needed to find another way.

But when she turned around, something was blocking the way back. A strange, silvery mist was creeping across the floor toward her.

She took a step back from it, closer to the all-wrong passageway behind her. She was going to have to make a choice, it seemed. This mysterious, ominous mist or the shadowy corridor.

A terrified whimper escaped her as she turned and fled down the not-right tunnel and deeper into the shadows.

Chapter 3

"The city's too big for me to see all of it," said Gina.

"Understandable." Albert didn't think it'd be as easy as her simply pointing to the temple entrance. But it was worth asking. Violet and Nicole both told them that Gina was uniquely psychic. *She just* knows *what's in her surroundings,* he recalled, remembering the way Nicole described it. *Like a human radar or something.*

He tried accessing his own psychic eye while Brandy was pressed against him in that archway and wasn't able to glimpse any kind of clear picture. All that came to him was a vague sort of image of those blocky stone structures stretching for miles down into a great depression in the earth and an enormous, towering structure at the very bottom of that depression, jutting up toward the angry heavens. But perhaps that was only his imagination...

"There's something about this storm that makes it hard for me to see much, too," added Gina. "It's distorting things somehow."

The four of them had withdrawn from the storm and backed into the empty passageway where the noise wasn't so loud. Nicole's flashlight was lying on the floor, offering its meager glow. He, Gina and Brandy were crouched around it to discuss how best to continue. Nicole was leaning against the wall a few paces away, still watching the storm.

Something seemed a little off about her. If they were back home, he'd think she was pissed off about something. But here, after all she'd been through, she was probably just tired. If she was anything like him, she was probably feeling demotivated by the fact that, for all their travels and ordeals, all the frights they'd endured, for all the danger they'd faced, they'd only found themselves back at another beginning.

"I can tell that we're on the very edge of it," explained Gina. Her gaze shifted toward the back of the tunnel. "The wall is right there."

Albert watched her, taking in the way her eyes moved, following all the shapes and contours that lay *beyond* these walls. She had lovely eyes, he saw. Soft and brown, like Olivia's. It was a difficult thing to notice, he realized, in worlds where the sun never shined. "And what are you able to see about the layout?"

"Not a lot. But enough to see that it's not really a city."

"Not a city?" asked Brandy, confused.

"Not really," she explained. "There are streets. There are structures that are shaped like buildings, but they're not really buildings. There aren't any doors or windows. No way in or out. No one ever lived here. The entire layout isn't practical. There are streets and walkways that go nowhere. Steps that just end. The whole thing feels like a giant maze."

"Of course it does," grumbled Brandy. "Why would anything be easy?"

"But there's more under us. Lots more."

"Tunnels?" asked Albert.

She nodded. "They go much deeper than I can feel. I couldn't even begin to make sense of them. It's too big. Too complex."

"An underground labyrinth," he sighed, glancing over at Brandy.

"Just like before," she groaned. "Under Briar Hills."

"I could sense the tunnels when I was there, too," Gina recalled. "It was strange. I've never been anywhere else with so much under my feet like that. But even that didn't feel like this."

"Briar Hills has its own labyrinth of tunnels to get through before you even reached the temple," pondered Albert. "Kneede played some part in that. It was his way of hiding it." It was one of the things he realized five years ago when he faced the old man down, trying to buy time for the girls to find and open the door. He didn't understand how he knew those things at the time, but he'd become fairly sure by now that it was the Keeper who gave him that information, using the same kind of psychic connection that the Sentinel Queen used to nudge him in the right direction when he was stumped.

"Don't wander too far," worried Brandy.

Nicole had walked back toward the open archway and was staring out into the storm, her hair blowing in the gusting wind.

Brandy turned and looked at him, a concerned look on her face. He didn't blame her. Something seemed to be bothering their friend. It wasn't like her to be this quiet.

Maybe she was worried about Andrea. *He* certainly was.

"The goddess didn't tell us anything about what to do once we were here," recalled Gina.

Goddess... That still sounded so strange to him. While telling their story, Nicole said she wasn't *really* a goddess. She was just a woman named Ada. But she'd been alive for an impossibly long time and apparently knew everything about everyone...which sort of sounded like a goddess to him… What exactly was the criteria for being a goddess these days, anyway?

"So we're just starting from fucking scratch?" growled Brandy.

"I'm sorry," said Gina.

Brandy blinked at her, confused. "It's not your fault."

"I'm not much help."

"You've already been a ton of help."

Albert remembered Violet saying that Gina was extremely quiet. And Nicole told them she apologized too much. He didn't care much for that. It made him wonder what the poor girl had been through before she came to Briar Hills. It sounded like the behavior of someone who'd grown up abused in some way.

"My abilities aren't reliable in all worlds," she explained. "This is like that. It feels like the storm is somehow blocking me. I may not be very useful here."

Brandy moved closer and grasped her hand. "We're all in this together," she promised. "Usefulness has nothing to do with it."

"That's right," agreed Albert. But when he looked over at where Nicole was standing, she was gone. He sprang to his feet, his heart leaping. "Nicole?"

Brandy was already moving. She rushed after her, calling out for her.

"Wait up!" he shouted.

But she didn't slow down. She ran out into the raging storm and he followed on her heels, determined not to lose sight of her. The cold rain immediately pounded his face and drenched his clothes. He could barely see. Only the irregular flashes of lightning illuminated the hazy landscape enough for him to keep following her.

What was Nicole thinking? Why on earth would she run out into weather like this all alone? Had something happened? Did she see something out here? Or worse, did something grab her while they weren't looking?

No, that couldn't be it. She didn't scream. She never made a sound. Unless the storm drowned her out, but he didn't think so.

Ahead of him, Brandy stopped and shouted Nicole's name into the deafening gale, her voice drowning away almost as soon as it passed her lips. She was trying to shield her glasses from the rain, but it was doing very little. She was as good as blind out here.

He seized her hand and held on for dear life. Then he turned and squinted into the storm. There was no sign of Nicole in any direction.

"Why would she do that?" shouted Brandy.

But he didn't know. It made no sense. Again, he remembered how quiet she'd been since they entered the city. He'd assumed it was just that she was tired and feeling frustrated by the prospect of whatever fresh troubles were waiting for them in this new place. But this wasn't just a little out of character for her. This was simply something she wouldn't do. He could think of no logical reason for it. Something was wrong. And he was kicking himself for taking this long to realize it.

"We have to find her!"

But he pulled her closer to him, holding her back. "We will," he shouted over the noise of the storm. "But we don't know which way she went. We need to think this through."

Gina appeared from behind them and grabbed Brandy's other hand. Then she pointed with Nicole's flashlight toward a shadowy shape visible in a series of lightning flashes. "She went that way."

The three of them hurried in that direction.

Again, Albert felt like an idiot. In his fear of losing sight of Brandy, he'd simply rushed off after her and left poor Gina behind. What if something had happened to her, too?

Although, all things considered, he was fairly sure Gina was the most capable of them all. Her psychic abilities were positively astounding. He might not have been wrong to be more worried about his wife than about her. But he still felt like a jerk...

They were moving downhill, he realized, the runoff rushing past their feet as they hurried onward. He made a mental note to be wary of slippery surfaces.

The shadowy shape ahead of them looked like a building when she first pointed it out in the haze, but just like Gina described back in the dry passage, it had no visible doors or windows. It appeared to be nothing more than a great block of gray stone, like every other surface they could see. It made no sense. What was even the purpose of such a thing? Was there anything inside it? Could it only be entered from the tunnels below?

There are structures that are shaped like buildings, but they're not really buildings, he remembered Gina telling them. *There aren't any doors or windows. No way in or out. No one ever lived here.*

Then why did the creepy cat lady call it a city? Why was it made to *look* like a city?

She led them around the thing that wasn't a building and down what appeared to be a sort of narrow street between several such featureless stone structures.

He couldn't help being reminded of toy building blocks, as if they'd found themselves in some giant child's playroom.

Another structure emerged from the haze of the storm ahead of them. An open archway under what appeared to be a bridge. They hurried under it, out of the pouring rain, where Gina stopped and let go of Brandy's hand.

She wiped at her eyes and turned around, scanning her surroundings. Her long hair was plastered to her face. Her blouse had gone completely transparent, revealing every detail of her modest bra. (But he tried not to notice that. It wasn't very gentlemanly.)

Brandy squinted into the wind and rain, a desperate panic painted across her pretty features. "Where'd she go?"

"She came this way," Gina shouted over the noise, "but I lost her. She just disappeared. I don't get it."

Albert squeezed Brandy's hand. "We'll find her. I promise."

Gina turned and looked back the way they came, then she looked up at the stone archway overhead. She even swept her gaze across the ground in front of her feet as if scanning those many tunnels she spoke of earlier. But finally she met Brandy's worried gaze and merely shook her head.

"I don't understand," Brandy cried over the din of the wind and thunder. She was shivering from the drenching rain, he noticed. Her lips quivered. And when she looked at him, those pretty eyes shimmered with tears.

"I won't stop looking for her," promised Gina. She looked down at the flashlight in her hand. She wasn't a very expressive person, he'd noticed, but right now she looked almost sick with worry. "I won't stop," she said again.

Brandy nodded and hugged her.

"We'll find her," agreed Albert.

Gina wiped at her face again, either at the rain running down it or at tears, it was impossible to tell which, and then she looked out into the rain again. She said something else, but a crash of thunder drowned her out.

"What was that?" shouted Albert.

She turned and met his gaze, her expression tightening. "I said we can't stay here." She pointed into the storm. "There's something moving around out there. Something bad."

He and Brandy both looked up and scanned the hazy downpour again. Lightning flashed, revealing a shadowy skyline looming in front of the towering stone wall of the city behind them.

Gina took hold of Brandy's hand and held on tight. "Stay together. I'll try my best to keep us away from them."

Chapter 4

Nicole stood staring up at the dead tree looming over her. It wasn't a night tree. But it wasn't anything else she quite recognized, either. It had strangely patterned bark and its bare limbs drooped wearily toward the surface of the water from which it grew.

It was a strange sensation. On one hand it was nothing more than a dead and rotting tree. But on the other hand, there was something profound about it, almost awe-inspiring, as if she were staring at one of the great mysteries of the universe. And at the same time, there was something positively *dreadful* about the sight of it.

Everything else in this space was darkness. She wasn't even sure how she was seeing what she was seeing. There was no light source.

And why was she standing in this water? She could feel the cold mud beneath her bare feet, squelching between her toes. It was a deeply unpleasant feeling. What reason could she have had for wading out here like this?

She crossed her arms over her chest and shivered. Had she been naked this whole time? A part of her insisted that she'd taken her clothes off hours ago, back when that freaky, naked man who had no eyes and crawled on the ceiling like some kind of bug took them away from everyone. And yet another part of her was sure that all happened a long time ago, that she was fully dressed only a moment before.

Where did everybody go? How long had she been alone?

Slowly, she tore her eyes from the dead tree and lowered her gaze to the black water. Why couldn't she remember coming to this place? How long had she been standing here? And just where was she?

(*Stay away from the meadow.*)

A terrible fear was slowly overtaking her body. Her mouth had gone dry. This wasn't right. Nothing about this was right.

(*There is nothing for you there but pain and death.*)

Something churned beneath the black surface of the water near the trunk of the tree. She uttered a startled yelp and stumbled backward. The sound of her voice and the splashing was almost deafening in the eerie silence. And the sound of it seemed to stir something up in the stagnant darkness all around her.

She wasn't alone. Unseen things were watching her, *staring* at her. Unnatural things. *Unimaginable* things…

How did she get here? *Why would she come here?* This was no place she ever wanted to be, not back then and certainly not now! She had to get out of here. But which way? She couldn't remember how she got here.

Again, something splashed in the water, this time somewhere farther out in the darkness. She uttered a choked scream and turned to run, but her foot sank deeper into the mud. She teetered for a moment, nearly falling.

(*Just leave us then.*)

She froze, her arms still raised to catch her balance. There was blood spatters on her skin.

(*Just let her die. What do you care?*)

A great, wet sob escaped her. That wasn't fair. She wouldn't do that.

No. This wasn't real. It was some kind of illusion. A dream, even.

Something cold and slimy slithered across the top of her foot. She cried out and tried to scramble away, only to fall and splash into the water. Cold mud squelched under her butt and between her fingers. There were things squirming in that mud. It felt like she was sitting in a great vat of wriggling worms.

She screamed and tried to stand up, but her foot and hand were both stuck. She couldn't pull herself free.

Something large and shadowy broke the surface as it cruised past her, bare inches from her face.

She wrenched her hand free and lifted it out of the water. It was covered in black mud almost to her elbow. And there were unthinkable things crawling over her skin.

She screamed and thrust it into the water, trying to wash it off. But she could feel them crawling over her other arm too. Her feet and legs. Her butt.

Something cold and awful was squirming against the flesh between her legs.

She needed to get up, but she could find no leverage. Every time she tried to push herself up, her hands sank down into that writhing muck.

She couldn't get out.

And she was *sinking*.

The water was up past her waist. She felt its icy touch as it crept over her bare breasts. That awful mud oozed between her thighs. Terrible, squirmy things were crawling up her back.

She cried out for help, but no one was coming. No one else was here. She was all alone in this hellish darkness.

Panic was quickly overwhelming her. Desperate, she began thrashing, struggling to free herself from the mud, but it only made her sink faster. She felt the wormy sludge swallow her hips. Grotesque, squishy things slithered all over her, prodding every inch of her body. Things were worming their way into her armpits and between her breasts, squirming in her hair, wiggling between her thighs, into every crease and crevice.

Now her head was sinking beneath the surface. She stretched her face toward the non-existent sky and screamed one last time.

She was going to drown. She was going to be sucked under this foul, infested water and die here. These filthy, slimy things were going to crawl into every orifice of her body and devour her from the inside out.

Murky, reeking water filled her mouth.

Something slithered into her ear.

The dead branches of that awful tree, the last thing she'd ever see, vanished from sight as the meadow swallowed her whole into its fearsome depths.

She screamed and sat bolt upright in the dark.

"Hey, it's okay!" Keith assured her. He wrapped his arms around her and pulled her close to him. "It was just a dream."

Her heart was pounding in her chest. She could barely catch her breath. Her skin was still crawling with that awful, lingering feeling. She buried her face against his bare chest and sobbed.

That was *terrible*. She'd never had a dream like that in her life. It felt so utterly real. She could still almost *taste* that filthy water on her tongue.

Keith kissed the top of her head and cradled her against him. "I got you," he whispered. "Just take it easy."

She nuzzled forcefully against him, trying to push away all those disturbing images. It wasn't real. It was only her stupid mind fucking with her.

It was probably that nasty business with Glum and his fucking melancholy nightmare apartments. Sinking into that cold mud wasn't so unlike what it felt like when that freak tried to swallow her the last time she was there.

"I got you," Keith assured her again.

She sniffed and pushed the thought from her mind, then reached around his body and squeezed him. He was always so nice to her. She really did miss moments like these.

"I got you…"

Wait…

She opened her eyes, confused. Keith shouldn't be here…

Slowly, she lifted her head and looked up at him.

Hotdog's bloated and rotting face grinned down at her. "I got you!" he snarled.

She tried to scream, but the monster's gory hands were already around her neck, strangling her. She stared up at him, her eyes bulging, and watched as terrible things squirmed from his bloody mouth and nose.

This wasn't real. This couldn't be real. She had to wake up.

But the world swam away from her. Everything faded.

Everything went dark…

Cold…

Silent…

She blinked hard, confused. What was she doing again?

Nicole stood staring up at the dead tree looming over her…

Chapter 5

The thorn was nothing like a key should be, Wayne observed. There was no perfectly sized hole, no tumblers, no latch, no dramatic grinding. There wasn't so much as a click. There was nothing physical about any part of it. Instead, there was a strange lurching sensation deep in the pit of his stomach, a sort of shockwave that passed through his body that sent a bolt of pain through the hole in his shoulder and a startled gasp from Olivia. And then he was suddenly standing at the end of a square tunnel that looked unsettlingly like countless dead-end passages deep inside the Temple of the Blind.

Olivia was clinging tightly to his arm, her chipped nails digging into his skin again, her pretty brown eyes wide and her mouth pressed tightly closed, looking as if she might throw up, which was perfectly understandable if she felt anything like he did at the moment.

"That wasn't pleasant," muttered Keith.

It certainly wasn't. That lurching feeling in Wayne's belly was lingering. He felt like he'd taken too many spins on a playground merry-go-round. He just wanted to lie down and close his eyes for an hour or two.

Olivia nodded, her mouth still pursed as if struggling to maintain her composure.

"Weird," was all Corey had to say about it. He was standing with his considerable bulk leaning against the wall, as if he might yet fall over if he wasn't careful.

Austin, however, didn't seem fazed in the least. He was already on the move, in fact, impatient to be on his way.

"Wait up!" Wayne called after him. "Some of us need a second." He was still holding onto Olivia, making sure she was steady.

But Austin ignored him and kept walking.

"Hey!"

But he never looked back.

"What's with that guy?" asked Keith.

"Rude," agreed Corey.

"To hell with him," decided Wayne as Austin's light dwindled away. He didn't have time to deal with some stranger's nonsense. He had his fiancée to look after. "We didn't need him to get this far. He can just piss off if he's in such a hurry." He shined his light around, scanning the stone walls. There was only the one way to go, but he wasn't eager to simply rush off down that unsettlingly familiar passage. Instead, he turned his light on Olivia. "You okay?"

She nodded that she was fine, but she still hadn't let go of his arm. "Why does it look like the temple in here?" she asked instead.

A good question.

"This was what Andrea was talking about?" asked Keith, surprised. He looked around at the smooth, clean stone, confused. "I pictured something a little more...Indianna Jones, I guess..."

"Kind of an alien vibe 'bout it," observed Corey. "Extraterrestrial base or somethin' like."

Wayne wasn't so sure about that one, but he didn't say so. "The sentinels built it all," he reasoned. "So I guess it makes sense it all looks the same."

"I guess," said Olivia. Finally, she let go of his arm and started to slip the thorn back around her neck, but she stopped and stared at it, confused.

Wayne saw it, too. "Where's the thorn?" he asked.

She never let go of it. She reached out and placed it in the hidden notch in the wall. Then her stomach did a summersault and she ended up here, feeling like she might puke. "I thought I was holding it in my hand..." But it was only the empty chain, with nothing on the end of it. She turned and shined her light at the floor around her. "Where'd it go? Did I leave it in the lock?"

All four of them turned and looked behind them, but the wall there was entirely blank. There was no sign of the round indention that contained the thorn's lock.

"That doesn't make sense," reasoned Wayne. If it was such an important item that it had to be delivered by Erin Laplede at the cost of her very life and then brought all this way through a fairy circle, a magic transforming train and half a universe of nightmare zombie forest, why the hell would it be designed in such a poor way that they could just leave it in the lock?

"Maybe it stays there 'til we're done," reasoned Corey. "So we can get back out."

"That's possible, I guess," said Wayne, but it still didn't feel quite right.

"I hope I didn't lose it," worried Olivia.

He shook his head. "No. Everyone keeps saying the Keeper

knows what he's doing. I'm sure it's supposed to be this way. Let's just keep going." He looked forward again. By now there was no sign of Austin. Even his light had completely vanished. Personally, though, he didn't really care if they never saw the uptight jerk again. What was his deal, anyway? Just who did he think he was?

But then again, a better question was how the hell did he know so much about this place? How'd he get to the gate so quickly? How'd he know about the thorn and the locks and the City Beyond Memory? Because no one had bothered filling *them* in on any of those details.

The four of them set off through the darkness.

He glanced over at Corey. "Back on the other side of the gate, *you* had the answer when I asked what would happen if we opened it and not everyone had arrived."

He nodded. "Left behind."

"How'd you know that?"

"Dunno. Just knew it somehow. Can't explain it."

"Like how Everett could see the mushrooms and smudges in Gutler's Weep," reasoned Olivia.

Wayne nodded. She had a point. It was likely that Corey was here for the same reason Everett was there.

"That guy knew a lot more than me, though," pondered Corey. "Dunno what his thing is."

"That guy was weird," said Keith.

"Somethin' strange 'bout him," Corey went on. "Feels funny. Like how *this place* feels funny. Can't explain it."

Wayne, for one, didn't like it. Maeve said that someone was interfering in everything. What if *he* was the "chaotic energy" that she warned them about back in her inner circle?

But if that were the case...then why in the hell would Max and Nadia have brought him here on the train? No, that didn't make sense...

Did it? He didn't exactly know anything about those two. Would it be any different than telling them to stay on the stone road and not mentioning that sandstone-like labyrinth they were going to have to navigate?

God, he was exhausted.

Ahead of them, the passageway ended in a T-shaped intersection. Austin could have gone left or right from here, and there was no sign of his light for them to follow. Thinking back now, they probably should've taken advantage of the fact that the jerk seemed to know exactly where he was going and kept up with him...

But when he reached the intersection and shined his light one way, then the other, he found only two dead ends waiting for them. "Wait… What the *fuck*?"

"Where's Rude Guy?" asked Corey.

"That's not possible," said Keith, turning and looking back the way they came. "There's nowhere he could've gone."

Olivia looked up at Wayne, her eyes wide and terrified. She didn't need to say what she was thinking. He was thinking it, too. It meant there was also nowhere for *them* to go. They were trapped in here.

"Don't make sense," muttered Corey. He walked up to one of the dead ends and shined his light over the stone.

"He came this way," reasoned Wayne. "We watched him."

"Secret passage," decided Corey. His big hand was prodding at the stone, searching for a switch of some sort.

"Maybe," agreed Keith. He turned and checked the other dead end. "But there's nothing here. It's not like there's a bookshelf or a fireplace or something."

Wayne recalled the way the tower at the end of the first temple's labyrinth fell apart after Nicole opened it. The smooth, gray stone simply dropped in sections, creating a passage leading down and under the chamber. If there *was* a passage around here that Austin used, it could easily blend in perfectly with the rest of the stone, meaning they could've walked right past it. He turned and looked back the way they came.

"Wait…" sighed Olivia. "Something's wrong."

He turned and watched as those pretty brown eyes grew wider and wider with mounting concern.

Something was about to happen, he realized.

The hair on the back of his neck stood up and he swung his light around. Was this some kind of trap? Were they in danger?

Olivia let out a startled gasp and rushed forward, wrapping her arms around him. In the same instant there was a reverberating boom that shook the very stone beneath his feet and a sudden rush of air in the otherwise stagnant passageway.

He stood there a moment, confused. The passages leading left and right were both gone, along with Keith and Corey, who had each been inspecting one of them. Instead of an intersection, he and Olivia were now standing there alone, staring down an open passage continuing straight ahead.

"What happened?" she squeaked.

"It shifted," he realized. It happened so quickly, it was almost impossible to see, but he managed just a glimpse of the wall in front of them slamming downward and opening up the new passage.

"Keith..." she gasped. "Corey!"

He stepped up to the wall that used to be a passage leading to the left and banged his fist on it. It barely made a sound. "Keith?" He called. "You okay in there?"

"Corey?" Called Olivia. She turned and looked back at him, her eyes wide with dread. "You don't think it crushed them, do you?"

"What? *No.* I'm sure they're..." He shook his head. "Why would the Keeper do that after all the work he did to get us all here?"

"Corey?" she called again. "I can't hear anything."

"It's solid," he said, banging his fist against the stone. "Thick. They could be screaming their heads off on the other side and we'd never hear them."

Olivia whimpered at the thought.

"But they're fine. I'm sure of it. A path opened up for us. I'm sure it did the same for them, too."

She didn't like it. She was pressing against the wall, as if she had any chance of moving it. He could hear her sniffling. Tears weren't far away. And he didn't blame her.

"It's like back in Gutler's Weep," he murmured. "Pulling us apart. Like it *wants* us to be alone..." He reached out and took her hand. "Don't let go of me. Not for *any* reason."

She nodded, terrified, and pressed herself closer to him.

He stared into the newly opened passage, his thoughts churning. Everett. Keith and Corey. Even Austin. Why did everyone keep leaving them? And did the Keeper intend to tear Olivia from him again, too, before this was over?

"I hope they're okay," whimpered Olivia.

"They're tough guys," he assured her. "Everything's worked out so far. We've just got to keep pushing forward."

She squeezed him and buried her face against his shirt again. "I don't want to do this anymore."

"Me neither." He squeezed her in return and kissed the top of her head. "So let's hurry up and get this crap over with."

She didn't reply. She didn't even move. She just stood there, clinging to him for several seconds, gathering her strength. Then, at last, she nodded and took a shaky breath.

Still clinging tightly to his arm, she allowed him to lead her forward.

If all this was really the Keeper's way, then this was simply where they were always meant to end up. They'd already conquered Gutler's Weep. They'd crossed the fairy circle and boarded the pale train. They'd navigated the stone road and passed through the impenetrable wall. This was the place they'd been trying so hard to reach, where all the scary things had led them. Through the gate with the lock that fit Yggdrasil's thorn.

This was the City Beyond Memory.

But he couldn't help wondering what new nightmares were awaiting them in these dark passageways and what they'd be forced to endure before they'd be allowed to finally go home.

Chapter 6

Keith wasn't sure what happened. One second, he was taking a close look at a stone wall in a dead-end passageway, trying to determine if there was some kind of secret door, of all things, as if he'd found himself in an episode of *Scooby Doo*. The next, the very floor dropped out from under his feet and he found himself plummeting through a black void.

He had just enough time to wonder if this was the end for him, if he was about to have his brains dashed across the stone floor several stories below, then he plunged feet first into a deep body of cold water. The unexpected impact jolted him, sending thunderbolts of pain through both the injury in his side from the bone monsters and his chewed-up forearm, as well as forcing a great deluge of water straight up his nose and into his screaming sinuses.

Dazed and half paralyzed by the pain, he kicked and clawed his way back up from the black depths for what felt like an eternity, until he was convinced he'd run out of breath and drown. But then he broke the surface, gasping and coughing and splashing.

Where was he? He turned all the way around, searching his surroundings, but he couldn't see. Everything was dark. In his startled panic, he'd dropped his flashlight.

Blinking back tears from his flooded sinuses, he looked down into the water beneath him and watched the glow of it sinking deeper and deeper. *Much* too deep, he immediately knew, to ever retrieve it. Was this some kind of underground lake? Was the stone labyrinth built on top of it?

Or was this like what kept happening back in the Denselands? Did he only think he fell straight down when in reality he'd been transported somewhere completely different?

Everything's crinkled, he recalled Gina warning them. He didn't understand what that meant when she first said it, but he thought he was starting to now. Everything out there was crumpled and compacted under the weight of all those dead worlds. And this place, here inside that impossible, impassible wall, was at the very center of it all. He probably couldn't even begin to comprehend what kinds of physics could be at work in a place like this.

But maybe he didn't have to comprehend anything. Maybe he wasn't lost at all.

As he watched his light dwindle far below him, he remembered something else someone said to him: *Where light fades into hazy depths, divide the feuding brothers.*

His light was definitely fading into hazy depths right now. As he watched, it winked out of sight completely. Cat Lady knew he was going to fall into this place. She was telling him that this was where he was supposed to be. But what the hell did "divide the feuding brothers" mean?

He didn't know what she expected him to do. He could only hope it would make sense in time. For now, he could only swim and hope that he was closer to land than he was to the bottom of this watery eternity.

Chapter 7

Corey was lying on his back in the empty passage, his flashlight lying beside him.

A moment ago, he was on his feet, searching for a switch to activate the secret passage he was convinced must be there. It was the only thing that made any sense, after all. They stood there and watched that rude Austin guy come this way. He had to have gone somewhere. And he was right! Although, he wasn't sure whether he found the secret passage or if the secret passage found him.

He wasn't aware of activating a switch. He didn't feel anything click or slide or turn or snap. He just sort of fell. Or, more precisely maybe, the floor fell out from under him and he fell with it. This entire eight-foot section of passageway was the same one he was just in. But now it had dropped into a space that was waiting directly below it. Now there was a dead end where there used to be an intersection and there was a passage where there used to be a dead end.

He didn't fall very far, thankfully. Maybe ten feet, give or take. Enough to bump his head and knock the wind out of him. Nothing he couldn't handle. He was tough.

It was a clever mechanism based off little more than gravity and balance, he found himself understanding. The perfect fit of the stone and the laser-like precision with which this place was constructed made it appear seamless and unmovable, but with an amazingly simple trick, the stone labyrinth all around them could be rearranged in very significant ways with only a few of these hidden mechanisms.

He still didn't know how it was that he understood these things. It wasn't as if he was able to see what happened. The entire process started and was over in an instant. And he was falling through most of it. It was a startling, jarring experience that left no room for close observation. But once it was over and he was lying here staring up at the ceiling, he just simply found that he knew what happened. It was as if he'd always known about things like this and just hadn't happened across them before.

(*I remember this place.*)

He frowned as an old memory stirred briefly in the back of his mind, but vanished again before he could fully grasp it. Something about stone like this.

He thought back to their first encounter with it, way back in Minnesota. A single stone at the bottom of the hole where they found the tokkatoks… Except…*was* that the first time? For a moment there, he thought he could recall an even earlier time…a dark and mysterious place *full* of that stuff…

But that wasn't possible. He wouldn't have forgotten something like that.

It was only his imagination. He pushed the thought away.

Again, he recalled that cold Minnesota January. And then again the following year in Arkansas, when Violet passed out and gave him a fright. He didn't understand how this stuff worked then. But on the other hand, those stones didn't really *do* anything. They were just markers of some sort. The same with the carriage house and the shadow road, the purpose of which were pretty obvious. They somehow created shortcuts through the weird physics of the Wood, which was beyond his understanding, but that was more about that strange forest than about these "sentinels," as Albert called them.

Who *were* the sentinels? How were they able to do all these things? Because it wasn't merely the ingenious design. The use of gravity as the main force behind these mechanisms meant that they could only be activated once. There was no room for a misfire.

He sat up, rubbing at the back of his head, and scanned the stone surfaces all around him.

No… It wasn't *just* gravity and balance. There was something else involved, too. The manner in which the mechanisms had stayed in place for all this time. And how, exactly, they were triggered. He could *almost* grasp how those things worked, he could understand that it was relatively *simple*…but something was missing. Something in the fundamental *science* of it all. It was as if he were missing an entire law of physics. Something worked in this place that didn't work in his own universe. Something basic, but utterly absent. The very *notion* of it was missing.

He'd already considered that there were entire concepts in past worlds that could never be dreamed up in their own world because the very laws of nature had changed. Whatever the other element in these ancient workings might have been, it was like that. He wasn't going to be able to imagine it, much less replicate it. And yet it still worked here. And after all this time.

"Cool," he muttered to himself as he rose to his feet and shined his light into the open passage waiting for him.

It looked as if he were on his own again. That was fine. He'd be okay. Hopefully he didn't worry the others too much. He didn't bother trying to call out to them. He was sure they'd already tried yelling and he hadn't heard so much as a mutter through all this stone. And it wasn't as if the "secret passage" was going to open again. He'd already determined that it was a one-time sort of deal.

He started walking, eager to see what awaited him up ahead.

Chapter 8

Austin walked through the empty passageways beneath the City of the Blind without looking where he was going. He didn't need to. He knew the way. He'd *always* known the way. Instead, he kept his light aimed at his book. He was almost done with it. These were the final chapters.

He turned down a passage that branched off to the right and heard the rumble and thud of the walls rearranging themselves behind him.

This was his path, laid out for him by the Faceless Ones eons ago. For him and him alone. Like the hidden path through the Denselands that bypassed the stone road's trials. The others had their own paths to follow. That was their responsibility. It had nothing to do with him.

He turned the page and pressed on, ever deeper into the darkness, alone as always, as it was meant to be.

Chapter 9

Everett had found himself in quite a few tough spots by now, each one more dangerous than the last. Landing in that broken place inside the fairy circle. Being sent away from Olivia and Wayne by the puzzle box and stranded in the Red Waste. Getting swarmed by the potato men and waking up locked in that suffocating, metal container. He'd faced a zombie bear, waste walkers and that horned monstrosity in the forest of copper rods. But somehow, this was the first time he'd truly found himself feeling unsettled.

He didn't like that Andrea had disappeared. Getting *himself* lost was one thing, but losing *her* felt wrong, even though it was no different, he supposed, from losing Olivia back in Gutler's Weep. Except he really didn't think there was anything dangerous in those woods at the time. He'd been there all day and hadn't seen a thing, after all. There were almost certainly unknown dangers lurking here on this side of that massive wall. And if he and Violet were both here, then Andrea, wherever she ended up, was very likely all alone now.

Violet ran her hand over the wall that was blocking the way back. There was no sign of the lock that brought them here. It was impossible to tell if it was a part of that enormous wall they found at the end of the lake road or just a random, *dead-end* wall. It seemed as if inserting the key inside the lock teleported them to the other side in the same way the puzzle box moved him around. But why did it split them up? Or did she, by some strange twist of fate, somehow get left behind?

It was a troubling thought. He suddenly found it far too easy to imagine her stranded all alone back there at that gate, with strange and dangerous creatures closing in around her.

No. What sort of sense would that make? Everything that happened here was supposed to be part of the Keeper's grand design. That was part of the knowledge the puzzle box forced into his head. There was no way he'd just abandon her out there.

No. That simply wouldn't make any sense. Would it?

As he watched, Violet reached into her shirt and withdrew what appeared to be a piece of blue glass hanging at the end of a necklace. She stepped back from the wall and lifted it to her eye, peering through it.

"What's that?"

"Complicated," she replied. She turned around, still peering through the shard at the walls on either side.

"Okay…"

"Sometimes it shows me things that are hidden."

"Cool. What's it showing you now?"

"Nothing," she spat, frustrated. She let go of it, letting it fall back to her chest, and then turned and pressed her hands against the wall again.

"Bummer," he said. And he meant it. He thought for a moment that the magic shard of glass might be just the thing they needed to find Andrea.

"The gatehouse isn't just what it appears to be," said Violet, seemingly muttering to herself. "Sometimes it changes. Hidden mechanics. Technology from a lost world. Impossible to explain, but still operational…" She frowned at herself. "I don't know how I know that…but I do…"

"That's a thing," said Everett. "Just knowing stuff. Like, I know this is the second gatehouse. What Andrea and her friends call 'temples.' It's sort of like a trial, I guess. We have to work together to solve it and find whatever's here."

"Doors," mumbled Violet.

"What?"

"That's what's here. What we're supposed to do. Find and open a door."

Everett nodded. "The Oblivion Doors." He wasn't sure where that knowledge came from, whether he'd known it since that painful download of information back in the stone circle or if it only just popped up now when she mentioned it, but he simply knew it to be true.

She turned and looked at him, her pretty face pinched with a combination of deep thought and worry. "Oblivion Doors…" she sighed. "Yeah. I've heard that somewhere before …" Then she looked up at him, those green eyes focusing sharply. "Who told you those things? Was it someone in a dream?"

"Dream?" he asked, confused. "No. I mean, I don't think so…" He frowned at himself. *Was* that like a dream? "I got it from a puzzle box."

Now it was her turn to look confused. "What, like from *Hellraiser?*"

"What's that?"

"Seriously? Do you not watch movies?"

"Not really. I was kind of a shut-in growing up."

"Huh..." She turned and looked at the wall again as she processed this. "Do you have this puzzle box on you now?"

"No. The Eeshee took it."

"The *what?*"

"It's kind of a long story."

"Okay."

She didn't tell him he sounded crazy, which was a little surprising. Even Andrea, with all she'd been through and seen, had told him he sounded crazy. And he could hardly blame her. Because he *did* sound crazy. But Violet only turned her back on the unhelpful dead end and started down the empty passageway ahead of them. Either she'd simply accepted that all weird things were possible or she'd decided it better to simply drop the subject.

He hesitated a moment, unsure that they should leave this spot just yet, but he knew it was pointless. He doubted that Andrea was just held up in traffic. The gate used some kind of lost technology to transport them instantaneously. She clearly wasn't here. She wasn't calling out from anywhere nearby. He already knew through the puzzle box that this place was enormous. It wasn't called the *Village* Beyond Memory. It was far bigger than all of New York City. And at least four times as deep as the tallest skyscrapers in the world were high. They had almost no chance of finding her, but they had *no chance whatsoever* if they stayed here. Their best chance of seeing her again was to simply find that door and finish what the Keeper sent them here to do.

He followed close behind Violet, his eyes open, alert for anything that might separate them.

"So tell me what you know," she said after a minute or two. "About where we are."

"Let me see..." He pondered it for a moment, trying to sort through all those alien thoughts the puzzle box poured into his brain. "I can't remember all of it. It was a lot. And it kind of comes back as I need it. But I do know we should be inside those huge walls now. That means we're inside the City Beyond Memory. I know it's *huge*. And it's an unsolvable maze."

"If it's unsolvable, how are we supposed to solve it?"

He creased up his face at this. It was a good question. "I mean, I guess...it's unsolvable to anyone who isn't *us*? Like, each of us brought something that unlocks or activates the way to the door. If *any* of us didn't make it, we might not ever be able to leave here."

"Well *that's* a shit deal."

"It's fine," he insisted. "The Keeper plans for everything, so it's pretty much impossible for us not to succeed."

"I'm not sure I share your optimism."

"You don't have to. I know what I know. And I'm pretty sure what *I* know is how to see spirits."

"You mean like Andrea?"

"No, she sees ghosts."

Violet glanced over her shoulder at him. "That's...the same thing."

"Not necessarily. She sees *human* spirits. Ghosts. I see *non-human* spirits. Fairies. Potato men. Eeshees, I guess. And toothpick men. Them too. Unless there's only the one of those. I don't really know for sure." The toothpick man... He'd forgotten about him in all that excitement.

(*Break the circle. For her sake.*)

He shrugged it off and said. "All sorts of stuff, I guess."

"Okay then," sighed Violet.

"What about you? What do *you* know? And you said it came to you in a dream? Because that's pretty cool."

"I don't know if it was a dream or not. I feel like I'm still missing some important details. But I know we eventually need to make our way to the highest point in the city. There's something we need to find there. The door, I think. Or at least something we need to open it."

"I think so, too. Except no one will be able to get there until all the conditions are met."

She glanced back at him again, one neat eyebrow raised. "Conditions?"

"I'm not sure what they are, but I feel like there are conditions. Like, locks that need opened or switches that need switched. Something like that."

She considered this for a moment and then nodded. "Yeah. That sounds right to me, too."

"Maybe that was why Andrea was taken away. Because she had something else she was supposed to do."

"Maybe..." Violet stopped walking and stared into the darkness looming ahead of them. Then she turned and grabbed his arm, pulling him closer to her. "I don't give a shit what the Keeper wants us to do. We stick together until this is done."

Everett felt a strange sort of flutter rush through him at suddenly being so close to her. He wasn't used to being around people, much less women. His mother had made sure of that. And as she pulled him onward again, he couldn't help feeling a flush rise into his face. "Okay…" was all he could manage to say.

Chapter 10

Andrea didn't want to be here. The wrongness of this passage only grew worse the deeper she went. She was trembling. Tears wouldn't stop streaming down her face.

She could no longer make out individual words. The ghostly voices had melded into a constant, ominous murmur with no discernable origin and random screams and wails that seemed to drift from somewhere far away. Instead, she found her head invaded by terrible thoughts. Every time she blinked, she saw blood and chaos. Crystal-clear images flashed through her head in vivid detail. Faces contorted in terror. Bodies sprawled on the ground. Glimpses of unthinkable *things* lunging from the darkness, teeth and claws flashing before her eyes.

She wanted to leave, but every time she looked back, she could just glimpse that strange, silvery mist lurking at the edge of her light, following her, pushing her forward.

Where was she being taken? What were they going to do to her when she reached the end of this horrible passageway?

She wiped at her eyes and kept moving. She didn't know what the silvery mist was, but she didn't have the courage to face it. She could only trudge onward and hope she didn't find herself trapped against a haunted dead end.

Again, something in that darkness ahead of her screamed, making her jump. A great sob bubbled up from deep inside. Why did she have to deal with this alone? She *hated* being alone! It was the worst!

"You're not alone," said a clear voice spoken directly into her ear.

She jumped and twirled around, jabbing her light into the darkness behind. Who said that? Who was there?

But there was no one else here. No one she could see, anyway…

She sniffled and wiped the tears from her cheeks. She was *certain* she didn't just imagine that. It was nothing like those other voices. It couldn't have been clearer if Nicole or Violet were speaking right to her face.

It wasn't Ghost Girl, she didn't think. It didn't sound like her voice. Which was good, since Ghost Girl turned out to be a backstabbing bitch who sold her friends out to Glum and trapped her in that dead spirit highway thing.

But then again, did ghosts always sound the same? What did she really know about being dead?

Something had changed, she realized. She stared into the empty corridor in front of her as she listened to the sudden silence. All those other voices fell quiet the moment this new one made itself heard, as if it were the one in charge.

The idea of a *boss* ghost was absolutely terrifying, and certainly the last thing she needed to deal with at this point, but that was only her betraying imagination still trying for some unfathomable reason to make the situation worse. This voice was different from the others. Though it had only spoken three words, it sounded kind. It sounded sincere. And more than that, it sounded *familiar*. She'd heard this voice somewhere recently.

She felt an icy prickling sensation on the back of her neck and turned around, thrusting her light into the corridor behind her. "Who's there?" she asked, her voice a bare squeak of a whisper.

That silvery mist had crept closer to her.

A fresh wave of fear washed through her and she took an involuntary step backward. But even as she felt that jolt of fear pass through her heart, she remembered where she heard the voice before. It was back inside the gouging station, in that dangerously unstable room. It was the voice in her head that told her she was the only one who could bring Violet back.

"Stop being afraid of them," said the misty vision drifting toward her.

Easy for her to say! She took one more step backward and then steeled herself to hold her ground.

As she watched, the thing that had been crawling along the floor slowly stretched toward the ceiling. She found that she could make out the shape of a dress in that silvery mist. Long and silky, luxurious, like something she might have seen on the red carpet.

"Trust me," pleaded the woman in the haze.

Strangely, she *did* find herself wanting to trust this voice. But should she? Or was this some kind of trick? She *had* recently been betrayed by another ghost who pretended to be friendly. This particular voice helped her wake up Violet, but that other voice saved her from Hotdog Creep. Twice.

It still didn't make sense to her, but now wasn't the time to try making sense of the insane actions of a crazy dead girl.

She glanced behind her. Did she even really have a choice? Was it possible to outrun a ghost? In a *labyrinth* of all places? She didn't know how much of what she knew about ghosts was real and how much was fiction, but that silver mist looked like something that could probably pass through walls if it wanted to.

And she *really* didn't want to be alone again…

"You're not alone," the spirit again assured her.

When she turned her light back onto the apparition in front of her, however, she found that *everything* had become a silvery mist. It was taking up the entire corridor.

No… It was right in her face!

She stepped backward again, trying to put distance between herself and it, but it wasn't just in front of her. It was everywhere. It *enveloped* her.

She felt lightheaded. She tried to cry out, but all that escaped her was a weary gasp. She felt herself sinking toward the floor. Her body had become so heavy. She couldn't breathe.

"It's okay," that ghostly voice assured her.

How was this okay? She felt like she was being suffocated! There was an unpleasant aching deep inside her chest and a tremendous pressure rapidly building in her eyeballs. She felt as if she were sinking into the depths of a great, black ocean.

Was she *dying*?

She tried again to cry out, but that cold, crushing darkness had swallowed her. There was nothing left but silence and darkness and a great, suffocating dread that felt like it was squeezing the very life from her heart.

"You're not alone," said the voice of the silvery mist as she felt everything, even her own body, fade into the black depths.

Chapter 11

There was something about the storm that raged over the City Beyond Memory that not only seemed to suppress Gina's psychic awareness of her surroundings, but also filled her with unease. It had a strange energy to it, one she felt distinctly with every lightning bolt that split the churning sky. It ebbed and flowed, sometimes receding far out into these queer, rain-soaked streets, allowing her brief glimpses of the layout of the land around her, but then sweeping inward again until she could barely sense things right in front of her face. And strangely, each time the storm eased and allowed her those teasing peeks farther out into the city, she could never quite visualize the exact layout or even focus on any given point in order to locate a possible escape.

This wasn't like Tristesse Lane or Hochog's nightmare hospital or the crinkled confusion that was the Denselands. This felt like interference, no different than a satellite dish having trouble receiving a signal in bad weather. But storms had never had this sort of effect on her before. Getting caught driving through a blinding downpour was one of the few times she actually appreciated this intrusive awareness of her surroundings. She didn't need to see the road or the other vehicles with her eyes to stay out of an accident.

The worst part about this was that she was having trouble tracking the things she felt prowling these drenched streets. There was one somewhere to her right, she could tell, far enough away to not be an immediate threat, but she couldn't tell exactly where it was or which direction it was moving. There was another one farther out a moment ago, but it had faded away and disappeared for some reason. And there were two others somewhere behind them that she wasn't aware of at all until just a moment ago, as if they'd simply appeared there.

She couldn't even get a proper read on what, exactly, these things were. She could usually discern a basic, physical shape at least, but these remained frustratingly evasive. And while the storm seemed to be muting her psychic awareness to a fair extent, she was sure that wasn't the only reason for her blindness to these creatures. It was as if they possessed some kind of natural camouflage against her inner eye.

What she *could* discern was that they were dangerous. Their very presence here filled her with an almost primal sort of fear. She needed to stay alert. One of these things could pop up anywhere, without warning. She needed to be able to react in an instant. And yet it was so hard to stay focused when she couldn't stop worrying about Nicole.

It was her fault. Looking back now, it was clear that something was wrong. She wasn't acting like herself from the moment they arrived. She should've taken it more seriously when she said something was following them. But she never felt anything to suggest that they were in any danger. None of the frightful things prowling the Denselands had approached them. Nothing she could feel, anyway.

And she couldn't stop thinking about the way Nicole just *disappeared* out there. That wasn't the storm. It wasn't one of those creatures. It was as if she just dropped through a hole in reality and vanished.

Something else was at work here. Something that could sneak past her psychic eye. Something that now had Nicole at its mercy.

Clinging tightly to Brandy's hand, she ducked down a narrow walkway between two huge shapes that looked like buildings but weren't and descended a set of steep steps that no human feet had ever tread before. A shadowy passage cut beneath a jutting section of one of the many not-building shapes that made up the city's strange skyline. Here, where they were finally shielded from the rain and where the din of the wind and thunder were much more muted, she stopped and wiped at her dripping face.

"I can't see shit," said Brandy, wiping at her glasses.

"There's not really shit to see," Albert informed her.

"We're safe here," said Gina. "For a little while anyway." Hopefully long enough for her to sense a safe path forward.

"What if those things find Nikki before we do?" worried Brandy.

"That won't happen. The way she disappeared back there… I didn't just lose track of her. I think she's gone below."

"Below?" asked Albert, looking down at the ground beneath their feet.

Gina looked up at the stone overhead. "This whole city is some kind of maze." Even with her senses stifled by the strange storm, she could tell that these structures didn't serve any *reasonable* purpose. The spaces inside were illogical. Tightly packed. Twisted. With no furnishings of any kind. And there was no way into any of these structures from out here. Instead, they were connected to the tunnels that ran deep under her feet.

"A labyrinth," considered Albert, nodding. "Just like the first temple."

"So we're near the second one?" asked Brandy.

Albert was looking back the way they came, out at the lightning-lit skyline above. "No. We're already there. This *is* a temple. This *whole city* is the second temple."

Brandy looked out there, too. "This is all another Temple of the Blind?"

"Maybe. I don't know. Or maybe it's a completely different temple. Maybe this is..." He shook his head as a great clap of thunder crashed somewhere overhead. "...the Temple of the Three Whispers," he decided.

Brandy glanced at Gina. "He likes naming things."

"What?" He looked back at her, embarrassed. "No I don't."

"You do." She insisted.

"Call it whatever you want," said Gina, "but we have to find a way below ground. It's not safe on the surface." She turned and looked out at the rain pouring down beyond the far end of the passage. The storm was ebbing again. The haze inside her head receded. She could make out several very large structures jutting up into the stormy sky in that direction. The whole city was sitting in what appeared to be a giant depression, like an enormous crater, with the wall encircling its outer rim. And those shapes that weren't buildings grew larger and jutted higher into the stormy sky the closer they were to the center.

"I mean, things *need* names," fussed Albert.

There was something about the area nearer the center. There was something there, she realized. Something profound. Something *significant*. It seemed to call to her, beckoning her toward it. That, she realized, was where they ultimately needed to be, down at the bottom of the crater, in the deepest of those strange streets, where the structures were the tallest. But they couldn't reach it from here. It was like *all* the structures she'd sensed so far, inaccessible from the surface, only from below.

But how did they get into the underground? She couldn't seem to sense an opening anywhere. It didn't make sense.

"We have to call them *something*."

"I know," said Brandy.

What she *did* sense was more of those storm-dwelling things. There were several of them gathered in an area to the left now, which was concerning. But she thought she could detect a path circling around the other direction that seemed safer. As she tried to focus her psychic eye on that path, however, she suddenly became aware of something else. "There's someone over there," she realized.

"Nikki?" gasped Brandy.

She shook her head. "No. Someone else, I think." She tried to zero in on the presence, but already the storm was swelling again. Everything was clouding over. "I think they're below." Was it Andrea? Or maybe Keith? Or Violet and Corey? It could've been more than one person. Sometimes when people were gathered in close proximity, they sort of blended together at first. And she only glimpsed them there for a second or two.

So many friends out there... So many dangers... She felt a sick knot of worry twisting deep inside her at the thought. If she let it, that worry would overwhelm her. She couldn't dwell on it. She needed to focus on the task at hand.

She switched off the flashlight. "We don't want to attract any attention out here," she explained, pressing it into Brandy's hand. "You keep it. In case we get separated."

"Are you sure?"

"Very." Then she grabbed her other hand and tugged on it. "This way. Stay close. And maybe keep quiet," she added as she led them back toward the pouring rain. "Just in case."

Chapter 12

Nicole opened her eyes, only to find that it didn't help. Everything was black. And cold.

She was having a dream...something scary, she thought...but already it was slipping away from her, sinking back into the depths of her mind where all dreams came from and returned to, she supposed...

She was so confused. So many questions churned inside her head. Where was she? What happened to her flashlight? Why was she *wet*? The last thing she recalled was that room at the end of the tunnel and that weird, empty hole in the wall that Gina said was somehow the gate they were searching for...and then...

She gasped and sat up. Hotdog was there! But he wasn't Hotdog anymore. He was something far more terrible. A foul, dead thing clinging to the ceiling like some monstrous spider. He lunged at her before she could even scream!

And yet...she wasn't hurt? Her clothes were drenched all the way down to her underwear but she didn't seem to have any injuries. Nothing hurt.

What walked away and remains out there is only an empty husk, she suddenly recalled Ada telling them way back in Cedric's Cove. *Only Goar Nangup remains.*

Was that what that thing was? Hotdog's evil god, using his rotting corpse like some gross marionette? It was an awful thought, made even worse by this strange darkness that enveloped her.

Just where the hell was she?

She reached down and felt the ground beneath her. Smooth, cold stone. The road? She reached out into the empty darkness and found a wall beside her, made of the same stone. Was she still in that room where Hotdog Thing attacked her? What had she missed? And where were her friends?

"Hello?"

Her voice echoed softly, the only answer she'd receive.

Where did everybody go? Did they pass through the gate without her?

No... Why would they do something like that? It made no sense.

They'd never leave her behind.

Slowly, she rose to her feet. It was more difficult than it should've been. She felt strangely exhausted. Her legs trembled a little beneath her, making her lean on the wall. Her calves were sore, as if she'd spent the past hour on a Stairmaster.

What happened to her? What couldn't she remember?

She pressed her back against the wall and reached into her shorts pocket. She still had her phone, if it hadn't gotten too wet. And it should still be fully charged. She hadn't touched it since they disembarked back at the dock.

The screen lit up immediately, giving her a tremendous feeling of relief that lasted only an instant before she looked up and saw that she was standing in what looked like one of the countless passageways deep in the labyrinths of the Temple of the Blind.

Her heart leaping, she turned and shined her light the other way.

A horrible image came floating back from somewhere deep in her memories, alone and naked in these terrible tunnels, staring in at the dreadful meadow the Keeper warned her to never enter.

(*Just leave us then.*)

A hard shiver raced through her. No. That was just a dream she had once. Or maybe it was more than once… But it *was* only a dream. One of countless nightmares brought on by those haunted tunnels. It didn't mean anything.

And the Temple of the Blind was gone. It fell apart beneath her very feet.

Besides, she wasn't naked this time.

Although, looking down at herself, she was surprisingly disheveled. Besides being soaked to the bone, her shoe was untied, her shorts were unfastened, there was mud on her shirt and her hair had fallen down at some point. She was sure her makeup was all but gone by now, too. She probably looked like a drowned rat. But now wasn't the time to fuss about such trivial things.

Why *were* her shorts undone? How did that happen? Was she struggling with someone? Did something attack her?

She fastened them and quickly tied her shoe. Then, while she was kneeling, she searched the floor around her. There was a puddle where she was lying in her drenched clothes, but there didn't appear to be any wet footprints or water drops to reveal which direction she came from. Did she just…drop out of thin air in here? Like back in Violet and Corey's camp at All Trails Crossing? Did someone carry her? It didn't make sense.

Finally, she picked a direction and began walking. Just a few yards, perhaps. Then she'd try the other way, just in case the way out was just out of sight. It wasn't impossible that she could accidentally wander in the wrong direction and miss her chance to leave this maze. After all, she had to have come from *somewhere* to get here…right?

The sound of her wet shoes squeaking on the stone sounded loud enough in this silence to be heard for miles. It was impossible to sneak around. If anything dangerous was lurking anywhere nearby, it wouldn't be hard to find her.

This was so weird. Her first thought was that she was back in that temple from five years ago, but this had to be somewhere different. The entire road leading here, including both docks, that creepy gateway with the giant, yawning mouth and even the city's impossible wall were all made from this same stone. Why wouldn't there be more tunnels like those here?

What she needed to focus on was that missing time. What happened to her between Hotdog's terrifying corpse and waking up in this darkness? How long had it been? Where did her friends go? Were they okay? And which side of that God-forsaken wall was she even on?

When nothing appeared in the passage ahead of her, she turned and tried the other way. *Now* there were wet footprints to follow. How could there not be any showing how she ended up in here?

She passed the puddle where she awoke and pushed through the darkness beyond. It seemed to be a straight corridor, with no turns, intersections or end in sight. She was starting to feel the suffocating grip of claustrophobia closing around her. What if there wasn't a way out? What if this was just some enormous circle? She wanted to tell herself that wouldn't make sense, but by now she knew damned well that sense had nothing to do with anything.

She stopped walking and stood there a moment, frustrated. She *really* didn't want to be doing this anymore. She just wanted to gather her friends and go home. What did she care about the Keeper's stupid plans? Nobody ever asked that monstrous little freak to interfere in their lives.

Of course, that didn't change the fact that without the Keeper's stupid plans, she would've never met Andrea. Or Olivia and Wayne. Or Gina. For all she knew, without the Keeper's stupid plans, maybe Brandy and Albert never would've ended up in that Chemistry lab together. Just how far back did the strange little creature's meddling reach, anyway? Was he the reason she and Brandy were seated next to each other way back on that first day of kindergarten? Was he the reason their families both lived in Briar Hills? How much of this reality did he write to ensure that the six of them ended up inside the Temple of the Blind that night?

She shined her cell phone light back the way she came, then turned and continued forward.

Albert sometimes liked to talk about that stuff, about how everything happened just the way the Keeper meant it to, that they didn't even really do anything because he'd already arranged it to happen that way. Did they really make any difference at all? Had anything any of them *ever* done made any difference?

She'd never paid him much attention. It all seemed a little too complicated for her. And she didn't care to think too much about it. She wasn't sure she'd like the conclusion she might come to. She just wanted to be happy for all the friends she brought back with her when it was all said and done. Was that so much to ask for?

This whole thing was really pissing her off, if she were being honest. It was getting old. Why did they have to go through all this nonsense? Just to open a couple of fucking *doors*? It was idiotic! If they were so important, why didn't the wrinkled little freak just go and open them himself?

"Stupid fucking bucket of skin..." she muttered under her breath.

Was the Keeper watching her right now? Would he be able to hear all the horrible things she wanted to say to him? Would he see if she showed him her middle fingers? And if she did, would it only be because he intended for her to do it?

This was all so fucking confusing.

Ahead of her, the passage split in two. One continued straight while the second veered off at about a thirty-degree angle. It looked just like countless intersections she remembered seeing in the Temple of the Blind.

Door number one or door number two? she thought, knowing it probably didn't matter. Both were probably wrong.

She continued on straight for no particular reason.

Trudging onward, her sneakers squeaking with every weary step, she thought about Gina. She hoped she was still okay out there. She'd promised to stay with her, to keep her safe... But like Andrea, she'd failed her.

They're dead by now...

She frowned at herself. What a terrible thought! She knew no such thing! Why would something like that even cross her mind?

Eaten alive...

She stopped walking and squeezed her eyes closed. What was with her? Was Glum still in her head or something?

Torn limb from limb...

"Stop it!" she hissed into the silence.

Choking on blood...

She frowned and opened her eyes. Something wasn't right. Those weren't her thoughts. That wasn't her.

Desperately grasping at their own entrails...

An awful chill rushed through her body as she realized that she wasn't alone in this darkness. Slowly, she turned and shined her light back the way she came.

A large and terribly familiar figure was standing there, hunched over, staring back at her with one cloudy dead eye. Its flesh was tattered and torn, pale and blotchy, covered in oozing black gore, but still she recognized that muscular form.

But was he always so *big*?

The mouth of the thing that used to be Hotdog Creep was moving, but no voice filled the silent passage. Instead, its words filled her head, in her own voice: *Begging and screaming with their final, tortured breaths...*

Nicole couldn't find her voice to scream, so she fled in terrified silence.

Chapter 13

Olivia was clinging to Wayne's arm, refusing to let go of him for even a second.

She couldn't believe they were back here again, inside these same stone walls. "I thought this was supposed to be a city. Why does it look so much like the temple?"

"Sandy told us there was more than one temple," Wayne reminded her. "The first one was plenty big enough to be called a city. You guys said it filled an entire mountain."

"I guess so..." And it sort of even made sense that the so-called City Beyond Memory that they were trying to reach would, in fact, *be* the next temple.

"I'm not going to complain," decided Wayne. "I was kind of expecting to get dumped in some ancient post-apocalyptic metropolis and then have to search the whole thing to find the second temple."

That was a pretty good point. And really, what did she expect an ancient city locked away behind a huge, impenetrable wall to look like? It wasn't like they were going to walk through that gate and see a Holliday Inn and a Buffalo Wild Wings.

Wayne turned and shined his light back the way they came. He kept doing that, even though there was nothing back there. They'd started at a dead end and hadn't found another path besides the two *other* dead ends that both vanished, taking poor Keith and Corey with them. But she didn't ask what he was expecting to see back there. He was only being cautious, she knew. Besides, if those two dead ends could disappear and open up this new path ahead of them, then it also easily could've opened up another path somewhere behind them. She just didn't want to think about that possibility. She much preferred to think that there could be nothing back there.

She was thankful that she had this strange psychic warning alarm, but it was still frustrating that she didn't know exactly what was about to happen when it went off or which direction it was coming from. If she'd been able to see exactly what was about to happen back there, could she have warned their companions quickly enough to have avoided being separated? Was it her fault it happened?

But then again, maybe Wayne was right about it all being a part of the Keeper's plan. Maybe it didn't matter what she did. Maybe they were supposed to go somewhere different. If those were their paths and this was hers and Wayne's, then it was possible everything was going to be this way regardless.

She certainly hoped that was the case…but how could she be sure?

"How're you doing?" asked Wayne.

"Scared," she replied without hesitation.

He gave her arm a reassuring squeeze. "Yeah."

"Thinking about Everett."

He nodded. "Yeah," he said again.

"Hope he's okay out there."

"I have no doubt he is."

She really hoped he was right. She still felt awful about leaving without him. She knew they had no choice, that they couldn't wait around forever, but still it felt wrong, like they abandoned him. The idea that they might have left him in that ancient darkness to die wouldn't stop haunting her. She couldn't help feeling sick with guilt at the very thought of him.

"That Austin guy was pretty insistent that everyone made it."

"That guy was a butt," she grumbled.

He chuckled. "Yeah, but that doesn't necessarily mean he was lying."

"Doesn't necessarily mean he was telling the truth, either."

"True. But I don't think he was wrong about everyone being where they were supposed to be. It just…*felt* right, you know?"

"I guess so." Everyone kept saying that the Keeper didn't make mistakes. Nothing happened without him intending for it to happen. If he really knew so much, then getting all of them to the three gates at the same time would probably be nothing to him. But she couldn't help it. She wanted to know for sure that Everett was safe. Keith and Corey, too. She wanted to see them again with her own eyes.

"Something up ahead," warned Wayne.

She looked up, distracted, her stomach giving an anxious twist. At the far reaches of their flashlights, the passage was finally coming to an end. There was a chamber up ahead, filled with the same darkness and uncertainty as everything else they'd found since stepping off that pale train. Her psychic alarm hadn't gone off yet, but she was certain it was only a matter of time. If this really was another temple, it was all but assured.

Wayne paused at the end of the passage and swept his light around the room that was waiting for them there. "Crossroads," he observed.

The space was roughly star shaped. They were standing at the end of one of five passages, all of them identical for as far as she could see.

He glanced back again, frowning. "Easy to go in circles," he worried.

He was right. If they took too much time poking their lights into each of those other four passages, they could easily lose track of which way they entered from and end up going back the way they came. And even more easily if they should end up circling back here.

"Last time, Albert brought a whole bunch of sidewalk chalk and used it to mark the way. Smart."

She remembered that. He was even clever enough to only mark the left wall, allowing them to know at a glance which way they were walking when they circled back to one or when there was a dead end. It wasn't foolproof, she didn't think, not in a labyrinth that complex, but it kept them from walking pointlessly in circles for endless hours. And even better, it had allowed her, Wayne and Andrea a means to catch up to them, even though they were hours behind.

But they had no chalk with them this time. Or anything else for that matter. She remembered Brandy saying that on their first trip she marked one passage with lipstick, but she didn't even have that option. Her purse was still in the Explorer, which was last seen on the back of Max's truck way back in Gutler's Weep. She stepped forward, careful to keep her back to the path they just came from.

"Does it even matter?" wondered Wayne. "I mean, we kind of started off lost, didn't we?"

"It matters," she replied. She very much doubted, after all they'd been through, that they were simply supposed to wander aimlessly until they just happened across something. She knew what she was supposed to do. Still clinging to his arm, still half-expecting to be spirited away from him at any moment like everyone else was, she turned her attention toward the first opening to the left. She stood there a moment, pondering the darkness beyond her light's reach.

But she couldn't feel anything.

She scrunched up her nose and squinted at it, as if maybe there might be a sign in there somewhere, if she only looked hard enough. But that wasn't how it worked. It wasn't about looking *harder*. It was more subtle than that.

She forced herself to relax.

She could do this.

She tried to imagine walking that way, pushing back that darkness with her light and forging ahead. But still there was nothing.

Disheartened, she turned her attention to the next passageway. Maybe Wayne was right. Maybe there was no right way. They'd started off lost and they'd remain lost. She might as well just choose this one.

But at the very thought, she felt a sudden jolt of fear deep in her gut, making her heart skip a beat in her chest and causing her to sink her nails into Wayne's arm again.

"Not that way," said Wayne. "Got it."

She looked down at her hand, at the fresh crescent marks she was pressing into his skin, and forced herself to relax. "I'm sorry!"

"You're fine. Don't worry about it. Just keep it up."

He was right. That was unpleasant, but it was a success. She knew there was something dangerous down that second passageway.

She turned her attention to the third. There was no strong reaction, like with the second passage, but for no reason that she could quite explain, she simply didn't like it.

Did that mean that it didn't lead to anything dangerous, but that it wouldn't take them anywhere good, either? A dead end? Or a circle? Or even just through something unpleasant, like that gross mud chamber back in the first temple?

She moved on to the fourth passage. Like with the first, she felt nothing.

She pointed to the passage on either side of the one they entered from. "Either of these should be okay, I think."

"Awesome," he replied. "You're like an old school video game cheat code."

She giggled a little at this. "Let's just hope I actually know what I'm doing."

"I trust you," he said, adamant. Already, he was moving toward the left passage. He didn't hesitate. "Let's see where this one takes us."

Her gaze drifted to the next passage and she felt that anxious clenching deep in her belly. Where did that one go? And would they be able to avoid places like that forever? Or was it only a matter of time before they had no choice but to face something terrible in this endless darkness?

Chapter 14

Keith wasn't sure how long he'd been swimming these black waters, but he was exhausted. His shoes were weighing him down. His teeth were chattering from the cold. And without any light, he couldn't even be certain he wasn't going in circles.

Cat Lady said he was supposed to be here, "where light fades into hazy depths," which sounded exactly like his flashlight sinking out of sight in whatever bottomless lake he'd landed in. But he was beginning to wonder if maybe he'd misunderstood the creepy woman's crazy talk.

Not that it would've made any difference, though. It wasn't as if he made the decision to jump into this water because of what she said. He was just sort of unceremoniously dumped here without any warning, so if she knew any of the stuff she claimed to know, then she must've known he'd end up here.

Right?

Sure. Because there was nothing in this weird world more trustworthy than the crazy babbling of some creepy-ass, dead-looking cat lady in a room full of scary, whispering cats.

(He was going to drown down here, wasn't he?)

He was running concerningly low on stamina. Pretty soon he was going to have to abandon his shoes before they dragged his weary butt down into the depths with his light. Maybe his blue jeans, too. That was a thing that happened, wasn't it? People who found themselves trapped and treading water were often found in states of undress after they drowned because the weight of their clothes made it too hard to swim. Then people started spreading rumors that you were murdered by some kind of crazed pervert... Not really how he wanted to go out, if he were being honest.

He splashed onward, convinced by now that he was only swimming in circles. Without any light, there was simply no way to prevent it. And for all he knew, there might not be a way out. Maybe that mechanism that dumped him into this bottomless pool was a booby trap. A one-way trip to a cruel, watery grave.

That would be just his luck, he supposed. Although it seemed to him a rather anticlimactic way to go after all he'd been through.

But then he caught sight of something new. There was a dim light in the distance. A faint, wavering glow in the water.

Encouraged, he picked up his pace and swam toward it. He was well aware that it didn't necessarily indicate a way out. For all he knew, that light could be a trap, enticingly dangled by the great, toothy maw of yet another ravenous monster. But anything was better than the endless nothing he'd been surrounded by all this time. At this point, he'd sooner take his chances with some monstrous anglerfish than keep treading water until he inevitably sank.

But there was no monster. The light was lying just beneath the surface of the water on a set of submerged steps ascending up onto dry land.

And it wasn't just any light. It was his flashlight! The very one he watched vanish into the depths below.

Breathless from the exertion, he snatched it up and then rose to his feet, shining it around, confused. How did this get here? He shined it down into the water, half-expecting to see a flash of some mysterious mermaid's tail. (At this point, there were precious few things he wasn't willing to believe in, he found.) But there was nothing in the water.

Nothing he could see, anyway, which didn't mean much.

When he turned and shined his light onto the steps, however, there were wet footprints leading up them.

Was someone else here?

Someone *barefoot*, no less?

And such *small* prints… A female? One of the girls?

He climbed the steps, water squelching from his soggy shoes, and followed the footprints up to a flat, open space, where he caught just a glimpse of a woman strolling away from him, a long, silvery dress glittering briefly in the glow of his light.

He hadn't seen anyone dressed like that… What did he see just now? Who was there?

But when he tried to catch up to her, she was nowhere to be seen.

"Okay…" he sighed wearily as he shined his light down at the floor where the wet footprints simply ended, as if the woman had vanished into thin air. "Now I'm seeing ghosts. Cool… Check that off my 'I've officially lost my mind' bingo card. Awesome."

There was something in the darkness up ahead, he realized. A shape just visible in the gloom beyond the reach of his light. He continued forward and watched as it materialized into two statues.

He swept his light up and down them both as he approached, frowning. He knew these things. Andrea had described them back on the trawler. She called them 'sentinels.' There was one standing at the far end of the dock where he picked the girls up in Cedric's Cove, but he never got much of a look at it. According to her, they were ten-foot-tall, naked, faceless men with freakishly elongated features, including, apparently, ridiculously long penises. And these two certainly fit *that* description. Those monstrous things were just hanging there, utterly uncontained, apparently just swinging around, ready to put someone's eye out.

She told him that the first temple had hundreds of these guys. Because why carve *one* freaky statue with a giant wiener when you could make an *army* of them?

These particular two appeared to be having a quarrel. They were facing each other, their fists raised, looking for all the world like they were about to throw down, even without the slightest hint of facial features to show expression.

Behind these two was a curved wall with three passageways leading out of the chamber. One in the middle and one on either side.

According to Andrea, these guys were typically just standing around, all stiff and straight, like a guard on duty—hence why they called them "sentinels"—but some of them acted out warnings about the areas ahead of them. Was that what this was? A warning? Or a clue of some sort?

But what did it mean?

She also mentioned those freakish emotion rooms, where the mere sight of the statues could apparently make people lose all earthly control. That still sounded like bullshit, to be honest, but he wasn't going to say so. Everything else was turning out to be real. And wasn't one of the rooms she described supposed to turn people hostile? Was that what the kickstand twins here were miming out for him?

He shined his light at each of the three passages. They were identical. And those ghostly footprints stopped well before they'd even come into view, offering no clues. So which way was he supposed to go from here?

(...*divide the feuding brothers*...)

"That's right..." he whispered to himself. Feuding brothers, the creepy cat lady said... And here these two were, clearly ready to brawl.

Divide the feuding brothers...

He shined his light at the passageway directly in front of him. If he walked between the two statues, he'd be heading straight for that one, meaning that was where he was supposed to go.

"'Where light fades into hazy depths, divide the feuding brothers,'" he recalled. Then he frowned. "Why the hell not just say, 'you're goanna drop your flashlight, then you wanna take the middle path'? What the hell's the difference?" He shook his head and walked between the bickering sentinels, his shoes still squelching with every step. "Creepy ass woman trying to be all mysterious... I'm soaking wet and bleeding. Do I look like someone who wants to play *Dungeons and Dragons* with the weird emo kid?"

He trudged onward, grumbling at the unpleasant chafing of his wet jeans.

Chapter 15

Corey was still wandering the empty corridors, one pudgy hand dragging along the stone walls as he contemplated the unseen workings hidden behind them.

Most of this place was exactly what it appeared to be. There was only the stone that made up the walls, floors and ceilings and the spaces *between* the stone that were the labyrinth's passageways. But sometimes there were workings concealed within the layout of the labyrinth. There were simple mechanics, like the one that separated him from the others. Strategically placed empty spaces to allow for movement of certain chunks of stone. Things that were perfectly sized and balanced, using gravity and leverage and even utilizing miniscule vibrations in the stone itself. Some of the passages carried water, like a sewer or irrigation system. And he was increasingly sure that there was a living ecosystem encoded into the layout as well, the bulk of it hidden away somewhere deep within.

And then there were all the things he couldn't understand. Strange fluids pooled in dark chambers. Empty cavities within the stone that weren't really empty at all. Devices that shouldn't work but were doing things he couldn't wrap his head around. And a persistent feeling like certain parts of the labyrinth overlapped themselves in some bizarre and maddening way. It was like walking through the bowels of some titanic alien spaceship filled with unfathomable futuristic technology, and yet every inch was made from nothing more than this same gray stone.

But even the stone itself had strange and curious properties, he realized. It was able to carry, hold and even direct that bizarre energy he first felt at that control panel back in the Denselands. He could feel the flow of it as he dragged his hand along the surface of the wall. It was what led him to Austin and the gate. And now it was flowing in this direction, leading him somewhere new.

He plowed ever onward, eager to see what awaited him in this fascinating machine.

Chapter 16

"Are you sure about this?" whispered Violet.

"Mm-hm," replied Corey. He never hesitated. He charged ahead, marching into the ominous cave without a glimmer of fear, just as he'd always done everything for as far back as she could remember. She recalled learning to ride bikes together. She wanted it so bad, but she was so scared of falling off that she couldn't make herself let go of the porch railing she was clinging to. But not ten yards away from her, out in the middle of the driveway, she watched Corey as he hopped on his own bike without a care in the world, wobbled three or four feet, fell over with a great thud, then simply stood up and repeated the process, over and over again until he got it down. He'd always been like that. And here he was again, completely unconcerned with the consequences. They said, "Curiosity killed the cat," but her best friend was a constant reminder that the lesser-known second half of that old saying was "but the satisfaction brought her back." Because no matter how careless he was, he somehow always managed not to get seriously hurt.

So far, anyway.

He walked on a few more steps, deeper into the larger chamber, then stopped and looked around. "Dark."

"Inside a cave?" she mocked. "*Weird.*"

He didn't acknowledge the dig. He never did. She could say anything she wanted to him and he'd just let it roll off him like it was nothing. Partly because that was the kind of person he was. He didn't see the point in getting upset about things people said. It wasn't worth his time. It never had been. But it was also because he knew that it *was* nothing. He knew she didn't mean it when she said things like that. It was just her sense of humor.

He stood there a moment, letting his eyes adjust to the gloom, then slowly crept forward, taking in the shape of the space.

She would've thought it was the coolest thing she'd ever found if not for the fact that they may have just followed an unknown intruder into this creepy darkness. She kept thinking of that strange, pale figure she glimpsed. She didn't get a good look at it, but Corey insisted it was too tall to be a person. She didn't really believe that. She seriously doubted that there were giants roaming her parents' vacation property. But there *was* something nagging her. Whoever it was didn't seem to be wearing a shirt, and something about that had struck her as odd. Now, as she stood crowded behind Corey, peering around at the naked cavern walls, it finally clicked. Why would someone be both shirtless *and* pale in late July? Wouldn't anyone with a tendency to go shirtless have a considerable tan by this time of year?

Vampires, she heard Corey saying in her head. The memory sent an involuntary shiver through her body. But of course there were no such things as vampires. And even if there were, they wouldn't be able to go out in the sunlight.

At least, that's how they were *supposed* to be...

(*Nobody's that tall.*)

She looked back at the sunlight they were leaving behind as they ventured deeper into the cave, uncertain. Corey was always going on about all the mysterious stuff in the world that was being covered up by the government or by secret societies or by big business or, on more than one occasion, simply by the creepy manager of their local Subway. (She wasn't entirely sure why he was so hung up on that guy, but whatever.) And there was simply something about a dark and creepy cave that made even the most absurd story seem eerily plausible.

"Goes back a ways over here," he reported, still moving forward.

"Don't get us lost," she said, not daring to raise her voice much above a whisper. "Caves can be dangerous, you know."

"Can still see daylight," he reminded her, stuffing his hand back in his chip bag.

"How can you still be eating?"

"'Cause they're good," he replied, as if he really didn't understand what she meant by the question.

"You're making too much noise."

"S'only that loud when you're the one eatin' 'em."

"What? Not the *chewing,* you big doofus! The *bag!*"

"Mm. Right."

She wrinkled her nose at him as she realized he was teasing her. She hated when he did that. It was so hard to tell when he was joking. "Doofus..." she said again, annoyed. She looked around. Her eyes were adjusting to the gloom, but she still wished she had a light. It was far too easy to imagine someone lurking in one of these shadows, watching them.

She was still looking back the way they came, so she didn't see Corey stop. She bumped into him. A startled squeak of a shout escaped her and she clapped her hands over her mouth to stifle any more sounds. "What's wrong?" she gasped, her voice muffled through her fingers.

"Steps."

She thought she must've misheard him. This was a cave, not a basement. Why would there be steps? But when she peered around him, she realized that he was right. It was hard to make out in the gloom, but there was a perfect set of stone steps leading deeper into the earth right in front of him. "Why are there steps here?" she asked. Did this used to be some kind of mine? Or an old root cellar? And why would they be hidden away down here in the dark? Maybe it was supposed to be secret. Some kind of clandestine meeting place? Perhaps it was part of the underground railroad back in the days of slavery. Or could it be some sort of old Cold War remnant? A bomb shelter of some kind?

She frowned at herself as she realized how much these crazy thoughts sounded like Corey.

But Corey didn't offer any guesses, crazy or otherwise. "Let's find out," he replied instead. Again, he didn't hesitate. He descended the steps, as if they hadn't just followed a mysterious figure that may or may not have entered this cave ahead of them, that may or may not have been inhumanly tall and that may or may not have been butt naked.

Unconvinced, yet unwilling to be left behind, Violet followed him down into the darkness...

Down into the earth...

Down...

Down...?

But down to *where*? She couldn't remember.

"You okay?" asked Everett.

Violet blinked and looked at him, confused. "What?"

"You zoned out there for a second."

Indeed, she had. She was still clinging to his arm, determined not to be separated again, but she'd stopped walking, her head filled with thoughts of a faraway cave. Was that a real memory? Or only a memory of a dream? It didn't *seem* real. But it was so *vivid*, right down to the dank smell of the earth around them.

She wished Corey were here so she could ask him if he had any such strange memory. But wishing never accomplished much.

"I'm okay," she assured him. She tightened her grip on his arm, pulling him a little closer in the process. He still seemed a little flustered at having her pressed so close against him. It was cute. Charming, even. She didn't get any kind of pervy vibes from him at all, which was always a good thing. A lot of guys underestimated her because of her petite size. She'd left more than a few overly handsy jerks with black eyes and bruised egos over the years. But she felt like she could trust Everett. He was a nice guy. "Just worried about everyone," she added, not wanting to talk about strange memories that may have been dreams or strange dreams that may have been memories.

"Yeah. Me too. I just keep telling myself that it's all part of that Keeper guy's plan, so it has to all work out, right?"

"Right," she replied, though she wasn't sure she really believed it.

She continued walking. The path ahead of them had been sloping upward for the past hundred yards or so, but she wasn't sure if that meant they were making progress.

The Keeper's plan... What *was* the Keeper's plan? What was *he*? According to their friends in Wisconsin, he was a scruffy looking older man they first spotted hitchhiking on the side of the road. But according to Albert and Brandy, he was some kind of monster, like a creepy Tim Burton version of Yoda or something. Was it some kind of shapeshifter? Or was it like a *Wizard of Oz* man-behind-the-curtain sort of thing?

Ahead of them, the passage leveled out and the first of the labyrinth's endless choices awaited them. They could go straight ahead. They could go left and continue upward. Or they could go right and back down.

"Keep going up?" she guessed. Continuing in the same vertical direction felt like a good idea at the moment. Going back down just seemed like a waste of effort after climbing this far.

"Sure," said Everett.

Easy enough, she supposed. She gave his arm another squeeze and pretended not to notice the way he stiffened at the feel of her body against him. Then, together, they continued upward through the darkness, both of them wondering where it would eventually lead them.

Chapter 17

Andrea gasped and sat up straight, confused. In an instant, that horrible, suffocating darkness was gone. And so was the stone corridor. Instead, she was sitting on a stool, her hands resting on the polished surface of a black, marble bar. She blinked up at a shelf full of liquor bottles as her mind struggled to comprehend how she came to be in this place.

"See? No harm done."

She turned and looked at the woman sitting next to her. She was tall and beautiful, with long, silky black hair and a friendly smile. She was casually swirling a drink in one hand.

"You were still resisting me pretty hard, so I had to give you a bit of a push. That probably wasn't pleasant. Sorry. But I *did* tell you to trust me."

Andrea couldn't form any words. She called it "a bit of a push," but…was she talking about that awful, suffocating sensation? Because that didn't feel like just "a bit of a push." It felt like she was going to *die* for a moment there.

"We had to make a short stop on the way over, too," the woman added. "Little errand I needed to run. Something lost that needed returned. Luckily, time's rather elastic out here. It happened so fast, I doubt you even noticed I was gone."

"What…?" She sat blinking at this beautiful woman sitting on the stool beside her, looking overdressed in her long, silvery gown, with her shoulder adorned in bright yellow sunflowers. She looked like something out of an old movie. The gorgeous and mysterious new love interest for the gruff main character, perhaps.

What was going on? Who *was* this woman? What was she talking about? And where did this bar come from?

"Wait…" she muttered to herself. This bar was familiar, she realized. She'd seen it before. When she had that strange episode while stumbling around alone in the dark inside the gouging station. This was the bar inside that mysterious club. "The Elysium Fog…" she muttered.

Finally, she broke free of her confused paralysis. She twirled around on her stool and looked out at the space behind her…but there was nothing out there. Everything beyond two or three feet of the barstools was empty darkness. It was strange.

"You've been here before," the woman realized.

She nodded. "With…" She held her hands up over her head and curled her fingers to mimic antlers.

The woman smiled. "Horatio. Yeah. He takes some getting used to, doesn't he?"

"Horatio…" So that actually happened? It wasn't just some kind of messed-up hallucination? Because that was *super* weird. "Yeah," she sighed. "Him. But it wasn't dark like this before."

The woman turned and cast her gaze across the room. "That's because it's not real."

"What?"

"It's only a copy," she explained. "A spiritual construct pieced together from my memories of the real one. It's not a perfect replica, but not bad, I don't think."

Andrea looked down at the bar again, confused. A copy? As in, none of this was real? It looked real. It *felt* real. But it was so utterly…*bizarre*… "I don't understand *anything*."

"That's okay," said the woman, smiling. "I didn't understand any of this either. Not at first."

She turned to look at the woman again, but she was no longer sitting on the stool beside her. Instead, she was standing behind the bar, looking over the bottles on the shelf.

"I only bothered manifesting the bar. It's only the two of us. We don't need much space."

"Makes sense," she lied.

The woman smiled. "I would've taken you to the real one, but no one, not even the dead, can pass through the walls of the City Beyond Memory."

"Dead?" She looked down at herself, confused, half-expecting to find herself covered in blood.

"No," laughed the woman, "you're very much alive. Unlike me."

She looked up, distracted. She remembered hearing her disembodied voice back in that creepy labyrinth. And how she spoke to her back in the gouging station. "You're…?"

She offered her an indifferent shrug as he plucked a bottle off the shelf and examined it. It was about three-quarters full of a clear, amber-colored liquid that looked like whiskey, but the label was in a language she couldn't read, or even recognize. "Deceased? Yeah."

She found her gaze drawn to the woman's shoulder, to those bright yellow petals. Something about the sight was strangely familiar. Had she seen those flowers before somewhere? She felt like she'd glimpsed them once in passing, but she couldn't remember when or where. "Who are you?" she asked, her eyes still fixed on the colorful tattoo.

"My name's Erin. I was the one who took you from your friends."

"You...? *What?*"

"Sorry about that." And she did, in fact, look sorry. There was a kind sadness painted across her pretty features. "I know I scared you. That was my fault. But you have an important job to do and there's something dangerous following you. I had to steal you away to be able to talk to you like this. And even now, I don't know how long we have." She glanced up, her lovely eyes drifting from left to right, as if searching for something. "Eventually, she'll find us. Even here. And when she does, I won't be strong enough to fight her."

This was too much. Her head was spinning. "Her *who?* What're you talking about?"

"The Priestess of Ruin."

"Who's *that?* Is it another of those monsters like Glum?" She recalled Gina saying something about there being *twelve* of those horrible things, come to think of it.

"No." Erin turned and plucked a second bottle off the shelf, those gorgeous black curls bouncing over her shoulders. She placed it on the bar next to the first. It was dark and smoky, with a heavy layer of dust settled onto it, with no label and an old cork. It looked like something that had been sitting there for a *very* long time. "Something worse."

Andrea shook her head, confused. What was worse than *Glum?*

Wait... Was she talking about the thing Ada warned them about? The thing that was hovering over them and attracting trouble? The reason Hotdog Creep was able to keep finding them?

(*There's another... Something far stronger than a mere spirit, something I can't see.*)

The memory gave her an uncomfortable chill that raised the hairs on the back of her neck.

(*It seems to attract unwanted things. And it delights in your misfortune.*)

Erin placed a glass onto the bar between them. "I don't have all the answers. I only know we have limited time." She poured a small amount of the amber liquid from the first bottle into the glass, then added a clear liquid from the second bottle and gave it a swirl. Then she slid the mysterious concoction toward her. "Here."

Andrea wrinkled her nose at it. She wasn't very fond of straight liquor.

"It's a Moris Special. Might not be as good as Moris, himself, would make you, but I know my way around a bar, too."

"Who's Moris?"

"He's the Fog's bartender. Big, hairy guy?"

"Oh..." She *did* recall glimpsing a man that fit that description standing behind the bar during her bizarre conversation with Horatio, now that she was thinking about it.

"You should drink it," she advised as she picked up her own glass and gave it another swirl. "It'll strengthen your bond with the Murk."

The Murk? Horatio used that word, too. He said that was what the other side was called. The afterlife. The spirit world. Which was something she didn't think she wanted to get any closer to under any circumstances. Not for at least the next sixty years or so, she didn't think.

She picked up the glass and sniffed it. It smelled strong. She couldn't quite place it. It looked like whiskey, but there was something else in it. Something that sort of shimmered in the light. She was more of a cocktail girl herself. She sat it down again, reluctant, and instead asked, "What is it about *me* that's so special? What am I supposed to do?"

"Hm... Let me see if I can explain it. It's a little complicated, but..." She paused, thinking it over, then she gulped down her own drink and grimaced. She set the empty glass aside and then leaned over the bar, those gorgeous eyes fixed on hers. "You've reached the very heart of the Denselands," she explained. "A place where the weight of countless worlds is constantly crushing down on the impenetrable walls of the City Beyond Memory, compressing everything inside, even reality, itself. Realms overlap and merge here, including the worlds of the living and dead. You're special because you can walk the fringe of both worlds at once. You can see the *other side of the city*. The side that exists in the Murk."

"Compressed reality? Overlapping realms? You know you sound crazy, right?"

Erin stared back at her, surprised, blinking, a bewildered sort of look on her lovely face. "Um... Yes?"

She nodded. "I mean I know this whole thing is crazy. But I just want to make sure you can hear it, too. Like, if I hadn't just been dragged through, like, *five alternate dimensions* to get here, I'd say you were a fever dream or something."

"That's fair."

Andrea leaned closer, squinting at her. "So are you really a ghost?"

Again, Erin looked surprised. "I am."

She reached out and poked her forehead with her finger. "You *feel* alive."

Erin laughed at this. "Of course I do. I'm as real right now as the stool you're sitting on."

She glanced down, half-expecting it to vanish at the mere mention and drop her unceremoniously onto her butt.

"The rules that apply to the living don't necessarily apply to the dead. It's a fundamentally different and usually entirely *separate* reality. I couldn't teach you to understand it all any more than you could teach a fish calculus."

She scrunched up her nose at this. "If you say so…"

"It's kind of something you just don't get until you're actually dead."

"Oh. Okay."

Erin smiled. It was a pretty smile. Very friendly. Very kind. She wanted to like this woman. But she was hesitant with her trust. "You're not going to double-cross me and strand me in a dead spirit highway like the last ghost I trusted did, are you?"

For the first time, Erin's kind face turned sour. "What? *No.* That's terrible!"

"I know! Don't wanna make *that* mistake again!"

She pressed her hand over her heart, looking flustered. "I'm *nothing* like that! I swear."

But Andrea found herself wondering if she even had a heartbeat in there.

Erin frowned. "Wait… That doesn't make any sense. That's not something a ghost would be able to do."

"Well that didn't stop the bitch!"

She stared at her for a moment, considering this.

"*And* she sold my friends out to Glum," Andrea recalled.

"I don't think that was any kind of human spirit."

"I don't know *what* she was. But we should've left her in that gross hospital…" She leaned forward, hopeful. "You seem to know an awful lot. Do you know if Glum still has my friends? Are they okay?"

"Glum doesn't have them. He can't. They all passed into the city through one of the other two gates at the same time you did."

She wilted with relief at this news. "Thank God."

Erin's kind expression faltered and she stood up straight, her gaze fixed on something in the darkness behind Andrea.

She turned to see what she was staring at but could make out nothing in that creepy gloom. "What's up?"

"She's closer now. We don't have much time."

Andrea glanced around, her stomach tightening with dread. The Priestess of Ruin… Who was she? *What* was she? And why was she so fixated on *her*?

Erin turned her gaze back on her. "Look, Horatio sent me to you because the Keeper chose me for that job. Just like he chose you for your job."

"My job?" She tilted her head and squinted at her. "I have a job?" Somewhere in the back of her mind, she heard Gina telling her that a goddess gave her a job. It felt like ages ago that they had that conversation. Had she somehow come full circle?

"Because of your natural connection to the world of the dead," she explained. "You're a bridge between the two realms, able to see what most living people can't."

"I don't *want* to be a bridge! It sounds terrifying!"

Erin's expression darkened at this. "No, terrifying is having some antlered monster tell you that your job includes *dying* and still having to do it."

Andrea stared at her, surprised.

She leaned toward her again, those lovely eyes gleaming in the haunting lights of the bar. "Listen. My job is to be the one standing on *this* side of the veil and helping you see through the murk. Your job is to *be alive* and on *your* side of it. That means you still have a chance at going home."

She wasn't sure what to say to that. This woman had actually *died* doing the Keeper's work? That was unsettling in itself. What proof did she have that they all wouldn't die out here. And yet she wasn't wrong. She wasn't dead yet. She could still hope for a happy ending.

"It's okay," said Erin, smiling that pretty smile again. "I made the choice myself in the end. I understood what I was doing. I know it's kind of hard to believe, but it *is* worth it."

Again, Andrea looked down at her drink. She really didn't want it. Drinking was the last thing she was in the mood for right now. Her head was spinning enough just from all the weirdness that kept happening. It felt like a metaphor for this discussion they were having. Regardless of how she felt about it, she was just going to have to take her medicine.

"In order to get where you need to go, you're going to have to navigate more than just the physical side of the City Beyond Memory. There are things that only the dead can see. Places only the dead can go."

"City..." muttered Andrea. "You mean where I was before? After the gate?"

"That's right."

"It looked like the Temple of the Blind, but that place is gone."

"The City Beyond Memory is the second gatehouse. I'm sure it shares a lot of characteristics with the first one."

"Second temple," Andrea realized. Ada said there was more than one. She thought the temple was hidden somewhere *under* the city, somewhere they'd have to find. But she was already there. It had already begun.

"That's right," said Erin. "And your job here is much like your job was there. Your friends will need you to light the way. They can't ever go home without you."

Andrea pouted at her. "That's not fair. If I screw up my friends are lost forever?"

"You won't screw anything up. That's the beauty of the Keeper's designs. Somehow, it always works out."

She sighed. "If you say so, I guess." She picked up the glass and peered into it again. She still didn't want to drink it. But she didn't want to open the mysterious red velvet package, either. Five years ago, in the deep, dark corridors of the temple, she didn't want to take her clothes off. She didn't want to climb that burning mountain. She didn't want to be stranded alone and frightened in that spirit highway. But if she hadn't done any of that stuff, she wouldn't have the friends she had today. And if she didn't do these things now, she might not have any of them tomorrow.

She threw back the glass and gulped down the drink. It tasted strangely sweet, but it also burned her tongue and throat. And its fumes sent her into a coughing fit. "Oh my god!" she wheezed, grimacing. "What *was* that?" It made her head swim. She gripped the edge of the bar to steady herself.

"Death in a glass," replied Erin.

"*What?*" Her heart was pounding again. Death? Was it some kind of poison? What did she just drink? Again, she felt herself sinking into that cold, dark silence, a fresh wave of dread filling her heart.

"You'll be fine," Erin assured her, her voice drifting away into the distance. "Just ride it out."

Chapter 18

Brandy couldn't see a thing through her rain-streaked glasses. She was aware of great, shadowy walls all around her and Gina's hand clinging to hers, pulling her along. She was aware of Albert, his arm linked in hers in a tight grip, keeping him as close as possible. And she was aware of the lightning and thunder flashing and crashing chaotically overhead. But everything else was shadows and haze and wind and rain that seemed to come from every direction at once.

She was shivering. She was tired. And she was scared, of course. Not only because Gina said that there were things lurking out here in the storm, but because all these shades of gray were unsettlingly familiar. Regardless of the rain and the wind and the lightning, she might as well have been back in the depths of the Temple of the Blind, creeping through the fear room, naked and vulnerable and at the mercy of anything that might be waiting in the unseen shadows.

The Temple of the Three Whispers.

Something about Albert giving it a name seemed to have strengthened her fear of the place. She kept wondering if they'd be facing the same terrors as before or brand-new ones. And she couldn't decide which would be worse!

But as frightened as she was of this place, she couldn't stop worrying about Nicole. There were few people in her life as capable as her best friend, but she just kept thinking about how strange her behavior was just before she vanished. What was wrong with her? Had something happened when they weren't looking? Had something gotten into her head? Her thoughts drifted back to Warner Harr and how he simply slipped inside people, wearing them like disguises, making them do whatever he wanted, like something out of a scary science fiction movie. If *he* could do that, then it was possible there were other things out there that could do it, too. Much *nastier* things.

And then there was Violet and Corey, who they left behind when she and Albert were snatched away by the psychic predator. Were they able to remain on the road? Or did something get to them, too?

Andrea was also lost out there somewhere. And Keith. And Probably Olivia and Wayne as well.

That was ten of them…

Twelve are fated to gather in City Beyond Memory, she recalled the mysterious cat lady telling them. *Twelve to do Keeper's bidding…but only ten fated to return.*

Those words sent a queasy warmth spreading through her belly in spite of the chill in the rest of her body. Every time she thought about it, she felt as if she might vomit. Only ten… But what of the other two? What was going to happen to them? And *which two?*

She couldn't bear the thought of losing any of her friends, old or new. But the odds simply weren't looking good…

Gina stopped without warning. She and Albert stumbled into her, knocking her forward. Before Brandy could apologize, she was pushing back against her, urging them the other way. She started to ask what was wrong but recalled being told to remain quiet and immediately clenched her jaw shut.

Something was there, she realized. Ahead of them. Unseen in the raging storm except to Gina.

Lightning flashed overhead, allowing a brief glimpse of their surroundings, but she could see nothing through the rain-drenched lenses of her glasses except those ominous shades of gray. She wished *her* psychic ability allowed her to see these things. She hated this blind and helpless feeling.

Gina pulled her hand again, guiding her back the other way, faster now than before. After a moment, they turned a corner and descended a short set of stone steps. Soon after, the looming shadows to their right withdrew and another flash of lightning revealed a river rushing past on that side of the street.

She stared at the churning water as Gina pulled her along, distracted. She could see that it was rolling past them, but she couldn't hear the roar of it over the howling wind and pouring rain and constant rumbling of thunder. It looked like it could sweep someone away in an instant. And how easy would it be for her in this mostly deaf and blind state to simply walk off a ledge and be washed away forever?

Another flash of lightning revealed a row of stone columns sticking up out of the rushing water and several large spheres lined up along the far bank, each one big enough to fit a full-sized pickup truck inside. And jutting up somewhere behind those spheres was what she was sure—in spite of her rain-streaked glasses—was a towering pyramid.

Did all these strange shapes have purposes? Or were the sentinels just a bunch of minimalist artists simply whittling basic shapes from stone? Nothing made any sense out here. She felt like Alice wandering through Wonderland.

Again, Gina changed direction, yanking at her hand, nearly pulling her off balance. They slipped between two great stone walls that Brandy, for one, couldn't even tell were two different walls, into a sort of narrow alleyway where they were shielded somewhat from the wind and where the noise finally receded a little, much to her relief. But she still couldn't see. It was much darker here. The constant, violent strobing of lightning was reduced to a narrow crack of flickering sky somewhere high above their heads so that very little of that light reached all the way down to them. But this extra darkness didn't slow Gina down. She plowed onward. Again, she yanked at her hand, pulling her in yet another direction. Then another. And another.

Brandy was already lost. Even if she *could* see anything, it would've been impossible to remember the way back. But that mattered little, considering there was nothing back where they started but a lonely dead end.

Besides, she trusted Gina. *Nicole* trusted Gina and that was enough for her. But it wasn't just that. There was something about this woman, something she'd been feeling since they joined up with her. What she'd thought all her life was a fairly accurate judge of character but might have always been her latent psychic power. Gina simply seemed like a good person.

Was that always the way it was? Was that how it was way back on her first day in kindergarten when she sat down next to the pretty brown-haired girl who would be her best friend from that day on? Or was it something that had cultivated inside her as she grew into adulthood?

Did she really choose her friends? Or did this strange psychic part of her do that for her?

And was there any difference?

This was all so confusing.

They turned another tight corner, but then Gina stopped again. She lingered there a moment, as if uncertain, then she backtracked and turned down another passage that Brandy, again, hadn't noticed before.

Now, even that narrow strip of sky was gone. It was utterly black in every direction. Had they entered one of these structures? Were they in some kind of tunnel?

She didn't like this. She couldn't see or hear anything. She didn't know what was going on. Why did they keep changing direction? What couldn't she see? How much danger were they in?

Gina steered her to the right and back out under that electric sky.

The wind and rain slapped her in the face, cold and sharp and stinging. They were darting across one of the city's wide streets. A massive lightning bolt revealed a great block of stone looming ahead of them. There was a large, round archway that reminded her for some reason of that great, yawning mouth the carriage entered when they first arrived in the Denselands. Just like in that moment, it felt like they were about to be swallowed!

Again, the deafening roar of the wind, rain and thunder and the blinding flashes of the lightning were muted. But she could already see the strobing light illuminating a space ahead of them.

Gina yanked hard on her hand again, steering her to the right, around a large column of the same gray stone as every other surface, then along what appeared in the subdued flashes to be some kind of stone lattice made of an intricately carved interlocking pattern that sort of resembled woven tree branches or vines.

Somewhere beneath their feet, she could hear the roar of rushing water.

What was this place? Why did it seem so different from those other areas with the overly simplistic blocks?

Again, Gina steered them to the right, through a gap in the strange, stone lattice. Then she stopped. For several seconds, she stood motionless, as if uncertain. Finally, with one last hard yank, she pulled them into a corner consisting of another large column and two connected stone lattices. She said nothing. Instead, she let go of her hand and reached out in the darkness, pressing the fingers of each of her hands against their mouths. The message was perfectly silent yet delivered loud and clear: don't make a sound!

Brandy pressed closer to Albert, making herself as small as possible, and then reached out and pulled Gina close as well. The three of them stood there, huddled together, hiding in the flickering darkness. Her heart was pounding. What were they hiding from? What was in this darkness with them?

Then a great flash of lightning lit up the space around them, accompanied by a deafening crash of thunder, and in this brief, disorienting light, she caught sight of a large, hunched shape disappearing behind a wall across from them.

She had to bite her tongue to keep from screaming.

What the fuck was that? It wasn't a person. There were strange, spiky things sticking out from its back.

When the next flash of lightning lit up the space, it was already gone.

And yet Gina didn't move. She remained motionless. Brandy could feel her shivering body pressed against her.

Was it not gone yet? Was it still lurking over there? Was it still likely to turn around and come back?

No… She felt the hairs on the back of her neck stand up. Slowly, she turned her head and looked at the stone lattice beside her.

Another flash of lightning illuminated the space for a split second, revealing strange fingers, long and sharp and thorny, curled in the gaps.

It was right there on the other side, mere inches away…

She felt lightheaded at the sight. Her knees trembled beneath her. She dug her nails into Albert's shirt and swallowed back the screams she felt bubbling up inside her.

In the next flash, the fingers were gone. Wet stone was all that remained as proof she didn't imagine it.

But she didn't dare let herself breathe. It couldn't have gone far. Could it see them in this darkness? Could it hear them breathing? Could it *smell* them?

Another flash of lightning again revealed nothing.

Was it moving away? Or was it sneaking around them? Gina said she could sense these things. She said that was one of her psychic abilities, to simply *know* her surroundings, even when she couldn't see. But she also said the storm was distorting this ability. Could she really keep them safe?

Again the lighting flashed. And then again a few seconds later. Both flashes revealed nothing frightening. Perhaps it *had* wandered off.

A much brighter flash flooded the space with light, revealing a huge, cloudy eye staring back at her from one of the gaps in the stone lattice.

She felt the world fading to black as she fought back shrieks of terror at the sight. If she'd been alone, she was sure she'd have fainted. She was barely able to hold onto Albert's arm.

What kind of creature had eyes like that? It looked like something that might have crawled up from the depths of the ocean, lidless, bulging, glassy, but also faded and scarred.

The thunderclap caught up with the flash, as sharp as a blast from a cannon, freshly startling her. This time, she couldn't be certain she was successful at holding in all of the screams. A small one may have escaped her, unheard over the crash.

In the next flash, the eye was again gone. There was no sign of whatever monster it was attached to.

Before she could torture herself with a million scenarios about what the mysterious storm-dwelling creature would do next, Gina gave her hand another tug and they were on the move again, following the latticed wall deeper into the shadowy darkness.

From somewhere within the cacophony of the storm came a sound that was almost a scream, but not quite. It was just faint enough over the rolling thunder that she might have believed she only imagined it from the constant howling of the wind, if not for the fact that she felt Gina's hand tighten around hers at the same moment.

She'd been wishing that she had Gina's ability to sense these things, but now, feeling that frightened grip, she found herself wondering if it would really be something she'd want. What sorts of horrible things was she really able to see out here? How frightening might it be inside her head?

Gina guided them around a corner and back the other way through a disorienting strobing effect of flashing lightning and several earth-trembling crashes of thunder. Light and shadow danced through the strange, interlaced patterns, casting unnatural shapes across the ceiling and floor and creating frightful, creeping forms everywhere she looked.

They seemed to be zigzagging through the stone lattice, back and forth as if following a long queue line in a theme park.

Or a maze…

(*This whole city is some kind of maze.*)

Albert said they were already inside the second temple. Another labyrinth, just like the first. And they'd literally barely scratched the surface. Gina said that they had to go *below*, into whatever was hidden beneath their feet. She said that was where Nicole went, too.

Gina abruptly turned and guided them into another corner, where they again stopped to hide.

Brandy bit her lip and crowded closer to Albert. She didn't like this. How long were they going to be able to keep it up? How had these things not already found them? This was their territory, wasn't it? Wouldn't they have the advantage in every situation?

Several small flashes of distant lightning cast an eerie glow across an opening in front of them, revealing something moving behind a low wall about thirty feet away. The sight made her heart stutter in her chest.

There was nothing between it and them. If it spotted them, where would they go?

Albert saw it, too. He slid in front of them both, determined to protect them. A sweet gesture, but she wasn't sure it would do any good. He wasn't Superman. And there were plenty of things out there capable of literally going right through him.

A much closer flash of lightning illuminated the space again, revealing a strange silhouette sliding past one of the columns so that all she could make out was that strange, bristly shape and a glimpse of a long, creepy arm.

Thunder caught up to the flash. A great, startling crash that nearly made her scream in spite of herself. Her poor heart wouldn't stop pounding. She hated this. She just wanted to go home.

Another bolt of lightning split the sky outside, illuminating the space in front of them. It had been only a few seconds at most, but already the thing was gone. Had it darted out of sight? Was it circling around to ambush them?

Gina tugged on her hand again. It was a harder tug this time. Urgent. "Hurry!" it said, and Brandy didn't dare hesitate. She seized Albert's arm and hurried after.

More blinding flashes in the sky, more disorienting shadows lurching at her from every direction, then the rain was back. They rushed out into the storm once more, across a stone bridge over a raging river and down another set of steps to an archway as big as the doors of an airport hangar.

Here, Gina abruptly changed direction, pulling them left instead of straight ahead.

Another of those eerie screams drifted through the storm between crashes of thunder, sending a fresh chill through her drenched body.

Brandy couldn't keep up with where they were going. Were they getting anywhere? Or were they just blindly winding through these confounding streets?

Now they were climbing steps. They'd been going *down* most of the time, hadn't they? Were they going back the other way?

At the top of the steps, Gina rushed forward. Another flash revealed that they were now on a raised platform of some sort, high off the ground, without so much as a railing to keep them from falling some forty feet to the stone below. The sight was freshly startling and she stumbled a little in the pummeling wind of the storm.

A moment later, Gina stopped again. She squatted down, so Brandy did the same, tugging Albert down with her.

What now? Were they hiding? Were one of those monsters nearby again? Worse, had one caught their scent and begun actively hunting them?

In the next flash of lightning, however, she saw it. Just above their heads, another platform crossed over this one. A hunched and prickly shape was crouched there, long, thorny fingers dangling down over the sides.

Even through the rain streaking down her glasses she managed to see that its cloudy white eyes seemed to be fixed on her.

Chapter 19

Nicole couldn't run any farther. Her legs were aching. She couldn't catch her breath. She leaned against the wall, panting, and shined her light back the way she came. She could see no sign of the monster, but she hadn't lost him. Not completely. She could still hear his awful words inside her head. Although for the moment they'd at least been reduced to an eerie muttering that she couldn't quite make out.

Why was the freak after *her?* Didn't Hotdog want the leaf? Did he think she had it? Not that she wished for even a second that he was out there tormenting poor Andrea, but what could it want with *her?* She was just the tagalong. Was he pissed about the fact that she was the one who killed him? Because that just seemed kind of petty, if you asked her. What choice did she have? He was trying to kill her friend! He totally deserved it.

Even dead, the creep was a pain in her ass.

She wished she could remember how she ended up in these awful tunnels. But of course she'd have probably gotten herself lost by now anyway, so she supposed it didn't matter.

Staying in one place felt like a bad idea, so she trudged onward, but slowly, leaning on the wall, conserving her strength. She still hadn't caught her breath. Her heart was still pounding. She was already tired when she woke up, after all. What did she do that she couldn't remember?

This was a pretty bad predicament. She was all alone again, with no key, no weapon, no supplies of any kind. She didn't even have a flashlight. How long would her phone battery last? And how much more terrifying was it going to be trying to run from that monster in pitch-blackness?

God, she hated this…

Ahead of her, the tunnel opened up. Something was standing there.

She froze, her heart pounding even harder.

But this didn't look the same as the monster that used to be Hotdog Creep. It was much taller. Much thinner.

She crept another step closer, her muscles tense, ready to bolt the second it so much as twitched.

But it wasn't going to move, she finally realized with a wave of almost dizzying relief. It was a sentinel statue. It stood stiff and at attention, its feet together, its hands at its side, its face forward, its huge, ridiculous dick dangling obscenely.

(Fucking freaks…)

It was standing in the center of a round room with four other passageways leading away from it, all of them identical to the one she stepped from.

Sentinels… Did its presence here mean that she was already inside the second temple? That would certainly explain the familiar look of these tunnels. But where was the so-called City Beyond Memory they were supposed to be searching for? Was Ada referring to the second temple all along?

And where was she supposed to go from here?

She shined her light up at the thing's blank face. "Not even going to point the way out?" she grumbled at it. It wasn't even facing one of the passageways. Its impossibly featureless head was fixed on the stone wall between two of them. "Thanks for nothing."

…*ripped flesh…shattered bones*…

She shivered and shined her light back the way she came. It was getting closer again. But was it still behind her? Or was it coming from one of the other four directions? The last thing her poor heart could take at this point was running headlong into that horror.

…*blood and bile*…

She was going to have to take her chances. She hurried past the sentinel and chose a path at random, her teeth clenched in expectation of a fearsome silhouette emerging from the darkness ahead of her with every step she took.

But the monster didn't appear. Instead, the passage began to slant. She was traveling down a gentle slope, descending deeper underground.

This couldn't be good. Didn't she want to be going *up*? She was already underground.

Or was she? She still didn't remember how she came to be here. She could just as easily be inside some kind of structure. The way out could very well be down. And at least if she were going down, she should be moving away from Hotdog Thing. Or she hoped so, anyway…

She shined her light back behind her. He wasn't creeping up on her. And that awful voice in her head had finally gone silent. Maybe she'd finally lost him. But somehow, she didn't think it would be that easy. That *thing* was no longer a mere man. According to Ada, it was some kind of ancient god who was imprisoned under the living universe…or something? She called it Goar Nangup, which was also the name Hotdog kept spouting whenever he was talking crazy.

Something about the mere name gave her chills, as if she instinctively knew somehow that it belonged to something evil.

Ahead of her, the tunnel ended. A dark emptiness loomed beyond.

Cautiously, she crept toward it, her light illuminating the way, revealing that the floor continued on, but only as wide as the passage, itself. On either side was nothing but darkness.

A bridge?

She stepped out onto it. The passage she'd just emerged from was merely one small opening in a massive stone wall stretching as far as her light would reach both up and down and left to right. There was another passage just visible below and to the left. And there was an opening with no bridge above and to the right, a reminder of just how dangerous it could be to run around blind in here.

She pressed forward, pushing back the darkness ahead of her. She'd seen a place like this before. There was an area like this in the first temple, but it wasn't this wide. Back then, she was able to see the end of the bridge and the next passageway waiting there. She remembered Albert talking about it a few times, how if he had it to do over again, he'd have packed some flares so he could drop one into the black abyss in an attempt to see how deep it really was. Personally, she wasn't sure that was something she really wanted to know. She wasn't afraid of heights, really, but something about the idea of seeing all the way to the bottom made her uneasy. Somehow, she felt that if she could see what was down there, she wouldn't have the courage to cross.

Her light receded from the wall behind her as she pressed forward and darkness swallowed it up again. For a moment, she was hovering ominously in her meager halo of cell phone light, in the middle of a vast void. The feeling was disorienting. Almost dizzying. She felt her stomach clench at the thought of stumbling and falling over the edge and considered dropping to her hands and knees to cross, just to be sure.

But then the next wall materialized from the darkness and the feeling passed. She could see the passage waiting ahead of her, an escape from the dizzying depths of this black abyss but not from the endless stone walls.

She felt more lost than ever. This was solid proof of just how enormous her problem was. She wasn't just lost in some unfamiliar part of town, after all. This place was massive. And it was literally a maze.

...*squeeze...break...burst...*

She gasped. A jolt of terror pierced her like a spear. That was strong. It felt *close*. She never heard that eerie muttering. Had it intentionally clammed up in order to sneak up on her?

But which way was it coming from? She turned and shined her light back the way she came, then forward, revealing nothing. Was it just out of reach, lumbering yet unseen toward her? Which way should she run?

...*crush...cripple...torture...*

Tears were welling up in her eyes as panic set in. She *hated* this! Why did she have to do this by herself? Why couldn't the freak just leave her the fuck alone? And why did everything have to be so fucking hard?

...*I see you...*

There was nothing in front of her. She turned and shined her light back the way she came, already backing away, convinced that it must be coming from that direction. But was it? She couldn't see it. Was it behind her *now*?

She felt as if her heart might explode in her chest.

Then something caught her attention. A sound? A motion in the dark? She wasn't sure. It happened so fast. But she thrust her gaze and her light *upward*.

The thing was plummeting toward her. It was there for only a split second, and yet it hung in her mind as if in slow motion. A great, broken figure sprawled against the blackness above. One dead eye like curdled milk. An awful, sneering grin.

She screamed and jumped backward, out of the way.

Hotdog struck the stone in front of her with a resounding and rather dreadful sound, like a wet bag of sand. Blood spurted from several open wounds, along with something black and viscous that looked an awful lot like the oily black stuff she saw spattered on the road before everything went blank.

She stood there a moment, her heart pounding, too startled to move.

What the fuck was that? Had it just killed itself in front of her? Again?

No... That definitely didn't sound right. There was no way this thing was done terrorizing her.

...*pitiful flesh...weak...fragile...*

She took a step backward as one of Hotdog's arms lifted off the ground. It was the one that was injured when he appeared in Cedric's Cove, raving like a lunatic. In addition to being burned and bloodied, it was now clearly broken. The elbow didn't bend, but instead folded hideously. She could see the snapped bones pressing against the discolored flesh from inside his forearm as it twisted. And yet he lifted himself off the ground and turned his gory face toward her. His nose was broken. Red and black gore oozed down his swollen lips. There was a fresh gash in his forehead through which she could see his cracked skull. His whole head was weirdly misshapen. (She supposed two multi-story falls onto solid concrete and stone would probably do that.)

...no point...no purpose...

She was still backing away, still watching the awful horror unfold itself into an upright shape before her eyes.

Hotdog's tee shirt was torn, revealing that one side of his chest was caved in as well, the ribs likely shattered. And yet still it managed to rise to its feet and take a staggering step toward her.

She thought it was the cramped passageway that made him look bigger than when he was alive, but it was no trick of the light. The man this thing started out as was tall, but whatever now occupied his corpse had stretched him to nearly seven feet. Parts of him were distended and bloated, like a poorly fitted costume.

...except to be devoured...

Finally, she turned and fled.

Chapter 20

Wayne kept glancing back the way they came. This all seemed a little too easy. Sure, they'd lost all three of their companions almost as soon as they stepped foot in this labyrinth, but aside from that, there had only been that one intersection, and Olivia had fairly easily sniffed out the safe passages. He was hardly complaining, but somehow he couldn't help feeling like they were overdue for something frightening.

"You're making me nervous," said Olivia.

"Sorry. We don't all have convenient spider senses. Some of us have to keep looking over our shoulder."

She scoffed. "Convenient my butt."

He turned his attention forward and made a mental note to stop looking back so much. But he couldn't help feeling uneasy, as if they weren't really alone in this darkness. Probably because the last time he saw passageways like these, he was dying. That sort of thing could make anyone a little uneasy, he was sure.

But he didn't care to think too much about death. Four times now he'd gone down that one-way road and somehow managed to find his way back again. Twice just *today*! That first time wasn't really his fault. That Erin woman was to blame. But when the scarecrow man's foul bird attacked them in that bone room, he made a conscious decision to grab that killing vine. It was a dangerous gamble, not merely that he was counting on being able to return, that he still had at least one retry left, but that he trusted he'd actually be able to do something after he crossed over. He could just as easily have dropped dead for good and left poor Olivia there to fend for herself while he floated around aimlessly (or whatever the hell the souls of the dead did when they found themselves evicted from their bodies).

Everything worked out in the end, of course. He kicked that maggoty feather duster's ass on the other side. (Though all of that was a complete blur.) And then he woke up and Olivia gave him a well-deserved scolding. But he wasn't sure why he did it. Why did it even cross his mind that the answer to beating the scarecrow man's filthy bird was to face it on the other side? Was it some kind of instinct he brought back with him from his time as a spook? Or was it something

Erin Laplede told him to do when she snatched him away on his third not-so-permanent demise?

He still felt like he spent a considerable amount of time with her. It seemed to him that they talked about a lot of things. And yet he couldn't have been gone more than a few minutes. If his heart had stopped for any longer than that, it would have damaged his brain.

What couldn't he remember?

And what did she want from him?

Ahead of them, the wall on the right ended. At first, he thought he was looking at another intersection, but it was something different this time. The other wall, floor and ceiling continued onward. But there was another passage running alongside this one, set six feet lower than the one they were walking in. When they reached it, he saw that the lower passage was connected to a tunnel leading farther to the right. And farther ahead of them, their higher passage turned left while the lower one continued forward out of sight.

"I remember seeing places like this," he recalled, shining his light down onto that lower floor.

Olivia nodded. "Scratches on the floor," she observed.

"Scratches," he agreed. The floor they were standing on was flawless gray stone. But down there it looked as if someone had been dragging heavy things across it for a very long time. There were even chips worn loose along the middle where the traffic was heavier.

Neither of them quite dared to say the word aloud, but they were both thinking it.

Hounds.

The very thought sent phantom pains shooting through the scars on his shin.

He reached around his fiancée and pulled her closer to him, away from that dangerous lower passage. They weren't supposed to be able to climb or jump, meaning it should be safe up here, out of their reach, but still he remained wary. These weren't just any dangerous animals, after all. These were *hounds*. They had claws and teeth, but they were also covered in a thick layer of scales that resembled square razor blades all standing on end. Even worse, for some ungodly reason each and every one of those scales could oscillate at high speed, slashing anything they touched, from every angle. They were power saws with anger issues.

Were these the same as the ones they encountered in the first temple? Or would they turn out to be an even nastier variety? On second thought, he didn't think he wanted to know. He was already moving, eager to be well away from this place before one showed up, even if they couldn't reach them.

But he was only halfway across when he heard the strange and familiar sound of one not far away. The machine-like drone of countless scales slashing back and forth, rubbing and grinding together, sent a wicked chill down his back, freezing him in place for a moment.

"I don't like that sound," whispered Olivia.

He nodded and continued onward, a little faster this time. It didn't sound very close. It seemed to be coming from somewhere ahead of them, in whatever mysterious darkness that lower passageway disappeared into.

Their path, meanwhile, turned left, away from the deadly lower section, and he eagerly followed it. But he found himself looking back as they walked away. Something felt off somehow, but he couldn't put his finger on it. Was it something Erin warned him about that his living brain was struggling to remember? Or just his nerves? He was deeply uneasy about being around those creatures again, after all, and not merely because of the scars one left on his body. The last time he saw those things, he watched them turn a six-foot-tall gorilla of a monster into a smoothie in mere seconds.

The memory sent a shiver down his back and he turned his attention forward again. He really hoped he wouldn't have to deal with too many of those areas down here. He'd rather spend extra hours wandering the labyrinth than risk crossing through their territory, letting them catch their scent.

Scent... He recalled the blind man back in the first temple telling them that they had to take their clothes off for exactly that reason, to prevent the hounds from being able to smell them. He and Albert had had quite a few discussions over the years about that particular detail. It didn't make sense. Their clothes wouldn't smell much different from their bodies, would they? Not to a scent-oriented predator. It still baffled them both to this day.

And now they were here again, back underground with those same monsters...and yet no one had told them they had to be naked here.

What did that mean? Was something different between that temple and this one? *Should* they be naked now? Or did the blind man lie to them last time and there was never any need for them to disrobe?

What was the real truth? Would they ever know?

Behind them, the hound's strange droning suddenly erupted into a furious explosion of noise, as if it had suddenly shifted its strange body into overdrive. Startled, both of them turned and shined their lights back toward the racket. The darkness had already swallowed the end of the passage, so there was nothing to see, but the sounds of clashing scales and snarls and growls seemed to roll toward them like something physical, making them both take a step backward.

Then there was a terrible sound, half shriek and half howl…and then everything went deathly silent.

"Two of them got in a fight?" suggested Wayne. A territorial dispute, perhaps? A quarrel for dominance? Those in the first temple had scuffled quite a bit, too, after all.

Olivia shook her head. Her mouth was pressed tightly closed, her pretty brown eyes wide open. She looked horrified, and he could hardly blame her.

The way it all just fell silent at the end… Was it attacked by another hound? Or was it attacked my something even more dangerous?

No. He didn't think he wanted to consider that option.

"I have a *really* bad feeling about that sound," she whispered.

He wanted to ask her what that meant, but of course she wouldn't know. Her psychic ability didn't work that way. It didn't give her details. It was little more than an early warning alarm. And if it was going off, the best they could both do was listen to it. "Come on," he said, urging her to keep moving. He wanted to be as far from this area as possible.

Chapter 21

Keith wasn't sure how long it had been since he left the feuding brothers behind. This passage hadn't branched or intersected any others. It simply went on and on. His shoes had stopped squelching by now, but they still squeaked, which was both annoying and a little worrisome, considering there was no reason to think that there weren't actual freaking monsters roaming this place that he wouldn't want to hear him coming.

He wondered how the others were doing. Olivia, Wayne and Corey. Andrea and Gina. Had that rude Austin guy found what he was looking for, yet? And then there was Nicole, who he'd rather *not* think about, but hoped was safe, regardless. He just wanted to stay the hell away from her. The fact that the two of them of all people ended up on that boat together kind of felt like the punchline of some cosmic joke.

Why *was* he here, anyway? Creepy Cat Lady said everybody would die if he didn't follow all her weird clues, but what difference could he make wandering these empty passageways all alone? Was she telling the truth? Was she really breaking the rules by telling him those things? Or was even that a part of the mysterious Keeper's scheme all along?

And just who was the Keeper? Cat Lady talked about him like he was some kind of god, setting everything in motion, planning every meticulous detail. And yet she also said that they were all going to fail miserably and die out here. So which was it? Did he have everything figured out or didn't he?

Ahead of him, something finally changed. The passage ended. He stepped out into a much larger space and shined his light around.

It appeared almost to be some kind of colosseum. He was standing on a walkway circling the perimeter of the room, with a second walkway protruding outward below him. The stone floor was just visible below that. Above him, he could see two more levels, each one a little wider than the one below it, like giant steps, each about eight feet high, with more passageways leading away from the room. There were no railings of any kind. It wouldn't be hard to fumble around in the dark and fall. Serious safety no-no right there, if you asked him. Very unprofessional.

It looked unsettlingly like the sort of place some terrible boss monster would be waiting in a video game, guarding the way to the next level.

There was a set of steps to his left, leading all the way from the top level to the floor below. He walked over to these and shined his light down them, trying to decide if it was worth investigating the other passages or if he should just immediately make his way down into the scary lion pit where he was almost certainly going to find himself anyway.

What was the next thing on Crazy Cat Lady's list of insanity? Something about an obsidian pool? Whatever the hell *that* meant...

He scratched at the stubble on his chin and glanced around. There could be dozens of passages leading off this chamber and he was willing to bet not one of them would have the courtesy of a convenient sign pointing the way.

He sighed and made his way down the steps.

There were no gates. If this were meant to be some kind of arena setting, it couldn't feature anything as dangerous as monsters. There would have been nothing to keep them in. Any fierce predator would be free to roam the labyrinth, which just didn't seem practical at all.

Also, there were no seats, now that he was thinking about it.

So not a colosseum. Probably.

But he paused at the bottom of the steps and listened for the sound of anything moving in the darkness, just in case.

(As if he really expected the monsters in this place to give him the courtesy of a warning.)

Everything was silent, so he continued forward, his eyes peeled and his ears open, his muscles tense, ready to flee at the slightest sound. But step by step nothing stirred.

What was the purpose of this room? What sorts of things took place here? There must have been some reason for it to be built.

Except...*did* this place ever have any kind of purpose? Or did it exist solely for *today*? He'd been thinking of all this stuff like he thought about the ruins they encountered back in the Denselands, things built by people in the distant past, by civilizations that existed on alien worlds that would have once been home. But this wasn't a fragment of the past discarded in that cosmic junkyard. Didn't Cat Lady basically say that this was all about the Keeper's plan? Andrea said that the temple they found five years ago collapsed after they opened the doorway hidden there. Clearly that place served its purpose in that moment and was done. If this were like that, then nothing would make any sense. It might be perfectly possible, then, that this room was built specifically for *him* and whatever he was going to do here *right now*. But that was such a strange thing to comprehend. There was no way someone like *him* ever warranted this much work and planning. Especially thousands of millennia before he was ever even born.

He turned all the way around as he made his way to the bottom, shining his light in every direction, uneasy. How big was this room? The walls had receded into the surrounding gloom, leaving only him here in this halo of light as he descended. With every step, he felt smaller and more insignificant, almost as if he were shrinking.

He didn't think he liked exploring this place on his own. He'd almost rather be stuck with Nicole again than on his own.

Almost.

Finally, something began to take shape in front of him. There was some kind of structure waiting in the darkness there. The sight of it made his muscles clench even tighter. If something bad were going to happen in this place, it would happen there. He was determined to be ready, but still he could see nothing to warrant his concern. No monster rushed him. No traps sprang. No alarms sounded. He really seemed to be alone in this place.

As he approached the structure, he decided that it looked sort of like a large gazebo. A raised stone platform, round, with steps leading up all around it and several columns of stone rising into the darkness above, far too tall to see their tops, but the shape made it easy to imagine a gazebo roof somewhere up there, out of sight.

Less of a colosseum feel to the space now, he decided. That was good. But now he was getting more of a human sacrifice altar vibe...which wasn't so good... But he trudged on up the steps, determined to see what was there.

He found no bloodstained altar waiting for him, thankfully. Instead, the center of the raised platform was an open pit, about twenty feet across, filled with what appeared to be some kind of fine black sand or powder, its surface so smooth and flat that he mistook it for a moment for water.

"Obsidian pool..." he muttered as he stood staring into it.

(*In obsidian pool undisturbed, sleep with the dead.*)

Seriously? She wanted him to take a *nap* in there? And what the hell did she mean by "with the dead"? Was that some kind of ancient crematorium ash or something? The thought sent a shudder of revulsion rushing through him. He didn't sign up for *that* kind of weirdness. In fact, he never signed up for any of this. Why was he even here? This was stupid!

But quitting didn't seem to be an option. He wasn't going back the way he came. For quite a few reasons. The quickest way back home to his perfectly dull and uneventful life was to just do these things and get them over with. It was extremely doubtful he was going to find a way around the creepy cat lady's bizarre instructions.

With a deep-suffering sigh, he hopped down into the pit. He expected to sink, but it was firm enough to stand on. And when he bent and raked his fingers through it, it felt like sand rather than dust or ash.

He lay down on his back, wincing at the cold feel of it against his bare back, and rested his hands on his chest with his fingers enlaced, as if he were lying in a coffin.

(Was this what the crazy cat lady meant? Or was he being too literal? He didn't even know.)

Sleep with the dead... he thought. He didn't like the sound of it. He could almost imagine dead, rotting corpses reaching up from underneath and dragging him down into some torturous, suffocating depths below. But he resisted the urge to flee. He lay there, his eyes closed, focusing on his breathing, trying to calm his thumping heart. Whatever this was, he was sure he could handle it. He'd already been through so much worse than a power nap in the dirt and some sand in his butt crack, after all.

He didn't think he'd be able to sleep, but a heavy drowsiness seemed to wrap his body like a blanket. In only a few seconds, he felt the world swimming away from him.

Chapter 22

Corey shined his light one way, then the other. There were two passageways laid out before him, one to the left and one to the right. It should have been as simple as heads or tails, and yet something wasn't as it seemed. That queer energy he felt moving through the stone didn't match what he was seeing.

He frowned and focused on the odd, alien sensation. It was difficult to put a picture to the feeling. It was almost as if he could tell that there was something *flowing* through here, but he knew that "flowing" wasn't quite the right word. It wasn't as if there were a pipe or cable running through the wall. It wasn't contained to one spot. It simply streamed through the stone itself, so that he could feel it coursing all around him, following the passages of the labyrinth. If he had to compare it to anything, the sensation was sort of similar to a magnet. Positive and negative. Push and pull. Attract and repel. Like an electrical current through a wire, this energy was carried by the stone. And strangely, that energy didn't turn to follow the other two passages. It continued straight.

He reached out and touched the wall in front of him. The longer he stood here, the more convinced he was that he should be continuing forward. Was there something hidden here like the mechanism that brought him to this area? Some well-concealed device?

He turned and looked to the left. Or maybe one of these passages circled back around to the other side of this wall.

Again, he frowned. No, that didn't feel right. He couldn't help thinking for some reason that leaving this spot would be a mistake. He might fall into some kind of trap. Or at the very least lose valuable time getting himself lost.

Something was hidden here. Something no one else would be able to see. He couldn't move from here until he figured it out. He was sure of it.

It was like those gut feelings he sometimes had about things.

And yet, he didn't know how to even begin. If he could sense what kind of mechanics were being used, he should have an idea how to work it, but he was drawing a blank.

Was this one of those things he simply didn't understand? Something to do with the differing physics between different worlds? Because if that was it, was it even possible for him to puzzle it out? What if the sentinels made a miscalculation and used elements that he couldn't process?

No. Again, that didn't feel right.

If there was one thing he was starting to understand it was that this place was built with a very specific intention. Everyone who came here had a job to do. And this was his.

That meant he'd be able to figure it out.

He sat down on the floor in front of the stubborn wall, his legs crossed under him, and stared at it. There *was* something… He just had to give himself time to see it.

He was sure of it.

Chapter 23

Everett stood there, staring into the raging storm.

Was this the way out? He'd expected to be wandering these dark corridors much longer than this.

They began hearing a distant rumbling noise not long after they passed through that first intersection. As they continued upward, it grew louder and more ominous. The stone had muffled it, making it impossible to identify until they turned a corner and began seeing flashes of lightning around the next corner.

"How is it storming?" asked Violet. She had to raise her voice to be heard over the wind and the rain. "There's no sky out here!"

That had been his thought, too. They were deep in the heart of the Denselands, which was, itself, deep in the Wood, a veritable eternity from any living world. Those places had no sun, no moon, no stars and no *clouds*. He never tried to make sense of it. He just sort of accepted it. He could see it with his own eyes, after all. It was right there, hanging over them that whole time. And once you accepted the bizarre fact that there was no sky, he supposed, you simply assumed there was no weather, either. But...what *was* the Wood, anyway? How could *anywhere* not have a sky? How did anything work in a universe like that? How was there gravity? How was there air? How was everything not frozen? It was as if everything science explained about the world was *wrong* here.

But there *had* been weather, he realized. There was *wind*. Nadia even told them that the wind in the Denselands always blew the same way, that it would point them toward their destination if needed. And where there was wind, why couldn't there be a storm?

"I guess everything's different on this side of the wall," he reasoned.

The path continued out into the wind and rain. It looked like a covered walkway, but it was already apparent that the narrow roof was doing nothing to keep the space dry. Every inch of gray stone was soaking wet from the blowing rain.

Violet was moving forward, cautious but eager to see what was out there. "Cold," she shouted.

It was, indeed. He could already feel it on his arms, legs and face.

The gusting wind whipped it into the passageway, blustering sheets of frigid mist. But it *was* rain, he was optimistic enough to notice. Not snow or ice. And it had been a few years, but he was fairly sure it was considerably warmer than the cold October lake water his deranged mother tried to drown them in that night.

They crept out onto the walkway, shielding their faces against the blowing rain, both of them struggling to see what was out here. Within seconds, Everett's clothes were soaked through in spite of the roof above him.

There were stone pillars holding up the roof in pairs, spaced about eight feet apart, but no kind of railing, which made it something of a shock when he squinted down over a dizzying drop waiting just beyond the edge.

Startled by the same sight, Violet pulled him back, nearly toppling him in the process. "Careful!"

"I'm fine," he assured her, although he wasn't sure his voice carried over the howling wind.

"Where are we?"

There was a steady strobing of lightning and the occasional hazy bolt flickering in the distance, illuminating great, shadowy shapes all around them, but as they peered out, a brilliant flash exploded from what seemed like right over the top of them, bringing with it an explosive crash of thunder that frightened a terrified scream from Violet and made her cover her ears and cringe against his shoulder. The feel of her there, so close to him, was a distraction, but not quite as much so as the strange and wondrous skyline that the bolt lit up for them.

Towering shapes loomed all around them, stretching high into the churning sky, most of them vanishing into the boiling clouds above. Some were blocky and squared. Others were tapered, like great, stretched pyramids. Still others were strangely rounded in places. Farther down, below them, there were smaller and more crowded structures, some of them massive in size. And there were dozens—maybe *hundreds*—of walkways like this one stretched between the various structures like the strands of a spiderweb, many of them hanging over terrifying heights. It truly did appear to be a city of some sort. A *metropolis*, even!

The City Beyond Memory, the puzzle box's painful information dump called it. The second gatehouse. The second temple, containing the second doorway…

But what doorway? Where did it lead? Where did the *first* one lead? No one had actually told him. Wayne and Olivia simply said that opening it caused the temple to collapse and that was pretty much the end of their story. Then they went home.

At the time, he was so intrigued by the concept of ancient temples and strange monsters and multi-dimensional college dormitories that he never thought to ask such a question.

Another bolt of lightning split the sky overhead with a deafening crash.

"Shit!" cried Violet, her hands still pressed to her ears.

He didn't blame her at all. Was it even safe out here?

He turned and looked back at the structure they'd just emerged from. It was enormous. Stone walls stretched away from them on either side as well as above and below them, well beyond his sight, even in the glare of the lightning strikes. But it didn't look like any sort of building. There were no windows. In fact, there were no features whatsoever. It just looked like a great wall of the same gray stone they'd been surrounded by since they arrived here.

"Should we hurry up and cross?" he shouted over the din of the storm.

He wasn't sure she heard him at first. She didn't respond. But after a moment—either to consider the question or to steel her nerves for the unpleasantness of the task—she straightened up, tightened her grip on his arm, and then, before he knew what was happening, she was pulling him forward through that raging tempest.

It was every bit as unpleasant as he imagined it would be. The storm blew the rain at them from every angle at once, it seemed, a cold, constant, unassailable onslaught that drenched them from head to toe before they'd made it a hundred feet and left them practically blind, presenting what was, to him at least, an entirely unanticipated extra level of difficulty. With no proper railing to guide them, and with the powerful gusting wind shoving at them from one side and then the other, if they became disoriented and veered off course just a little, it would be frightfully easy to simply step off the edge and plummet to a swift death below.

They couldn't even communicate over the screaming wind, the near-constant thunder and the raging roar of the rain pounding on the stone roof over their heads. He was deaf and blind and disoriented.

This was crazy awesome!

He hoped he survived to tell someone about this.

Clinging to each other with one arm, shielding their eyes with the other, bracing against the pummeling winds, they plowed forward.

It was such a strange sensation, being so close to a woman like this. He never interacted with *anyone* but his mother until she was gone, after all, much less any *girls*. She'd made him believe that every other person in the world was a monster. He never had any friends. And after she was taken away, he didn't set out into the world to make any, either. He was on a mission. He was searching for the truth about the universe. And about the angel he saw that night. But when he stumbled into that fairy forest and found Olivia, she hugged him. That was the first remotely intimate contact he could remember experiencing in his life. And then later, when Andrea found him, she took him by the hand and led him through that darkness. It was an odd feeling, one he'd never thought about before, a tingling, distracted sort of sensation deep inside that was a weird mixture of excitement and awkward embarrassment. And now Violet was clinging to him much the same way he saw Olivia cling to Wayne back in Gutler's Weep after they all found each other again. He could almost sort of see why it troubled him so much to lose her if it felt this nice with someone who was still little more than a stranger.

It didn't help that all three of them were remarkably pretty. He hadn't met very many women who were so distractingly attractive.

Another great flash of lightning split the sky, accompanied by an almost instantaneous explosion of deafening thunder, and Violet jumped, startled. She pressed herself against him again, sending another of those weirdly awkward sensations rushing through him.

He couldn't let himself be distracted, though. The wind was getting stronger. It was harder to walk in a straight line. Something about how high they were, perhaps? Like the powerful winds that were said to whip past the upper floors of high-rises in big cities? Wasn't that a thing? He was fairly sure he heard that somewhere once or twice.

Violet was still pulling him along by his arm, still leading the way, reminding him that she wasn't clinging to him because she was afraid or fragile, but simply to keep from losing him like they'd lost Andrea.

He was simply along for the ride. And he'd better keep up.

Around them, the wind continued to rage, threatening to blow them off their feet, forcing him to focus on his footing. How long was this bridge? He couldn't see the far side through the haze of the storm. He couldn't even see another structure waiting for them out there.

Violet jerked him to a stop, startling him. "Did you hear that?" she shouted over the storm.

"Hear what?" He shined his light at the path ahead of them, but it wasn't very useful in this haze. He could see better by the lightning. Then he turned and pointed it back the way they came. There didn't seem to be anything on the walkway with them. Not as far as the beam reached anyway. But then, that wasn't very far…

She turned and looked out over the storm-soaked city. "There it was again!"

Out there? But they were so high off the ground. What could be out there?

But then he heard it, too. It was a strange sound, almost buried under the cacophony of the storm, but it was there. A strange, almost *moaning* sound that could have been the wind howling through the eaves of a building or the branches of a forest…except of course for the fact that there was nothing like that out there. Was it only a trick of the wind in the bridge itself, as it gusted through the stone pillars? But then why did it sound like it was coming from out in that haze?

Violet held up a dainty finger in a gesture that said, "*There!* Hear it?"

And he *did* hear it. It was a strangely eerie sound in spite of the noise of the storm. He turned and peered out the other way, over the drenched city. Maybe there was some sort of structure supporting the bridge under their feet, where they couldn't see it. Maybe the wind was rushing through that.

"It sounds like voices!" she shouted.

"Just the wind," he shouted back.

But when he looked at her again, she was suddenly nose-to-nose with him. Those lovely green eyes were wide open in spite of the blowing wind and rain that kept forcing him to squint. And there was something strangely distant about those eyes, as if she weren't looking at him at all, as if she weren't looking at *anything*. "Drafts!" she said in a voice that was both hers and not hers.

"What?"

"Born from the storm. Ever drifting through the currents above. Able to drain the life from the living on contact. Don't linger on the city's high bridges."

He stared into those strangely empty eyes, confused. Drafts? Something alive in the storm?

Again, he heard that creepy moaning sound from somewhere out over those hazy heights and he glanced in that direction. When he looked back again, Violet was blinking away the rain in her eyes.

"What're you doing?" she shouted, pushing him away from her.

"Me?" he shouted back. "You're the one being weird!" *This time,* he added in his head, understanding all too well the irony of telling *other people* they were being weird.

"What?" But she didn't wait for an explanation. Another of those creepy moans gusted over them from the storm and she turned and looked out over the city. "What *is* that?"

This was strange. Didn't she just tell him what it was? Something called a "draft"? And that it was dangerous for them to be standing out here like this?

If that wasn't her, then who was it?

Thinking back now, didn't she do something like that after she woke up back in the gouging station, too?

From the corner of his eye, he glimpsed something. A shadowy shape whipped past them. It looked like a piece of fabric or plastic caught in the wind, visible for only an instant. He turned for a better look, but it was already gone.

And yet, when he turned back to face Violet, he saw it again on the other side of the bridge, and ahead of them. It should've been within her line of sight, too, but she didn't seem to notice it. Was it one of those things only *he* could see? Like the mushrooms and smudges in Gutler's Weep?

"We have to go!" he shouted, pulling at her arm.

"What's happening?"

"No time!"

They hurried forward, plowing their way through the wind and rain as more and more drafts whipped past them in the surrounding tempest.

Chapter 24

Andrea blinked her watering eyes and found that everything had changed again. The Elysium Fog's phantom bar had vanished. She was back inside the stone walls of the temple labyrinth, still clutching her flashlight, as if everything that just happened was nothing more than an intense hallucination. Except this wasn't even the same place she was before she was stolen away to that displaced bar. She was now standing in a *curved* passage.

"What happened?" she gasped. She felt weirdly lightheaded. She took a step forward and staggered. Everything felt like it was slowly spinning. Was she swaying on her feet? How strong was that drink?

She reached out and leaned against the wall. In front of her, there was an opening on the right, revealing another corridor running beside this one. She turned around and shined her light behind her. There was another opening on the other side back there. She remembered areas like this in the Temple of the Blind, too. Areas of the labyrinth that were confounding concentric circles or spirals filled with dead ends.

"Erin?" She faced forward again, sweeping her light across the opening and the next passage. "Where'd you go?"

"Here," Erin replied.

She turned and squinted into the darkness. That strange, silvery mist she encountered before she was sent to that bar was hovering back there, barely visible in the gloom.

"Focus on my voice. Don't rely on your physical eyes."

"Wha...?" She squeezed her eyes shut, confused.

"I'm right in front of you."

Again, she opened her eyes. This time, Erin was standing there, just on the other side of that farther opening in the wall, still dressed in her slivery dress. But she looked oddly blurry, as if she were looking at her through a dingy window. Or like when she woke up and her eyes were all blurry and gunky. But at the same time, her sunflowers were crisp and unnaturally bright, seeming almost to glow in the gloom, as if giving off their own light.

(Was that silvery mist some kind of manifestation of her ghostly dress? Was that a thing?)

Erin reached up and pointed her first and middle fingers at her own eyes. "Hold my gaze for a little bit. Memorize my eyes."

"I still feel funny from that drink."

"That'll pass. Trust me. You're almost there."

"Almost *where?*"

"You'll see."

This was so frustrating. What did Erin's ghost eyes have to do with anything? Was she just toying with her? Her belly felt wonky. Everything seemed to be tilting to one side. It was only one shot. What did she pour into that glass?

"There." Erin smiled at her. "Now look around."

"At *what?*" she asked. There was nothing here but the two of them. It was an empty corridor. But even as the question passed her lips, she realized that something had changed. There were strange, shadowy shapes clinging to the stone like creeping vines, but lumpy and strangely oozing. She looked down at her feet and saw that she was standing on one, but she couldn't feel it beneath the sole of her shoe. She reached up and tried to touch one, but her fingers passed right through it. Aiming her light at them didn't make them stand out any more or less. Although she could see all of them clearly, it felt for some reason as if they didn't really exist.

She turned and looked the other way. It ran the length of the corridor in both directions, as far as her light would reach. There were dozens of tiny dark specks floating about, too, she realized. They blossomed in and out of sight, sort of like fireflies, except...well...*opposite.* They *darkened* into existence instead of brightened. It was bizarre. She kept trying to blink them away as if they were specks of dust in her eyes. "Seriously," she breathed, "what was in that drink?"

"It won't last long. Just enough to train your psychic eye to focus on them."

"What are they?"

"Things fundamentally connected to the Murk."

Look for the Murk, she thought, remembering Horatio's mysterious instructions. *Sometimes it bleeds.*

Someone muttered something behind her and she twirled around, startled...but there was no one there. As she stared down the corridor, she heard what sounded like a distant scream from the opposite direction. This time, when she turned, her light fell on something strange and twisted. The dark, emaciated thing she glimpsed before Erin spirited her away to that imaginary fragment of the Elysium Fog.

"They're not what they appear to be," said Erin.

Her heart pounding with fright, Andrea squeezed her eyes closed, then looked again. That creepy shape was still there, but it had changed from a freestanding, skeletal thing into what amounted to nothing more than another shadow writhing on the wall. As she watched, it withdrew into the shadows as if *it* were afraid of *her*.

"Your living brain is constrained by the senses you use to perceive the world around you. Whatever it is you think you're seeing and hearing is just your mind doing its best to tell you what's there."

"So they're not really what I'm seeing…because I wouldn't understand what they *really* look like?"

"Sort of? It'll make sense after you're dead," she promised.

Andrea decided to drop the subject. She was in no hurry to understand it if that was what it took. "This is so *weird*…"

"Being dead isn't the same as being alive," explained Erin. "There's no equivalent in the living world. You're not born. You don't require food, water or air. Your existence isn't defined by your heartbeat or electrical synapses in your brain. Or by the environment human beings evolved to live in. You're not bound to a physical body or to the limits of biological senses. Even our earthly sense of *time* becomes meaningless. After we die, we're only a fraction of what we were in life. Little more than a shadow in comparison. But we're also so much *more*."

"Is this going to be on the test?"

"You've been given the ability to see the other side. That's your gift. And that's the role you've been given here. You can do this. You're the *only* one who can do this."

"If you say so…"

Erin turned, frowning, her gaze distant, as if she were looking not *at* the walls, but *through* them. "She's coming. We're almost out of time."

Andrea followed her gaze, frightened. "The Priestess of Ruin," she'd called her. Something somehow even worse than Glum. "What is she?"

"I don't know that. I don't know if *anyone* does anymore. Something ancient beyond words. Something *primitive*. *Primal*. She's neither living nor dead. I don't know if *evil* is the right word, but she's certainly *dangerous*. And she's particularly focused on *you* for some reason."

She groaned and swept back the crowding darkness with her light.

"It'll be fine," Erin decided, turning those pretty eyes back on her.

"It really doesn't sound like it!"

"Quick. Look in this one," she instructed, gesturing toward the passage behind her.

Andrea stepped through the opening and shined her light one way, then the other, frowning. "There's nothing in this one." It looked just like every other corridor.

"Exactly. Which corridor overlaps with the Murk?"

"Oh... Okay. I get it." She turned and looked back at the mysterious shapes clinging to the stone in the first corridor, only to find that Erin was standing several yards away, in front of another passage. She looked back again, half-expecting there to be two of her.

"I'd start here," she instructed.

Andrea squinted at her in the gloom. "The last person I met who could teleport tried to drop me off a roof."

Erin tilted her head to one side, confused. "I'm...sorry...?"

She closed her eyes and sighed. "This is all kinds of messed up. You know that, right?" When she opened her eyes, Erin was standing right in front of her again, giving her an apologetic shrug. "That's freaky. Do you just *know* how to do that when you're dead?"

Erin frowned. "I guess? Lots of stuff doesn't translate very well between living and dead."

"Oh." She rubbed her eyes, still trying to shake off the weirdness of that drink. When she opened them again, Erin was back by the other passageway again.

"She's getting closer. Take this passage. Follow the murk. It'll lead you."

She squinted at one of those shadowy tendrils, confused. "Wait..." Follow the murk? "Is the Murk a place...? Or is it this black stuff?"

"It's both. The Murk is the entirety of the spirit realm, just like all the various worlds you've been through are part of the physical world. But anything that bleeds through into the living realms is also murk."

Sometimes it bleeds, Andrea recalled again, shuddering a little at the words. Why did it have to sound so creepy?

"It's confusing, I know. Chalk it up to the whole 'things don't translate well' thing."

"Okay..."

"Now hurry." Again, she gestured at the passageway. "We're out of time."

Andrea stared at the passage. Thinking about it now, was that particular opening even there before? There was the one she was standing in and that other one on the other side some distance away... But she didn't remember seeing that one when she first looked around.

(*In the places where the living and dead overlap, there are often more than one path to choose from.*)

She frowned at the memory. Was Horatio telling her that there were passages down here that could only be seen using her strange connection to the dead?

This was exhausting. Why did *she* have to be the one doing all this?

"Okay," she sighed, stepping forward. "I can do this. It's only the dead."

"That's the attitude."

"They can't scare me."

But when she shined her light into the next tunnel, she froze. The ceiling in there was crawling with strange, black shapes. Squirming streamers of black mist dangled down and shapes like eerie, oozing hands reached out of the walls. There was an entire *swarm* of those little black shadows, like a dense and churning cloud of flies.

She could hear dreadful voices drifting from somewhere down there. Mutterings and murmurings…sobbing…distant screams… It was as if she were standing at the very mouth of hell itself, listening to the moans and wails of the suffering damned.

And as she stared into that horrible, writhing passageway, she clearly heard something in there *growl* at her.

Erin offered her a sympathetic frown. "Well…I didn't say you wouldn't be *scared*."

Chapter 25

Albert remained crouched on the floor of the stone platform in front of Brandy and Gina, his free hand shielding his eyes from the onslaught of the wind and rain so that he could keep his gaze fixed on the strange, shadowy shape looming above them. Even without the rain hindering him, he couldn't see it clearly. The only light sources were those flashes of lightning, bright enough to allow glimpses of these alien surroundings but far too brief and infrequent to allow him a clear grasp of what was really there.

What were these things? How did they live in this place? What did they eat? He was reminded of the hounds back in the first temple, and how it never made any sense that a predator of that size could thrive in such a desolate place with no obvious food source, much less an entire *pack* of them.

Then again, he supposed the real mystery was why he kept looking for logical explanations in a world where things like this existed.

And then there was the matter of his priorities. Far more important than the diet sustaining these things was their mobility. How fast could they run? Could they jump? Could they climb or swim? This one was just lurking there. It wasn't moving. He never saw it blink that one visible, cataract eye. Was it able to see them? Or was it blind? Was it even alive?

How long had they been here? His legs were starting to get sore from crouching and the thing hadn't so much as twitched.

It didn't seem to be aware of them. He was fairly sure it would've done something by now if it had. Maybe they could sneak under it.

But the very next bright flash of crashing lightning revealed that it had vanished.

He shot to his feet, startled, his eyes wide and alert. Where did it go? Was it about to attack? Already the light was gone. He was blind.

But Gina was again on the move, pulling on them, leading them under the upper platform. In an instant, the rain and wind were blocked, the noise suddenly muted.

It felt so strange, observing her. She didn't wait for the lightning flashes to light her way because she didn't need them. She could essentially see in the dark. *She just knows what's in her surroundings*, he recalled Nicole telling them when they first met her. *Like a human radar or something*. It was almost the same thing Violet said when they first arrived in the Denselands. (*She knows things, too. Lots of things.*) They didn't say she "sees" things or "feels" things.

He was still interested in having a proper conversation with her, but now certainly wasn't the time.

He looked back the way they came and a flash of lightning revealed something prickly perched at the far end of the stone bridge where there wasn't something before.

They passed through an opening much smaller than the one they entered through and out into the rain again. Once again, the cold hit him like a punch in the gut, taking his breath away. This was every bit as miserable as those frigid pools of water in the first temple. They'd be lucky if they didn't end up sick after this.

Gina steered them left, then right, then right again, weaving through towering walls, rows of columns, and more of those strange stone spheres. The structures that resembled buildings were getting bigger, slowly turning from office buildings and apartment complexes to sprawling factories and towering high-rises. And yet none of them were any such thing. Just as she'd told them, there were no doors or windows leading inside, no sign of people, present or past. Just miles and miles and miles of featureless gray stone, no different, really, than the first temple.

Gina stumbled to a stop and immediately turned and pulled them both back the way they came.

What did she sense? He looked back as he hurried along, but he could see nothing in the hazy flashes of the storm.

They turned and fled into a narrow alleyway—if that was what you could call a gap between two big stone structures that weren't actually buildings—and then turned again, only to stop and change direction once more.

In another flash of light, he saw the pinched look on her face. Something was frightening her. She couldn't seem to find a safe route. And he had no idea how to help. His own psychic abilities weren't nearly as strong as hers. And to use them, he'd need to stop and get handsy with his wife, and now simply didn't seem like a good time for that.

They hurried back out into the open, past more thin columns of stone jutting toward the boiling sky and then across another bridge.

It was here, as a great, lingering flash of lightning forked across the sky, that he glimpsed the sentinel.

It was standing on a platform of stone in the middle of the raging river and looked exactly like every other sentinel statue they'd seen. Immaculately carved stone in exquisite detail, ten feet tall, muscular and naked, its body stretched grotesquely. Like most of those statues, it was standing stiff, feet together, faceless head forward. Ridiculously enormous penis dangling limp between its thighs. But instead of its hands hanging down at its sides, it was holding a great, round bowl of some sort out in front of it with its elongated hands and fingers. The rain had filled the bowl to overflowing and water was pouring down the sides and into the river.

Gina reached the far side of the bridge and turned right, but immediately stopped and went left, instead.

But again she stopped.

This wasn't good. He didn't need to be psychic to figure out that they were running out of directions to run.

She struggled for a moment, then she turned around and fled back across the bridge. But she stopped again. She looked one way, then the other, her expression filled with mounting fear.

He looked back and forth, too, but he could see nothing but gray stone and sheets of rain in the flashes of lightning.

She backed into Brandy, pressing herself against her, frightened. "I don't know what to do!" she shouted over the din of the storm. "I can't find a way past them!"

Brandy wrapped her arms around her and looked up at Albert, her pretty face stretched into a terrified expression behind her rain-streaked glasses. But he didn't know what to do, either. He couldn't even see the things she said were closing in around them.

But they couldn't just keep standing here, either.

Again, lightning split the sky. This time, he *did* see something. It was creeping along the river's edge toward them, something large and prickly in the shadows.

Another bolt followed the first and he looked out at the shadowy sentinel, at the water pouring from the bowl.

He grasped Gina's shoulders and leaned over her so that his face was hovering right above hers. As loudly and as calmly as possible, he spoke to her: "You said we have to go *down*."

"There isn't a way down," she shouted over the storm.

"Then where does the water go?"

She blinked up at him in the electric strobing of the sky for a moment, confused. Then her expression bloomed with understanding.

He watched as she squeezed her eyes closed, focusing her psychic eye on the space around them. She turned her head left, then right...upward...then she blinked and squinted up at him again. She nodded. "It's possible!"

"What's possible?" asked Brandy.

Gina glanced over her shoulder, then grabbed both their hands and pulled them toward the side of the bridge. "No time! You have to trust me!"

As Albert turned, he saw another shape moving in the haze of the storm. The strobing lightning gave it an eerie effect, as if it were flickering in and out of existence, drawing closer with each flash.

Gina stepped up to the edge of the bridge and looked down into the rushing river. Then she gave them each one last pull.

"You're crazy!" shouted Brandy.

But Gina had already let go of them both and jumped.

"Oh my god!"

Albert didn't have time to convince her. Monsters were closing in on them. At least four. No...at least *five*. He grabbed her arm and threw himself into the water, taking her with him.

She had just enough time to scream.

He had just enough time to hope she'd forgive him when this was over.

Chapter 26

Nicole ran. She had no clue where she was running *to*. She didn't take the time to consider which direction she was going. She turned blindly, from one passage to the next, deeper and deeper into this abysmal darkness until she was almost certainly too lost to ever be found.

That awful voice in her head had died down to mutters again, but she could still hear it. It was still out there. And for all she knew, that monster could make itself sound like that no matter how far or near it was, fooling her into believing she was getting away right up until she ran headlong into it.

And that didn't even include whatever other horrors might be down here. The first temple had no shortage of monsters. Why would this one be any different?

She kept hoping to glimpse a light somewhere in this darkness. Even just the briefest confirmation that she wasn't really alone. Was that too much to hope for?

Breathless, her legs aching, she turned another corner and began to slow down. She couldn't keep doing this. She was in better shape than most, but she was only human. And she was already weirdly exhausted when she arrived here, as if she'd run miles during that missing time between Hotdog's terrifying reappearance and waking up in the dark.

She really hoped her luck changed soon. This would be a really shitty way to die.

She turned another corner and pushed onward a few more steps. Then she stopped.

There was a room ahead of her. But something was dreadfully wrong about it. Her light hovered over the floor beyond the end of the passage. The familiar smooth stone gave way to coarse, black earth.

"No..." she gasped. It couldn't be. Not another one.

Her knuckles white on her phone, she crept forward, pushing back the darkness, revealing more and more of that black soil.

Dreams came rushing back to her. *So many* dreams. Far more than she remembered until just this second. Dreams of being lost in this very darkness, sometimes naked, sometimes not, but always alone, always afraid...and always ending up *here*...

She could see water farther out. Its surface still as glass. And above it, unsettlingly familiar branches.

(*Stay away from the meadow.*)

A terrified sob escaped her before she knew it was there. Why was she looking at the meadow right now? It should have been swallowed with the rest of the temple's horrors that night.

And why was she suddenly remembering all these dreams? And in such detail? How many times had she been here these past five years? She remembered staring in at it just like this countless times, at the unmoving surface of that water, at the drooping branches of that dead tree...

But there were also times where she found herself *in* that terrible meadow, surrounded by dreadful things. And sometimes her friends were there, swallowed up in the darkness, lost to the horrors within.

(*Just let her die. What do you care?*)

She turned and fled back the way she came, tears streaming down her face.

Why had the meadow been haunting her like this? What did it mean? And why was it still here? Nothing made sense. Nothing *had* made sense from the moment that disgusting barely-there got into her head at the wedding.

The creepy muttering was getting louder again. Startled, she realized she'd forgotten what she was running from *before* she stumbled across the meadow. If she wasn't careful, she'd run right back into that monster's broken arms.

She turned left. Then right. Then left twice more. At this point in time, she realized she was *trying* to get lost. The more lost she became, the less likely she was to be found by Zombie Hotdog.

And it wasn't like she had any idea where the fuck she needed to go anyway.

This passageway was curving to the right now. Ahead of her, a new passage branched off to the left. She chose it without pausing to think it over, not daring to waste a single second.

But she stumbled to a stop as the way forward opened onto black soil again.

She cursed and backed away. Had she merely gone in a circle?

No... The first time she was here, the passage wasn't curved like this.

It was like this five years ago, too, she recalled. They kept finding themselves back at the meadow for a while, as if *all* the passages led to it.

She retreated back to the last intersection and continued to the right where she last chose left. A few minutes later, she found an inter-secting passageway and chose right again, only to find herself staring at a dead end a moment later. Retracing her steps, she chose left, then left again, then right, which brought her to another dead end. Frustrated, she hurried back, took the other path, only to find herself back at the meadow.

This was frustrating! Why did she keep coming back here? She was wearing herself out and getting nowhere in the process!

She stared at that awful black earth as she backed away, her frightened mind dragging her back to that night five years ago, when she and Brandy and Albert were here.

It had a strange effect on Albert, in particular, she recalled. There was a moment when he was actually about to step off the stone and onto that awful dirt, almost as if something inside were luring him in. When it was all said and done, they'd all simply dismissed it as his natu-ral curiosity. That was, after all, what had lured him into those tunnels in the first place. But now that she was back…now that she was finding herself staring into it again and again…and after all those dreams she'd been having… Was it possible that there really was some sinister intelli-gence in there somehow drawing her back?

If she wasn't careful, could she, too, forget herself and step blind-ly onto that black earth?

She turned and fled again, back the way she came, but after a few minutes, she found herself at an intersection that she remembered en-countering before…except, she couldn't remember which ways she'd been.

Run all you want…

She clasped her hands over her ears, knowing it would do no good. She wasn't hearing the words with her ears. They were still inside her head, in her own voice, pretending to be her own thoughts.

You can't avoid me forever….

"Bitch, watch me!" she grunted, choosing a direction at random.

But almost immediately, she arrived at another dead end. A des-perate panic was building up inside her. She couldn't afford to deal with dead ends. She needed to get far away from here.

She ran back and chose a different direction. Was this the same passage from before? Was she just retracing her own steps at this point?

She turned left, then right, then right, then left, then cursed as she once again found herself back at the meadow.

Anun amum ut mu.

Again, she retreated. Again, she chose paths at random, hoping each one would take her somewhere different, somewhere far away from this part of the labyrinth.

Her cell phone light pushed back the darkness as she fled. Would it reveal another dead end or another doorway leading into that wicked meadow? Either one might be her last. She was getting nowhere and she was running desperately low on time!

But something different appeared from the gloom ahead of her this time.

She stumbled to a stop, a great startled gasp escaping her.

This wasn't the meadow. There was none of that raw black earth. In fact, there was no ground at all. She stood at the edge of a sheer drop into utter darkness.

She was back at the bottomless chasm. This was where Hotdog Corpse dropped from the ceiling and almost landed on her. She was standing in one of the passages that didn't open onto a bridge. If she'd been running any faster, she might've fallen to her death without any help from her undead stalker.

She swept her light back and forth, up and down. There was a bridge above and to the right. Another one was just visible far off to the left. A third was below her, about twenty feet down and a little to the right again.

A dead end after all.

She turned to flee back the way she came, only to find the hulking monster lumbering out of the darkness at her.

Anun amum...

She cried out, half cursing and half crying, half frustrated and half terrified. This wasn't fair! Why wouldn't this monster leave her alone?

She turned and shined her light back down at that lower bridge. It was too far to simply drop down onto and too narrow to reliably land on. The slightest hesitation and she'd fall to her death. Best case scenario she'd break an ankle. But there was no other choice.

Cursing, she dared a few steps toward the monster, then took a running start.

No hesitation. If she let so much as an ounce of fear hold her back, she'd never make it.

She leapt.

Her scream echoed through the chasm, but she barely heard it. Her mind was numb with terror.

Her feet struck the surface of the bridge with a bone jarring jolt and she tumbled forward, stumbling, tripping. She had too much momentum. She couldn't catch her balance. She was going to fall off the other side!

She shoved her weight into the stone grasping at it, trying desperately to stop herself.

Her right arm and leg slipped over the edge. She found herself staring down into that bottomless blackness.

But she'd stopped.

She wasn't sure if she was screaming or cursing or praying or crying or some combination of them all, but somehow she made it!

As she crawled away from that deadly ledge, however, she heard a familiar sound behind her. That wet sand sort of sound of something heavy and gross slamming against the stone floor.

She looked over her shoulder to see the broken form of Hotdog Corpse sprawled on the bridge, his broken arms already working to pick himself up again.

This guy seriously didn't know when to give up!

She scrambled to her feet and ran from the bridge, back into the winding depths of the labyrinth, desperate to put as much distance as possible between her and that festering freak.

Her heart still racing from that terrifying jump, she could barely think straight. She turned left at the first intersection she found. Then right.

Left.

Right.

Right again.

Left.

God, she was tired! How much longer was she going to be able to keep running like this?

The passage was curving to the left now. She tried to remember how many turns she'd taken, which direction she was going, but it was impossible to think straight.

Another split in the path. Left or right? This was all so frustrating!

If she was already veering left, then maybe right?

She picked up her pace and kept running...but all she found was yet another dead end.

This time, when she turned to flee, a great and dreadful shadow was blocking the way back.

Anun Goar Nangup.

She backed against the wall, a terrified sob escaping her. There

was nowhere left to run. She was trapped.
And no one was coming to save her.

Chapter 27

Olivia had a bad feeling.

It started as they were walking away from that hound passage. It wasn't one of those intense, imminent peril feelings like back in Dunnen when they tried to leave the city or in the fairy circle whenever those nasty never-children were about to strike. It was much more subtle than that. More of a constant, looming dread kind of thing that she felt deep in her stomach, a continuous, aching sort of anxiety that was slowly making her feel sick to her stomach.

Was it something to do with whatever they heard going on with that hound? Like Wayne, she'd found herself wondering if there could be something in these tunnels even more dangerous than a hound, something capable of actually preying on them regardless of those deadly scales. Maybe it was nothing more than that idea floating around in her head, of some *ultimate* super predator lurking somewhere in these gray walls. The thought was more than terrifying enough to fill her with this kind of anxiety. But she didn't think it was only her imagination at work.

The passage they were currently following kept inclining and then leveling off again, over and over, carrying them up one level after another. Five times now, if she hadn't lost count, but she couldn't quite tell how far each incline carried them upward, or even if they were ascending the same distance each time. The Temple of the Blind wasn't like the mazes on the backs of cereal boxes. It was more than an enormous, sprawling labyrinth. It was *countless* labyrinths, all stacked on top of one another, stretching from the top of that burning mountain to deep beneath the streets of Briar Hills. And this was no different.

How could they ever hope to find *anything* in a place like this? Were they doing it right? Were they *supposed* to be going upward? No one had given them any direction to follow. Were they at the bottom, trying to get to the top? Or were they going the wrong way and their goal was hidden somewhere far below? What if they started out exactly where they needed to be and immediately did something wrong?

She didn't like mazes very much, she decided. They were very impractical.

Ahead of them, the passage finally opened up. There appeared to be a chamber of some sort waiting up there. She hoped it wasn't more hounds. Those things freaked her out.

But when they stepped out into the open and shined their lights around, they found something completely new.

The space before them was less a chamber than a bottomless abyss. They were standing on a small platform, overlooking a huge, cylindrical shaft that their flashlights barely reached halfway across. That dark, empty space was crisscrossed with walkways of the same gray stone they'd been walking on this whole time, but were all frightfully narrow, barely more than a foot wide, most of them sloped up or down, with no visible supports holding them up.

"This is just stupid," grumbled Wayne. "What's the point in something like this? It looks like a lame video game level."

Olivia stared at the walkways in front of her, her stomach twisting into a terrified knot. "There's no way," she breathed.

He pulled her closer to him and hugged her. "Yeah. Heights aren't really your thing."

It wasn't as if she were cripplingly phobic. She could climb a stepladder. She could ride a Ferris wheel. She could even fly on an airplane. Things like that didn't bother her very much. But standing at the top of an observation tower, for example, looking down over some flimsy railing, with nothing but a harrowing drop and the hard ground waiting to catch her... Or one of those ropes courses like they had at the vacation resorts her family had always visited in the summers, where they tethered you to a track and set you loose to explore an obstacle course of tightropes, balance beams and all sorts of wobbling, spinning, twisting things three stories above the arcade floor... That sort of thing made her weak in the knees. But being up high like this, on narrow platforms, with no railings, no tethers, no *anything* to keep her from tumbling over the edge and plunging to her death was an absolute nightmare.

There was one place she saw in the first temple that looked like this. But it wasn't a single, vertical hole. It was a horizontal chasm between two massive stone walls, with bridges connecting openings across the gap. But those bridges were the same width as the passageways on either end of them. She'd simply kept to the middle. It was only when they were climbing the burning mountain outside, when the path required them to climb in places and even sidle across narrow stretches of path between sheer walls and dangerous drops, that her fear of heights really began to kick in.

And she still had nightmares about that corpse monster dropping her through those night tree branches in the dark and stranding her in the Wood. That was an absolutely traumatizing few seconds when she had no idea how high up she was or where she was going to land.

And of course when Brandy opened the door and the temple collapsed. That was even worse. She experienced true freefall for a few seconds there before Andrea caught them in her weird little portal. That was terrifying beyond words, like living her worst nightmare. She was fairly sure she wet herself on the way down, but she'd never admit that to anyone. (And since she was naked at the time, no one could prove it, either.) She *never* wanted to experience something like that again.

But this...

Each walkway began and ended at a rounded platform just like this one, and each platform had two or three walkways protruding from it, connecting multiple passageways at different heights. But not all of the platforms had passageways leading from them. In fact, most of them didn't, which meant they'd have to cross several narrow walkways in order to reach a way out.

She shook her head. No way. She couldn't do it.

Wayne was sweeping his light across the room, from one narrow platform to another. She could almost read his mind. He was wondering if the labyrinth was designed so that they wouldn't be able to avoid something like this, if they'd only be wasting time trying to go around.

"Strange," he said after a moment. "It's a lot wider than a balance beam. It wouldn't cause a lot of people problems. But for someone afraid of heights..."

She frowned up at him. "You think they made this deathtrap just for *me?*"

He shrugged. "No clue. But it's just odd that they'd have something like this. Kind of specific, isn't it?"

"I'm not going out there."

"I know. We passed an intersection a ways back. Let's try one of those paths."

The relief she felt hearing him say that was almost enough to leave her lightheaded. She thought for a moment he was going to try to talk her into it. But there was no way. Not a chance. She'd definitely start crying. She might even have thrown a full-blown tantrum.

Wayne gave her a gentle squeeze, then turned and started back the way they came.

Ever her hero.

She pressed herself closer to him, thankful. Sometimes he could get careless, like back in Gutler's Weep, when he insisted on going up that ladder. He'd promised to stay by her and he went up it anyway. That wasn't nice. She still wanted to smack him for that. But most of the time he was considerate.

Besides, that was how they met Everett, so she couldn't be *too* mad about it.

"There was a lot of weird stuff in the first temple," he recalled. "Like that one super narrow tunnel we had to crawl through. Remember that?"

"I barely fit my chubby butt through there. I thought Andrea was going to have to pull me out by my feet."

"Your butt's not chubby. It's perfect."

"Aw. Yours, too."

"Thanks."

She smirked up at him. "I should know. I could see right up it when we were crawling through there."

She couldn't help giggling at the way that made him grimace. "That couldn't have been flattering," he grumbled.

She shrugged. "It obviously didn't scare me off," she said, flashing him her engagement ring.

"I guess that's true…"

She remembered that part of the journey pretty vividly. The passage kept getting smaller and smaller, making her duck, then hunch, then stoop, until eventually they had no choice but to get down on their hands and knees and crawl. She remembered fumbling with her flashlight and wondering just how small it was going to get when she happened to look up… She was pretty sure she turned every shade of red possible. It still kind of made her blush to think about it to this day, if she were honest. It was so startlingly shocking that it didn't even occur to her until later that Andrea had the same view of her and it was only marginally less embarrassing than it would've been if Wayne had been behind her instead.

"But the reason I brought that up," Wayne went on, "was because I remember talking to Albert once about how there were so many places in there that would've been impossible for someone claustrophobic to pass through."

He was right, she knew. There was a point when she wasn't sure she was going to make it. It shrank down so small that she could barely move. It was really scary.

"Or anyone with a significant disability."

"Or anyone any fatter than me," she added.

"You're not fat. You're perfect. Stop that."

"What? I like making you compliment me."

"That's not healthy self-esteem."

"I don't care," she told him, nuzzling his arm. He was right, of course. But she couldn't help herself sometimes. It just made her happy to hear him argue with her about it.

"And anyone who couldn't swim or had a crippling fear of water wouldn't have been able to cross those flooded areas," he went on.

"Oh yeah…" There were several places like that. She remembered how cold the water was and feeling like she was going to catch pneumonia before the night was over, but what would she have done if she hadn't been able to swim? She never would've made it. And she wouldn't have been there to pick the correct paths up the mountain…

"Much less if someone was afraid of the dark. Or even a significant fear of spiders or rats, considering we had to go through the city sewer tunnels to even *get* to the temple."

"You think the sentinels really built this place with us, specifically, in mind?"

"I mean…when you really think about it, how else could they be sure we'd even make it this far?"

She wasn't sure if she liked that thought. It sort of felt like the sentinels had already written her life for her, long before she was ever even born. It was a strangely suffocating kind of feeling.

Ahead of them, the intersection came into view. It was a single passage branching to the right. If they went straight, they'd go back to where the hounds were. Hopefully going right would take them somewhere less scary.

But as they reached the intersection and Wayne started to turn, she paused, her gaze fixed on the darkness straight ahead of them.

"You okay?"

"Yeah…" she replied. But that feeling of something not right was still lingering. And it felt like it was getting stronger.

What did it mean?

Chapter 28

"I don't want to go anywhere today," sighed Amber as she nuzzled against him. "Let's just stay in."

That sounded perfectly fine to Keith. He could use a break. It'd been a long week.

"I don't want to leave this bed until you have to go back to work."

"You'll probably have to use the bathroom before then," he reasoned.

"Future Me's problem." She rolled onto her back and stretched, the sheets falling away in the process, revealing all of her slim, naked body. His gaze washed over her. Those unimpressive little breasts, the overgrown tuft of stark black hair between her thighs. There was a certain roughness about her body that had never been his idea of feminine perfection. Those protruding hip bones. The hard ridges of her ribs and sternum as she arched her back. She hadn't even shaved her armpits very recently. But none of these things bothered him, he found. There was something nice about the stark honesty of her body, the level of trust and ease that it represented. She had a comfortable sort of beauty about her that was both familiar and intimate.

And yet for some reason something about her felt very *unfamiliar.*

She rolled over and snuggled up to him again. She kissed his chest. Those messy black curls tickled his chin. Her small hand slid up and down his bare chest and she draped her leg over him.

He stared at that big, gaudy tattoo on her thigh. That was the only thing that really still bothered him. It simply wasn't very attractive. Why did it have to be so big? And did that shield always have an image of a gnarled tree embossed on it? He thought it used to be something different...

"I still kind of can't believe it," she said. She lifted her hand and looked at the shiny new ring on her finger. "It's crazy, isn't it? Like, who'd have thought we'd end up like this?"

He lifted his hand and looked at his own wedding band. How *did* it end up like this? Amber had never been the kind of girl he pictured as *anyone's* wife, let alone his. It was so out of character for her. She was a wild spirit, too in love with her own freedom to ever tie herself down. She was the girl who came and went like the seasons. He didn't even really know all that much about her, when he stopped to think about it. What she did when she wasn't with him. Who she spent time with. Who she slept with...

That seemed like a lot of distance for two people to travel...

(...*we're a long way from home. A lot farther than we should've been able to go in that time on an ordinary boat...*)

What was that memory just now? It surfaced for just an instant, then vanished again. But for that one second, it felt like there was somewhere else he was supposed to be right now.

He stared at his ring, frowning. How *did* they get from there to here? They were casual lovers. Friends with benefits. He couldn't quite remember when that relationship changed, when it turned into something serious.

He couldn't remember when he proposed to her...

Or even their wedding for that matter...

He sat up, confused and looked around.

"What's wrong?" asked Amber.

This wasn't right. This was his bedroom, but where was the window? There was nothing but a blank wall where it should've been. "Where am I?"

She sat up and gave her head a too-familiar tilt. "What're you talking about? You're at home."

No. This wasn't home. If he were home, there'd be a window right there. He stood up and stepped out into the hallway. The doors to the bathroom and his mother's room were open. He could see that the windows were missing from there, too. He turned and rushed out into the dining room. *All* the windows were gone. And so was the front door. There was no way out.

Amber's body pressed against his back, startling him. Her arms were around him before he knew she was there. He never heard her approaching. "Come back to bed," she whined.

He looked down at those slender hands, at the glint of reflected lamplight off the diamond on her ring.

It looked like Amber. It *felt* like Amber. But this couldn't be Amber.

"What are you?" he asked.

She didn't answer at first. She simply stood there, her naked body pressed against his back, her hands clutching at his chest. She seemed to be pondering the question. Then she surprised him by asking a question of her own: "What do you want?"

"What?" He was still staring at the ring on her finger, distracted. Something about the way it glinted in the light was strangely familiar.

Somewhere nearby, he thought he heard voices muttering. Somewhere beyond those imprisoning walls, perhaps?

"What do you want?" she asked him again.

"I want to leave," he replied.

She stepped around him and kissed him. It caught him off guard. He stumbled backward, confused, and tripped over something.

He fell…and he fell…and he fell… A long, long way, it seemed. Everything went fuzzy and upside down and backward. And the whole time he was falling, she kept kissing him.

This wasn't right. Why was everything so confusing?

"Mmm…" she sighed.

He was sitting down now, his back resting against something soft and cozy. Where was he? What happened? He could feel her hand on his bare chest, her fingertips gliding over his skin. His body felt damp with sweat and his heart was pounding.

She was warm. Her skin smelled like sunscreen. Her lips tasted like red wine.

Slowly, she pulled away and smiled at him.

He stared back at her, disoriented.

"Did I break your brain again?" asked Nicole, giving him that familiar, sultry grin.

They were in a hotel room. He was sitting in the armchair and she was straddling his lap. They'd just made love. And it was *exquisite*.

She snuggled up to him, her full breasts pressing against his skin, and kissed his neck. He loved when she did that… It sent shivers down his whole body. He closed his eyes and savored the feeling. What was he thinking about? He couldn't quite remember. She *did* have that effect on him, it seemed. She was the most amazing lover he'd ever had.

(*What the fuck are* you *doing here?*)

His eyes flashed open, confused. What was going on? Something wasn't right.

But she was kissing him again, making it hard to think.

This time, when she pulled away, he found himself leaning into her, pursuing those sweet lips, yearning for more.

She smiled and then reached up and swept her long hair back over her shoulders, the motion lifting those perfect breasts, softly bouncing them before his eyes. She had the sexiest tan lines. And yet it was a subtle glint of shining gold on her wedding ring finger that drew his attention.

His gaze shifted toward the closet, to the white gown and veil hanging there.

Of course. The wedding. Such a gloriously beautiful day. Such an angelically gorgeous bride. The beginning of a happy life together.

Something tugged at the back of his mind like an impatient child at the tail of his shirt. His head was fuzzy. He was forgetting something important. But then Nicole kissed him again.

That's right... That was simply what it was like when she kissed him. It was always hard to think when she did that. She was so amazing. Sometimes he could almost believe she was an actual goddess sent down from the heavens.

The world seemed to swim away as she pressed herself more firmly against him.

This was nice... So much better than...

(*You stay out of this! No one invited you!*)

Again, his eyes snapped open. "Wait..."

But she wasn't going to wait. She was already moving her hips. His body shuddered with anticipation.

"Something's wrong," he said.

"Nothing's wrong," she assured him. "Everything's exactly as it should be."

"Then where's the door and window?"

Just like last time...just like it was with Amber...

That place looked just like his house but there were no windows or doors. And this hotel room was exactly the same. It was perfect in every detail, but there was no window. No door. No way in or out.

From somewhere beyond those walls, he heard that ominous muttering begin again.

"What's happening?" he demanded. This wasn't Nicole. She'd never kiss him like that again. The real Nicole hated him. Nothing here was real. It was just like that dream he had where he met the creepy cat lady. Except this felt different somehow. There were no cats here. And there was no cat lady. This was something else. "What are you?" he demanded, staring into those deceptively familiar eyes.

But she only sat there staring back at him while that strange and ominous muttering continued.

Then everything went silent again. The Not-Nicole blinked. "What do you want?" she asked him.

Again, this caught him off guard. "What?"

"What is the thing that you really want?" she pressed.

"I told you, I want to *leave*. I want to go *outside*."

Before he knew what was happening, she was kissing him again. The world faded into confounding darkness. He felt himself falling.

Then he was staring up at a moonlit sky full of stars. What was happening? Why did he keep getting so confused? Time seemed to have passed, but he couldn't tell minutes from hours from years.

He was lying on a picnic blanket in the back corner of the fairytale playground in the park over by the river. His mom used to bring him here to play when he was a kid. And then when he was older, he used to sneak in after dark with...

"I could stay here all night," sighed Ramona.

Keith turned and looked into those bright blue eyes, his head still swimming.

She leaned over and kissed him. It felt like it had been ages since he felt her lips...and yet...weren't they *just* kissing? Hadn't they been here for the past couple hours, just lying under the stars together?

Why did everything feel so disjointed? What was wrong with his head?

"There's live music at the riverfront tomorrow," she informed him. "We should go."

"Sounds fun," he agreed, still feeling numb.

Ramona Swarter. His high school sweetheart. His first love. The sweet girl he dated all through senior year, who he took to prom, the first he ever made love to... He remembered all of those things clearly.

But didn't they drift apart after graduation?

No. Why would he think that? Theirs was a perfect romance with the perfect ending.

She reached up and tucked a strand of golden hair behind her ear. He stared at the wedding ring on her finger, watched the moonlight glint off it. Somewhere, in the far back of his mind, he wondered why that kept coming up. What was so significant about those rings? But those thoughts kept dissolving before he could become fully aware of them, leaving only that strangely slippery sensation of some important fact continually evading him.

She smiled that lovely smile. She was so pretty, sitting there in her flowery summer dress. And so *young*... Did she always look so young? She leaned forward and kissed him again. What a warm and wonderful sensation. This was nice. He wanted to stay here with her.

(She shouldn't be here at all.)

She made him so happy.

(She ended up with someone else.)

There'd never been anyone else but her.

(Seriously?)

This was so perfect.

(This was so *wrong*.)

He winced and squeezed his eyes closed. What the hell was going on? Why were his thoughts so muddled?

"Are you okay?" she worried.

This was wrong. It was just an endless loop of lies. He opened his eyes and met her false gaze. Though he was looking into those lovely blue eyes, he wasn't seeing what was really there.

Because she didn't have any eyes.

Chapter 29

Corey sat cross-legged on the floor, his gaze still fixed on the unremarkable wall standing stubbornly in his way, still processing the strange feelings these stone passageways filled him with. It was hard to comprehend it all. The feelings themselves were as alien as these empty walls and the unfathomable technology hidden within them, and yet they remained at the same time strangely familiar somehow.

A part of him itched to get up and simply try exploring one of the two passages. There were almost certainly more interesting things to be found in this labyrinth, but he remained convinced for some reason that those were the wrong way.

His path lay directly in front of him.

He just had to figure out *how* to get there.

Violet was always asking him how he found some of the things they'd discovered, what convinced him to take a closer look, to dive down that particular rabbit hole. And he would always reply that it was just a "gut feeling." But the truth was that he simply didn't know what it was, or even how to describe it. There was no magic formula, no key detail, no absolute clue. *Was* it a gut feeling? Somehow, those stories he found had simply spoken to him. They captured his attention and drew him in. He wanted to know more. That was all there was to it.

But *why* did those particular stories speak to him? Because it went much farther than just a personal interest. It wasn't just the rumors he found online. When he found a place that was merely interesting and it turned out to be nothing, he shrugged it off and moved on. But when he found a place that was real, he remained fixated on it until they found it. Like he did that day in Arkansas, with the mysterious field of stones in the forest.

Was there something more to it? Gina just knew things. Albert and Brandy just knew things. They were psychic. Some mysterious part of their brains spoke to them, giving them information that their ordinary senses couldn't possibly detect. Did *he* have something like that, too?

No… That didn't seem right. It was different for him. But he couldn't explain exactly *how* it was different.

He just simply knew which strands were worth following.

He stared at the empty wall before him, his thoughts focused on that bizarre energy he felt flowing forward even though there was no opening to be seen.

Temple stone, Albert had called it. The sentinels used it to make the three roads, the impassible wall and these temples, as well as the curious stones he and Violet had discovered in Minnesota and Arkansas. They used it to make statues with impossible detail that had the power to instill intense emotions in anyone who looked upon them. And somehow they'd used it to communicate with him, across impossible ages and entire universes!

This was about them, he realized. Whatever his gut feelings were really made of, it had to do with the sentinels. *They* were why he knew these things.

Temple stone was the canvas they used to create their art. And their art was how they did all the amazing and impossible things they did.

Time wasn't constant. It was variable. His research into portals and gateways had taught him that. Just as intense gravity could affect the flow of time out in space, so could the boundaries that separated the many worlds out there. And that meant that time could be manipulated. The sentinels had done just that. They used time as a tool and they used this stone to reach across eternity and speak to him.

All he had to do was listen to them…

The answers would come.

He just had to be patient.

Chapter 30

Violet wished she could see what was going on around her, but the wind and rain made it nearly impossible for her to even open her eyes as she ran through the raging storm.

What was going on? What were they running from? And just how long was this bridge? It felt like they'd been running for miles!

And what was with Everett back there? She looked away for a second and suddenly he was right there in her face. Was he trying to kiss her? What the hell? She really hoped she wouldn't have to deal with that kind of shit. This was *not* the place. And he was too young for her taste anyway.

Something was going on. Something about this storm. That strange noise was louder now. It seemed to come from every direction, yet she couldn't *see* anything. It was such a weirdly disturbing sound. Although it was reminiscent of the eerie noises the wind made on gusty nights, it most definitely wasn't that innocuous. It filled her with a strange and urgent sort of anxiety, as if it reminded her of some long-forgotten nightmare that she didn't dare try to recall.

"Keep moving!" shouted Everett.

"Do I look like I'm thinking about stopping for lunch?"

"Um…? No?"

"You just worry about keeping up!" she told him.

"Okay!"

He was cute. She sort of liked his awkwardness. It was disarming. It was even kind of charming. But it made him seem even younger than she first judged. Could he still be in high school? She didn't know anything about him. She simply woke up in that awful gouging station—whatever that place was—and he was just sort of there. They made their way outside and the city wall was looming over them and then they lost Andrea and…well, they simply hadn't stopped moving long enough to really talk. She'd have to ask him some questions when they weren't preoccupied with…whatever the hell was going on right now. Have a real conversation. Get to know him a little. People worked better together when they weren't complete strangers.

Everett suddenly stopped and yanked on her arm, nearly knocking her over. "Get down!" he shouted.

She didn't know what was going on, but she didn't hesitate. He dropped down to his hands and knees and she threw herself to the ground with him. An instant later, that awful sound rolled over them, louder than before, seemingly passing right over their heads.

She dared a look upward as it began to fade, but the rain made it impossible to see anything. Was there something disappearing from sight up there? Something wispy and shadowy? Or was that only the water in her eyelashes?

"Okay! Keep moving!" Everett was on his feet again in a flash, pulling at her arm, helping her to her feet, although she probably could've stood up faster on her own than with him tugging at her like that. He was only managing to get in her way.

But he was trying. That was sweet of him.

"What is it?" she asked as they hurried forward again.

"How do you not know what it is? *You're* the one who told *me*!"

"That doesn't even make any sense! I don't know anything about this!"

"But *you* said they were drafts!"

She scrunched up her nose, confused. "Drafts? It's like a *hurricane* out here! I'd say that's *way* more than just a *draft*!"

"Not that kind of draft!" he huffed. "They're *called* drafts! You really don't remember telling me that?"

"Obviously not!"

"And you can't see them?"

"I can't see *anything* in this storm!"

"So weird!"

She shined her light back the way they came, little good that it did her. It was better than going completely blind between flashes of lightning, but there was nothing to see but hazy shades of gray everywhere she looked. It was probably more likely to attract unwanted attention than actually show them anything.

A great gust of wind caught her by surprise and she stumbled sideways, her heart leaping at the thought of tumbling over the edge. She was between the stone pillars, too far away to grab one of them. Instinctively, she clung to Everett instead. It was a natural instinct. Corey was always there to catch her if she tripped in unfamiliar terrain. But Everett and Corey were two very different people. And two very different *sizes*. For one heart-stopping moment she thought she was going to drag the both of them right over the edge and down untold stories to their deaths.

But Everett managed somehow to steady her.

She stood there a moment, hear heart still in her throat, slowly realizing that she was still clinging to him. "I'm okay," she said, pulling away from him before she could give the poor kid the wrong idea. But he grabbed her instead, startling her again, and shoved her backward two more steps, even closer to that awful ledge.

"Look out!" he gasped.

Before she had time to react, another of those terrible moaning noises swept past them, this time close enough to send a chill racing through her body. She could almost *feel* something passing by them, directly behind his back. The world swam out of focus for a moment. She felt strangely lightheaded.

Was that another of those draft things?

"You okay?" he asked her, looking terrified.

She couldn't seem to find her voice for a second, so she merely nodded.

"Good," he said. But his eyes were so big... He looked like he'd just seen something straight out of his darkest nightmares. He was actually *pale*. "That's good..." he muttered.

She tightened her grip on his arm, concerned. "Are *you* okay?"

He didn't answer her. Instead, he only said, "We have to keep moving. Can't let them touch us."

She glanced around, nervous. She didn't like this. Why did he look like that? Did something happen? He pushed her out of the way and shielded her from it, but maybe he wasn't quick enough to get himself out of harm's way. Did it do something to him? Was he hurt? But he was right. Now wasn't the time to stop and talk about it. "Keep moving," she agreed, already pulling him along again. "You just keep watch for us, okay?"

He nodded. He looked so strange, almost dazed, but he was moving, at least, going wherever she guided him.

How much farther did they have to go? Where was the end of this awful bridge? And once they reached it, would it finally be safe? There was no door of any kind blocking access to the passage they exited from, nothing to keep anything out. What if whatever was out here followed them inside? How long could they avoid them in those shadowy passageways? She still couldn't even properly *see* them!

She realized that Everett was muttering something, but she couldn't hear him over the howling wind. "What?"

But he didn't seem to hear her. He was staring forward with those big, startled eyes.

"Everett?"

He turned those wide eyes on her, but his lips continued moving. She still couldn't hear what he was saying. And yet somehow she understood him.

"Don't let them touch you..." he muttered, the words immediately carried off by the storm. "Don't let them touch you... Don't let them touch you..."

Chapter 31

Why me? wondered Andrea. *Who thought* I'd *be a good candidate for this job?*

She was standing alone in the dark passageway, her head down, her flashlight aimed at her feet. She was surrounded by those creepy, seeping shadow things. They seemed to be growing on the walls and oozing from the ceiling. And sometimes they broke apart into those tiny little black particles that floated and darkled in her path. They looked like little specks of ash floating in the air, but they weren't disturbed when she walked past them. Neither her movements nor her breath affected them in any way. She seemed to walk right through them as if they weren't there. And she couldn't feel those creeping shapes on the floor when they grew too thick, leaving her no choice but to tiptoe through them. They filled her with the same kind of cringing revulsion she felt walking into the reptile house of a zoo, making her skin crawl with every step, but she didn't seem to be capable of physically interacting with them in any way.

Every now and then, however, that creeping darkness gathered into a softball- or even basketball-sized lump on the wall, floor or ceiling, with a much more solid appearance. It became a darker-than-dark mass with weird little strands of more darkness sticking off them and wavering like something hairy underwater.

She didn't think she was just being squeamish. She distinctly felt as if something bad would happen if she touched one of these particular shadows. They seemed to take on a more ominous sort of life than the rest. She'd found several of them already, and they always seemed to be *aware* of her as she crept past them. They stretched toward her, pulling at the connecting shadows and taking eerie, hand-like shapes that visibly *reached* for her.

But fortunately, they'd all seemed to be stuck in place.

Until now.

Now she found herself frozen to the floor in fear as the biggest glob of shadows she'd yet seen—a great, undulating mass roughly the size of a German shepherd—oozed from one side of the corridor to the other, stretching and twisting like some kind of oily blob. As soon as her flashlight fell on it, the thing twisted itself around and let out a sound like something strangling to death, startling a scream from her, which only made it flop over and stretch itself toward her.

She wasn't sure what made her realize that she needed to freeze rather than run, if it was some instinct associated with her ability to see these things or if it was perhaps some fact that Erin planted into her brain, but she knew almost immediately that she needed to lower her light, remain still, make no sound and not look directly at it.

Sort of like what the actor in *Jurassic Park* said to do when the T-rex attacked, she supposed. Mixed with when you saw those people at the mall with the clipboards.

And it seemed to be working. As soon as she lowered the light and began focusing intently on her shoes, the thing calmed a little. It was still agitated, of course. She could hear it squelching back and forth, searching for her.

What *were* these things, anyway? She thought she was supposed to be able to see ghosts. Why was she seeing shadow monsters? Were *these things* ghosts? Were they, like, the ghosts of plants and animals or something? Things that were native to whatever world this so-called City Beyond Memory was built it? Or was this what ghosts of humans became when they spent untold eons languishing in the depths of an inescapable labyrinth? She didn't understand what the connection was.

If you stay down here long enough, Stella's entirely unhelpful voice informed her from whatever part of her mind was responsible for such mentally unstable thoughts, *they'll eat your soul.*

You shut up! she snapped back at her. But she could almost hear her laughing at her.

She wondered what the real Stella would think of all this. Would she delight in all the strangeness like she did with all the normal, *real-world* mischief she loved getting into? Or would the horrors of the Wood have been enough to scare her straight by now? Either way, it was probably better that she didn't go back for her at the reception.

Was the thing getting closer? She didn't dare look up at it. She was afraid she'd see something staring back at her. But she could still hear it moving. And she could sort of see the shadows undulating at the far top of her vision.

You should run, warned Stella.

No. She absolutely shouldn't. Something inside her was adamant about that.

Fine. Don't run. Then, in a creepy singsong voice: *But you're going to get eaten.*

140

"You're doing great," whispered Erin, surprising her.

At least…she *thought* it was a whisper. It might have been in her head like Unhelpful Stella. But it seemed so much more real. She could almost feel her breath on her ear.

"It'll be gone soon."

"Gone…" echoed a ghostly voice that seemed to drift up from somewhere at her feet. It was the first actual word she'd heard in a while. The voices had mostly dulled into an unsettling sort of constant muttering and moaning as the shadows thickened around her. She didn't like them at all, but the fact that it repeated something Erin just said meant that it wasn't merely her overactive imagination. She was here with her right now. She wasn't alone.

Why would you trust some dead slut? Didn't you learn your lesson the first time?

She's being more helpful than you *are!* she snapped. She had to make a physical effort to not say these words aloud. What was up with her head? Why was she like this?

She realized the gross squelching noises were growing more distant and dared a quick peek at it. It was making its way farther down the passage. There was an intersection up there, she realized, a chance to move away from the thing without going back the way she came. But she couldn't get ahead of herself or it would notice her again.

Slowly, she crept forward, still keeping her light aimed at her feet, careful not to get too close. If it kept moving, she could slip around the corner and put a wall between her and it.

She wished she didn't have to be alone in here. She missed Nicole and Gina. She missed Everett and Violet. But even if they were here, would they be able to see these things? And would that gross, squelchy thing be able to hurt them?

Maybe it was better this way after all. She didn't have all the answers. Or hardly any of them, for that matter.

It sounded like Erin might still be nearby, which was something, at least, but she couldn't see her. She could have already left again. She warned her, after all, that she wasn't strong enough to fight the Priestess of Ruin, who was supposedly stalking her through this nightmare shadow labyrinth. She might only be able to communicate briefly with her and then retreat back into the darkness.

She reached the next passageway and hurried into it. It was infested with shadows like this one, with those black, mossy fingers crawling over every surface and fluttering flecks of darkness drifting lazily through the air, but she didn't see any more *large* clumps of shadows.

She should be safe for a little while.

Why bother? asked Stella. *You're gonna die out here anyway. It's only a matter of time.*

"Don't listen to her," whispered Erin. "She's not who she pretends to—"

Andrea stopped as the voice seemed to suddenly recede into the distance. "Erin?" she whispered.

Somewhere overhead, several disembodied voices whispered the name as well, seemingly mocking her. The sound of them made her skin crawl.

Forget about her. She's just another dead bitch trying to get you killed.

She stood there a moment, her eyes wide in the darkness. This wasn't just her frightened mind manifesting her friend's voice in order to speak the thoughts of her subconscious, she realized. This was the thing Erin and Ada both warned her about. The primitive entity that was following her. The thing that was attracting all the trouble.

The Priestess of Ruin.

She was here. She'd been here throughout her journey, hiding inside her own head.

Such fun… sighed the voice that wasn't Stella inside her head.

Chapter 32

Gina wasn't the strongest swimmer. She'd never spent much time in the water, after all. It wasn't as if anyone ever took her to the beach or invited her to pool parties. The best she could do was a sort of weak doggie paddle, which did her little good in the raging current coursing down the slopes of the City Beyond Memory.

Between the sporadic flashing of the lightning and the waves that splashed up over her face, she had only brief glimpses of her surroundings, enough to see those false stone buildings flying past her at startling speeds.

She was terrified enough at the prospect of drowning in these raging rapids, but at this velocity, if she slammed into one of those stone columns or another of those scary statues, she wouldn't stand a chance.

Where were Albert and Brandy? Were they still behind her? She couldn't see them anywhere, but she also wasn't really able to look behind her. She hoped Brandy didn't resist too much. Those monsters were closing in on them, far too close for comfort. If they'd lingered too long, things could have turned very bad very quickly. Jumping into the river was something she didn't even think of in her state of panic. (And no wonder, given her lack of confidence in the water.) It was Albert's idea, not hers. And he was right. Even as she struggled to keep her head above water, she knew it was the only way out.

But it was still terrifying.

And then there was the lightning. A blinding flash. A crash of thunder she could hear even over the raging water. What if one of those bolts struck the water while she was in it? Would it be enough to kill her?

She felt herself swept over a ledge. A waterfall. In an instant, she was plummeting blind through the darkness, her vision blurred so that even the flashing lightning revealed nothing more than endless shades of ominous gray. She screamed. And then she was under water, struggling to reach the surface, still fighting the speeding current. The world around her was reduced to a blurry void of darkness interspersed with flashes of hazy white.

Why did she scream? She wasted her air! And now she couldn't find the surface! How far down had she gone? Was something pulling her? Was she caught in an undercurrent?

Her chest was aching. Stark terror was welling up inside her. She didn't want to drown. After all she'd been through, it wasn't fair. It was downright *cruel.*

Something hard slammed against her right shoulder, surprising another great belch of bubbles from her already starved lungs and twirling her around, disorienting her.

Seconds later, something struck her foot. Then her flailing hand.

Would she be bludgeoned to death before she could drown?

But then she felt herself swept over another waterfall. She managed one desperate gulp of air before crashing beneath the surface again.

Enough to keep her alive, she wondered, or merely delay the inevitable?

She tumbled over another waterfall, then another.

She was growing tired. She wasn't strong enough to keep this up for long. She'd never been very fit. It had always been more comforting at home, locked away in her room, her nose in her sketchbooks. It always felt safer there, where she could be alone, away from all the mean people in the world.

Finally, she broke the surface and gasped. Lightning flashed overhead, revealing in the shadows on either side that the current was still carrying her along at a troubling speed, but now the river had widened considerably. And it was much deeper than before. It was no longer rolling.

Did she hear a shout from behind her? Was that Brandy and Albert? Were they still with her? She tried to look back, but she was struggling to stay afloat. Her arms and legs were aching. There was a stitch in her side. And she couldn't seem to catch her breath.

Then another great bolt of lightning shot across the sky, revealing more enormous shapes looming in the hazy distance. It looked like towering skyscrapers stretching up toward that boiling sky. And at the center of them all, her psychic brain informed her, something far more massive still, a towering structure like nothing she'd ever seen or sensed before.

She remembered feeling something at the center of the city when she first cast her psychic gaze out across it, when the storm's haze ebbed outward, offering that first, tantalizing peek. There was something profoundly important there, something that almost seemed to be calling out to her. And these rushing waters had already swept her most of the way there.

That feeling of *significance* was almost overwhelming.

But in the next flash of lightning, she realized that she wasn't being carried toward the tower, but to an ominous darkness directly ahead of her. The river was pouring into a great, yawning blackness.

Then where does the water go? she recalled Albert asking her. After all, the water *had* to go *somewhere.* And water always ran downhill. Even here in the middle of the Denselands, where concrete concepts like gravity and time and distance didn't even work well, water still followed its own laws.

And now she was barreling toward the answer to that question, toward an unsettling darkness that was about to swallow her whole. There was something dreadful about the idea. She felt a sudden and overwhelming fear of that darkness. A panic overcame her and she tried to swim the other way. But her pitiful paddling was no match for the powerful current. She was swept into the inky darkness and enveloped by it.

Was this a mistake? Was she about to be plunged into some underwater cavern, never to surface again? Somehow, the thought of not merely drowning, but of being swept forever into some pitch-black watery grave was even more dreadful.

Then she was once again falling. In one awful instant, she found herself plummeting through a hopeless darkness, the heavy water pushing her down. Seconds seemed to drag on, as if she'd fallen off the edge of the world and into a bottomless abyss. And in that crawling, agonizing moment, she felt an odd sense of surrealness, as if she'd just crossed into an entirely new universe. Endless winding passages of stone filled her thoughts. Mysterious chambers bathed in perfect eternal darkness. Unthinkable dangers. Monstrous presences. And *time*, like eternal ages piled atop one another, stretching back so far that even attempting to comprehend it felt like madness.

The Temple of the Three Whispers, as Albert called it, went far deeper than she ever could have imagined, as if it had spent all its countless centuries *growing*, its fearsome roots snaking deeper and deeper into the cold, black depths.

This was no temple. This was a universe unto itself, dark and hopeless and eternal. How could she ever have thought she could hope to return from somewhere like this? It was impossible. It was going to swallow her soul and keep her here forever.

Then she hit the water.

The impact knocked the wind out of her and left her dazed and disoriented, sinking for a moment into the suffocating darkness.

She needed to snap out of it. She didn't want to drown. She didn't want to die that way.

She tried to swim back to the surface, but she was so tired. Her arms and legs felt like lead. She felt as if she were moving in agonizing slow motion.

She was almost within reach of it. She felt the cold air on her skin as her hands and forehead broke free, but she was too weak to force her head up enough to allow her a saving breath.

She couldn't keep doing this. She was fading. Her flailing grew weaker and weaker. She began to sink.

Hazy light danced through the darkness above her, taunting her as the last of her breath bubbled away from her.

Then someone was there. Strong arms grabbed her and yanked her upward. She was out of the water, gasping and coughing.

"I gotcha!" gasped Albert. "Hold on!"

Stars were dancing before her eyes and everything was spinning. She clung to him, terrified and dazed. She could hear Brandy calling out from somewhere nearby.

It was so hard to think. She could barely comprehend the feel of the body she was clinging to. But still she was able to understand that this wasn't some subterranean deathtrap. She wasn't going to be swept into an eternal watery grave.

This was an underground chamber. Part of a sort of reservoir system. There was a walkway circling them. Brandy had climbed up onto it. That was where she was calling out to them from. She could see the glow of the flashlight through her streaming tears.

She might yet die in this place. She might yet die *today*. But it wasn't going to happen just yet. Thanks to Nicole's friends. Andrea's friends. Violet and Corey's friends.

Her friends…

Chapter 33

Nicole stood in the darkness, staring wide-eyed at the undulating shape twisting and writhing its way across the empty sky.

Was she screaming? She couldn't quite tell. The noise of this place was like a thousand screaming power saws inside her brain, making it impossible to hear her own thoughts, much less her own screams. But she *wanted* to scream. The mere sight of that strange shape overhead filled her with terror like she'd never felt before, making her feel as if the only thing she *could* do was scream. And her throat felt raw and bruised, as if she'd been screaming a *long time.*

Her eyes and lungs were burning. Her skin felt cold as ice. There was a stabbing pain deep inside her belly and a pins-and-needles sensation up and down her back.

What was this place? She saw everything and nothing at the same time. There was no light in this horror-soaked world, but there was no darkness, either. Everything was painted in shades of maddening nothing, constantly shifting shapes like ever-evolving inkblots across a landscape of blood and ash.

She wanted to run, but there was nowhere to go. Everything was wet and crumbling and bloody and foul. And even if there *were* anywhere safe for her to go, her body wouldn't work. When she took a step, she could feel her legs moving, she could feel the poisoned ground squelch beneath her shoes, but her surroundings never changed. She could do nothing to escape the unthinkable things that crawled across the noxious ground and burrowed into the tainted earth below.

Shapes like groping hands reached out for her. Gaping holes in the earth and sky alike cracked and spewed and yawned open like screaming mouths. Every surface seemed to be alive and writhing. She could feel them crawling on her skin, beneath her clothes, in her hair, even inside her body.

So many horrible things…and yet there was only one. The thing in the sky. The things on and in the earth. The things in her flesh. They were all the same. They were all *him.*

Voices somehow wormed their way through the maddening cacophony and burrowed deep into her brain, chanting eerie words that she didn't understand but had heard before: *Anun amum ut mu. Anun amum ut mu.*

She didn't want to hear these words. Somehow they were worse than the deafening din that swallowed even the sound of her own screams.

Anun amum ut mu. Anun gan sutol um go. Bog tok na shivta sa.

She could make no sense of these alien words passing through her head like a shrieking locomotive, but something about them filled her with unspeakable terror. Somehow she simply understood that if she *could* understand what these words were saying, they'd drive her insane.

Anun amum ut mu. Anun amum ut mu.

She couldn't stand this. It was too painful. She needed to find a way out of this place!

Except this was no place at all. This was the nowhere that existed in the sealed depths somewhere *under* the living universe. She couldn't move because she wasn't really here, she realized. This wasn't her body. This was only her mind. If her body were here, it would instantly have been crushed beneath the unfathomable weight of all existence.

Anun amum ut mu. Anun Goar Nangup.

Goar Nangup... That was the name Hotdog kept spouting whenever he stopped pretending to be a good guy, the name of his foul god, the one Ada said was imprisoned "beneath the weight of the living worlds," and wanted to break the cycle in order to be free again.

This was *his* world. His *prison*.

Was this where Elias Hochog sold his soul to become Hotdog Creep? Was this what drove him mad? Or was he mad to begin with? He would've had to have been to come someplace like this willingly.

Anun amum ut mu. Anun amum ut mu.

She couldn't stand it any longer. Everything hurt so badly. Her lungs were on fire. Her heart felt like it was going to burst from her chest.

She wanted to give up. She wanted this agony to end. Death had to be less cruel than this, even out here in the vast depths of the Wood where the dead remained stranded for all eternity. Nothing could be as painful as this. But she didn't even know how to give up.

Because she wasn't really here...

Because this wasn't really a place...

Chapter 34

Wayne paused at yet another intersection. They turned left at the last one after descending another sloped passage, moving down what felt like at least two or three levels. But he'd lost track of where they'd been. Was this where they turned right before? Or was that the one that merged with two others from the left? After being lost in here for so long, it was all starting to blur together. Not that it would likely do them any good even if he could remember every turn they'd taken since they arrived here. It was a maze. Left could be right, right could be down and straight ahead could take them in a circle. The whole point of a labyrinth was to confound.

Olivia stepped forward and shined her light one way, then the other. The last several hadn't given her any information. It seemed that if there didn't happen to be imminent peril waiting directly down any of the passageways that she considered, her psychic power wasn't particularly helpful, which made sense, really. It was a warning alarm, not a compass. It pointed to danger, not to the exit.

But this time she lingered longer than any of the previous times, her pretty face pursed in an adorable expression of deep thought.

"Feel something?" he asked.

"It's weird," she replied. "It's not exactly an aversion, like before, but it doesn't feel *pleasant*, either." She turned and shined her light the other way. "It's the same with both directions."

He frowned. "So...either one, then? Or should we go back the way we came?"

She turned and shined her light behind them, her perfectly shaped brow deeply creased and an uncomfortable expression overtaking her soft features. "No... I don't like back," she decided. "Something feels wrong about back."

He shined his light back as well. That was concerning. Why would *back* feel bad? Was something behind them? Had they attracted something's attention?

"Sorry," she said, looking left and right again. "This all still feels strange to me. I'm not sure if I'm doing it right."

"You're doing great," he assured her.

"Let's try this way." She turned right and started walking.

He kept pace with her, still clinging to her hand, determined not to lose her like he did the others. Not again. Those hours he spent looking for her back in Gutler's Weep were pure torture. He hated every second of it.

But then again, that wasn't so different from every day. He *always* wanted to be with her, every minute of every hour. He was happiest when she was right here at his side. He kept thinking she'd get annoyed with him, that she'd tell him to stop suffocating her, the way Nicole grew frustrated with Keith, but she put up with him so well. She let him follow her around like the lovesick puppy he was, never seeming to mind one bit.

She was far too good for him.

Again, the passage sloped downward. Again, they found themselves descending lower. And again, he wished he knew where it was they were trying to go.

At the bottom of the slope, she paused and tightened her grip on his arm.

"You okay?"

She shook her head. "I'm not sure," she whispered. "Feels dangerous. Like something's going to happen."

"Want to go back?"

She stood there a moment longer, considering, then she shuddered visibly, her whole body giving a hard tremble. "No," she said firmly "Not back." This time, when she started walking, she was moving faster.

He cursed under his breath and shined his light back over his shoulder. Was something chasing them? What did she feel when she considered going back? He didn't like not knowing what was happening, but he also didn't want her to try explaining it. It would take too much time. And he doubted that speaking her worries would make them any less frightening. He was better off simply staying alert.

They continued forward, slower now, their eyes peeled.

There was another intersection ahead of them. A big one. There was a small open space with six passages branching out, including the one they were in. Olivia immediately shook her head and pointed to the one directly ahead of them. "I don't like that way."

He frowned at the darkened corridor stretched out before them. "Not that way," he agreed. He wished he could see what was down there.

Occasionally, when the two of them had sat down and discussed the temple and all the lingering questions they still had, Albert talked about how he'd do things differently if they ever did it again. He had a lot of ideas. He talked about bringing more chalk, of course, for marking paths. And flares. He thought they'd be useful for tossing from high areas to illuminate the dark spaces below. Or possibly to distract or frighten off hounds or other creatures. One of his more ridiculous ideas, he thought, was to bring an arsenal of remote-controlled toy cars outfitted with cameras for scouting ahead. He remembered just nodding politely, thinking it was a stupid idea. But now he was really kind of wishing he had one of those cars...

He might owe Albert an apology.

Olivia turned and again shined her light into each of the remaining passages, her pretty features scrunched up like she used to do when she was studying hard for one of her nursing classes. He used to love watching her study. She was so peaceful. And so adorably expressive when she was all wrapped up in her work. But those faces didn't have the same magic down here in these dark passageways. There was a layer of fear shining through from underneath that made him ache to simply scoop her into his arms and carry her somewhere safe.

"I don't really like *any* of them," she said, her full lips pushed into an unhappy sort of pout. "I can't decide."

He shined his light into the nearest of the openings. Why was she having trouble picking one? Did it mean that none of them were safe? Had they made a wrong turn somewhere and now they were moving inevitably toward some unforeseen peril?

She let go of him and walked a few steps into the tunnel to her right, then stood there, contemplating it.

He didn't try to stop her, but he kept his eyes on her, not daring to even glance away. He needed to give her space, he realized. This was the time for letting her work. Her abilities were the reason she was here. And for all he knew, the only thing keeping the two of them alive.

Besides, he didn't have anything useful to contribute at the moment. He frowned at the realization that as long as his heart was beating, he was just an average shmuck without any particularly useful talents.

"I guess this way's as good as any?" She turned and looked back at him, her face uncertain.

"Sure," he replied. "Let's see what happens."

She reached out her hand, her fingers splayed. She had such dainty hands. And she always kept her nails so perfect and pretty. It still bothered him to see them scuffed and chipped like that. He felt terrible for all she'd been through. Especially since much of it happened when he allowed her to be separated from him in that nasty forest.

They pushed onward in silence, their eyes peeled for anything out of the ordinary. For the next couple minutes, there was nothing but the one empty passage, the same featureless walls, the same gray stone. Then they stepped out into another room.

Wayne shined his light around, confused. This was a little odd. There was nothing here. Certainly, there was nothing dangerous he could see. It was a completely empty chamber. Not even a very large one. It was about twenty feet wide by about forty feet long. It was taller than most, about thirty feet high. The passageway continued onward at the far end. It was bigger than the corridors leading in and out of it, but otherwise, it was just another hallway in a maze of smaller hallways. What was the point in it?

And yet, there was something familiar about it…

Olivia crept forward, her head tilted, her pretty eyes scanning the stone surfaces all around them.

"What do you feel?" He realized he was whispering, but he wasn't entirely sure why. There wasn't anything to hear him.

"I don't like it here," she whispered back.

"Do we need to go back?"

But she was already shaking her head. "No. I don't think we're in danger. Not exactly…"

He scowled at her, concerned. Not exactly? Were they or weren't they? He wished he could feel what she felt. He wished he could do *anything* to help her. It seemed like this was difficult for her.

She turned her light up to that high ceiling and stood there, staring up at it, one ear tilted toward it, her earring twinkling as it reflected his own light back at him.

"Hear something?" he whispered.

"Chains."

"Chains?" He looked up at the ceiling. A deeply unpleasant chill settled over him as he finally remembered when he last saw rooms like this.

The Sentinel Queen called these rooms psychic traps. Something dreadful was bound to them, something not of their world, something intangible to most of them. Only those with extraordinary psychic abilities would be able to perceive what was there.

People like Beverly Bridger…

The sight of her screaming up at the ceiling of that room in utter terror still haunted him. He was still occasionally reliving that moment in his nightmares. Those bulging eyes… Those hideous screams… And of course the way his hand grazed her skin as he snatched for her, trying to save her…only for her to fall into that gruesome pit…

A psychic trap. A device to keep people from cheating. Because the temple had a way of subconsciously luring sensitive minds to it. People like her and Wendell Gilbert.

Olivia shuddered and pressed herself closer to him. "We should keep moving."

He nodded. She'd get no argument from him.

He took her hand and the two of them continued into the next passageway and onward through the dark.

But Olivia looked back as they pushed forward, a deep concern painted across her face. "I don't think that room is dangerous to us," she said, her voice still hushed. "But I still have a bad feeling."

He pulled her close to him and kept walking.

Chapter 35

The old playground had only one gate leading into it. You had to go through the little fairytale city with all its arches and stairs and ladders and towers and cross the shaky little bridge to reach the grand gate. It was a safety feature to make it easier for parents to keep track of their kids. It was remodeled and enlarged when he was in middle school, but much of it was still original and had been there as long as he could remember.

This, however, wasn't that playground.

Just like in that mockery of his house and that prison of a honeymoon suite, there was no way out. The ten-foot-high, faux stone walls encircled the entire plot, including at the end of the shaky bridge where the castle drawbridge was supposed to be, preventing him from escaping. Even if he tried to climb over it, it wouldn't work. Somehow, he understood that everything *above* the wall was only an illusion. There was no sky up there. Not really. Even the moonlight and the cool night air on his skin was a trick of his mind.

"Come back," urged Ramona. "You're being silly."

"Silly," he laughed. He thrust a finger up at that false sky. "You think I can't hear those voices?"

That same, ominous murmuring swept across the playground like a cold breeze, making the hair stand up on his arms. He could almost *see* them… Great, towering, shadowy figures looming over him, staring down with empty faces like titanic, cosmic judges deciding his fate.

"What do you want?" she asked him.

"*Why do you keep asking me that?*"

"So we can see the way inside you."

"*What?*"

He was surprised by arms reaching around him from behind.

"No one here wants to harm you," Amber assured him.

He blinked at her, confused. When did they move from the playground to that fake version of his bedroom? When did they lie down? How did he get naked again? Nothing made any sense. This was all so confusing.

"This is how it's supposed to be," said Ramona as she crawled onto the bed with them. "This is the message we've brought you."

"What message?" And why was *she* naked now?

"Your way forward," explained Nicole as she reached around him.

This bed was getting crowded. He probably shouldn't be complaining, but he was outnumbered and feeling *very* self-conscious.

"It's like a map," explained Andrea. What the hell was *she* doing here? She wasn't even someone he'd slept with! And yet there she was, right on the other side of Nicole, peering over her shoulder at him, her piercings glinting in the lamplight. "You'll need it for what lies ahead."

"But we can't give you the message," added Gina from the other side of the bed, "until we establish a common language between your mind and ours."

He rubbed at his eyes, confused. He couldn't even keep all the faces straight anymore. "What do you mean, 'common language'? You're speaking to me right now."

"For the purpose of this sort of communication, this language works fine," Gina replied. "But the information we need to pass onto you must be exchanged at a much higher level of consciousness."

He opened his eyes to find himself back in the captain's chair of the trawler, idling between those towering, rock walls. Except this time the cliffs were blocking the way forward and back as well. Even out here, he was trapped.

Gina was standing beside him, her gaze fixed intently on him. Andrea and Nicole were standing behind him. All of them were dressed, thankfully. They looked just as they did hours ago when they were really on the boat together. But there was something eerily unnatural about the way they all stared at him like that. Something about their eyes didn't quite reach him. It was as if they were all blind.

For some unfathomable reason, he found himself thinking that their faces were nothing more than masks and that there was nothing underneath them, that they were as blank as the faces of the sentinel statues.

Sentinels, he found himself thinking. The word sent a strange shiver through him. "What are you?" he asked again.

"Messengers," replied Andrea.

"Our spirits have lingered here in these walls for eons," explained Gina.

"Waiting for the day you finally arrived," continued Nicole.

Keith frowned. "You're...sentinel *ghosts*?"

"In a sense," replied Gina.

"A simple way to put it," agreed Nicole.

Sure, he decided. Why not? He was pretty sure he was *way* past calling *anything* impossible. At this point, if the dead sentinels' message turned out to be that he needed to go and fight Santa Clause and Edward Scissorhands in Smurf Village for a magic eggplant, he was just going to have to go with it.

And yet...then again... Didn't the cat lady say as much would happen?

(*In obsidian pool undisturbed, sleep with the dead.*)

He laid himself down on that black sand and began dreaming *this* weirdness. So didn't that mean he was now, in fact, "sleeping with the dead"?

That mysterious cat lady... This was *so* much like the dream he met her in, right down to the naked and overly familiar Amber and Nicole. Why did these freaky dream people keep trying to hook him up with his exes? It didn't make any sense.

(*Death waits in City Beyond Memory.*)

Right... She made it sound like everyone was going to die if he failed. In all the chaos and confusion of...whatever *this* was right now...he'd forgotten about that part. He should probably be working a little harder at this...

(*Ten will return. No more. No less.*)

But how did he even get out of this place? He looked up at those towering cliffs. "Those are the *city walls*, aren't they?" he finally realized. Like the fairytale park and that hotel room and the imperfect version of his own home, there were walls, but no windows or doors, no way out. Just like the walls surrounding the City Beyond Memory.

"A manifestation of the limits of this dream realm," affirmed Gina.

"Ordinarily, dreams are not subject to the limitations of distance, dimension or time," explained Andrea.

"But here inside the Impassible Wall," Nicole continued, "we are isolated. Even in our dreams."

"The Keeper gives us what we need to succeed," said Andrea.

"But it is up to each of us to do our part," finished Gina. "Or we all fail."

That sounded like an awful lot of pressure. He reached up and rubbed at his face, weary. "You said something about a...'higher level of consciousness,' was it? How does *that* work?"

"By allowing our minds to meet," replied Andrea, as if that made any more sense.

"A union of awareness," added Nicole.

"An emotional bond," said Gina.

"I don't really follow…" He opened his eyes to find that he was standing in front of Andrea. She was dressed in a flowing white gown and veil. She was clutching a bouquet in front of her with strangely naked hands. There were rings on only one finger. An engagement ring and a wedding band glinted dramatically in the soft lights of the windowless church they were both now standing in.

"Do you prefer this one?" she asked him.

"Or this one?" asked Gina.

He turned to find that she was standing there in her own wedding gown, her long, brown hair trailing down her back, her own wedding band glinting on her finger. "For God's sake, *slow down!*" he cried.

"This is what you want," said Nicole.

He turned to face her, expecting to find her all dressed up, too, but instead found himself back in that fake hotel room again, lying naked in bed with her. "What are you talking about?" He was trying his best to stay calm, but all this jumping around was disorienting. He needed a little damned space. Why the hell were they trying to *marry* him?

"We've seen inside you," said Amber. She was snuggled up on a couch with him, dressed in comfy pajamas. There was a fire smoldering in a fireplace in front of them and the room smelled like gingerbread. "You want companionship. With no family left, you feel alone in the world."

"You're afraid of an empty life," said Ramona. The two of them were sitting together in a large bathtub, her shoulders leaning back against his chest, white bubbles rising up around them. "A lonely life."

"You want to have a family again," said Nicole. She was lying with her head on his lap, her long, brown hair spilling over his leg, her bare feet stuck out over the arm of the loveseat, dressed in only a pair of panties and an oversized tee shirt.

"I don't know *what* I want!" he snapped at her. "How can *you* claim to know?"

"We just do," she replied.

He sighed. "I don't know. Maybe you're right. Maybe I do want that. But what am I supposed to do about it? I'm still working through a lot of stuff. You can't just barge into my head and tell me what I want. I need time."

"But there *isn't* time," said Nicole. She stared up at him with those gorgeous eyes he once found so fascinating and a ping of painful regret rang through his heart at the familiarity of the sight. "Enemies of the cycle have slipped through the gates. Without you, no one will leave this city and everything will crumble."

Disaster looms ahead, he thought, remembering the creepy cat lady's ominous warnings. *Death will take them all.* Again, he sighed. Why did *he* have to be the one responsible for something this important? What did he even really have to offer? His only talent seemed to be falling unconscious and having freaky dreams.

"Fine…" He met those fake Nicole eyes, his heart fluttering at old memories stirring somewhere inside. "Tell me what I need to do."

Chapter 36

There it was.

Corey stood up and stretched his legs, his eyes remaining fixed on the wall in front of him, not daring to look away and risk losing it again. He couldn't stay here all day, after all. He still had to find Violet. She was probably worried about him.

He stepped up to the wall and pressed both his hands against it, feeling the coolness of the stone against his palms. That strange energy was pulsing forward. He couldn't see it. He couldn't even feel it. Not physically. At first he thought he could, but that was just his brain processing a brand-new sensation and not knowing how to present it to him. This was an entirely new sense. It was as if he felt it *under* his skin, as if the energy passed into him and then flowed through his very veins, but always coursing in the same direction.

It wasn't an optical illusion, exactly. There was no angle he could look at it from to reveal it. There was no trick of light or shadow or shading. It was hidden some other way. And his mind couldn't seem to grasp it even now that he knew it was there. The closest his brain could come was that it made him think of a four-dimensional tesseract. Something beyond his brain's ability to fully perceive. He needed to reach *into* the stone, not around it.

It was something he shouldn't have known how to do. Humans were three-dimensional beings, after all, in a three-dimensional world. And yet somehow, as he sat there, staring at it, letting the sight of that plain, gray stone soak into his head, he found that he *did* know what to do. But it wasn't something he could ever hope to explain to anyone else. It was sort of like that old Leslie Nielsen skit where he caught a woman's hand when she tried to slap him, then caught her other hand when she tried again, only to then get slapped with a third hand. That was only a silly gag, of course, good for a chuckle in a goofy spoof movie, but this somehow felt sort of like that. It was impossible, it made no logical sense, yet it was happening. His body didn't move that way, wasn't shaped like that, and yet he was able to do it. This was the real world, and yet it was like something out of a cartoon. It was as if his fingers had reached out in several directions at once and found a way inside the very molecular structure of the stone. Or, at least, that was as close as he could come to describing it. He doubted it had anything to do with actual molecules. Those would be far too small to interact with in such a way. But it was as if, instead of a single slab of stone, it was some sort of complex structure made up of many smaller stone pieces that merely *mimicked* a single block of stone and he'd somehow found his way into the miniscule cracks between them.

Regardless of the details, however he might have done it, and whatever it was he did, it worked. Because something happened.

That was pretty much all there was to it. Just…*something happened*. Because he couldn't describe it. It was like a subtle lurching in his gut and a brief wave of dizziness. It felt like he saw something for a split second, but he couldn't remember what that something was, if it was a light or a shadow or a movement…or even if it might have been a sound, instead. It was baffling.

But now there lay before him a brand-new passage leading forward where there wasn't one before, just as he'd sensed there was.

That strange energy was flowing into it, urging him forward.

"Cool," he said into the endless silence. It seemed to sum up the whole experience well enough.

And yet, as he stood there, a slight frown creased his pudgy face. As indescribably strange as that was, he suddenly felt as if he'd seen something like it somewhere before. But if he'd ever encountered anything like this, he surely would have remembered it… It wasn't the sort of thing he'd have forgotten. Was it simply some kind of side-effect of exercising whatever seldom-used part of his brain was needed to comprehend things alien to his natural environment?

(That was a good one, he decided. Very scientific sounding. He should try to remember that when he told Violet about all this later.)

Yet, something was stirring somewhere deep in his subconscious. An old and long-forgotten memory was trying to wriggle its way up from some dark and forsaken tomb at the very bottom of his mind.

Something about…a cave? In the forest?

But already the memory was fading again, slipping away, descending back into the mysterious shadows of his subconscious.

Violet was there… he thought, though he wasn't sure why. Violet was *where*? What was he thinking about? He couldn't remember. And besides, Violet was *always* there. They were best friends. They grew up together. They did *everything* together.

He shook the strange thought away. He couldn't remember it, so there was no reason to spend any more time on it.

He continued on, advancing deeper into the mysterious darkness, wondering what other curiosities were waiting for him up ahead.

Chapter 37

"Don't let them touch you... Don't let them touch you... Don't let them touch you..."

Everett struggled to shake it off. He was lucky. That draft only grazed him as it whooshed past, its feathery, gossamer form merely skimming his back and shoulder as the wind whipped it past them. It lasted only a fraction of a second, but that was more than enough for him. What an absolutely *dreadful* feeling. It was cold and lonely and hopeless and unforgiving, making him think for some reason of the cruel and unforgiving hand of death that eventually closed around everyone. But death could sometimes be peaceful. Death could sometimes be merciful. He felt no peace or mercy in that ethereal caress. He felt only a raw, carnal hunger, cold and emotionless. And an icy, sinking certainty that he'd avoided a terrible fate by less than the width of a very fine hair...

(*Able to drain the life from the living on contact.*)

He shuddered at the memory of those mysterious words. And yet Violet denied saying any such thing. She claimed to know nothing about the drafts. And he truly didn't think she was lying...so who *was* that?

He realized that he was muttering those words to himself. ("Don't let them touch you...") and clenched his teeth to silence them. He needed to snap out of it and focus. Those things were still out here, fluttering through that never-ending wind. He'd only barely escaped the last one, he needed to wake up and be ready to react.

He pushed the awful thoughts from his head and looked out over the ancient cityscape illuminated in flickering lightning. He could see them out there. Wispy and shadowy, formless, little more than sheets of mist. They had no bodies. They had no means of moving on their own. They were at the mercy of the storm itself. And yet they were very, *very* real.

Was this why he was here? Because he could see things like these? That felt like a tremendous amount of responsibility. He could see them, sure, but would he be able to protect anyone from them? They moved so fast. And so erratically.

"I really wish you'd talk to me," shouted Violet.

He glanced over at her, saw her worried expression even as she squinted through the rain, and realized that all of these feelings were painted on his face for her to see. He made a conscious effort to push it all aside and focus on what was important. Another one could be whipping past them at any second and he was the only one with any chance of seeing it coming. "Sorry," he said.

She looked relieved. "You okay?"

"Just had a little...um..." But he wasn't sure how to explain it. A little *what*? A little *scare*? That sounded utterly inadequate. It was *terrifying*. And yet he wasn't sure he could fully explain *why* it had terrified him so much. More than that, he found that he didn't want to talk about it. The ordeal had left him feeling shaken. "I'm okay," he said instead. "Don't worry about me."

"Don't do that to me!" she snapped, surprising him.

"Sorry," he said again. He looked back over his shoulder, then out over the city, first one way, then the other, his eyes peeled for darting misty shadows. They seemed to all be farther out right now, but they were much too fast to underestimate. They could be on them in an instant.

He needed to stay sharp. He needed to keep his attention reigned in as tightly as possible. They could come from any direction and at any time. If he dropped his guard, even for a moment, it could be bad.

But another great gust of wind washed across the bridge and threatened to topple them over, forcing them to stop and brace themselves.

It was a desperately vulnerable feeling, standing out here in the open, unable to move for fear of falling to his death, unable to open his eyes against the onslaught of wind and rain, unable to even hear over the howling of the storm hammering at his ears, all while knowing that *they* were all around them, whipping this way and that, perhaps zeroing in on them at this very instant.

It seemed to go on and on, much longer than the last one, and each second passed like the tolling of an ominous funeral bell.

Eventually, however, the gale eased. He opened his eyes and looked around. Several of those misty shadows flitted past them, much too close for comfort, but not right atop them, as he'd feared.

"You okay?" he asked.

She nodded and stood up straight. "Look!"

Ahead of them was an enormous, towering shadow illuminated by the haze of the flickering lighting. The other side at last?

"Come on!" she shouted, pulling at his arm. "We're almost there!"

He considered arguing that they couldn't really see how far away that shadow was but decided against it. They could use all the optimism they could get out here. Instead, he focused on the bridge itself, and on those barely visible monsters blowing in the wind like wayward shopping bags.

Another great crash of thunder and lightning split the sky overhead, startling them both, but also revealing the stone wall they were rushing toward. Like the one on the other side, it looked like a towering skyscraper, but lacked windows of any sort, making it look less like a building than some kind of massive stone monument.

It sort of made sense, he supposed. The "structure" they exited from on the other side was no building, either. It didn't contain rooms and hallways. It contained those dark, empty passages.

Did the labyrinth fill *all* of these structures? Did it make up this entire "city" from top to bottom? Just a convoluted way to make it as hard as possible to navigate?

A draft was rushing toward them from the left. He pulled at Violet's elbow, stopping her, his eyes fixed on it, watching its every move. It was heading this way, but not directly at them. At this rate, it would pass in front of them. But if it swerved a little, they'd need to rush backward, out of its way.

Instead, it rustled strangely in the wind and was swept off the other way, missing them by several yards.

Still too close for comfort, though.

"Now!" he shouted over the noise, tugging her onward.

The next flash of lightning illuminated an open doorway ahead of them. Less than a football field's length away! They could do this!

Violet saw it, too. She was moving faster now, pulling him along by his arm.

Two hundred yards…

One hundred fifty yards…

A hundred yards…

He looked out into the storm. There seemed to be less of them now. Perhaps they couldn't drift around like that too close to the walls. Maybe it was safer for them to keep their distance from the structures.

But when he looked back, he saw one gliding along the surface of the bridge, seemingly chasing them.

It was a big one. There wasn't going to be room to move aside for it. And it was too low to duck under it as they did that first one. They needed to run!

It was his turn to hurry them along. He picked up his pace, pulling at Violet's arm hard enough to communicate a proper amount of urgency, which she read loud and clear because in the next instant they were both sprinting through the storm toward that opening in the wall, running for their very lives.

His heart was thundering more than the sky by now. He could see the opening leading back inside and away from the nightmare storm, but could they really reach it in time?

He risked a look over his shoulder, only to find that it was closing in on them. It wasn't as fast as some of the other shapes whipping about out over the darkness, but it had a strange sort of intention to it, as if it were overriding its natural currents specifically to chase them down.

Focusing his attention forward again, he ran.

Almost there…

Almost…

So close…

He expected at any second to be overrun, to feel that awful, death-like coldness envelop him and carry him off to wherever the dead ended up in places like these.

But they rushed through the doorway and into the dark passage beyond, the raging chaos of the storm immediately becoming muffled as they left the wind and rain behind.

He ran on for another twenty yards before turning to see how far the monstrous mist had made it.

It was right in front of him.

He stood there, frozen, as it drifted slowly along the floor, great misty tendrils of ethereal shadows stretching toward him, reaching, groping.

But without the wind of the storm, it had no power left…

He watched it settle to the floor and melt into nothing.

He stood there a moment, his heart still pounding, unable to quite make himself believe that they'd escaped by such a miniscule margin.

"Are we safe yet?" asked Violet from behind him.

"I think so," he replied, breathless. "The drafts can't reach us in here."

"You're sure?"

He stared down at the floor where the strange, gossamer shadows had just melted away. Clearly, she didn't see how close it came to catching up to them. It was still mostly invisible to her. And maybe it was better if he kept it to himself. "Positive."

"Thank God!"

He nodded. Thank God, indeed. He felt lightheaded after that.

He *really* hoped they didn't find themselves needing to go back the other way.

"I'm soaked to the bone!" grunted Violet. The din of the storm had eased enough now that he could hear the shivers in her voice, reminding him that his own teeth were chattering from the frigid rain.

He turned away from the stone bridge and the swarms of storm drafts and shined his light over the stone walls on either side of him. Wanting only to be helpful, he started to ask if she thought they should crowd close together to utilize their body heat until the chill passed, but thankfully he quickly realized how that would sound and swallowed the words before he had a chance to open his mouth. What an embarrassing thing to say aloud. ("Hey, you look cold. Wanna snuggle?") The very idea made him cringe a little.

Yeah, that was more of a last resort sort of option when you barely knew each other. He could almost feel himself blushing at the very thought of it.

He turned to face her, trying his best to act like he wasn't thinking something completely inappropriate, only to find himself watching her wring out the tail of her shirt. He could see her lean belly shining beneath it, her wet skin glistening in his light. At the same time, her neckline was drawn downward, revealing a glimpse of a lacy black bra and the mysterious blue glass shard hanging in the teasing curves of her modest cleavage. The wet cloth had stretched tight over her small breasts, which, he realized with a great bolt of embarrassment, he was blatantly aiming his flashlight at, mesmerized by the tantalizing, visible shapes of her hard nipples poking through from underneath.

With a not-very-well-repressed jolt, he turned his back to her and pretended to be watching the entrance for any more approaching drafts.

Did she notice? He didn't dare look again. He could feel his face burning. How embarrassing!

On the other hand, at least he suddenly didn't feel quite so cold anymore...

Chapter 38

Andrea crept through the mossy shadows, tiptoeing over and around them whenever and wherever she could. She wasn't sure it was worth the extra effort. Her sneakers passed right through them when she had no choice but to wade through the unnatural darkness. There seemed to be no substance to them, no material, no mass. It was as if they were nothing more than an ocular illusion, a hyper-vivid hallucination. Yet she remained convinced that somewhere in all that darkness would prove to be something dangerous. And when it eventually and inevitably happened, she wasn't going to be caught entirely off guard by whatever nightmare experience was sure to follow.

She hadn't seen any more of those larger, *mobile* clumps of darkness, but she'd seen several more of the smaller ones that merely twisted and reached toward her with that creepy underwater-hair sort of motion as she passed them. And those icky looking strands of darkness dangling down from the ceiling were thicker here, too. She did her best to avoid them, but far too many kept passing through her shoulders and head for her liking. She couldn't feel anything, but the very thought of it happening never failed to make her shudder.

Were they actually phasing through her body? Were these creepy, black danglers sliding through her head? Through her *brain*? She couldn't help wondering if they could be leaving something behind in there. She imagined slimy black stains lingering deep inside her, poisoning her blood and organs.

But that was only her imagination, of course. Erin and Horatio both told her she was supposed to go this way.

And you trust those two?

Right. What proof did she have that they were telling the truth? She knew nothing about any of this. But what else could she do? She sure as hell didn't trust the Stella Pretender.

She cringed as she walked through another dense curtain of dangling darkness. It was strange how they passed in front of and even *through* her light without even casting a shadow. It was like the special effects in old video games that hadn't perfected the graphics yet so that it didn't quite look real. When she looked too hard at it, it made her feel kind of queasy. It was as if her mind couldn't handle the wrongness of it all.

From somewhere behind her came a long, mournful wail that sent the hair standing up on the back of her neck and froze her in place.

"I really hate that," she breathed.

All around her, those ghostly voices awoke at the sound of her voice, echoing her in their own eerie whispers.

"Hate that…"

"Hate…"

"Really hate…"

"Hate it…"

She shivered and started walking again. "Oh my god," she groaned.

Somewhere directly over her, something replied, "No God here…"

She clenched her teeth and pushed on, following her light into the infested tunnel ahead of her. There was a chamber waiting for her there. She could already see that it was just as infested as the passage she was in, but at least it was a larger space. The things on the walls and ceiling wouldn't be crowding her so much. She picked up her pace a little, eager to be out of the passage.

The space was about forty feet across, round, with a domed ceiling and no other way out. A dead end. But at the center of the room was a circle of six stone columns stretching from the floor to the ceiling. Those creepy shadows all seemed to be bending and stretching toward these columns, encircling them, clinging to them like vines. Long, thin tendrils of oily darkness were woven between them, twisted and tangled like black cobwebs. And there were several of those condensed balls of darkness growing in the knotted mass, each of them subtly twitching and writhing.

They all seemed to turn toward her light as she approached.

Her eyes, however, were drawn toward the floor *between* the columns. There appeared to be a hole there. The shadows were growing down the sides, like moss and roots creeping down the walls of an old well.

Still tiptoeing through the ribbons of darkness at her feet and remaining ever cautious of those reaching globs of *nope* clinging to the columns, she crept closer. Something about that hole seemed weirdly important. *Significant*, Albert would've said. Maybe it was that strange connection Gina said she had to the spirit world, trying to tell the normal part of her brain something. Or maybe it was just that it was the only thing here and she *really* didn't want to have to go back the other way.

Or maybe it was because these columns looked familiar. Beneath those gross, oily looking shadow things, they looked like the stones she saw back in that chamber beneath the ghostly cemetery, way back in All Trails Crossing.

(*They go deep.*)

The memory made her shudder. What did that mean? Why did she keep thinking that? She remembered thinking the same thing when she found Violet asleep in that dreadful gouging station. She still didn't understand what exactly happened back there. She remembered feeling as if she were looking deep inside her—whatever kind of sense that made—and then feeling as if she could see her. But she could see her just fine. She was literally only inches from her face. And yet the moment she thought that, Violet woke up.

She shined her light up into the black shadows between the columns, still wary of any more of those big crawling blobs, but she could see nothing through the darkness. Then she stepped between two of the columns and shined her light down into the hole.

Deep...

Again, she felt that word echo through her mind.

"Deep hole..." she muttered under her breath. It wasn't exactly rocket science. Calling a mysterious hole in the ground inside a massive stone labyrinth "deep" didn't seem the same as using the word to describe tombstones or columns. Or *people*. It was just a deep hole... And yet it was nothing as simple as that. Not at all. The word seemed almost to thunder through her mind, ominous and strange. *It goes deep... All the way into...* "...somewhere else..." she whispered.

She shuddered and took two steps backward, as if afraid it might suck her in.

She turned and shined her light around the room, half expecting something to have crept up on her while she was distracted, but she was still alone.

More or less, she supposed.

"Down the hole..." drifted the eerie, singsong voice of a child from somewhere below. "Down...down...down the hole..."

She stared down into the darkness, a chill washing over her. Was this somewhere she was supposed to be? Or was this some kind of trap? How was she supposed to know the difference?

Deep, she kept thinking. She was sure it was her own voice saying that word, not the thing that sounded like Stella. She hadn't heard much out of her since realizing she wasn't just her own discouraging thoughts trying to sabotage her. But now that she'd become aware of it, she couldn't help feeling as if there were an unpleasant presence nearby. Something was watching her, she realized. And it had been watching her at least since she left the wedding reception with Gina.

She stood there, staring into the mysterious hole, distracted, that word circling around and around inside her head.

Deep...

Deep...

Deep...

"Great," she grumbled to herself. "So what am I supposed to *do* about it?" What good was having some kind of psychic ghost-seeing power if all it did was say the same stupid word over and over again. Unhelpful much?

"Great..." mocked the cackling voice of an old woman.

"What to do..." whispered something that sounded like a young boy.

"So lost..." bemoaned a mournful-sounding woman.

She ignored them and leaned over the hole again, farther this time, her light illuminating the shadow-infested stone as it sank down into the black depths.

Wait... When did she step closer? Didn't she just back away from it? She had no memory of approaching it again. The realization sent a startled flutter through her heart. And yet, she didn't back away. She was still staring down into that eerie darkness as if it were pulling her gaze down into it.

(It goes deep...)

This wasn't just some random dead end, she realized. There was something about this chamber.

(All the way into...)

Was she always meant to be here? Was this what she was looking for?

(Somewhere else...)

What was down there? What couldn't she see? She felt a wild urge to drop the flashlight and see how far it fell, but she tightened her grip against the ridiculous notion. She still needed it. Without it, she'd be stranded in the dark with these shadow things, unable to see what might be crawling across the ceiling and walls toward her.

She felt strangely dizzy as she stared down into the hole. The world seemed to spin. She reached out to steady herself on one of the columns, but it wasn't there. It was behind her. She was standing on the very edge of the hole, the toes of her sneakers already hovering over it.

She was getting closer and closer without even realizing it.

She was going to fall!

She gasped and threw her weight backward. Her butt struck on the hard, shadow-infested floor, her heart suddenly pounding.

What just happened?

Somewhere in her head, she could hear Stella laughing at her.

Was that her? Or rather, the thing that made itself sound like her? Did it just get inside her head and try to make her fall down that hole?

What a *bitch*!

She scrambled to her feet, unwilling to spend any longer sitting in those gross, pulsating shadows, and shined her light around again. For a moment, she couldn't quite process what she was seeing.

The passage she entered the room through was gone. There was no trace of it.

And on the far side of the room was an opening that wasn't there before.

She walked around the hole, giving it a wide berth this time, and hurried toward it. In addition to moving closer to the hole, had she also unknowingly circled around it so that she was facing the other way? That seemed like the most logical explanation. If one could even apply something like logic to places like these, she supposed. But it wasn't the same passage that brought her here. Instead of a shadow-infested corridor, she found herself looking down a shadow-infested stairway.

"Seriously…" she sighed as she stared down into the waiting darkness. "What was in that drink?"

Chapter 39

Brandy sat on the stone floor, soaking wet, shivering. Gina was lying with her head propped on her thigh, coughing, recovering from her close call in the water. Albert was sitting beside them, still catching his breath, worrying over her.

They all needed a moment. It was a terrifying experience, being swept down that river at what felt like perilous speeds, tumbling over waterfalls, bouncing off stone columns. She was going to be covered in bruises tomorrow. (Assuming she lived that long, she supposed.) It was a wonder no one hit their head and drowned.

Although she'd held fast to Albert's hand the whole way down, not daring to lose track of him, Gina had jumped in ahead of them and immediately vanished from sight. She wasn't sure if it was basic intuition or her newfound awareness of her strange psychic abilities, but her first thought when she splashed into this room was to find her. She was worried about her, of course. She didn't want to lose track of any more friends. But more than that, it was as if she simply *knew* that something was wrong, that Gina was in imminent danger. She forgot about getting herself out of the water and fumbled the flashlight out of her pocket to look for her. It was this light that allowed her to catch sight of her flailing arms just as she sank below the surface. If she'd taken just a few seconds longer, she might not have seen her in time.

And for that matter, she wouldn't even have had the flashlight if Gina hadn't given it to her on the surface, telling her she should hold onto it in case they became separated. If not for that one thoughtful gesture...

Well, she didn't care to think about it.

Gina rolled over and pushed herself onto her hands and knees, still coughing.

"Take it easy," worried Albert. He had to raise is voice to be heard over the roar of the nearby waterfall.

"I'm okay. I just needed a minute."

"We have more than one to spare," Brandy assured her.

"We need to keep moving." She was putting on a brave face, but she was shivering hard. Her arms wobbled as she lifted herself off the ground. Albert pulled her out in time. She only inhaled enough water to send her into a coughing fit. It wasn't as if she needed mouth-to-mouth or anything. But she looked so beaten down and weary. That rough ride had clearly taken a lot out of her.

"We need to take care of each other," Brandy countered. She raised up onto her knees and hugged her, nearly pulling her off balance in the process. "*That's* what's important."

"We will," she promised, distracted. "But..." She coughed again and looked up at the stone walls around them. "...this place is big. And the layout is so complex. I don't know how long it's going to take to find whatever we're here to find."

"It'll take exactly as long as it takes," said Albert. He looked up into the shadowy darkness overhead. "This isn't *our* job. It's the Keeper's. We're just playing his game. And whatever happens will be exactly what he *intends* to happen. No matter what we do." He lowered his face and met her bloodshot gaze. "So we'll take all the time we need."

Gina stared at him for a moment, as if trying to find a flaw in his logic.

Brandy hugged her again, then pulled her back down onto her butt and sat with her.

She coughed again, then frowned. "I'm okay," she insisted, trying her best to clear her throat. "It's like when you take a drink and choke. Down the wrong pipe, or whatever. Not bad...just...kind of irritating..."

"I know." She pulled her closer, sharing what warmth she had with her. There was something about her. She'd felt it for a while now, but it seemed stronger now. Sharper. She sensed a lot of pain inside her. Loneliness. Inferiority. And a *lot* of fear. With every ounce of her being she just wanted to protect this person. "Just a little while longer, okay? We want to make sure everyone's had enough rest."

Gina laid her head against her shoulder, surrendering. "You're cheating," she said in her quiet, sleepy voice, barely audible over the roar of the falling water.

She blinked, surprised. "What?"

"Your psychic ability. It lets you see inside my head, doesn't it?"

"Um..." She looked over at Albert. "Kind of? I think?" She felt suddenly ashamed and embarrassed, as if she'd been caught reading her diary or something. "I didn't mean to. I'm still new at this psychic stuff."

"Please don't treat me like a little kid."

"I'm sorry. I didn't mean it that way."

"I know. You're really nice. I appreciate it. I do. But I'm not a kid anymore. I can decide for myself when to rest and when to keep moving."

Brandy nodded. "Okay. That's fair." She glanced up at Albert again, uncertain. "We just want to take care of our friends. That's all."

"That's right," agreed Albert.

"You guys are nice," she said again.

Brandy stared at her. She remembered the first time Violet spoke of her, how she said she was extremely quiet. Shy. And then later Nicole told them that she had a bad habit of apologizing too much. Between that and her outwardly timid nature, the quiet way she talked, she supposed she did sort of see her like a child. She seemed too innocent for the horrors of a place like the Denselands. She seemed so *fragile*.

But she wasn't fragile. She wouldn't be here now if she was. Because things that were fragile broke in this world. That was why there was nothing left out there but steel and stone. Everything weak had shattered or crumbled or simply rotted away.

Gina sighed and stood up. This time, Brandy didn't try to stop her. Instead, she and Albert stood up, too.

"On the other side of these walls are more walls," she said. "Lots more walls. Even down here, the storm's still clouding everything, so I can't see very far. Not nearly far enough to see a way through. But I can see enough to know that it's enormous. It's above us. And below us." Her gaze sank to the floor. "Way below us. Like it goes on forever."

Brandy shuddered a little at the thought. That was how it was before, too. Deeper and deeper they'd gone, under the streets, under the steam tunnels, under the sewers…until they were under *everything*. She recalled the City of the Blind, deep within, with towers stretching upward and holes plunging downward, each one covered in little openings like some great insect hive, each one a living space for countless generations of the Sentinel Queen's eyeless children… Albert had often wondered just how many levels the city had. Just how far up and down did it all go? He'd theorized that the temple was far larger than the mountain that contained it, that it might have stretched countless miles below the surface, deep beneath the zombie-infested Wood.

Gina stood there a moment, pondering what she could feel of the space around her, then she turned and looked out into the darkness of this room. "This walkway circles around the water," she reported. She had to speak louder to be heard over the waterfalls, but even so her voice remained soft and sleepy. She sounded almost bored. "There are six channels carrying it out." She pointed at each one, starting on the far side of the waterfall and working her way counterclockwise to the nearest, which was just out of sight from here. "There are more tunnels underwater, too," she added. Then she coughed again and cleared her throat. "But those won't do us any good. They're too deep. Too long."

"I'd rather keep my head above water," agreed Brandy.

"I can't say which channel we should take, though." Her gaze was shifting from one to the next, considering each of them in turn. "I can feel things moving in the passages around us, different from the things on the surface...dangerous things...but I can't tell which passage leads where." She scrunched up her face, frustrated. "I'm sorry. The storm's clouding over again. I might not be much help."

"You'll be fine," Albert assured her. He was already walking. "We all have our limits."

Brandy followed him, her light pushing back the gloom between them and the first of the six channels, revealing it to be a tunnel about eight feet wide, with a narrow walkway leading down the left side. A flat stone bridge crossed over the water, allowing them to walk around to the next channel. "There were places in the other temple that looked like this," she recalled.

He nodded. "I remember. Some kind of reservoir system. It was like the entire place was built on top of an underground spring and certain tunnels were designed to carry water to different places. This might be the same concept, except..." He glanced back at the waterfall. "Upside down?"

"There are a lot of elements at work here," said Gina. "There are whole concepts that exist here that we can't understand within the context of our own universe."

"Different laws of physics," he pondered.

"Like you and Corey were talking about," recalled Brandy. Things that once existed but no longer did. Things that exist now that never were before. "That stuff made my head hurt."

"On the surface, this place only looks like stone," marveled Gina, "but it's much more than that. I can feel things that I can't explain. Things I can't even describe."

"So business as usual," grunted Albert.

Brandy nodded. "Yeah, we weren't exactly expecting anything to suddenly make sense."

Albert turned and scanned the chamber they were in. "What *can* you feel about the layout of our immediate surroundings?"

"This is one of several flood chambers," replied Gina, still raising her sleepy voice to be heard over the rushing water. "All the rain that falls outside is directed downhill through a system of channels toward the center of the city, where there's some kind of tower structure." She lifted her face and looked up into the darkness above them. "We need to get inside that, I think."

"We're supposed to be up *there?*" asked Brandy, surprised. Had they already messed up?

But Gina shook her head. "No. There wasn't a way inside from up there. We can only get there from somewhere below it. The entrance is hidden somewhere in all these winding passageways."

"And it's too big for even you to see a path leading there," said Albert. It wasn't a question. He wasn't asking. He was working through this new puzzle in his mind. "Which makes sense because what kind of challenge would *that* be? If you were always meant to be here with us, then the sentinels would've made sure that even you couldn't find your way through this labyrinth easily."

"You really think they knew it'd be *us* who did these things?" asked Brandy. She couldn't even comprehend it. How many generations of their ancestors had been born and died between the construction of this place and their own births? How many very specific events must have taken place in all that time to ensure that the right two people came together at just the right time, over and over again, to ensure the birth of each and every one of those people throughout history? It was enough to make her head spin.

"That's how everyone keeps describing it. Just another part of the Keeper's ridiculous design. Shanzer told us we were all just parts in his machine."

"That guy was a pervert and a whack-job," snapped Brandy.

"I know he was," he replied.

"Machine..." pondered Gina. "That sounds right."

"*Nothing* about that guy was right," grumbled Brandy.

"If we're meant to find our way through this thing, we're going to find our way through it," reasoned Albert. "What we have to worry about is traps and monsters." He turned his gaze on Gina. "Which is something *you're* great at."

"That's right!" gasped Brandy. "Like with those things on the surface!"

But she didn't look very convinced. "I can't promise to see every danger. I didn't see Glum when he separated us from Andrea and Keith. I didn't see what was wrong with Nicole."

"But you're a lot more than we had last time," said Albert. He turned and pointed at the nearest channel. "Feel anything dangerous near any of these?"

"No."

He flashed her one those charming smiles. "See? Already helping."

Gina still looked unconvinced, but she nodded anyway. "I'll do
my best," she promised.

Chapter 40

Keith opened his eyes and blinked up into the darkness. The obsidian pool... That felt like so long ago now... He'd almost forgotten about it.

His heart broke as the dream images evaporated from his mind and the real world came flooding back.

(*You must let yourself be swallowed by the dream. Let it take you where it will. You'll find what you need in the depths of the reality your mind weaves.*)

And the dream did, indeed, swallow him. He felt as if years had gone by. *Decades.* He lived an entire life in the course of the visions that followed. He married. He had children. He grew old. He loved and he cherished. He held grandchildren. He made a brand-new family, one that stayed with him until the very end.

He felt tears roll down his cheeks. What a full and meaningful life. What a spectacularly happy ending. He struggled to hold onto all the beautiful memories, but they were slipping through his fingers like fine sand, impossible to grasp, year after year simply melting into the haze.

Faces of loved ones...

Children's laughter...

Irreplaceable magical moments...

All of it fading like a dying candle.

He took a great, shuddering breath. No... He didn't *want* to wake up. He didn't want to come back to *this* reality. He couldn't take it. It was too much for him to bear. He wanted to stay in the dream. *Forever.*

"Oh god..." he gasped, the heels of his hands pressed against his streaming eyes. "Oh god..."

Why? Why would they put him through something like that? It was so beautiful...*too* beautiful... It would be too much for *anyone* to bear!

But an icy chill washed over his body as he lay there, taking his breath away and startling his eyes wide open.

That feeling just now... Was someone there?

"Endure..." whispered a soft voice in his ear.

He scrambled to his feet and shined his light around, confused. Who said that? He was sure he didn't imagine it.

But there was no one. He was all alone in this place.

Endure... he recalled. The cat lady used that word, too, now that he was thinking about it.

(*Endure what is not and follow the spark.*)

"Endure what is not..." he breathed. As in, endure what isn't real? Endure his grief for a life that was never even his? Was that what she meant?

And it wasn't real. It was only a dream. Sure, it was an incredibly vivid dream, full of haunting emotions. But he was no stranger to intense dreams. He needed to let it go.

He couldn't remember most of it now anyway. There were only a few fleeting glimpses remaining. A few grains of sand left in the palms of his hands. Feelings, mostly. Love and laughter. Comfort. *Home.* And a vivid picture of a wedding band glinting in the sunlight.

He couldn't even remember who he chose. Did he spend that life with sweet Ramona? Or did he find happiness with Amber, instead? Or did he find himself growing close to Andrea or Gina? He could remember that he spent a lifetime with her, but he couldn't quite recall her face. He only knew that it was precious to him in that false life...

He took a shuddering breath and shined his light back and forth. He was feeling better now, more rational. Did he only imagine that voice? It felt so real, but maybe *it* was part of the dream, too.

And yet the thought had barely crossed his mind when he looked down to see a set of footprints that weren't his own. They looked just like the wet footprints that led him to the feuding brothers, barefoot, considerably smaller than his own. And just like those, they belonged to someone who walked right up to where he was lying and then simply vanished.

He took a deep breath...held it...then slowly let it back out.

There was no sense in dwelling on weirdness in a weird world.

He stepped out of the obsidian pool and looked around. "Endure what is not..." he muttered to himself, "...and follow the spark." But he didn't understand that last part. What did she mean by "spark"?

Somewhere in the darkness behind him, something broke. He jumped and twirled around, ready to defend himself. But nothing was there. Everything was silent.

It sounded like glass, but there was no glass down here. There was stone. There was that black sand. And there was some water back a ways. That was pretty much it.

But as he crept toward the source of the noise, he saw a flash of reflected flashlight beam. Lying there on the floor before him was the mysterious bottle he found in the ruins of that building, way back before he was separated from the girls. He'd forgotten all about that.

But why was it broken on the floor? His hand went to his pocket, only just now aware that it was missing. He still didn't even know what it was. What was it for? Was it important? Had he screwed up? Did his wallowing in self-pity allow that ghost to steal it from him and destroy it?

He knelt down and picked up the largest piece of it, then held it up in front of his eyes, searching for that mysterious light inside. But it was gone.

What did it all mean? What was he supposed to do?

But as he knelt there, pondering it all, he caught sight of a familiar glint of light deep in the darkness ahead of him.

"What the hell…?"

He stood up and walked toward it. Was that his imagination?

No. Again, he saw it. A glint of light, without any source. Just like the one he saw inside the bottle. Was it something alive? Something that had been released now that the bottle was broken?

(…*follow the spark.*)

He picked up his pace. This was part of the Keeper's ridiculous plot, too?

The light was coming from a passage up ahead. He rushed into it, pursuing it, desperate to keep up with it, lest he lose his way and his chance.

Ahead of him, the path split.

Again, he saw the light. It glinted deep in the darkness to the right. And it was strangely familiar.

It was just like the glinting of the wedding bands in those dreams, he realized.

This was where he was supposed to be. This was how he was going to protect everyone.

But he couldn't wrench his thoughts fully from the remnants of that dream. It lingered in his mind, haunting him, making him wonder what it all might cost him here in the waking world…

He went through all of that so that those dead sentinels could give him a message… But what message? He didn't have any information now that he didn't have before he fell asleep in that obsidian sandbox. Did he do something wrong? Did their messenger get lost? What happened?

Why the hell did he have to go through all of that?

He tried to focus on the light ahead of him. The glint. The *spark* he was supposed to be following. Whatever was making it seemed to be looming just beyond the reach of his flashlight, no matter how fast or slow he walked. It would disappear for minutes at a time, until he thought he'd lost it, then it would flash again. And at every intersection he encountered, it was there, showing him the way.

What was in that bottle? Was it some kind of spirit? Had he been carrying around some kind of ghost this whole time? Did it have something to do with the woman in the silvery dress and those ghostly footprints?

And where was it leading him?

He stepped into a room with eight passages branching off it. For a moment, he stood there, looking around, his flashlight sweeping across every option, confused. Did he lose it? He didn't see the strange glint anywhere.

But when he turned around again, he saw a *different* light. There was a soft glow at the end of one of them, growing brighter at first, then dimming.

A flashlight? Was someone there? A fellow traveler lost in this same darkness?

He hurried after it before it could fade away again.

The path forked ahead of him. The light was fading from the one on the right. He hurried in that direction. Immediately, he could see that the light was moving to the left in an adjoining passage.

Someone was definitely there!

But when he turned the corner, he froze.

Ahead of him, the passage opened into a large, empty area with a bridge stretching out into the darkness. On that bridge, a hulking, bloodstained figure was slowly trudging away from him. With one twisted and distended arm, it was dragging a startlingly familiar body along the floor behind it.

Nicole!

He wasn't sure what he was looking at. She looked unconscious. She wasn't struggling at all. And yet she was still clutching her phone in one rigid hand, its flashlight still shining. It was the very same light that he followed to find her here.

And just what the hell was *that* thing? It looked sort of like a man. It was *dressed* like a man, in filthy blue jeans, work boots and a blood-soaked tee shirt. But it was *huge*! And it looked beat all to hell, as if it had just crawled out of some kind of horrid industrial accident!

He didn't have time to process the scene. He rushed forward, a cyclone of emotions and thoughts raging through his head.

"Why is it always *you*?" he shouted.

Chapter 41

Anun amum ut mu. Anun amum ut mu.

Nicole felt as if her very mind were about to shatter. She couldn't take it any longer. The pain…the madness…the *terror*…

Why was this happening to her? Why had God forsaken her to this terrible place? What had she done wrong? She didn't ask for any of this. All she wanted was to protect her friends.

Anun amum ut mu.

But of course she'd already failed to do that. She lost Andrea. She lost Gina. She lost Brandy and Albert.

Anun Goar Nangup.

Was this simply what she deserved? Was this her punishment for sticking her nose where it didn't belong? For butting in after Gina warned her she wasn't involved?

It wasn't fair…

Then a voice tore through the chaos and the pain, far louder than the horrible constant chanting: "Why is it always *you?*"

She gasped. Fresh air suddenly filled her lungs and startling silence swallowed her. The foul and crushing inkblot nowhere world broke apart, replaced with a myriad of colorful stars that danced in the darkness before her startled eyes.

Keith?

"Snap out of it!" he shouted.

She blinked the tears from her eyes and focused on the awful face of the undead abomination looming over her. The sight sent fresh terror jolting through her.

She was on her back on the cold, stone floor. Hotdog's monstrous corpse was hunched over her, one broken hand closed around the straps of her tank top, dragging her by it. Unconscious and oblivious, she was sliding across the floor like a piece of cheap luggage, her dirty, disheveled bra on display and her breasts popping out.

Somehow, she was still clutching her phone in her hand, allowing her to see the monster standing over her. But there was another light, too. One that was shining onto Hotdog's moldy back from behind.

The thing let go of her shirt and turned to face the man standing there now.

Keith took a step back as the grotesque corpse turned its attention on him. "Whoa... Okay... Um...definitely see why you'd resort to roofies, not gonna lie... But it's still not cool man!"

Nicole stared up at the filthy walking corpse of Hotdog Creep, her mind reeling. That awful place. That writhing thing in the sky that was also all the writhing things in the ground. Goar Nangup. An actual fucking *god*...

"Get up!" he shouted at her. "Get out of here!"

"Hold on!" she shouted back, yanking her shirt down and adjusting herself. "My tits are out!"

"What do you care? Your tits are always out!"

"Not for *you*!" Her tank top was all stretched out now. And a little torn, she realized. That really pissed her off. She didn't have any spare clothes.

The monster lurched toward Keith and he backed away, his gaze washing over it, taking it in, measuring it, calculating his odds, which clearly weren't very good.

He looked pretty rough, himself, she realized. He was no longer wearing his shirt. Instead, it was wrapped around his arm in a makeshift bandage. And there was dried blood on the lower left side of his abdomen, staining his jeans. She wondered briefly what he'd been through since Glum separated them, but decided quickly that she didn't care. It wasn't like he was her responsibility. Which was good, since he was armed with nothing more than his flashlight. What was he going to do? Have a pretend lightsaber duel with the thing? Idiot.

She turned and shined her own light around, confused. Where the hell was she? This wasn't the dead end where the thing cornered her. This was... She peered over the edge and into the black abyss stretched out beneath her. Why was she back *here* again? Where was the dead freak trying to take her? What did it want with her?

Nothing made any sense!

She looked back in time to see the monster lunge at Keith, its powerful, unbroken arm lashing out. But Keith was faster. He scurried backward, out of reach. In almost the same motion, however, the thing swung its other arm. Somehow, it maintained control regardless of the broken bones within, but it was a stomach-turning sight. The arm bent and twisted horribly as it arced toward him, and seemed to unravel itself, the muscles and tendons stretching between the detached bones, extending its reach much more than he anticipated. He couldn't back away fast enough, so he lifted his arm to shield himself, only for it to connect with the part that was wrapped in his shirt.

He let out a painful shout and staggered backward, dropping his flashlight.

Nicole's heart leapt as she realized he was approaching the edge and the deadly drop beyond. "Be careful!" she shouted.

"Don't yell at me!" he shouted back through clenched teeth. "You're the reason I keep getting into these messes!"

"So fucking *sorry!*"

He was still backing away, but he was moving away from edge now. That was good. At least the moron was aware of his surroundings. This was a terrible place for a fight, like something from a video game. And it was hardly a fair fight. On one hand, there was the muscle-bound, mind-controlling, teleporting pervert's already imposing body, zombified by an evil ancient god and supersized for good measure. And then there was skinny Keith, who was far more likely to be found helping some little old lady get something off a high shelf in a grocery store than engaging in a fight.

Why did it have to be *him?*

She gathered her frustration and ran at the monster's back. She didn't want to be so close to the thing. It reeked of rotten meat and rancid blood. But Keith wasn't going to be able to beat this thing fighting it face-to-face.

"What're you doing?" shouted Keith.

She rushed right up to the thing's back, grabbed the belt loops of its filthy jeans and kicked. She might not have been as strong as Wayne or as clever as Albert, or possess any kind of impressive supernatural abilities like…well, *everyone else in this fucking place*, apparently…but she was in fantastic shape and very flexible. She could do a standing split. So even at his increased size, her kick connected with the monster's groin.

"Ouch…" said Keith.

She let go and backed quickly away, avoiding any flailing elbows.

She expected the thing to drop to its knees, the way it did back in that hospital hallway when it was still Hotdog Creep, but the thing only turned around and began lumbering after her.

"Oh come on!"

"Get out of here!" Keith shouted again.

"You don't get to tell me what to do!"

"Why are you so stubborn?" Now that the monster's back was turned to him, he rushed it, too. But he didn't bother with its zombie junk. He went for the structural weakness. He kicked the back of its knee.

The thing's leg buckled, sending it tumbling to one side. Now its increased size had become a liability. It thrust its good arm down to catch itself but missed. Its weight carried it over the edge.

"Yes!" cheered Nicole. But it was too early to celebrate. Its other hand grasped the edge and it hung there instead of falling. "Fuck!" she amended.

Keith rushed over and stomped the thing's fingers.

She wasn't sure what he thought that would do. If a swift kick to the balls didn't make the thing flinch, she doubted it would squeal in pain over a sneaker to its knuckles. And she would've told him that, too, if there'd been time.

The thing's other arm shot up and snagged his foot. In the same moment, its grip slipped.

The monster disappeared over the edge.

And so did Keith.

"*No!*" she screamed. She squeezed her eyes closed, her heart plummeting into her belly. "*Please no!*"

Chapter 42

Olivia shined her light down into the dark abyss far below. "Here again..." she groaned, staring out at all those terrifyingly narrow walkways.

"With all the paths leading out of this room, it's no wonder we'd circle back to one of them," reasoned Wayne.

She supposed he was right. But she couldn't stop thinking about what he said earlier about the temple being designed to test them. What if the sentinels intended to force her across one of those deathtraps? It wouldn't be hard. They didn't choose where they entered the labyrinth from. They were just sort of dumped here when she used the key. And then they were separated from the others. For all she knew, the only way to the exit was through this room.

How totally unfair would that be?

"Come on," said Wayne, pulling her closer to him as he turned and started back the other way.

It was frustrating. It was getting harder and harder to pick out the safest paths. And going backward like this felt extra wrong. It seemed to her that something deeply unpleasant was in here with them, getting closer and closer the longer they were here.

She couldn't stop thinking about the Caggo in the first temple, that great, pale pile of gross, jiggling flesh that bounded up the sloped sides of that central tower like some kind of jungle predator. Did this one have something like that guarding it, too? Was that what she was beginning to sense? And could it have already caught their scent?

Or was it merely that some subconscious part of her psychic brain already knew that this awful labyrinth was eventually going to force her to cross that terrifying room one way or another?

The last intersection wasn't very far back, but even making this short trek was almost painful. Something inside her didn't want to go this way. Daggers of dread seemed to dig into her gut with each step she took. And when she finally reached it, she wasted no time contemplating the best way. She pulled on Wayne's hand and dragged him to the right without hesitation.

But this way didn't feel good, either. It was as if she were locked in a room with walls closing in around her. That claustrophobic feeling was gripping her again, squeezing like a python, making it harder and harder to breathe.

"You okay?" worried Wayne.

She didn't reply. She wasn't sure she could. If she opened her mouth, would words come out or would she only utter a strangled sob. There was a desperate panic welling up inside her, building pressure like a geyser. Instead, she gave her head a hard shake, her hair whipping about her face.

"I'm here," he promised, quickly glancing back.

He was definitely here with her. He had little choice in the matter. She was clinging to his arm with a death grip. And she had no intention of letting go any time soon. Maybe not until they were safely back home.

Ahead of them, the path split again. Right or left.

No, as she drew closer, she realized that there was a third passage branching off from the one on the left just a little farther. Right or left or...*more left*, she guessed. But which way was the safest? She didn't like the feel of *any* of them.

She didn't want to waste time, but she couldn't choose. She stopped and shined her light one way then the other. Each option filled her with that sickening feeling of mounting dread. She could feel herself digging her nails into Wayne's arm again, but she couldn't help it.

What was happening?

"Did you hear that?" he asked.

She glanced up at him confused. He was standing there, shining his light into the passage on the right, squinting to see into the darkness. "Hear what?" she gasped. She heard nothing, but it wasn't really a surprise, given how loudly her heart was pounding at the moment.

"I don't know."

She held her breath and they stood there, motionless, listening.

Then she heard it, too. Very soft. Very faint. It reminded her for some reason of playing cards being shuffled. "What *is* that?"

The sound came again, but from the leftmost passage this time. Both of them swung their flashlights toward it.

Wayne cursed under his breath.

That sensation of overwhelming panic was swelling faster now. Something was about to happen. "Back," she whispered, already tugging at his arm. "We have to go back. This was the wrong way."

The sound came again. But she couldn't tell which direction this time.

They swept their lights from left to right as they backed up, wary. Something in the middle passage flittered briefly into view. Some kind of bug? A moth of some sort, maybe?

No. Nothing so benign if this mounting feeling of terror was any indication. Bees, maybe? Wasps? A killer *swarm*? Her mind flashed back to that ancient forest and those vile little monsters who dropped a hornet nest on her. That wasn't something she wanted to relive. She turned around, tugging hard at Wayne's arm, and fled back the way they came. Behind them, that strange fluttering noise erupted into a frenzy.

It reminded her a little of the sound the hounds made, which didn't make the situation any better at all.

This was bad. They were being boxed in. Her every instinct told her not to take the path to the right when she returned to the last intersection, but there was nowhere else to go besides back to the bottomless shaft and its dreadfully narrow walkways.

Barely holding back a scream, she turned right, praying that there'd be another passage to flee into before she encountered whatever it was that was sending her psychic alarm into the red.

But almost immediately, something glinted in the light ahead of them. It darted from the floor to the ceiling, then zigzagged left to right, then flashed over her head, wrenching a startled scream from her.

Wayne cursed and spun around to follow it.

When she looked up, he had a fine red line drawn across one cheek. A single drop of blood beaded in the middle of it and slid slowly down his face.

He reached up and wiped at it with the hand gripping his flashlight, then looked down at the blood smeared on his finger. "What was that?"

Again, something glinted in the beam of the flashlight. A strange shape fluttered clumsily in and out of sight, still making that bizarre shuffling sound.

Another flutter. Another flash. And then a sharp pain on her forearm. She cried out, startled, and looked down to see the same fine line drawn across her tanned skin.

"What the *fuck*?" shouted Wayne, pulling her closer to him.

Another flash and flutter. Another pain, this time on her elbow. At the same time, Wayne gave a painful shout and jerked his head back, a bloody line now drawn across his forehead.

What was happening? What were these things?

Again, something tiny and noisy shot past them. Again, a searing pain blossomed on her skin, this time across her upper shoulder. She sucked in a painful gasp and looked down to see that there was a slit in the sleeve of her tee shirt, as if someone had slashed at her with a box knife.

Were these things *cutting* them?

She yanked at his arm again. They had to get out of here. They'd disturbed something nasty.

This was her fault, she realized. It was a mistake refusing to cross that room. They'd wasted time, stumbled around until they found something worse than her fear of heights. If she'd just sucked it up like a big girl and crossed those platforms, would they have avoided this fresh horror?

More frenzied wings flapping. More flashes in the gloom. More burning slashes across her skin.

She was screaming, though she couldn't quite remember when she started. This was so much worse than hounds! At least the hounds they could keep away from for the most part. They remained contained in those lower passageways, unable to escape. But how were they supposed to keep away from things that could *fly*?

Another glint in the flashlight beam. Another flutter of incoming wings.

This time Wayne swatted at the thing, knocking it out of the air and against the wall, bloodying the back of his hand in the process. But the thing was down, whatever it was. It hit the ground and he stomped on it. "Fucking thing!"

He shined his light down at the remains, trying to get a look at what they were dealing with.

Olivia stared at it. What she saw was confounding enough that she forgot to keep screaming. It wasn't a bug at all, as far as she could tell. In fact, it didn't seem to be anything at all. It was just a smear of blood between two strange, rectangular wings.

Wayne bent and picked one of them up, "This is…?"

"What?" she asked, still shielding her face from any more arial attacks.

"I've seen these before," he breathed, shining his light down at the one remaining wing on the floor. That one was twitching, as if it longed to get back up and attack them again, but there was no body attached to it.

She shined her light onto the one in his hand, confused. Was she supposed to know what it was?

"It's a scale," he explained at last, looking dazed. A look of deep concern crossed his handsome face. "A *hound* scale."

"These things are like the hounds?" It was a terrible thought.

But he was shaking his head. "No... This *was* a hound."

"*What?*" But a thunderbolt of dread shot through her heart and she twirled around. Something was approaching from behind them.

Wayne turned and aimed the light toward it. "It's him again."

"What? *Who?*" But then she heard the voice. It was garbled and strange, like something alien and horrible attempting to *mimic* human speech.

"What fascinating creatures..." it said in a strange series of burbles and grunts that set the hairs on the back of her neck standing on end.

The thing that stepped out of the gloom was unthinkably horrible. Its feet were bloody claws, broken and splayed apart. Its legs were raw bones knitted together with knotted entrails. Its arms were flaps of razor-lined strips of flayed flesh ending in individual claws that dangled like macabre wind chimes. Its torso was little more than a ribcage with two spines, dripping with dangling organs and tattered flesh. And its head was the monstrous, gaping maw of a dead hound, a tongue covered in sharp, thorny barbs dangling from between its bristling teeth.

"I can play with these for a *long time*," growled the scarecrow man as hundreds of razored insects swarmed from behind him.

Chapter 43

Austin stuffed his book into his bag.

That was it. The last book. There were two more in the bag, just in case. And he was disappointed that he wouldn't get to them. And there were plenty more still out there in the world that he'd wanted to read, but there was no more time. He was almost at his destination.

Disappointing. He liked reading. Of all the ways to spend his time—and he'd tried a great many—it was his favorite. There were so many stories out there, after all. So many adventures. So many mysteries. So many discoveries.

So many different *endings*.

But he had a job to do. And it was almost time to do it.

He turned a corner and marched straight ahead. Behind him, a reverberating boom sounded as that section of passage dropped downward, simultaneously closing the way back and opening a new path elsewhere in the sprawling labyrinth.

Such clever architects, the Faceless Ones, able to create such intricate machinery from little more than blocks of stone. Of course, this particular kind of stone wasn't ordinary by any definition. This particular material had unique polarizing properties, allowing them to direct and utilize exotic energies in ways that hadn't been possible since universes long forgotten. It was quite extraordinary, really.

But it didn't distract him from wanting to pick up another book. His fingers reached automatically for his bag, caressing the leather, yearning to reach for the next. But the only thing more frustrating than not being able to read was not being able to finish something he started. And right now he had something far more important to finish.

In just a few more hours, he'd finally be at the end of this maddeningly long journey. He could almost taste the freedom the stoneworks promised.

Again, he turned down a new passage. Again, the stone rearranged itself with a resounding boom and a brief gust of displaced air.

He didn't need to think about which way to go. This was a path that had been programed into his brain all his life. It had always been there, nagging at him, pulling at him, like an itch he couldn't reach. And there was nothing he could do about it. It was his curse to wait for the Keeper's tools to assemble here.

And wait...

And wait...

And wait...

Books were his only escape. And even now, as he was finally within reach of scratching that infuriating itch, he still wanted to open the next one.

He marched onward, toward what appeared to be a dead end. And in many ways, he supposed, it was exactly that. The wall in front of him dropped down into the floor and vanished. The dark chamber revealed beyond was his destination. The end of his journey. The end of his very *meaning*. He had no intention of leaving this chamber.

This was the job he was given. His purpose in life. What he was made for.

He walked into the chamber without looking around. He didn't need to. He'd been seeing it in his mind all his torturous existence. Eight triangular columns stretched from floor to ceiling. A roughly hourglass-shaped stone in the middle. Several blocky protrusions jutted out from the wall, each one riddled with dozens of small, round holes, less resembling a part of the gatehouse than some kind of insect hive. The rest of the walls were dotted with rounded bulges of textured stone that was a stark contrast to the other surfaces which were all smooth and featureless. And there were ten thin, stone cylinders protruding down from the ceiling, only about an inch in diameter and varying in length from eight inches to almost a yard long.

To anyone else, none of this would make any sense. But this was Austin's purpose. His fate. His destiny. Whatever you wanted to call it. He walked around to the other side of the central stone structure, laid his bag down on the floor at his feet, and then reached up and laid his hand against a flat oval of stone.

He could feel the energy that passed through this room. Exactly as he knew it would feel. Everything was precisely as it was supposed to be. It had been waiting for him here this whole time. Because he was as much a part of the gatehouse as the stone itself. Because he was—

No... Something here *wasn't* as it should be.

He turned, frowning. What was that? Was something here?

He circled the central structure, back toward where he entered, and looked up at the ceiling behind one of the triangular columns. There was something there, something *not* of stone.

"You're not supposed to be here," he informed it.

It sprang from its hiding place, a great, twisting heap of shadows from which sprouted an explosion of hands and claws and teeth.

He stumbled backward, surprised for once, as the thing descended on him, enveloping him before he could react.

He didn't scream. It never even occurred to him. There didn't seem to be a point in it. It wasn't as if there were anyone here to come to his rescue. He didn't even feel any fear, exactly. He felt only a great and overwhelming *bewilderment*.

This wasn't supposed to happen. Something was wrong. Why would it be different? Why would this thing be here? It made no sense. The Keeper didn't make mistakes.

But it mattered none that it was wrong. The monstrous conglomeration of claws and teeth that wasn't supposed to be there tore Austin in half.

Chapter 44

Violet shined her light around the next corner. She'd grown a little jumpy after that harrowing journey across the storm-swept sky. She kept expecting something to leap out at them as they wound their way through the stone labyrinth.

It hadn't been very long since they ducked in out of the storm—twenty minutes, maybe half an hour, certainly not long enough for them to have dried off much—but already she didn't think she'd be able to find her way back to that bridge if she wanted to. And it wasn't really any surprise, given the size of this structure revealed by the lightning outside.

She kept a firm grip on Everett, their arms linked. First Albert and Brandy, then Corey, then Andrea... If it happened again, she'd be all alone. And she wasn't very fond of being alone. She was used to having Corey around. There wasn't much she did without him. She hadn't realized how much of a comfort his presence had become for her. And she was beginning to worry she might've taken that for granted.

She really hoped he was safe out there. She simply didn't know what she'd do if she lost him.

The passage turned sharply to the left and she again peered around the corner.

Another dead end. Was that the fourth or the fifth in this tower? The sixth? She'd lost count. There were a lot more twists and turns in this part of the city and less of those long, empty corridors. It was a little unsettling. Almost claustrophobic. She didn't care for the idea of being this lost.

They turned around and backtracked through the empty darkness, both of them clutching a flashlight and yet both of them fundamentally blind. Would it have made any difference if they'd been stuck here in the dark? There was nothing to see. They had no clues to tell them where to turn next. Every corridor looked exactly like the last. Was it even possible to navigate something like this? She *saw* the city spread out around them in the flashes of lightning back there. If this was what was inside all of those structures, how could anyone ever be expected to find their way *anywhere*, much less to a single doorway?

(*Except no one will be able to get there until all the conditions are met.*)

She frowned. Everett said that back when they first arrived. A part of the mysterious knowledge he claimed to have received from a puzzle box, of all things.

(*Like, locks that need opened or switches that need switched.*)

Conditions…

He theorized that these conditions might have been the reason they were separated from Andrea. If that were true, then it wasn't by chance that she lost Corey. That meant it wasn't her fault…

She glanced over at him as they walked, curious. "How did you get caught up in all this, anyway?"

"Me?" he asked as if there were anyone else here she could have been talking to. "I was just in the right place at the right time. I've been exploring places all around the country. Looking for proof that the world's not as small as people think it is."

Well, *that* sounded familiar…

Then he frowned. "Except…I guess maybe it wasn't by chance at all. Wayne said the Keeper arranged it somehow. Made sure I arrived exactly when and where he wanted me to be so I'd run into him and Olivia." He stared down at the floor in front of him as he walked, pondering it. "Thinking about it, I'm not sure anymore if I ever did anything at all on my own."

This made *her* frown. She recalled the Tunipet Boom. Jeremy Gleer falling from the sky. Black shadows stalking them through the night. Was it possible the Keeper arranged all that, too?

For some reason, she recalled that strange dream she had when she first awoke on this side of the wall. She and Corey, only ten years old. A mysterious figure in the forest. A cave she was fairly sure didn't exist.

(*…in the dreamy in-between…*)

Again, she frowned. What was that just now? Was that a part of the dream, too? Something she'd forgotten? It sounded so weirdly familiar, and yet she couldn't quite place it. In fact, it was already fading from her memory again, drifting into the murky depths with the rest of her forgotten memories.

Everett looked up at her, those bright, youthful eyes fixed on hers. "Is it a good thing if your future's already mapped out for you because you can't fail? Or does it just mean that your life isn't yours and never was?"

Violet stopped walking at this, surprised. "That's some epically deep shit for someone your age," she told him.

He smiled that charming smile and turned his attention back to the passage before them. "Yeah, sorry. That kind of talk probably isn't helpful."

"No, it's fine. I just mean…" She reached up and brushed back her unkempt hair. "I hadn't thought of it that way is all." *Was* it a good thing? She couldn't decide. It would be nice to know that somewhere out there someone was choreographing all of this, planning out every step, making it so that they couldn't fail, so that they'd all make it home again. It would be nice to know she'd be reunited with Corey and go back home to see her parents again. But on the other hand, what would that really mean? Was free will nothing more than an illusion? Was *any-thing* they did or said real? Or was it all part of some cosmic control freak's convoluted script?

They continued walking.

Ahead of them was an intersection. Was that where they turned left earlier? Or had they already passed that? It was getting harder and harder to keep track. But Everett seemed to remember because he chose what would have been the only other option without taking any time to consider it.

It was probably a good thing he was with her. If they all had a purpose for being here, like he said, then maybe *his* purpose was simply to keep *her* from walking in circles the whole time.

After only a moment, a new intersection appeared ahead of them. Again, they chose a direction at random. Again, they hit a dead end, backtracked and tried another way.

She doubted if this would make for a very thrilling movie.

But when they reached the end of this newest passage, something different finally awaited them. There was a set of stairs leading upward.

"You think we're supposed to keep going up?" wondered Everett.

She opened her mouth to say that she had no earthly idea, but instead, she found herself saying, "The higher you climb in the towering spires of the City Beyond Memory, the more detached you become from your own world and your own reality. Proceed with caution."

Everett turned and looked at her, confused. "What?"

She blinked back at him, unsure what to say. "I don't…know where any of those words came from…"

He stood there staring at her, looking as if she'd just randomly declared herself queen of the hamster people and demanded he pay her tribute. And she couldn't exactly blame him. Who the hell said that? She heard the words come out of her own mouth. She felt them form with her own lips and tongue. But they weren't *hers*. How could they be? She didn't know any such thing about this place.

"Okay," said Everett, turning his attention to the steps ahead of them. "Got it. Stay alert."

Now it was *her* turn to stare at *him*. "What do you mean, 'Got it'? Random words just spill out of my mouth on their own and all you say is, 'Okay, got it'?"

"And back on that bridge you told me those things were called 'drafts,' that they were born from the storm and that we shouldn't let them touch us. I think we're a little past the whole, 'this is getting weird, maybe we should just go home' stage, don't you?"

She blinked at him, bemused.

"You said you just knew things. That you saw them in a dream or something. That doesn't sound much different than my puzzle box."

He had a point, she supposed.

He gave her arm a gentle tug and they continued toward the steps. "Maybe it wasn't a dream," he pondered. "Maybe it was somebody talking to you."

Someone talking to her? She recalled that strange, alien landscape beneath that weirdly colorful sky. That unusual body that wasn't her own.

"And maybe," he added, "they're *still* talking to you."

Chapter 45

The shadow-infested stairs seemed to descend for hours, although Andrea was quite sure it was probably more like twenty minutes. But maybe it had been days. What did she know? Gina had warned them over and over again that time was weird in places like these.

Gina... The very thought of her sent a pang of guilt and regret through her heart. She didn't like not knowing if her friends were safe. Were Gina and Nikki still together? Was Keith still with them? And what happened to Everett and Violet?

Dead by now, insisted Not-Stella. *Almost certainly.*

"Shut it," she grumbled. She wasn't going to take *her* word for it.

Besides, Erin assured her they all made it safely through the wall, just as she did. But then again, she didn't know for sure that Erin wouldn't lie to her about something like that. Or something could've happened to them since they arrived. If only she could just call them and make sure they were still safe.

Stupid alien worlds with no cell service...

But then, her phone was dead anyway. And it was soaking wet. Would it even work next time she plugged it in?

You'll be dead soon, too.

"Oh my god, shut up!"

"Quiet..." hissed a ghostly voice from the darkness.

"Hush..." sighed another.

A third cried out in anguish.

A fourth merely wept.

"Lost little girl..." taunted another.

"Swallowed by the darkness..."

She picked up her pace a little, hoping to leave some of these annoying voices behind. Who were these people, anyway? What were they doing here? Why were they being so creepy?

And how were they speaking English, of all things?

"They're not what they seem," whispered Erin.

She stopped walking, confused. Not what they seemed? What did *that* mean?

"No human spirits linger in these passageways. Only the voices of the murk itself."

Lies, purred that awful imitation of Stella.

Andrea felt a strange sensation in the stagnant atmosphere around her, like a candle winking out in the suffocating darkness, and she realized that Erin had been sent away again.

She'll betray you as soon as you let your guard down.

"I'm not listening to *you*," she murmured.

All around her, those ghostly voices mocked her again.

She made a face at them and kept moving. She couldn't decide which was worse, the voices in the murk or the one in her head. Whoever this Stella impersonator was, she was as bad as Ghost Girl.

But she stopped again as the realization finally struck her. *You're her, aren't you?* she thought at it. This so-called primitive entity that both Erin and Ada warned her about. The Priestess of Ruin. It was the same thing that pretended to be a helpful ghost girl and then stranded her on that dead spirit highway!

Should've seen the look on your face, said the voice, perfectly mimicking Stella's laugh.

"Bitch!" she shouted. Then she clasped her hand over her mouth as she realized that she was still alone in this darkness and there could be more of those crawling shadow blobs lurking just out of sight.

"Bitch…" echoed the many voices of the murk.

"Bitch…"

"Bitch…"

"Bitch…"

The biggest *bitch!* exclaimed the unpleasant voice inside her head. These words, in particular, were so familiar. How many times had she heard Stella say that? It was one of her favorite lines. Ironically, she didn't think the real Stella was very bitchy at all. She was just mischievous. Perhaps a little annoying and immature at times. She loved stirring up trouble, which made plenty of people mad. But the two of them had always gotten along fine. There was a good person under there. You didn't need to look hard to see it. So why was this evil thing imitating *her* of all people? What made Stella the perfect voice for all these negative words? She'd had plenty of friends who were gone now, who never talked to her anymore, who she could easily imagine saying such cruel things.

She continued down the stairs, pushing the invasive voice from her mind. Whatever the thing was, it hadn't done her any harm directly. It just kept trying to frighten and demoralize her. Right now, those big shadow blob things were more of a threat. She needed to keep her eyes peeled. The last thing she wanted was to get distracted and walk face-first into one.

Ahead of her, the steps began to widen. She thought for a moment that she'd reached the bottom, but instead, the stairway split into two, each one curving outward.

She paused, uncertain. Was she supposed to know which way to go? She shined her light left, then right, examining each, hoping that one might have less darkness growing in it, but they looked the same. Should she just pick one and hope for the best? It seemed reckless and dumb, but was there any other way to solve a maze besides trial and error?

Somehow, she sensed that it would be more dangerous to stand in one place too long than to just pick a direction and go, so she chose left and started down.

After only four steps, however, something in the darkness below *growled* at her. She cried out, startled, and rushed back up, taking the other stairs instead.

That was one way to decide, she supposed... But she had no idea what she'd do if there was a growling thing in *this* stairway, too.

Ahead of her, the shadows grew thicker. It was impossible to avoid them all, making her tiptoe through the intangible gloom and creep through the dangling streamers of darkness. Those little flying specks were starting to look like clouds. And every one of them was still making her skin crawl.

Down and down she crept, her eyes peeled for any of those freaky reaching clumps of darkness. She had no desire to find out what would happen if one of those hand-like things closed around her ankle. But it was getting harder to see anything. There was less and less gray stone peeking through the unnatural darkness with each step her light revealed.

Had she made a mistake? Was she supposed to brave the growling thing instead?

No... That didn't seem right. If the Keeper was supposed to be able to plan everything down to the most minute detail, then he would've known she wouldn't be brave enough to go that way.

But nothing else made sense, either. Why didn't the little monster just do it all himself if he already knew what was going to happen? This was all so weird.

Lies... whispered Stella's voice inside her head.

She frowned. Lies? As in the Keeper *didn't* have it all planned out?

No. Why would she believe anything *she* said? *She* was a liar, saying all those awful things about her friends being dead...

But was *anyone* telling the truth in all this madness? Was Ada? Erin? Horatio?

The fact was that it didn't matter. She didn't have time to think about any of that right now. Truth or lies, it made no difference. From the moment Hotdog Creep appeared in front of her at Brandy and Albert's reception, she never had a choice in any of this. And she wasn't going to get to go home until she did whatever it was the wrinkly little weirdo wanted her to do. Thinking about who was lying and who wasn't wouldn't change that. All she could do was push forward and hope everything worked out.

There was barely any stone visible at all now. It was hard to see anything. She was feeling her way down each step, struggling just to keep from falling and breaking her neck.

What was she getting into? Her light was almost useless now. It couldn't penetrate the shadows and the shadows covered every surface. All it illuminated was her own body as she crept through the unnatural darkness, making her feel as if *she* were the ghost.

And maybe she was, for all she knew. How many times now could she have died? Between Hotdog trying to strangle her and those terrifying horsemen and Tristesse Lane and...

No. That wasn't helpful. She needed to stay focused on the present, on these steps.

She could see no stone now. The murk had covered every surface. She could see nothing except her own body and even that ended a little above her socks. Everything was inky, all-consuming blackness.

She tried to take another step and stumbled when there wasn't one. She'd reached the bottom. She stretched her arms out and tried to feel the walls, but there weren't any. She was in another chamber of some kind. But everything was utter darkness.

Somewhere above her, she heard another low growl. The sound of it filled her belly with dread. She wanted to run, but didn't dare. There was no going back the way she came, after all. And she had no idea what might be waiting ahead of her, concealed in the intrusive black.

She steeled her nerves, set her jaw, and crept forward, wondering what unpleasant surprises were waiting unseen for her.

Chapter 46

Albert led the way through the flood tunnels beneath the City Beyond Memory. This was almost certainly where they were supposed to be. Gina told them they needed to get to the passages below, but couldn't find a way in. The most logical solution he could think of was that the way down was somewhere she hadn't thought to look, somewhere that might not have seemed like a way down. And while he didn't know how an endless thunderstorm inside a giant sealed container in another world might behave, he knew that all that water had to go *somewhere*. Even if they were dealing with principles of science that didn't exist anymore, there had to be some mechanism keeping the city from flooding.

It was still a risk, of course. There was no guarantee that they wouldn't just end up landing in some vast subterranean lake and drowning. And the current was a lot rougher than he expected it to be. They were lucky one or all of them weren't bludgeoned unconscious by one of the many obstacles they sped past, rather than merely leaving a few painful bruises. But when he saw the sentinel statue holding the overflowing bowl in its freakishly long hands, he knew this had to be the way. Because that's what the sentinels did. They showed him the way.

The proof was in that room where they landed. The platform and walkway surrounding it weren't there for decoration. Their only purpose was to allow someone to climb out of the water and enter the labyrinth.

"It's just like the sewers under Briar Hills," whispered Brandy, her nose crinkled and her expression pinched. "Like we're really making our way back down there again."

The passageway stretched out before them did, indeed, resemble a sewer, but they didn't look like the ones they crawled through that night. There was a rather high ceiling and a raised area on one side for them to walk down. This looked like the kinds of tunnels they always showed on television and in the movies, which were far larger and more elaborate and would have been completely pointless in a city as small as Briar Hills. Most of the tunnels this size were near the beginning of their journey, in the machinery-filled utility and steam tunnels beneath the university. Also, these passageways were considerably *cleaner* than any they found between the university sidewalk and that first, sentinel-occupied chamber of the temple. Every surface here had the same strangely pristine look about it, as if it had just been built yesterday. But of course he knew that wasn't really her point.

Regardless of the purpose of any of the tunnels they explored that night six years ago, that bizarre adventure basically began in the sewers. And like her, he couldn't help but feel as if they were only just now beginning the real journey.

Back in Briar Hills, they were able to see the lights of the city above for a while through the various storm grates. And they could hear traffic droning overhead. Here there were no streetlamps or vehicles, but there was a storm. And now that the sound of the waterfall behind them had faded to a distant roar, he found that they were still near enough to the surface to hear the occasional crack of thunder overhead, although so muted that it was something more felt in the vibrations in the stone beneath their feet than heard with their ears.

The more he thought about it, the more he realized how right she was, how very much this here and now resembled back there and then. Even the tower Gina said was waiting for them at the center of the city was reminiscent of back then. They descended beneath the streets of a city, deep into the earth, only to have to make their way to the top of the burning mountain on the other side.

He said nothing more about it. He simply gripped her hand a little tighter and pushed onward. They'd do whatever they needed to do so they could finish this and go home. And they weren't leaving without Nicole. Or *any* of their friends for that matter.

And yet, even as he steeled his determination, he heard the cat lady's voice far in the back of his mind reminding him that only ten were supposed to return…

No. He couldn't think about something like that.

He reached up and scratched at his chest. While being tossed around in that raging river, he lost the seed's chain. There was no telling where it ended up. Probably at the bottom of that reservoir they landed in. He doubted if it mattered—the seed had vanished the moment they passed through the wall, after all—but he felt a twinge of regret at losing it. He'd considered it something of a keepsake. It was a part of that whole business with the Temple of the Blind, meaning it was a part of his and Brandy's story. But there was no helping it, he supposed.

Ahead of them, an opening appeared in the wall. The first of what would doubtlessly be a great many choices they were going to have to make.

The water continued straight ahead, as did the narrow walkway they were following. This new passage was dry. It was also square, like the one they arrived in, back before they lost Nicole, and like so many of those passages from five years ago.

Gina walked up without hesitation and peered down this new passage. She didn't need to wait for Brandy to light the way. Though dulled, it seemed her senses still stretched farther than the meager reach of an ordinary flashlight.

He didn't ask her which way they should go. She knew better than they did what might be waiting for them in any given direction. And there was no reason to rush her. He stopped and waited for her to finish observing the space.

After a moment, she chose to leave the flood tunnel and he and Brandy followed.

Soon after, the sound of rushing water began to grow louder again. They were approaching more of the ancient city's waterworks. Had they just found a passage connecting two of the channels leading from the reservoir where they entered?

His gaze washed over the stone walls as he walked, recalling those from back then. He'd prepared a little better for that. That big container of sidewalk chalk in his backpack, allowing them to see at a glance if they'd already explored a passage or not. This time, he'd been allowed no such advantage.

He wondered if Gina's psychic awareness also allowed her to know if they'd already been somewhere before. Did it work that way? Or would it all look the same, even to a psychic eye?

Ahead of them, she paused, distracting him from his thoughts. "That's the third time I thought I felt someone moving around somewhere down here." She pointed at the floor several feet in front of her and a little to the right. "That direction, I think. But pretty far away still."

"Nikki?" hoped Brandy.

"I can barely feel them, much less identify them. The storm's still distorting everything. And it might not just be the storm. It might be something about this stone, too. It has properties that I don't understand."

Properties she didn't understand? As in something that once existed but not anymore? He couldn't help being intrigued. The idea was fascinating. What kinds of things could have existed in worlds where science itself was fundamentally different? But he didn't say anything about it. He didn't ask any questions. He didn't want to upset Brandy. And he very much doubted the answers would come any time soon, much less make any difference to whatever it was they were doing here.

Gina pushed onward, her gaze fixed on the darkness up ahead. "If you want to find her, you'd probably do better searching for her yourself. With your ability."

Brandy wrinkled her nose. "Yeah, that's…*tricky*. Mine apparently doesn't work unless I get really *horny*."

"So?"

She looked up at Albert, surprised. "So…it's kind of *awkward?*"

"I don't mind."

"Well *I* do!"

"Oh. Sorry. I didn't realize it was personal."

"I mean, it's *sex*. Why *wouldn't* it be personal?"

He'd already noticed that she didn't show very much emotion, but she looked embarrassed. "I know you said it was sexual," she explained, her voice a little quieter. "But also that it didn't actually require you to have sex."

"It'd still be awkward!"

"Sorry. Forget I said anything."

"It's fine," Albert assured her. "It's no big deal." Then, to Brandy: "She's not wrong. With your connection to *people*, you might be able to find her. And it's not like we actually have to strip down and screw in front of her to make the magic work."

"I know she's not wrong, but I still feel weird about it. And this place doesn't exactly put me in the mood."

She had him there. Cold and wet wasn't exactly ideal romancing mood, much less dark and creepy.

The roar of rushing water was getting louder. They were approaching the source of it.

"I *have* been trying, though," said Brandy. "I keep trying to feel her out there. Andrea, too. But I'm not getting anything. I guess the pervert was right and it only works if I get all hot and bothered." Her expression soured at the mere mention of Shanzer. "Fucking asshole."

Gina stopped. Ahead of her, the floor ended in a sheer drop.

The water they'd been hearing was rushing from an opening above them and plunging into a deep, dark well of a hole. To their right, a set of stone steps led downward, circling both the room and the falling water.

"No railing," observed Brandy. "Typical."

"I don't think safety was their primary concern when building these places," reasoned Albert.

"What gave it away?" she asked. "The hounds? The Caggo? Or the fucking *spike traps*?"

"Exactly."

She tightened her grip on his arm as she looked down into the darkness below. She wasn't just making small talk about there not being a railing, he knew. She'd never been the biggest fan of heights. And this was just the sort of situation that made her nervous.

"It feels like we'll have to go deeper before we can get inside the tower," explained Gina. "And this feels like it'll take us deeper faster than anywhere else nearby."

He nodded. "Good thinking."

"I hope so," she replied. She looked over her shoulder at them. "There's something about this place that I really don't like. It scares me."

Brandy reached out and took her hand. "We're right here with you. Stay close and we'll get through it together." She glanced at Albert. "Right?"

"Absolutely." Although he felt like a liar. They were ambushed by a psychic predator and lost Violet and Corey, then they let their guard down and allowed Nicole to run off into that storm. They weren't very good at holding onto friends. But he really didn't want to lose Gina, too.

She started down the steps, one hand pressed against the wall, taking her time, and he and Brandy followed.

Chapter 47

No... Nicole was clutching at her head, her eyes closed tight, her teeth clenched. That didn't happen. She didn't just watch Keith vanish into that bottomless abyss, leaving her all alone again. She couldn't have seen that because that would be all her fault. He was here to save her, though she couldn't imagine why on earth he'd do such a thing. She'd never given him any reason to put his life on the line for her. Or to do *anything* for her, really...

No... God, please no...

"Little help?" grunted Keith.

She gasped and opened her eyes. He was clinging to the edge, clawing at the smooth stone, struggling for a grip. *"Keith! Oh my god!"* She rushed forward and grabbed his arm, pulling at him, but he immediately let out an agonized cry.

She'd seized his injured arm.

"Sorry!"

"Forget it!" he grunted through clenched teeth. "Just focus on pulling me up!"

She didn't think she'd ever feel so relieved to see him. She was *sure* she saw him vanish over the edge. He must've managed to reach up and grab it the very instant she shut her eyes.

Almost there...

He hooked his leg over and finally managed to pull himself up onto the bridge. Then he rolled onto his back and lay there, clutching at his injured arm and panting.

"That was *too fucking close!*" she gasped.

"*You think?*"

She sat down on her butt and tried to catch her breath. How much more could her poor heart take?

"Thanks," gasped Keith.

She shot him a dirty look. Why was he thanking her? She was entirely useless for a moment there. She froze up. She just sat there, being no help at all. And where did he get off making her have to save his sorry ass, anyway?

But those were only her wild emotions talking. God, why did he get under her skin like that? What was wrong with her?

He didn't seem to notice the look. He was lying with his eyes closed, still clutching at his arm.

"How'd you get that?" she asked. That bandage was still a shirt last time she saw him. He looked like he'd been through some serious shit.

"Same day, different monster," he replied.

"Didn't you have first aid supplies in that bag you were packing around?"

"Lost it dealing with the same monster."

"Gotcha…" But then she frowned as she remembered the last time they were together. "Wait…*where's Andrea?*"

He opened his eyes and stared at her. "She wasn't with you? All three of you disappeared at the same time. I assumed she went wherever you guys went."

"Glum captured me and Gina. Dragged us back to Tristesse Lane."

"That depressing apartment building weirdness Andrea was talking about?"

"Yeah. Fucking sicko crept up on us somehow. Gina didn't see him coming. But we never saw Andrea. Gina said she didn't feel her in there. We thought she was still with you."

"No. I was left out there all alone. And believe me, I started missing Gina *really quick.*"

She knew *that* feeling. Gina's psychic abilities allowed her to steer them away from trouble. Without her, she had no idea how she'd have made it this far. But if Andrea wasn't with him this whole time, then where did she go? A sick knot of worry was tightening in her belly again. She didn't like not knowing where her friends were.

"Where *is* Gina, by the way?"

"I got separated," she confessed. "Because of that thing just now, actually. Last I saw her she was with friends of mine. She should still be with them, safe."

"Right, that reminds me…" He sat up. I ran into some friends of yours too. It was one of them patched me up." He held up the bandaged arm. "Ophelia? No…that's not right…"

"Olivia?"

"Yeah. Her."

"And Wayne?"

"Him too."

She nodded. "Just like Albert said," she recalled. "All six of us are here. All of us who were in the temple that night. All of us to finish what we started."

"Albert," said Keith, nodding. "Corey mentioned that name.

"You guys found Corey?"

"Yeah. He was just waiting at the gate with this Austin guy. Kind of an asshole, that one. Austin, not Corey. Really rude. Corey seemed nice."

She didn't know anyone named Austin. He must have arrived with Olivia and Wayne. "But Violet wasn't with him?"

"Corey mentioned a Violet, but he said they got separated."

She didn't like that. Why was everyone getting separated? But if Corey was able to find his way to one of the gates, then Andrea and Violet could have done the same.

Albert said the Keeper probably meant for this all to happen. He theorized that the little creep had even gone so far as to arrange it so that their entire lives had been orchestrated in order to bring them all to this very time and place. That was why those involved were turning out to be people like her ex-boyfriend and Gina's friends. They were all connected in some way.

But it was so hard to imagine that her entire life might be part of some ugly little goblin's grand scheme to open mankind's way to the next universe…

Kieth rose to his feet, grunting, and then walked back to collect his dropped flashlight. "We should probably keep moving. If this place has any bottom at all, then Big Ugly probably isn't done."

He had a point. She'd already tried dropping him off a roof. It didn't stick. She stood up and shined her cell phone light around.

"Where was that thing taking you, anyway?" he wondered.

"How the fuck should *I* know?"

He pointed past her. "It was dragging you in that direction."

"Last I remember, the freak had me backed against a dead end in the labyrinth." She remembered the awful dream she had, those undulating inkblot shapes in shades of nothing, the deafening din, the agonizing, endless pain. It felt like *hell*. But that was all in her mind. Her body was here, being dragged across the ground like a bag of garbage, stretching her shirt out.

But Keith had a point. Goar Nangup had every opportunity to kill her. Instead, he sent her into that nightmare and then dragged her unconscious body here. So where was his undead lapdog taking her? What was it going to do with her? She steeled her nerves and stalked past him. "If that thing was taking me *that* way, then I'm going *this* way. Because *fuck him.*"

She left the abyss behind and set off back down the dark passageway.

"What's the deal with that thing?" asked Keith as he followed behind her. "It didn't look like any of the other zombies out here."

"It used to be Hotdog Creep."

"Seriously? The guy who tried to murder Andrea?"

"The same. I knocked him off a building back in Cedric's Cove. He's dead."

"He looked it."

"That's not Hotdog Creep anymore. It's just a meat puppet now. With some old-as-fuck god pulling his strings."

"Wow… Just when I thought I'd reached my limit of things I shouldn't be able to believe…"

"Tell me about it."

Chapter 48

Wayne couldn't run very fast *and* protect Olivia from the razor-winged abominations that were swarming the dark passage behind them. All he could do was stay behind her and try his best to shield her with the bulk of his body. But he wasn't sure how long he was going to last with the freaky things slashing at his back.

Who the hell let the scarecrow man get his morbid hands on a fucking *hound corpse* of all things? How was *that* fair? Wasn't there supposed to be rules? Wasn't that what everyone kept telling them? Sandy. Nadia. Maeve. They were all only allowed to help so much because of the Keeper's rules? So where, exactly, was it stated in the *Keeper's rules* that the *fucking telekinetic death-obsessed lunatic* could have a fucking *hound corpse*? That was what he wanted to know. He thought the *bear* was going too far! But now all he could think about was how Zombie Yogi fucking *exploded* and unraveled itself into a giant pile of *minced-bear spaghetti* and reeled him in like a prize marlin. Those claws and teeth that dug into his flesh were nothing compared to a whole pelt of *hound scales*! It was going to be like getting lassoed with razor wire and dragged through a pile of freshly sharpened knives.

He needed to get himself and Olivia as far as possible from this monster and well out of reach of *that* horrific scenario. And given that things didn't seem like they could get much worse, he didn't bother pausing to let her psychic thread thing do its work. He simply picked a path and urged her forward.

He could feel those freaky hound-bug things slashing at the back of his shirt and pants. His backside was burning. At this rate, he'd be skinned alive. But every one of those things that was tearing away at him was one more that wasn't doing the same to his fiancée, and that was all he really wanted. If only he were big enough to shield her completely. Unfortunately, they kept zipping past his head and legs and darting at her, wrenching terrified, painful screams from her that felt like someone ripping out his heart.

Why was this happening? Why couldn't he protect her? Every second of this was pure torture!

He didn't understand how the scarecrow man could even be here.

How did he get through the gate? Did he sneak in when they used the key? Was he simply lurking somewhere nearby this whole time, just waiting for something he could use as a corpse puppet?

Olivia turned at the next intersection and plunged down a sloping passageway, still screaming. The hound bugs kept pace with them, kept slashing at them as they ran.

They were too fast. They weren't going to be able to get away.

Ahead of them, the passage opened up. He knew immediately that they'd circled back around to the bottomless chamber with all its narrow walkways.

There was no way around it. He needed to get Olivia out of here and the only answer he could think of was to drag her through the worst kind of hell he could imagine.

"Just go for it!" he urged, raising his voice to be heard over the shuffling-droning racket of the razored swarm behind them. "It's plenty wide enough! Just keep going and don't even think about it!"

He didn't think she would. He thought she'd freeze on the platform. He thought they'd be swarmed for sure. But she didn't hesitate. With a terrified squeal, she set off along the middle walkway with him right on her heels.

They might just make it across, he realized. And then if they just ran fast enough and far enough, maybe they could lose the freak and his gore circus.

Except now that they were crossing the room, the swarm was free to spread out around them. Those razor blade scales were darting every which way, swooping in from both sides and above and below. He could feel the sting of their sharp wings all over his body.

In front of him, Olivia's upraised arms were bleeding. And he could see the many cuts in her shirt and pants. The sight made his heart ache. And it pissed him off. That was his fiancée the freak was hurting!

Goddammit! He felt so useless right now. What could he even do? He didn't know how to make it better! He couldn't turn around and fight these things. There were too many of them. And every last one of them was armed!

Seriously, how was this not against the fucking rules?

He'd never met the Keeper, but if he ever did, he was going to kick his freaky little ass.

One of the hound bugs swept down and slammed itself against Olivia's chest. She let out a shrill scream and turned, trying to knock it aside. But it was slashing at her instead of flying away. She grabbed her shirt, yanking it, trying to flick the little abomination away. It seemed to be caught in the loose fabric just below her bust, tangled up as if it meant to bore into her chest and pierce her heart.

She was teetering. She was going to fall. He grabbed her arm and then snatched the thing off her with his hand. He could feel it biting into the flesh of his palm and fingers, but he didn't care. He squeezed as hard as he could, crushing the foul little thing, then flung it aside, only to watch it flutter away, unharmed.

Was it even possible to kill them? They were just two scales connected by a little strand of twitching meat.

Olivia was clinging to him now. She'd managed to push through the fear thus far, but with her balance thrown off, she was sliding quickly toward full panic.

"We're past the halfway point!" he told her. "Almost there!"

But she was shaking her head. Slowly, she was folding herself up, crawling down his legs, her knees too weak to continue holding her weight.

The hound bugs zipped past her, slashing at her exposed arms, tearing at her shirt and pants. He was trying to bat them away, but there were too many of them. There were more and more with each passing second, far more than he could keep up with. And each one he managed to hit simply circled back because there was nothing about them that he could kill.

He turned and looked back the way they came.

The scarecrow man was there, a foul perversion of an already unthinkable monster, just standing and watching, enjoying this moment of terror.

Bastard.

One of the hound bugs attacked his hand, chopping with those fluttering razorblade wings at the back of his knuckles, and he jerked away from it. The motion caused him to lose the grip on his flashlight. It fell.

He bent over his screaming fiancée and watched it drop into the black abyss below them as the nightmare swarm descended over him.

All the way down…

"Aw fuck…" he grunted. This was going to seriously suck.

Chapter 49

Corey stood at yet another crossway in the endlessly jumbled stone walls, pondering his choices. This didn't seem like one of those places where something was hidden. But the energy was flowing in more than one direction, presenting him with a conundrum.

Which flow should he follow? Was there a difference? No individual stream seemed stronger or weaker than the others. But he doubted that they all went to the same place.

The longer he was in here, the more important it felt to stay on the right path. He had a job to do. A *crucial* one. And if he made a mistake, he might not be able to finish that job. He didn't have the luxury of trial and error. This labyrinth was enormous. He could walk around for months and never find his way back to where he started. He had to figure it out as he went. He had to get it right the first time.

He should probably be frightened. He felt confident that screwing up here could have severe consequences. At the very least, he might not make it home. More likely, Violet and all the others might never make it home, either. And that was something he couldn't let happen, no matter what it took. But he found that he *wasn't* really scared. Instead, this was strangely *fun*. *Exhilarating*, even. It was what he and Violet had been searching for, after all. The truth about life beyond the borders of their own world.

It was sort of like a video game. Solving mazes and puzzles and riddles, avoiding traps, unraveling an ancient mystery. Who wouldn't find that at least a *little* exciting? He was like Bilbo Baggins, off on the adventure of a lifetime.

He smiled a little as he remembered growing up with Violet. Their fathers were best friends and business partners who built one of the biggest tech companies in the Midwest. They used to go on little adventures all the time, exploring their thousands of sprawling acres of land. They might have been spoiled rich kids, but they were always adventurers at heart. They used to talk about traveling the globe and seeking out all the world's mysteries. But it turned out that the biggest mystery of all would drop right out of the sky one sunny spring day.

Jeremy Gleer. The Tunipet Boom.

Before they knew it, *the world* didn't seem so interesting anymore. They wanted to explore what was *beyond* it.

He wasn't really sure if he believed in God or not. He was still sorting that sort of stuff out. But he definitely wasn't ready to discount the possibility. And the fact was that he firmly believed Jeremy fell into their lives for a reason that day. Not just a sign, but an entire *road* spread out before them, inviting them along on this incredible ride.

Maybe God sent Jeremy to them specifically so he could be right here, right now, doing this very job. Or maybe it was the sentinels who did it. Or maybe God was the *reason* the sentinels did it. But the fact was that it happened and it led him to this moment and this place.

It was inevitable.

And as long as he believed that, then he could believe he was going to figure this out.

He aimed his light down one path, then the next. Then the next. They all looked the same. They all felt the same. They were all dark and silent and spooky.

It was hard to see. He almost missed it. A strange, barely perceptible shimmer that was less seen than…well he wasn't really sure *how* he detected it.

That energy he felt—or whatever it was, since he couldn't say for sure that it was *energy*, per se, but wasn't entirely sure how else to describe it—was branching away from three of the four paths laid out before him, breaking apart, feeding into other lines.

Of course, just knowing this didn't do him any good. Was that a good thing or a bad thing? And yet somehow he simply understood that he needed to take the one path in which the energy remained together.

He continued forward without hesitation, wondering if maybe those others might have been traps. He sort of doubted it, though… That didn't quite feel right. But they were definitely the *wrong* path to follow, wherever they went. Certainly wrong for *him*.

This was kind of fun. He was enjoying himself.

He hoped Violet was having as much fun wherever *she* was.

Chapter 50

"This is *not* fun," grumbled Violet.

How long had they been climbing these stairs? Everett had kept himself in pretty good shape. He was always moving. Some days he walked miles in his incessant search for the universe's truths. But this was a lot. He was out of breath. His calves were burning. He was starting to feel an ache in his gut. It felt like they'd climbed thirty stories! Although it was probably more like ten or twelve, realistically. It didn't help that these steps were steeper than average, requiring more effort than strictly necessary.

He shined his light up ahead, but the scene there hadn't changed. An endless stairway of stone emerging from the ever-present darkness, up and up and up, like some kind of storybook curse. He could almost imagine that they weren't really going anywhere, that they were just spinning their wheels, trapped in an endless loop of torturous stairs with no escape.

"That's it!" Violet huffed, her mind made up. She stopped climbing and seated herself defiantly on one of the steps. "I'm taking a break!"

"Sounds good to me," he panted. She was in better shape than he was. He was ready for a break a while ago, but he'd suffered onward, not wanting to be the one to hold someone else back. (And of course because he didn't want to look like a wimp.)

He sank to his knees on the next step and leaned forward, trying to catch his breath—without *looking* like he was trying to catch his breath, if possible—and willing that ache in his stomach to ease.

On the more positive side, at least he'd warmed up a little. The extra exertion of this monstrous stairway had offset most of the discomfort from his wet clothes. He might even have been sweating a little.

"What made you decide to start looking for weird shit in the first place?" asked Violet.

He looked up at her, surprised. Those piercing green eyes were fixed on him. He could hear that she was still breathing hard and could see the exaggerated rise and fall of her chest, but there was no sign of that breathless weariness in her pretty face. She seemed to be entirely focused on him.

"You said you were looking for proof that there was more to the world, or whatever," she recalled. "Was it just that you were into paranormal shit or…?" She gestured with her hand, inviting him to fill in the blanks.

He turned around and sat down. He was a few steps lower than she was, looking up at her. He found himself looking at her black boots. They were some style of army boot, he was pretty sure (though he was hardly a shoe expert) and were kind of clunky, yet somehow they still managed to look perfectly feminine on her. It reminded him of Andrea with all her piercings that was a striking contradiction to her girlish face and sweet personality. "It's kind of a long story," he said. "I didn't know anyone here until yesterday." Then he frowned. "Or however long it's been, I guess…"

Violet gave a huff of a laugh. "No shit. I think we're *all* on different times by now."

"For me, it started when I died and saw an angel."

This made her eyebrows raise. "You mean, like, one of those near-death experience kind of things?"

He nodded. "I nearly drowned."

"Wow."

"I had kind of a…unusual childhood. My mom was mentally ill. She told me a lot of lies about the world. Discouraged me from believing in anything. There was no such things as magic or fantasy, not even a Santa Clause."

"Wow. That's a shitty deal."

"I know. She even convinced me that heaven wasn't real."

"Wow." She sat up, looking uncomfortable. "That's awful."

"Yeah. But seeing that angel was proof that she'd been lying. It changed everything. I was an entirely different person practically overnight."

"So…you're looking for this angel?"

"Sort of, I guess. I mean, I don't know if I could actually find *her* again…but I knew that if she was real, then there's *way* more to the world than my mom wanted me to believe. Maybe more than anyone knows. So I've been looking for proof of *that*. An afterlife, I guess, sure, but even *more* than that. Because if she was lying about what happened after we died, then maybe she was lying about what could be real right here in our lives, you know?"

Violet smiled. "Yeah. I'd say I understand that."

"I started by exploring a bunch of famous haunted places, but they didn't do anything for me. I found out that I already believed in ghosts and souls and an afterlife. Some disembodied footsteps and a few shadows moving around on their own didn't impress me. I was convinced there was even more out there." He grinned at her. "And boy was I right."

She chuckled. "Like drafts and potato men."

"Yep."

They sat there a moment in silence, letting their breathing slowly return to normal, resting their weary legs, their heads swirling with thoughts.

Again, he found himself wondering if all the things he'd seen, all the things he'd done on this journey, everything that he'd suffered through in his life to get here, could all really be thanks to some mysterious being known only as the Keeper.

He thought about Wayne, so big and strong and courageous and…well, *grumpy*. But he could hardly blame him. He couldn't wrap his head around the lifestyle of a kid not much out of high school wandering around dangerous forests all alone and acting like every scary thing he heard was an opportunity for a new adventure.

He thought about Olivia, so kind and sweet and pretty. She kept defending him, telling Wayne to be nice to him. But she couldn't have thought he was normal by any stretch of the imagination. There were frightful things in her past that still haunted her, things revolving around that temple Wayne told him about. And a marvelously terrifying place called Gilbert House. She could easily have taken Wayne's side, but she didn't. She was nothing but nice to him, even when he was being insensitive on the train.

He thought of Andrea. She was kind like Olivia, but also cautious, like Wayne. She didn't trust him immediately, and he could hardly blame her. They were both lost in that darkness, at the mercy of who-knew-what. And when she found him, he'd been stuffed into some kind of metal canister with no lid. How did one even go about explaining something like that? He was lucky she didn't just assume he was some kind of trick and leave him there.

And of course there was Violet sitting here with him now. Kind. Smart. Courageous and strong.

These people were all strangers, and yet there was something about each and every one of them that felt like so much more than that. It truly didn't feel as if they'd come together by chance. It felt like he was always meant to be a part of this.

As cliché as it sounded, it felt as if he'd found his people.

Or maybe that would be too presumptuous. He was still just a kid compared to most of them. He wasn't even old enough to drink yet.

"An angel…" pondered Violet.

He glanced up at her, distracted.

"I've seen enough proof to know that there's an afterlife. But angels and demons? I don't come from a very religious background but I think I've always believed in some kind of God. That said, though, I can't say I've ever been all that sure of concepts like heaven and hell. I'm not sure it's ever crossed my mind to run across something like an angel." She stared down into the darkness below them as she contemplated the possibility. "I wonder how finding something like that could change a person."

Change? He sat watching her as she thought about it. *He'd* definitely changed. He turned from a meek and frightened child into what he was now. Adventurous. Unafraid to take risks. Curious about the shadows that used to petrify him in the dark hours of the night. He even told Wayne that he wasn't afraid of dying anymore. It was his answer to why he took so many risks. And it was the truth. If anything, he found the idea of seeing what waited on the other side *intriguing*. A whole new adventure, just waiting for him.

Something strange broke through the silence that had settled over them, scattering his thoughts. It was like a long and mournful sigh that seemed to resonate from the very stone around them.

Violet shot to her feet, startled, as Everett shined his light back and forth, up and down. He couldn't discern which direction it was coming from. Something following them? Or something blocking the way forward? It was impossible to tell.

"What was that?" she whispered when it had faded back into the silence.

But he didn't know, of course. He'd never heard anything quite like it before. It sounded like something *alive*, but what could live in a place like this?

"We should keep moving," decided Violet, already continuing upward. "We don't know how long we're going to be stuck down here."

He nodded and followed her lead. Yes. They should definitely keep moving. Even if there weren't ominous sighs emanating from the walls, moving was better than sitting around thinking. They'd never get anywhere just thinking about it.

The two of them continued upward and onward toward a future

as dark and unknown as the labyrinth lying beyond the reach of their flashlights.

"What about you?" asked Everett. "How'd you end up doing this sort of stuff?"

"Just a hobby," she replied.

Chapter 51

Andrea couldn't imagine a more unsettling feeling than this.

The darkness was growing deeper. It was up past her knees now. It was like wading through a dense and utterly black fog. Except fog would at least feel *damp*. This strange, unnerving darkness felt like *nothing*. She could see her thighs, her shorts, her tee shirt, her flashlight and the arm that was reaching out with it. But it was as if nothing else existed in this place. It was strangely disorienting. Surreal. She felt *lost* in it. The longer she was here, the more it felt like it went on forever, like she'd never find her way out again.

Worse still, she could no longer see those creepy, groping hand things. With every step she took, she kept expecting something to grab her leg. She wouldn't be able to see it coming. And as frightened as she already was, she wasn't so sure the shock of something like that wouldn't be enough to scare her to death.

What was the point in being able to see something other people couldn't if what you could see *blinded* you? What kind of tradeoff was that? Did that mean that anyone else who came here with her would be able to see perfectly fine with just a flashlight? What kind of sense did that make?

At least whatever it was that growled at her when she first entered this chamber hadn't made another sound, threatening or otherwise. Either she'd moved past it or it had retreated from her path. Or it was simply biding its time, she supposed, watching her from the oppressive gloom, waiting for a chance to pounce.

She still didn't understand what this stuff was. Erin had said that it was something "fundamentally connected to the Murk," whatever that meant. And that it wasn't what it appeared to be because the limited capabilities of her living brain couldn't comprehend the reality of it. The deeper this darkness became, the more she found herself understanding what she meant by that. Only being able to perceive things from that other world with her living senses must be sort of like someone born blind trying to imagine a specific color. Or like a mermaid trying to grasp the concept of fire.

Horatio was the first to call it "Murk." The spirit world. The afterlife. It was kind of ironic, she realized. There were people out there who were obsessed with searching for the answer to the question of what happened after death, and here she was, literally *wading through it.*

And she'd bet money that not one of them would believe a word of it if she tried to tell them.

She reached up and raked her fingers through several wispy tendrils dangling down from the ceiling. They passed right through her, completely undisturbed, as if they weren't really there.

Or as if *she* weren't really there...

There was something extra disturbing about *that* particular line of thought, so she chose to push it right back out of her head and focused instead on the murk. What *was* this stuff? Why did it look like inky black fog? What was it that her living brain couldn't comprehend about it?

Was it *ectoplasm*? Was that a real thing too? Some kind of ghostly residue, like those old spiritualists used to believe in way back in the days before there was the internet and Netflix to help people kill time? Back when seances and spirit boards were all the rage?

Movement caught her eye in the shadows somewhere to her right and she froze, her flashlight pointed uselessly in that direction. It was subtle, but she was sure she didn't imagine it. Something in that all-consuming gloom just shifted. Or...maybe it was more of a twitch...or a bubbling? Or maybe a churning sort of motion...? But it was definitely *something.* Was it the growling thing from before? Or was it another squelching thing? Or were the growly thing and the squelchy thing the *same* thing?

God, she wished she could see!

What was this place, anyway? Was she even getting anywhere? Or was she merely wandering in circles?

She stood there a moment, listening, her heart pounding, waiting for some inevitable fright. But it didn't come. Slowly, her light still aimed toward the sound that startled her, she continued creeping forward.

They're gonna get you, whispered Not-Stella.

She ignored the obnoxious voice.

Nothing jumped out at her from the right, so she turned her light forward again, her eyes still peeled. She hated this. How long was this room? When was she going to reach the end of this darkness?

She took a few more steps, then stopped. There was something there, she realized. Right in front of her. A column of darkness, barely visible against the surrounding black.

She stood there a moment, staring at it, watching for the slightest movement, but it didn't seem to be one of those concentrated blobs of darkness. It seemed to be something enveloped in the murk, like the floor and the walls. Some kind of support beam for the chamber? She took a cautious step toward it, her body tense, ready to flee at the slightest sign of danger.

Was this something important? Something she should investigate?

Curious, she reached out and slowly pushed the end of her flashlight into the darkness. It was immediately and completely swallowed...and yet she found that she could still see her arm. When she withdrew it, the light came back, but the brightness around her didn't change.

How did that work, exactly?

She passed the flashlight into the darkness again, watched the beam vanish into the murk without taking its light with it.

Weird...

But thinking back, she recalled noticing how those dangling black tendrils never cast shadows as she passed through them. The murk didn't seem to interact with the light at all...almost as if the two existed in entirely different places...

Did the murk only affect what she could see?

Erin said she wasn't capable of fully understanding the murk as long as she was still alive. This was probably one of those things. It was weird. Kind of trippy, even. But she wasn't going to get anywhere standing around wondering about it.

What she needed to focus on was the thing in front of her. What was it? Was it important? Was it dangerous?

She hesitated, still uncertain, then slowly reached in with her left hand.

For a moment, there didn't seem to be anything. But then she reminded herself that the darkness on the floor was more than knee deep. This was probably the same. Biting her lip in anticipation of something unpleasant, she reached in farther, past her elbow, until her fingers brushed against something cold and hard.

Stone.

But not a column, like the ones back in the hole room. This felt like...a pipe? She closed her hand around it, then slid downward, tracing the shape of it. Some kind of pole? It had an unusual texture, not entirely smooth, but not rough. She found the bottom of it and felt creases and a rougher, rounded tip.

Not a pipe, then. A lever of some sort? But it didn't move when she pulled or pushed on it.

She let go of it and moved her hand over. More stone. Wider, this time. Smooth and curved. She ran her hand upward, feeling ever higher, following the curious shapes. She felt a series of shallow creases. A pattern. Sort of like...

Then it dawned on her. This was a statue. Those were muscles. She reached up higher and felt the familiar curves of a human torso. A rib. A chest. A nipple. All of it stretched out of proportion, far too tall to be human, befuddling her mind as she groped blindly at it.

A sentinel.

She reached down and grasped the pipe thing again. What the heck was this thing, then? Was he holding some kind of staff?

Then she remembered the vulgar monstrosities that dangled between their legs.

"*Ew!*" she cried in revulsion, snatching her hand back.

Why were they like that? *Why was it at that height?*

Around her, the ghostly voices of the murk mocked her.

"Ew..."

"Yuck..."

"Gross..."

"Yucky..."

"Disgusting..."

And was that the sound of Stella laughing somewhere in the back of her mind, or only her imagination? The real Stella would've laughed her butt off, she knew. And she wouldn't be satisfied with just laughing. She'd tease her about it *forever.* She could almost hear her. ("I didn't even know you could put a smile on a sentinel's face!") Seriously, she'd never hear the end of it. But this wasn't Stella. This was some kind of ancient and powerful...*something*...using her voice to get inside her head. Did this thing even have a sense of humor? Did it really even know what laughter was? Or was it only imitating Stella from her memories?

Either way, it wasn't very nice.

She wiped her hand on her shorts as if she'd just touched actual flesh instead of cold, lifeless stone. "Gross," she grumbled. Now she was mad. Why was there a sentinel here anyway? What purpose could it serve somewhere it couldn't even be seen? "Stupid thing!"

"Stupid..." mocked the voices of the murk.

"Idiot!"

"Useless..."

"So stupid..."

Andrea clenched her jaw, frustrated. "Shut up already!"

"Quiet..."

"Shh!"

"Be quiet..."

"Silence!"

"Hush..."

She closed her eyes for a moment as the voices faded away again. She took a calming breath. She needed to relax. Her emotions were all over the place. The darkness was getting to her.

You're just not cut out for this sort of thing, sighed the false Stella.

Andrea ignored her. She still didn't understand what this thing wanted with her, of all people, but she was starting to understand that acknowledging the awful things she said wasn't going to get her out of this mess any sooner. She opened her eyes and took a step forward.

Somewhere in the darkness behind her, something let out a deafening shriek. She screamed and twirled around, her free hand clasped over her mouth. She let the stupid, obscene sentinel and the obnoxious fake Stella distract her. She forgot where she was. She forgot about the things lurking in this darkness.

She stood motionless, holding her breath, listening through the booming of her heartbeat in her ears.

Something was back there. Something that scratched and squelched. Was it on the ceiling? Had she passed directly under it on her way in?

Was there more than one of them?

Unwilling to stay and find out, she turned and crept past the murk-enveloped sentinel and away from whatever was moving behind her.

Why did she let the stupid sentinel get to her like that? That was so dumb!

She pushed deeper and deeper into the oppressive darkness, struggling to remain as quiet as possible, desperate to put as much space between her and the scratchy-squelchy thing as possible.

Then something cold and vile closed around her ankle in the darkness.

She wasn't strong enough to stop herself from screaming.

Chapter 52

Gina was relieved to finally be approaching the bottom of these spiraling steps. It was a much deeper descent than she first realized. The water pouring down from above had broken from a steady stream to a cold mist and finally to a heavy rain that once again drenched their clothes and left every surface wet and slick. For a long time, she expected her feet to slip out from under her and either send her tumbling down the stairs to break her neck or over the perilous edge to plummet into the black unknown below. But somehow, they'd made it past the worst of it without heinous injury.

And yet it was a shallow relief. Because the deeper she descended into these dark depths, the more uncertain she felt. There was something here. Something vaguely familiar, but too elusive to fully grasp. She kept finding herself thinking of Glum and that nightmare cobblestone street for some reason.

"I'm *so* ready to be done with this shit," shouted Brandy, her voice barely carrying over the rising roar of rushing water.

Gina certainly didn't blame her. Her legs were aching from all those steps. She'd been wet and shivering since Nicole disappeared into the storm, almost since they arrived here. And all this noise was starting to make her weary head hurt. They were descending into another reservoir chamber, not unlike the last one, complete with a walkway circling most of it. But in addition to what was pouring down from above them, there were two other openings allowing water to gush into the room, one that they passed over a short while ago and which was now above and across from them, and another one much closer to the surface of the pool just below them. It was getting more and more difficult to communicate, especially with the stone walls echoing and amplifying every sound.

When she finally reached the bottom, there were only two channels leading out of the room, compared to the six in the first one. Both pointed in opposite directions. The nearer one would take them toward that significant-feeling tower structure at the heart of the city, but that didn't mean very much in a maze. She tried to focus on those specific paths and where they went, how many other passages diverged from each, whether there was anything they should avoid, but it was difficult to concentrate. It was all so confusing, even without the storm clouding her psychic senses and the roaring water hammering at her ears. Again, she felt as if the very *walls* were somehow fighting her, preventing her from using her abilities to their fullest potential.

In either case, it didn't appear that there was any immediate danger, so she chose the nearer one simply to escape this noise faster.

Neither Albert nor Brandy questioned her choices. They followed close on her heels as if they really believed that she knew what she was doing, which made her feel guilty, since she was very much winging it. It was all she could do to simply keep steering them away from trouble.

As the noise faded to a much more tolerable rumble, she again turned her inner eye to the space around her, searching for anything that might have that same *significant* feeling as that tower and therefore might help them reach it faster. But still she couldn't quite comprehend what she felt.

It was strange. There were, indeed, more passageways on the other sides of these walls, as well as above and below them. But there were also gaps that she couldn't quite understand. They weren't simply areas of solid stone, but they also weren't exactly empty spaces, either. Were there areas down here that were hidden to her? She didn't understand how something like that would even work.

She stopped walking and placed her hand on the smooth stone of the tunnel's left wall. "There's something moving over there," she reported. "But I can't tell what it is."

"Hound?" worried Brandy.

"I don't know what that is," she informed her.

"There aren't any scratches on the floor," observed Albert. "I've been keeping an eye out for that."

"Those nasty hairy octopus things, then," she said with a look of such disgust that it caught Gina off guard.

"Oh yeah," said Albert. "I forgot about those things." He looked back the way they came. "They liked water."

"I don't know what it is," Gina said again. "But I don't think it's somewhere this passage is connected to. Not nearby, anyway. I just wanted you to know that it was there. Because if there's one, there's probably more."

"Gotcha," said Albert.

Brandy was still wrinkling her nose at the memory of the hairy octopus. (Whatever that was.) "It *still* makes me queasy just thinking about those fucking things."

"I know," said Albert.

Gina pushed onward. Hounds. Hairy octopi. And Andrea mentioned something called a Caggo… She wasn't looking forward to meeting *any* of these things. And she was quite sure she wasn't going to be lucky enough to avoid everything.

She'd never been very lucky.

And then there was that *other* feeling, the one that kept making her think of Tristesse Lane. It seemed to grow stronger the deeper they went, but she couldn't quite pinpoint it. It was strangely distorted. And it seemed to be coming from multiple directions. It was less a single origin than a sort of spattering, as if whatever it was had been scattered throughout these strange corridors. Yet she was confident that there was only one.

Behind her, Brandy stopped and shined her light back the way they came.

"You okay?" worried Albert.

She nodded. "That was weird. I thought someone was behind us for a second there."

"There's someone in a passage below us," said Gina. "I felt them too."

She looked forward, her expression hopeful. "Nikki?" But then she frowned. "No… I guess not. You'd have probably said something."

"I would've," she promised. If she knew Nicole was still alive after the weird way she vanished, there was no way she'd keep it to herself. She'd want them to know. She'd want to relieve them of that worry. And she hoped that someone would do the same for her. "But I couldn't tell who it was. They just sort of flickered in and out of my head for a few seconds. It's kind of hard to explain."

Brandy looked back for a moment, thoughtful.

Gina didn't try to convince her to try using her own psychic ability to search for Nicole. She supposed if hers worked the way theirs did, she wouldn't want to use them in front of anyone, either. But then again, she was humiliated so many times growing up, maybe it wouldn't even matter that much to her.

But as she stood there, giving Brandy the moment she seemed to need, something new blossomed into her awareness.

She turned and stared through the wall beside her, confused.

Something was there. Something deeply unsettling. It wasn't quite like anything else she'd ever felt before. It had an entirely different kind of feeling about it.

And it felt as if it were as aware of her as she was of it, like it was staring right back at her from the other side of the wall. Something dreadful and unnatural. Something that filled her with an intense fear. Something she didn't want seeing her…

"Gina?" asked Albert.

She blinked and looked back at him. She felt dazed and distracted.

"You okay?" He and Brandy were both staring at her. They must have seen something troubling in her expression. And it was no wonder. Her heart was pounding. Her hands were clenched at her sides. She didn't try to speak. Her mouth had suddenly gone dry. She nodded instead.

When she looked at the wall again, the feeling was gone. There was nothing there. Could it have merely been her imagination? Just once, that would be nice…

"You sure?" worried Brandy.

"I'm fine. Just trying to understand this place." She turned and continued onward. "There's an intersection up ahead," she reported in her usual sleepy voice. "I don't think it matters which way we go."

Chapter 53

Keith took the lead with his flashlight so Nicole could save her cell phone battery. But he had no idea where he was going. It was, after all, a labyrinth. "I bet this place is a piece of cake for Gina," he reasoned. "She might already be waiting for us at the end of this thing."

"I wouldn't doubt it," grumbled Nicole. "And here I am stuck with *you*."

"Ditto, Princess."

"Fuck off."

He missed Gina's psychic abilities. It made life a lot easier. His arm was proof enough of that. She was able to steer them clear of trouble the whole time they were together, yet he ran afoul of that monster within minutes of being separated from her.

But it was far more than just about what she could do. She was a sweet girl. Polite and kind. She and Andrea both. He'd happily be stranded out here with either of them. Or back there with Olivia and Wayne. They were nice, too. Why did it have to be his bitchy ex he kept ending up with? He'd rather be stuck traveling with that Austin asshole than with her.

But here he was.

He tried to focus on the passages in front of him. Andrea talked to him for a while about the first time they did this, about the place they called the Temple of the Blind. She described tunnels exactly like these. Miles and miles of them, supposedly, filled with all sorts of scary things. But if it was really as big as she said it was, how would it even be possible to navigate it? They could walk themselves to death and never find a way out. It was too complex. Too deep. Too much ground to cover. This was exactly what made spelunking such a dangerous hobby.

Ahead of them, another path merged with this one. He shined his light down it but saw nothing. It was just another dark passageway leading God-only-knew-where, like thousands of others all around them, he was sure. He started to ask Nicole's opinion but decided against it. He didn't really want to talk to her. It wasn't as if *she* knew the way, either. She'd probably just swear at him.

Foul-mouthed pain in his ass…

He chose to continue straight ahead without a word.

The empty passageway stretched on for several minutes, ever deeper into the unending darkness. Then another intersection appeared up ahead. Another passage crossed this one, presenting him three options. Left, right or straight. His first instinct was to ask if his companion had any opinion on which way to go. It was only right, given that he had no clue. Even a random gut feeling might be worth checking out. But again, he decided it was better to choose at random than to try starting up a conversation with someone who was only going to respond with something nasty.

He went straight through the intersection. It seemed the least likely to curve back around and return them to that bottomless chasm anytime soon.

If Nicole had any objections, she didn't voice them. She followed a few paces behind him, silent. She'd obviously been through some crap. Her clothes were wet. Her hair was a mess. She had a number of scratches and bruises. That hulking dead brute had stretched her tank top out so much that one of the straps wouldn't stay up and was hanging off her arm, exposing the left cup of her dirty bra. But he didn't dare ask her about any of it.

He hated this. Why couldn't she just be civil. He had no delusions of getting back together with her. She'd made it perfectly clear that their entire relationship was a terrible mistake. But they were stuck down here together, whether they liked it or not. (And he didn't.) So why did she have to keep acting like this?

Yet another intersection appeared ahead of him. Only left or right this time. He chose left entirely at random and kept walking. He didn't even want to pause to consider the options, giving her so much as a second to spit some snarky comment at him.

Nicole stopped and looked back the other way.

He paused, distracted. He went as far as to open his mouth to ask what was wrong, but he managed to snap it shut again. He simply shined his light back where she was looking and watched for a moment.

But she turned and continued forward without a word, so he did the same, pushing on ahead of her.

God, but it was hard to imagine that this was the same woman he dated a year ago. That Nicole was nothing like this one. She was sweet and passionate and playful in all the right ways. He really thought he'd found someone special. No matter how he tried, he couldn't understand how it all went so wrong. It was like she just simply flipped a switch and started despising him.

The path split again. Left or right, like before. Not wanting to end up going in a circle, he chose right this time.

That other her really was amazing, though... So sexy and sensual. He'd be lying if he said he didn't miss *that* Nicole. It never failed to make him sad when he thought about it. He just couldn't make himself believe that he'd ever be with anyone like her again.

She was literally too good to be true, he supposed.

Ahead of him, the walls and ceiling ended. The passage opened up onto a chamber of some sort. Maybe he'd get lucky and it would be wherever it was they were trying to go.

Whatever the space was, the floor was different. It looked like the stone gave way to bare earth. Was it some kind of natural cavern? Or could they have actually found their way outside?

Before he could step out of the passage, however, Nicole made an audible gasp and grabbed him by the waistband of his jeans. "Stop!"

He frowned back at her, confused. "What?"

"That's the meadow!" she breathed.

"The what?"

"The Keeper said we can't go in there." She was whispering, as if something might hear her. It was strangely unsettling. "It's a bad place."

"You've talked with the Keeper?"

"Last time we were here."

"You've been here before?" What the hell was she talking about?

"No. In the first temple. But there's one here, too."

He shined his light into the space ahead of them. Why would anyone call it a meadow? Weren't meadows supposed to be grassy? Grass wouldn't grow underground with no light. And what made it such a bad place? He didn't understand any of this.

"We have to go!" she hissed, pulling him backward by his waistband.

"Okay!" he grunted. "Fine. Just let go."

"Move your ass!"

He pushed past her and made his way back to the previous intersection. They'd try the other way, then. Hopefully it didn't take them somewhere else she'd freak out about.

"It's a bad place," she said again. "It gets in your head. It tried to lure Albert in. It was scary." And she really did look scared. Gone was the stony expression, the hateful glares, the mean attitude. She suddenly seemed so much...*softer.*

"Okay..." he replied, unsure what else to say. "Stay away from the meadow. Got it. Whatever you say."

But as he continued onward, he couldn't help wondering what made someplace called a "meadow" such a terrifying place.

Chapter 54

Olivia had gone completely numb with terror. She couldn't get control of herself. She was teetering over the edge of that black abyss, screaming her head off, clinging to Wayne's pantlegs. She was trembling so badly she could barely even breathe, and yet she just kept screaming.

Everything was chaos. It was like every atrocity the never-children threw at her in Gutler's Weep, but all at once, her mind unable to keep up with it. There was a monster chasing them, wearing the mutilated, patchwork corpse of a *hound*, of all things. There was a swarm of slicing, carving *bug things* pieced together from the same hound's *razorblade scales*. She was bleeding. Her skin felt like it was on fire. *And* she was about to fall to her death, because apparently things just weren't horrifying enough right now.

She *hated* this place!

Why would Sandy send her here? She was supposed to know everything that was going to happen. Why would she let her go through this? What could possibly be worth all this trauma?

Wayne was trying to protect her, she could tell. He was leaning over her, trying to shield her from the bug things. But they weren't going to stop. They were going to keep cutting and tearing and slicing until there was nothing left of her. It was only a matter of time.

"Aw fuck…" she heard him grumble, but she barely registered the words through her crippling panic.

A sharp, searing pain drew itself across her ankle.

A stinging heat blossomed at her elbow.

Wayne pressed his face close to her ear. "Do you trust me?" he shouted over the shuffling-droning cacophony of those monstrous bugs. But she couldn't stop screaming.

One of them slashed her thigh, cutting right through the fabric of her dirty khakis and into her tender flesh.

Something bit into her hand. Then her neck.

"Olivia!" he shouted. "Do you trust me?"

She nodded. Of course she trusted him! She always trusted him! He was her fiancé. Was now really the time to have a heart-to-heart about it?

"Good!" Then he wrapped his strong arms around her, lifting her a little. Frightened of falling, she grabbed him back, holding on to him for dear life.

Then, absurdly enough, he pushed her.

He.

Pushed.

Her.

For a moment, she was so utterly shocked that her screams went silent. Her heart seemed to stutter to a stop in her chest. All the breath flushed from her lungs. She couldn't believe it. And yet it happened. He simply shoved all of his weight against her and knocked her backward, over the edge of the already too-narrow walkway.

He didn't let go of her. He was coming with her, all the way, his strong arms enveloping her completely. But in an instant, all of her worst fears were realized.

She was falling.

Falling...

Plummeting into the black abyss below.

She saw the other walkways flashing past her in the light she was still clutching in her hand. The sight of them was surreal, like something she was watching through a television screen rather than in real life.

How did it come to this?

These were her last moments. The end of the line. The end of her story.

Just...*the end.*

Finality.

What did she do? How did she even begin to process something like that? Was this the part where her life was supposed to flash before her eyes? Was there supposed to be some grand realization about the purpose of her brief existence? Because all she felt was a desperate longing for more. It was too short. She hadn't done all that she wanted to do. She hadn't even made it to her own wedding yet!

Her insides seemed to have come untethered and were floating within her as she sped downward. Wind whipped through her hair. Her tears flew away as quickly as she shed them.

In her terrified panic, she imagined that she glimpsed death itself as a great, black, swirling vortex waiting to swallow her soul forever.

She finally remembered to scream, but it was too late. She never got the chance.

The black bottom of the abyss rushed up to meet her and she was swallowed whole into the cold and silent darkness.

Chapter 55

There was something on the other side of this wall.

Corey stood there, his hand pressed to it, concentrating. Something was right there. He was sure of it. And if he could somehow knock down the wall between him and it, he was also quite sure it would kill him quickly and without mercy.

Luckily, that wasn't where he needed to go. His path remained forward, following that queer energy flow that continued on down this passageway. He was simply distracted by this feeling as he passed this particular spot and paused to investigate.

That wasn't something any of them were meant to run across. It was in a separate area, unreachable to the twelve of them wandering this labyrinth. A sort of security feature for *other* kinds of trespassers…although he wasn't entirely sure what that meant. What "other kinds" of trespassers were there? And how? Who else could possibly reach this place?

It didn't matter, he supposed. What was important was that he was in no danger here on *this* side of the wall.

But it was such an odd feeling, knowing with such certainty that whatever was sending off those dangerous vibes was right there on the other side of this stone, that it was big and dangerous and mean and impossible to escape, that this wall was the only thing keeping him alive right now. And yet he was also *fascinated*. What *was* it? What did it look like? Was it furry or scaly? Did it growl or hiss? Did it bite or slash? He couldn't help himself.

Violet called them "crossers." Creatures from other worlds, ranging from the mundane to the strange to the downright ludicrous. Everything from slight variations in birds and squirrels and snakes to bizarre creatures that defied categorization to things that were nothing short of *monsters*. Literal living proof of the worlds they'd visited. Like those fascinating tokkatoks.

But could they still be called crossers if this was *their* world and *he* was the trespasser? The thought pulled a hint of a frown on his face. Wouldn't that, technically, make *him* the crosser? But that wasn't really important. It didn't matter.

Violet often told him he had a habit of thinking too much. (Which was kind of weird since she also had a habit of informing him that he didn't think nearly enough...) She was always telling him that sometimes you had to just keep moving. And she was almost always right. She was smart, after all.

He removed his hand from the wall and continued walking, but his thoughts lingered on that creature for a moment longer, wondering all his wonders about whether it might have scales or fins or feathers or some other sort of thing he'd never even imagined before. He probably shouldn't be this entertained. Violet would scold him for that, too. She liked his enthusiasm, but she worried that he was going to get himself hurt one of these days because he was going to be wondering when he should be doing something else. Like running.

He glanced back one last time and then fixed his attention forward, frowning a little.

He missed Violet. It was always too quiet when she wasn't around. And they couldn't look after each other if they didn't stick together. He hoped she was safe, wherever she was. And he hoped she wasn't too worried about him. She knew how easily he could be distracted...

The passage split ahead of him, but he didn't need to think about it. The energy was flowing to the right.

This was getting easier. He was having less trouble detecting it. Was he finally getting that strange extra sense warmed up? Or was the energy getting stronger, meaning he was getting closer to something? Or perhaps it was both at once.

He continued onward. Twenty yards. Forty. Sixty. The floor was sloping upward. He was ascending. Almost immediately, he felt the strain on his legs and belly. He was in pretty decent physical shape for his overall size, but he wasn't exactly the fittest specimen roaming these corridors. At some point, he was going to have to start taking better care of himself. He wasn't going to be able to protect Violet if he gave himself an early heart attack.

It was steeper than he first realized. He was already starting to sweat, which never failed to feel a little embarrassing when he was around people. He was fine being the fat guy, but he didn't care much for being the *sweaty* fat guy. It made him self-conscious.

Maybe he should take a little break. If something dangerous was waiting up ahead, he wouldn't want to face it gasping and wheezing.

But he realized that something about this passage was changing. The energy around him was definitely getting stronger. And at an accelerated rate. There was more of it flowing in from somewhere. He shined his flashlight around, aiming it at several points where he could feel it welling up within the stone. There was one above and behind him. Another on the wall a few paces ahead. Two more in the floor farther up. And more beyond that.

Yes…like flowing water. Like the little creek that ran through his parents' property back in Missouri. That was what this energy reminded him of. Except water always flowed downhill. Gravity had nothing to do with this, hence the fact that he was following it uphill at the moment. But these wellsprings of energy reminded him of the cold spots he'd found wading the creek, the springs that fed the stream from deep underground, in the places where the watercress grew and the water was purest.

He was following the creek right now, he realized. The main flow of energy. And it was growing bigger as it flowed, fed by these little springs that seeped from other areas deeper in the labyrinth.

An energy gathering system for some great machine, he realized.

He was close to something.

He aimed his light straight up the sloping path before him. The space up there was different. It felt like somewhere he wasn't supposed to be. And yet at the same time, it felt like *exactly* where he wanted to be…which of course was confusing. Which was it? It should be one or the other, shouldn't it?

Distracted from his physical strain by the pull of his overwhelming curiosity, he pushed onward up the hill, wondering what was waiting for him at the top.

Chapter 56

"You guys are professional *portal* hunters?"

"I guess," replied Violet. "Sort of." She never used the word "professional." Nor did she refer to herself as a "portal hunter," but she supposed it was an accurate enough description for what she and Corey did.

"That's *awesome!*"

She wanted to ask him if he was always so easily impressed, but she decided not to be rude. Besides, it was sweet that he was so enthusiastic. Most people just sort of looked at her like she was crazy. It was kind of refreshing.

But then again, she didn't usually find herself describing what she did to someone who'd already traveled across the *Denselands*, of all places. *Of course* he didn't think she was crazy.

They still hadn't found the top of these endless stairs. She was starting to think they weren't ever going to end. Was this really where they were supposed to be? Or had they made some sort of mistake?

The only thing she knew with any certainty was that she was going to need to stop for another rest soon. She was running out of steam again.

"How many have you found?" he asked, looking like a kid on Christmas morning.

"Quite a few." She couldn't remember exactly how many they'd documented. It wasn't a number she memorized. For one thing, there was a little gray area surrounding a number of those locations. She and Corey weren't entirely in agreement on whether *all* of them were really portals. Many times it wasn't clear where the actual transition was located, or if there weren't more mundane explanations for things.

"*So cool!*"

She shrugged. "Most of them are pretty boring, actually. You wouldn't know them if you saw them."

"Still!"

She stopped walking and leaned against the wall. "Seriously, what's with all these stairs?"

"Tired," he agreed, seating himself on the steps again.

She turned and shined her light down the way they came. It was the first time she'd looked back in a while. She had to make a conscious effort to stop doing that when they first started climbing. She was freaking herself out more and more as she pushed forward. Something about that deep, dark stairwell plunging into the inky darkness, like the gullet of some gargantuan snake about to swallow them whole. It was unnerving. And it didn't help that it reminded her of those creepy basement steps you saw in horror movies, the ones where the light switch was always at the bottom and you had to race to the top to escape the monsters, whether real or imagined.

But as she cast her light down into that darkness now, something about it looked strangely—and *dreadfully*—familiar.

Hadn't she seen steps exactly like these somewhere before?

(*What's wrong?*)

(*Steps.*)

(*Why are there steps here?*)

A strange shiver raced through her body. That dream she had when she stepped through the lake road's gate… Why did that keep circling back to her like this? It wasn't real. There was no cave. She'd have remembered something like that. She was sure of it. They probably would've spent the rest of their summer playing in such a place.

And yet she could so vividly recall peering around Corey and looking down these same ominous stone steps into that same, empty darkness…

(*Even if we go down there, we won't be able to see anything. It's too dark.*)

(*There's a light.*)

(*What? Where?*)

She turned away from that plunging darkness, frustrated by the impossible memories.

Did it have something to do with those dreams she had between being attacked by the Not-Jeremy and waking up with Andrea and Everett? Something about that mysterious voice she heard? Maybe these false memories of her and Corey as children were a part of *that* dream that her mind had somehow churned back up.

"What was the weirdest thing you ever found in another world?" wondered Everett.

"You," she replied without thinking about it.

He stared at her for a moment in silence, long enough for her to wonder if she might've hurt his feelings. This wasn't Corey she was traveling with, she had to remind herself. But then he burst out laughing.

She smiled. He really was a nice kid.

But his laughter was cut short by another of those long, creepy sighs that seemed to come from everywhere and nowhere at once.

They both shined their lights back and forth, startled, but there was nothing to see above or below them. Was it something on the other side of the wall? Was something keeping pace with them, following them as they ascended this bizarre labyrinth? It was a deeply unpleasant thought, but she wasn't sure how else to explain it.

Everett, on the other hand, seemed up to the task. "It's like the *walls* are breathing," he observed.

She wrinkled her nose at him. What an incredibly creepy thought that she wished he'd kept to himself. Back in their own world, she could've dismissed it as a mere figure of speech, but this wasn't their world and this wasn't the reality they knew. Now she couldn't help wondering if that sound might actually be coming from the labyrinth itself.

He stared down into the darkness behind him. "For all we know, this entire place could be alive."

"Let's just say it's not and forget about it," she countered. Like Corey, he didn't seem to know when to stop talking about creepy stuff.

He glanced up at her, distracted. "Huh?"

"Come on. Let's keep going." She didn't wait for him to agree. She was already climbing upward, eager to reach the top of these exhausting stairs.

Higher and higher they climbed.

They'd better be going somewhere. If she reached the top only to find a dead end, she was going to be pissed.

(*Someone down there.*)

She squeezed her eyes closed as Corey's voice rang through her head again. What was it with that? One part of her kept insisting that it was all just a dream. Another part, however, kept asking if she was sure about that, if it wasn't like that field of curious stones in Arkansas. She didn't remember that until the mysterious voice in her dream told her to remember it.

Except that was different. Frightened by her sudden collapse, Corey carried her out of that garden of stone and they never dared to go back. But they spent countless hours playing in those woods throughout their childhood. They explored every inch of that property over the years, including that place where those two bluffs met. And she distinctly remembered there *not* being a cave nestled between them.

Not only did they never find it again, she had no recollection of even *looking* for it. She didn't remember *remembering it* until now. If they'd actually entered that cave and then found it gone, there was no way she—much less Corey—would ever stop trying to find it again, if only to prove to themselves that they weren't crazy.

Above her, something new appeared out of the stubborn gloom at last. The steps ended. She could see the ceiling of the next passage.

"Finally!" she gasped.

But even as she climbed the last few steps, she heard the ominous sigh again, much louder than before. It no longer seemed without origin. It sounded like it was coming from ahead of them.

"Something's going to happen, isn't it?" whispered Everett.

She couldn't tell if that was normal trepidation in his voice, or un-ashamed eagerness, but she found herself leaning heavily toward the latter. "Just take it slow," she told him. "Be ready to run back the way we came."

"Okay."

But of course going back down all those steps was the very *last* thing she wanted to do. Especially while fleeing some ungodly monster, one slight misstep from falling and breaking their necks or fracturing their skulls.

She stood on the top step, shining her light into the dark passage that waited there for them, listening to that ominous sigh that seemed to go on and on, sending chills racing down her spine. She was tired. Her legs ached. Her heart was thumping. She *really* wanted a break. But they couldn't let their guard down.

Something was in here with them.

Someone's there, she heard Corey say inside her head again, making the hair stand up on her arms.

"Be careful," she whispered. Then she crept onward into that all-encompassing gloom.

Chapter 57

Andrea struggled to pull her leg free but whatever was in the black fog refused to let go of her. It felt awful in ways she couldn't even describe. Like every creepy, crawling, slithering, slimy, corpse-like thing her frightened mind had ever imagined magnified by every fear of every dark place she'd ever glimpsed in all her worst dreams. She couldn't make herself be quiet. All that mattered was getting free of this awful, disturbing thing that wouldn't let go of her ankle.

She shook her foot. She yanked at it. She kicked at it with her other foot. And then she pulled with all her might.

She was making *far* too much noise. She could almost feel things closing in all around her. She needed to break free and run.

Finally, the thing released her. It didn't feel as if she broke free, exactly, but rather as if it just *let go*. It happened so suddenly that she fell backward, startled, and landed on her back in the depths of that unnatural darkness.

Everything went black.

Terrified, she sprang to her feet. But she'd dropped her flashlight! It was on the floor somewhere, down in that eerie black fog, its light swallowed by the unnatural darkness as quickly as it passed through the lens.

She could still see herself. Mostly. The light was still reaching her from wherever it lay. But there was nothing *else*. The murk was everywhere, plunging every surface into inky darkness, making it hard to see. And she certainly wouldn't be able to leave this room without it.

She had to find it!

She dropped to her hands and knees and searched, her fingers sliding across the cold stone floor, her mind screaming at her that there were monsters everywhere, that those blobs of living darkness were going to grab her again.

She couldn't help holding her breath, half-convinced that if she breathed in that black fog it would somehow infect her lungs, filling her with this evil darkness and poisoning her.

And throughout it all, she was sure she could hear the unnerving scratching-squelching sound of something awful oozing across the ceiling, following the sounds of her clumsy movements, zeroing in on her.

She needed to get up. She needed to move. They were going to find her. But she *needed* her flashlight! Without it, the entire temple might as well be filled with this ghostly darkness. She'd be blind again, like back in that enormous gouging station, lost and alone and terrified.

Where is it? she screamed inside her head.

She could feel tears welling up in her eyes again. This was *so* unfair. Why did she have to be here alone? She couldn't order a drink without having to show her ID but she was grown up enough to travel to the middle of *hell itself* and do *this* all on her own?

Her hand finally struck the flashlight, only to knock it away. She couldn't stop herself from letting out a startled cry as she crawled after the sound of it.

Panic was rapidly enveloping her. Everything was spiraling out of control. Tears were spilling down her cheeks again. She didn't want to do this anymore. She didn't want to be here. She didn't want to be alone.

She hated this!

Then something in the darkness grabbed her elbow, wrenching another terrified scream from her. It felt vile against her skin, slimy and dank, like something from the cold, wet depths of the sea.

Was it the same one that grabbed her before? Or was this a different one? She couldn't tell. And she was still blind! She couldn't pull away enough to lift her head above the surface of the murk.

She struggled against it, yanking at it with all her strength.

There was no way she wasn't attracting the attention of the scratchy-squelchy thing. It was probably descending on her already, reaching out with ghastly claws.

Desperate, she twisted around and kicked at the thing that was clinging to her. Her foot found nothing, and yet it let go of her elbow anyway. Did she strike close enough to make it flinch? Or did she somehow break apart one of those shadow blobs?

Did it matter? Why was she wasting brainpower analyzing it? It was gone. She was free of it. That was all there was to it.

She scrambled away from the spot where the thing grabbed her and again struck the flashlight, knocking it away again. But when she lunged for it this time, she caught it.

She shot to her feet, flashlight in hand. It was surreal rising out of the black fog, her body blooming into view from the darkness.

But which way was which? She'd lost her bearings!

It struck her that it was eerily quiet. Those creepy voices that kept echoing and mocking her each time she spoke had gone completely silent. And in that silence, that awful squelching noise came again. She followed the sound of it and glimpsed a great, bulging shape churning through the darkness above her, far closer than she was comfortable with.

She lowered the flashlight and looked down at her feet, like she did the first time. If she tried to run, it would chase her. She didn't know how she knew this, but she did. It was already almost on top of her, probably following all the noise she was making on the floor. If she'd sprang to her feet a few seconds later, would it have attacked her before she even spotted it?

She stood as still as she could, but her body was trembling. Her hand was closed so tightly around the flashlight that her knuckles ached. Tears were still flowing down her cheeks.

She kept her eyes down, but she could still see the dark shape moving up there. And as she stood beneath it, unable to move, it descended toward her. Its shape didn't make any sense. It was just a glob of darkness with no discernable features, but something about it was absolutely dreadful. The sight of it there made her skin crawl.

And it was getting closer!

It was just above her, she realized, moving toward her face.

Was she too late? Was it going to attack her?

Every fiber of her being wanted to run. She could feel her muscles tightening, her nerves twitching. She was teetering on the very edge of her fight-or-flight response. And yet she somehow knew that she had to resist it. If she panicked, it would be over.

The thing let out a long, low growl that made her knees feel wobbly and the blood drain from her face.

If she passed out now, she'd never wake up again.

Oh god…oh god…oh god oh god oh god oh god oh god…

What was this thing? It looked like a glob of shadows, but it was far more than that. She was in terrible danger right now. She might as well be staring down a hungry tiger.

It was too late, she understood. She'd made too much noise searching for the flashlight and fighting with those creepy grabby things. It already knew she was here. Running would be the end of her, she knew, but it wasn't going to matter because it was already the end.

As she stared with terrified eyes at the darkness swallowing her feet, she could see the *other* darkness descending from above, unraveling itself in front of her lowered face, revealing shadowy teeth like dripping daggers, one after another, row after row, lining an impossibly deep chasm of a maw.

How could it be so big inside? How was that possible?

Mercifully, the tears welling up in her eyes blurred out whatever horrors were revealed next. She felt the world sway before her eyes.

It was over, she realized. This was how her journey was going to end.

(*Your friends will need you to light the way. They can't ever go home without you.*)

Her heart broke as she realized that she'd failed everyone.

It was all her fault.

Because she was too weak.

Chapter 58

Brandy tightened her grip on Albert's arm as they crossed the stone bridge. The channel was about thirty feet wide and too deep for her flashlight to reveal the bottom. She didn't care much for the idea of going back into that water. This far down in the labyrinth, she might never come back up. And while the current passing beneath their feet was hardly the raging rapids they rode down from the surface, it was moving at a pretty good pace, still much too fast for her to swim against if she should be so unlucky as to choose this moment to slip and fall.

"There are things living at the bottom," Gina informed them as she crossed ahead of them, as if she were merely commenting on the weather, but Brandy felt her heart leap at this sudden revelation.

"What kinds of things?" she asked in a voice that was embarrassingly shrill, making her clear her throat.

"Nothing dangerous," she replied. "At least, I don't think so. They don't feel like the kinds of things I usually feel when I cross bridges."

"You can do that?" asked Albert, curious.

"It's not an exact sort of thing. I can't sense every single fish, frog or snail. But I can feel a sort of 'carpet' of living things covering the bottoms of most bodies of water. And there's usually other sorts of things in there, too."

Albert's face drew downward in a thoughtful frown. "What kinds of 'other things'?"

"Scary kinds of things," she said in the most deadpan tone Brandy had ever heard, as if this weren't absolutely *terrifying* information she was sharing with them. "The kinds of things most people can't see. Or maybe just won't see. I'm not sure how it all works. But it doesn't really matter. No one but me ever sees them, so it's like they don't even exist."

"If they don't exist to anyone else, then they can't hurt them, right?" reasoned Brandy.

"No, they definitely can."

"Oh…"

"Are there 'unnatural things' in *this* water?" asked Albert.

"Yes. Lots of them."

Brandy gripped her husband's arm a little tighter and gave him a push, urging him to speed up.

They crossed the bridge and continued on without being eaten by anything, natural or otherwise, but for a while, she kept glancing back, half expecting to see something dripping and horrifying come flopping after them.

Albert, however, was still pondering this new information she'd shared with them. "Unnatural..." he muttered. "Shanzer said something about that," he recalled. "He talked about the natural world, the supernatural world and the *unnatural* world. Remember?"

"I try not to," she grumbled. Why did he keep bringing up that pervert? She never wanted to think about that creep again.

Ahead of them, the path diverged. They could veer left or right. Gina chose right without pausing. In fact, she picked up her pace a little as she passed the other one.

Albert noticed it, too: "What did you feel in the other direction?"

"Screaming," she replied in her usual sleepy voice, as if she were reporting the time rather than something horrible that sent the hairs on the back of Brandy's neck standing on end. "Pain. Lots of blood."

Brandy crowded even closer to Albert and shined her light back toward the intersection. What the fuck kind of answer was *that*?

Albert gave her an encouraging squeeze. He didn't press for any more details, thankfully. He could tell how much it spooked her, she was sure. He really was good at protecting her. He was always careful not to bring things up that disturbed her. Like the temple. Sometimes she felt bad, making him keep his thoughts to himself. She knew how much those unanswered questions nagged him. But she couldn't help being scared of that place, even once it was gone.

Except it wasn't gone. It was waiting here for them this whole time. They were always going to come back to these terrifying passages. The fucking Keeper had made sure of that.

She needed to get her mind off these claustrophobic tunnels. She needed to focus on something else. But the only thing her mind kept returning to was Nicole. Where did she go? And why? What was going on with her?

If only she could turn on that awareness she felt back in the hallway outside Trixie's room at will, when she was suddenly able to see the entire hotel and everyone in it. But was that even her? Or was that all Trixie? *She* was the one filled to bursting with that intense sexual frustration.

But then again, she sometimes felt things without being in a sexual mood. Like just a little while ago, when she thought for a moment that someone was behind them. Gina said there was, indeed, someone there, but in a different tunnel, somewhere below them. So why couldn't she use that ability any time she wanted? Why did it have to be *dirty*?

Still clinging to Albert's arm, she closed her eyes and tried to clear her mind of all the fears and worries of this awful place.

She knew Albert was there. She could feel him. The warmth of his skin. The muscles in his arm. The sound of his footsteps. The movement of his wet clothes. And Gina, too. She could hear her sandals clacking softly on the stone several steps ahead of them. But *who else* was here?

She squeezed her eyes closed tighter, frustrated. She wanted to make this work. She didn't want to have to do it the pervert's way. She wanted to do it on her own terms. She wanted to *defy* him, to prove him wrong.

But she didn't even know what she was looking for.

How did it happen before? Was it an image she saw in her head? No... She didn't think it was like that. There were too many people in the hotel for her to have pictured each and every face. It was more like...seeing a map, maybe? Like the app on her phone, showing various locations?

No, she was thinking visually. And that wasn't quite right. She didn't think she *saw* anything. She just...knew it?

She just knows things, she remembered Nicole telling them about Gina when they first met her. Was that how psychic stuff worked? Was it just a very distinct and certain *knowing* of things?

This was so confusing.

Again, she tried to relax. She forced herself to stop squeezing her eyes closed. She willed the tenseness to leave her body. She pushed all the other thoughts from her mind and focused on only the one thought.

Somewhere in these sprawling passageways was her best friend. And the others, too. Andrea. Violet and Corey. Keith. And probably Olivia and Wayne. There were supposed to be twelve of them here. But where was everyone? If her brain was supposed to be so psychic, why wouldn't it show them to her? Why would it be dependent on her being *horny*? That was just so *stupid*!

Now she was just getting pissed off.

"There's something strange up ahead," reported Gina.

Brandy opened her eyes. The passage ahead of them was still the same empty stretch of tunnel they'd been following since the intersection that led to "screaming" and "pain" and "lots of blood" that sounded like ever so much fucking fun.

"Strange how?" asked Albert.

"Weird energy," she replied, as if that explained anything at all.

The three of them stepped out of the passage and into a small, empty space with a high ceiling.

"Here?" asked Brandy, worried.

"No." She pointed forward, toward the next passage leading out from here. "Farther ahead." Then she lowered her hand and looked up at the ceiling. "This is…something else…"

"I remember these empty rooms," whispered Albert.

Brandy did, too. It was one of these rooms that killed Beverly. Some kind of psychic trap. The Sentinel Queen made it sound as if it were designed to keep out people with really strong psychic abilities, people who could potentially cheat their way through the trials the temple was supposed to represent, she supposed.

Gina looked back at them, her sleepy eyes narrowed. "This room looks empty to you?"

She glanced at Albert, confused. "Um…yeah? I mean…*isn't* it?"

"What do *you* see?" asked Albert.

Again, she turned her gaze up toward that high ceiling. "Chains," she replied.

Brandy felt a hard shiver race through her. Chains?

As if on cue, she heard a distant clattering of metal.

Without saying anything more, Gina crossed the room and continued forward.

"Wait," called Albert. "What was chained up in there?"

"I couldn't see," she replied. "And I didn't want to. Something was telling me it'd be really bad if I could see it."

He and Brandy exchanged a worried glance. She knew exactly what he was thinking. "Really bad" might have been an understatement if Beverly's reaction to one of those rooms was any indication. The sight of it had been so utterly terrifying that she lost her mind and stumbled backward into that pit of spikes. The sound of her screaming had haunted her for months.

"Come on," said Gina, passing through another intersection as if she knew exactly where she were going. "The space ahead is where it feels strange. It might be important."

Right. The "weird energy" she mentioned. Something even more disturbing than those murderous psychic trap rooms, she was sure.

She gripped Albert's arm tighter as they followed her.

Several minutes passed, considerably longer than Brandy thought it would take them. Just how far away was it? She thought her psychic senses were dulled in this place.

But then again, they seemed to be going in a straight line. Maybe that made a difference.

Gina stopped.

"What's up?" worried Albert.

"I don't know," she replied, shaking her head. "Something about this space. It feels…oppressive, somehow. I don't think I've ever felt anything like it before. I don't sense any danger, exactly, but I also don't want to keep going forward."

"Should we turn back?" wondered Brandy.

"I want to say yes," she replied. She looked back at them. Unshed tears were welled up in her eyes, gleaming in the glow of the flashlight. "But a part of me feels like we have to go in there. Like we can't avoid it."

She and Albert exchanged a worried look. What could be affecting her like that?

"You said you didn't sense any danger…" he reasoned.

"But that doesn't mean there isn't any," countered Brandy.

"True," he agreed. "But we should at least try to see what's up there." He glanced back the way they came. "I mean, I'd rather not spend any more time than necessary backtracking through rooms like that last one."

He had a point, she supposed.

He nodded, managing somehow to look confident about himself. "We'll get eyes on whatever's up there. Decide from there if we need to go back."

Gina didn't look happy. In fact, she looked like she was on the verge of crying. Not just the tears glimmering in her eyes but the way her lip curled and quivered as she turned away from them. But she didn't hesitate. She pushed forward, still not bothering to wait for Brandy to light the space in front of her.

A few dozen paces farther, a chamber opened up before them.

As soon as they entered, she knew exactly what sort of horrors awaited them. "No!" she cried. She backed away, dragging Albert with her. "I can't do that again! No fucking way!"

Gina turned and looked back at them, surprised and confused by her sudden reaction. Her tears were now streaming freely down her face. "What is it?" she asked.

On either side of her stood a row of sentinels lined up along the walls. The first two were standing in that default pose, feet together, arms at their sides, chests puffed out, featureless faces aimed forward. But ten feet farther into the room, the next pair of statues was different from the first. It wasn't profound. It was a *slight* change. Their bodies had slightly slackened, their knees slightly bent, their arms slightly raised, their heads slightly lifted.

"Emotion room," breathed Albert.

Brandy was shaking her head. No. She wouldn't go through that again. The sex room. The hate room. The fear room. All of them filled with such agonizingly intense emotions that they could drive a person utterly mad.

But which emotion was this?

Albert took the flashlight from Brandy's hand and drew it back. In a swift motion, he arced his arm in a low, underhand throw and sent the light sliding across the empty floor, its glow revealing the scene hidden in the shadows.

From the darkness, the three of them watched the sentinels as, pair-by-pair, they lifted their arms, their impossibly long fingers curled in agony, their knees bending and spreading, their heads thrown backward in a silent wail. And then they collapsed onto the floor and curled themselves into a miserable heap.

The flashlight stopped just short of the door on the far side. A man's face took up most of the wall, so startlingly realistic that Gina staggered backward at the very sight of it. Tears streamed from his eyes. His mouth was open in a terrible howl. Abject misery oozed from every pore in his stone flesh.

"Sorrow..." whispered Albert.

Brandy met Gina's streaming eyes and realized that she could feel mirrored tears rolling down her own cheeks. "Oh god..."

Chapter 59

"We're back here again," groaned Nicole.

Ahead of them, the passage again opened onto the raw, black earth of the meadow. Why did they keep coming back to it? Was it bigger than it looked? Did it take up most of this part of the labyrinth? Or were all these passages designed to funnel back to it somehow? Or was there some other kind of force at play that just kept steering her back here? Because it was starting to creep her out a little, if she were being honest.

"Strange," Keith muttered. "I was specifically trying to choose the paths that didn't seem to circle back."

"Well great fucking job with that."

He turned and stalked past her. "Come on."

"Don't order me around."

He stopped and turned on her. "Feel free to lead the way," he snapped.

"I might as well," she snapped right back.

"Better yet, feel free to go your own way."

"Why not? I never asked for a babysitter!"

"And I never asked to babysit your spoiled ass!" He turned and walked away.

She lingered a moment. She wanted some space. But as his light receded she found herself far too aware of the meadow looming behind her back. The idea of standing this close in the pitch-black darkness of the labyrinth's depths was more than she could handle, so she started walking.

But at a distance.

Why did he infuriate her so much? She didn't understand it. She knew he wasn't trying to be an asshole. She knew she was the one starting these fights. She knew she was the problem. *Everyone* knew it. When her friends all asked her what happened and she tried to explain it, how he wouldn't stop *doing* things for her. They all had the same perplexed look on their faces.

Because it didn't make sense.

They all thought it was because he wasn't like the other guys she'd dated. The selfish ones. The verbally abusive ones. The *toxic* ones. Like fucking *Earl*. He was the worst. Her own personal rock bottom. He was the one they always brought up. The one they used to measure her. The gold standard in shit boyfriends.

They thought she'd rather have an Earl in her life than a Keith...

But that wasn't it at all.

Her thoughts flashed back to that bridge, to that monster dragging Keith over the edge, how he disappeared for a second and she thought he was gone... Even the memory of it made her heart sink. And the thought that it was *her* fault, that he risked that to save *her*, even though she treated him so poorly, even though he had every reason in the world to walk away and let that monster have her...

Ahead of her, he made his way through the winding passages, choosing paths seemingly at random. She didn't fail to notice that he didn't bother asking her opinion. It wouldn't matter anyway. She had no fucking clue which way they should go. But it wasn't about choosing directions. It was about avoiding conversation.

She looked back over her shoulder, but she couldn't see anything. The light was aimed forward and she was hanging too far back. Something could sneak right up on her before she'd see it. The thought sent a shudder through her and made her pick up her pace a little.

"This is new," said Keith.

She looked forward again to see that he was approaching a wall. It was an offset passage, set about six feet higher than the one they were walking in. They'd have to climb up and over to continue forward.

Something to trip up unwary travelers in the dark? Or did it serve another purpose? Back in the first temple, offsets like these were used to separate the areas where the hounds were bound.

But there were no telltale scratches in the stone floor to indicate the presence of hounds.

Keith didn't waste time analyzing it. He gripped the wall and jumped, hooking his leg over the edge and then hoisting himself up. It was a little awkward with his injured arm, but he managed well enough.

He shined his light into the upper passage, checking for any dangers, then he turned and offered her his hand.

She ignored him and climbed up herself.

"Right," he muttered, standing up. "My bad." He continued forward ahead of her.

"I can do things for myself," grumbled Nicole.

"That's what my mom always said, too." He glanced over at her, a pained expression on his face. "You think I should've just sat back and let her? Ignored the fact that I could see how much she was hurting? How tired she obviously was?"

She stared at him. That caught her off guard.

"I know that's not the same thing, but just because someone says they don't need you, doesn't mean you should stop trying to show them how much you love them." He shook his head and continued walking.

She stopped and stood there a moment, watching him walk on.

That wasn't very fair, dragging his mother into it.

"Look," he growled, "I get it. Now more than ever. You've been through some shit. You're the stronger one. You're the braver one. You've literally been through hell and back. You never needed me and I had no business trying to be anything to you."

She didn't even notice the darkness swallowing her as he walked away. She'd forgotten about it. She'd forgotten about the dangers.

No… He didn't get it at all. How could he when *she* didn't even get it?

He was such a nice guy. He stayed by his mom's side until the very end. She couldn't imagine how much that must've hurt, how much strength and courage that must've taken. And it wasn't like he had any other family. His mother was all he had in the world. He did all that *alone*.

She could've changed that. She could've been there with him while he was going through that. But she was so stuck on this one meaningless idea that she didn't *need* to be taken care of, that she didn't want to be treated like some helpless child.

Why did it matter so much that he wanted to take care of her? Shouldn't that be a good thing? God knew none of her *trash* ex-boyfriends ever cared anything about her.

God, she was so confused. What was wrong with her? Was she really nothing more than a colossal fuck-up?

Realizing that he was getting farther and farther away from her, she started walking, her mind churning with confused thoughts.

Chapter 60

Olivia couldn't breathe.

She couldn't move.

She was being swept away by a cold, black current far too strong for her to fight.

She struggled to swim, but was she even moving? She couldn't see. She couldn't feel anything.

Where was Wayne? Why couldn't she feel him anymore? When did he let go of her? Why as she alone again? She hated being alone!

Then, suddenly, she broke the surface and gasped for air.

The terror she'd felt was still with her, still numbing her poor mind, making it hard to process it all, but somehow she'd landed not on hard, bone-shattering stone, but in lifesaving water. Now she was being dragged along, at the mercy of the current, unable to fight it, unable to even *see*. She'd dropped her flashlight at some point. Everything was darkness and chaos.

But somewhere in that darkness, she heard Wayne shouting for her.

Where was he? She tried to shout back to him, but water filled her mouth as soon as she opened it.

She was having trouble staying afloat. Where was she being washed away to? And was she being pulled *under*?

Again, she heard Wayne shouting for her, but she was sucked downward, her body thrashed around in a great swirling vortex.

She grabbed at her nose and mouth, struggling to keep what little air she had left as the current quickened, carrying her deeper and deeper.

How could she have survived that fall only to drown in these black depths? What kind of cruel irony was that? And how far down was she being dragged? How long before the pressure became too much and burst her eardrums?

She couldn't hold her breath much longer! The never-children were going to get their way after all…

Her body was jolted hard to one side. She struck something hard, sending a thunderbolt of pain through her shoulder and wrenching precious breath from her aching lungs.

Her head was spinning. She was going to black out. And then she'd never wake up again.

But suddenly, and bewilderingly, she was *airborne*.

She gasped for breath, startled, and seemed to float for a second or two in the inky blackness before landing in the water again.

This time, the current was weak. She popped up, coughing and crying, and started swimming. A moment later, her feet found mud and she struggled through it, clawing her way forward until the water was shallow enough for her to collapse onto her hands and knees, exhausted.

Behind her, she heard more splashing. Then Wayne's voice called out for her again.

She tried to call back, but she was still coughing. She felt like she'd swallowed at least half a gallon of water.

She heard more splashing. A light blossomed in the darkness, sweeping across the water's rippling surface toward her.

Then Wayne was there, his strong arms around her again. "You okay?" he asked.

"Remind me to never trust you again," she coughed.

"Fair enough." He sat down next to her, out of breath. "One of those things nicked my hand pretty bad," he said, holding up a bleeding fist. "Made me drop my flashlight. When it fell, I watched it fall in the water. We needed to get out of there fast. It felt like the only option."

She sat up, still coughing. "It felt like I landed in a *washing machine...*"

"Maelstrom," he said. "Whirlpool. Part of some kind of huge reservoir system, I guess. We got sucked through the pipes and spit out here." He shined his light out into the open darkness around them. "Wherever here is."

"That was the absolute worst..." she groaned. "And I've literally almost been eaten by a horde of zombies!"

"Yeah... Sorry." He turned the light on her and then lifted up her tee shirt.

She slapped it back down. "Hey!" She thrust a finger at him, poking him in the chest. "You're on the naughty list after that stunt! No boobs for you!"

"What? I'm not—" He pushed her hand aside, annoyed. "I'm trying to see how bad you're *bleeding*, your highness."

"Wha...?" She looked down to see that her tee shirt was stained with blood. "Oh..."

Again, he lifted up her shirt and shined his light at her belly. There were several cuts just beneath the bridge of her bra where the hound bug became tangled in the loose fabric of her shirt, but they weren't deep.

That thing was the reason she freaked out and lost her composure. Until then, she was frightened out of her mind but at least still moving forward. If not for that, she might have made it to the other side.

Maybe.

"Does it hurt?"

"Little bit," she replied. Not any worse than any of the other dozens of cuts those nasty little things left on her. She could feel them up and down her arms and legs, across her back and even a few on her forehead and cheek. She could see little slits all over her shirt and pants, as if someone had taken a razor blade to them. Wherever her clothes were loose, like her sleeves and the tail of her shirt, she didn't feel many cuts, but the more snug areas, like her butt and thighs and shoulders, burned. And her exposed arms, of course, had taken the worst of it. She had blood smeared all up and down them from dozens of little nicks. And then there were the burning cuts on her face… She *really* hoped they wouldn't leave any scars for her wedding!

He looked over the rest of her belly, prodding at a few cuts, then turned his attention to her back. "It'd be better if we had some bandages for a few of these, but I don't think there's any we really have to worry about." He pulled her shirt back down and looked over those on her arm. "Seems like they didn't have enough mass to cut very deep."

She pursed her lips at him, still mad. "You scared me half to death," she informed him.

"I know. I'm sorry."

She sniffled and wiped at her face. She knew why he did it. What other choice did he have? She was freaking out. She wasn't going to make it across that walkway. And those bug things weren't going away. Eventually they would've opened up a vein somewhere. Or put out an eye. He had to do something. And he did. He saved her.

But she still wanted to smack him.

Wayne shined his light back the way they came. There was a huge opening in the stone over there, dumping water into this… Was it a lake? There was mud beneath them, not temple stone. Just where had they landed? They didn't get flushed all the way out of the city, did they? That didn't seem right. "We should go before that freak jumps in to see where we went."

He stood up and she followed his lead.

"Our flashlights got washed here, too," he informed her, handing hers back to her. "Let's get as far from here as possible."

That sounded good to her. She switched on her light and followed him.

But she gasped as she caught sight of the blood soaking the back of his tee shirt.

Chapter 61

Corey stood in the gloom of the passage, one hand again pressed against the wall in front of him. Except it wasn't really a wall. Not exactly. A wall's only purpose was to separate two spaces. This stone wasn't doing that. Instead, it was holding *multiple* spaces together and even allowing them to overlap in ways that shouldn't be possible.

This so-called city was far more complex than anything he ever could've imagined. It was fascinating, *intriguing*, and not least of all because he shouldn't be able to comprehend these things. How did he know what he knew? How was he able to understand this stuff? Had he been here before in some past life or something? His curiosity was overflowing. It was *maddening*.

To his left, the passage continued on into the darkness. To his right, just out of sight, was the slope he'd been climbing for some time. There was no other passage, no third option, and nothing visible to indicate that this particular part of the wall should be any different than any other he'd walked past in all his time here. Yet he somehow knew as soon as he arrived at this spot that there was much more here than his naked eyes could perceive.

That feeling of drawing nearer to something had only grown stronger as he made his way to the top of the slope, urging him onward even as his body grew weary. He was breathing heavily now. His heart was thumping in his chest. There was an unpleasant feeling deep in the pit of his stomach telling him he'd pushed himself too far. And he felt slick under his armpits and around his neck from sweating. But he was barely aware of any of this discomfort. Something about this section of smooth stone wall had captured the entirety of his attention.

Was this where he was supposed to be?

The energy—or whatever it really was—didn't turn here. It continued onward. That still felt like the right way. But there was something about this one spot that made him stop.

It was important somehow.

By now he couldn't dismiss these feelings. He'd found things down here that he was quite sure no one else would have been able to find. It felt like this was *his* path, like it was specifically designed and built for only *him*.

Sentinels...

He turned his head and looked down the dark corridor where that strange energy was flowing, pondering it all.

What he needed was to zoom out and look at the bigger picture. But this wasn't his cell phone. This was reality. People didn't come with features like that.

And yet somehow, this idea stuck with him.

Zoom out...

Pinch...

Shrink the image...

It felt absurd, yet there was something distinctly *right* about it, too. He needed to broaden his perspective. He was too close to it.

He took a breath, calming his still-thudding heart, and closed his eyes. He could feel the energy flowing past him. He could sense the strangeness in the stone still pressed against the palm of his hand. He didn't need to see any of it. He didn't need to touch the stone to feel it. There was something else inside him that could sense all of these things in an entirely different way. That was the part of him he needed right now.

Was it a psychic sense? Like Gina had? Was this what it was like for her when she sensed things others couldn't?

That would be cool. He'd like to be psychic. But somehow, he found himself thinking that this was different. It was more like...*familiarity*. As if he'd once known this stuff and had simply forgotten it all.

It didn't make any sense, of course. But why would things such as this *ever* make any sense? Sense and logic...even *reality*...were all words for things that were bound by the rules that were understood about a universe. Those things all lost their meaning once you crossed a border. Eight years of research had taught him that much.

Zoom out...

He imagined it exactly as it would be if he were holding his phone and "pinching" the screen to shrink the image.

The effect wasn't exactly the same. It wasn't as if he left his body and floated upward, giving him a birds-eye view of the surrounding space. It was a lot more complicated than that. His awareness *did* seem to expand, but it came to him in what felt like multiple *layers of information*. Like a three-dimensional model constructed from a multitude of two-dimensional images inside his head, except the result was something *more* than three-dimensional. Focusing too hard on the result sent bolts of pain shooting through his skull like arcs of lightning. Instead, he found that he needed to relax his mind and let the maddening images play out like a television droning on in the background.

Then it was over.

Again, he looked at the wall his hand was resting against. It drew his attention because it *was* important. There was something right here that he needed. But not *here*. Not *now*. If he continued forward, following that strange energy flow, he'd eventually circle back to this area, approaching it from another angle.

That was where he needed to be.

Satisfied, he lowered his hand and started walking again.

That was a crazy sort of experience. He wasn't even sure how he'd describe it to Violet when they finally met back up. But he was confident she'd think it was cool.

He was also confident she'd probably yell at him for taking risks and say that he was lucky he didn't give himself an aneurism or something. She was like that. She worried about him.

But he knew what he was doing. In fact, he knew a great many things.

Chapter 62

The passage at the top of the stairs curved slightly to the left at first, then gradually became tighter, circling in on itself. Everett and Violet found themselves spiraling inward until, ultimately, they found another set of steps leading farther up. Unlike the last stairway, however, this one was short enough to see the top immediately. And there was no visible ceiling hanging over it. Instead, the space waiting there for them was cavernous and strange.

Everett hurried to the top and shined his light around. He was taking it all in, processing every detail. It was as if they'd climbed all the way to the highest level of the labyrinth and had now found themselves looking down from atop the towering walls. Laid out before them was a twisted landscape of narrow stone pathways winding through a gnarled tangle of deep, dark chasms. Great, towering pillars stretched high into the darkness above, holding up the hidden ceiling and whatever even higher floors yet waited to be explored.

And they weren't alone in this place. He could hear that strange, sighing noise again, coming from somewhere in the open passages below them, along with a low, barely audible rumbling and something else that he couldn't quite make out but sounded a little like creepy whispers and faint cries.

Beside him, Violet's hand tightened on his elbow. "This is…"

"*Cool*," he finished for her.

"Nope. Not the word I was looking for."

He kept forgetting that not everyone shared his endless enthusiasm for these strange new places. And *this* place was definitely strange and new. It was *thrilling*. Ever curious, he shined his light downward, into the darkness that blanketed the depths below, and found that he could just make out something moving through the shadows. He leaned over the edge, trying to get a better look, and felt Violet's hand tighten even more, begging him to be careful—or, more likely, he realized, warning him not to do anything stupid—but he couldn't help himself. He wanted to see what was down there. Frustratingly, however, he was unable to distinguish any details from this height. Whatever it was, it was very large. It moved very slowly. And something about the shapes he could glimpse made him feel a twinge of indescribable dread deep inside his gut. The longer he stared, the more he found that his thoughts were filled with weird, unsettling images that he couldn't seem to comprehend, images that gripped him with a series of complex and contradicting emotions. Sad elation. Enraged calmness. Euphoric terror. Stranger still, as he stared down at the one below them, he found that he could somehow see *all* of them. There were *dozens* prowling the sprawling corridors down there, and he was able to sense exactly where each one was, whether it was moving, which way it was going and other details that didn't quite make any sense for some reason. The one nearest to them, for example, dreamed in shades of wind and time…whatever that meant…

He took a step back from the edge and rubbed at his head. All this bizarre information was leaving him disoriented. It reminded him of the painful download from the puzzle box.

"You okay?" worried Violet.

"Yeah. Just…" He shook his head. "That was a lot just now."

"What happened?"

"Can't say." Again, he peered over the edge and down at that distant, shadowy shape. Suddenly, the lack of any kind of wall or railing felt much more profound. "But I feel like we *really* need to stay out of that area."

She shined her light down there, too. "No arguments here. But why? What do you feel?"

He glanced up at her. "Can…you not see them down there?"

She looked up and met his gaze. "Um…?" Again she looked down. He could tell by the way she was sweeping her flashlight back and forth that she wasn't fixing on the shadowy shape deep down in the gloom. It wasn't an easy thing to see anyway, but somehow he understood that these things were like the mushrooms in Gutler's Weep and the drafts out on that storm-drenched bridge. "I don't see anything," she confirmed. Then she locked eyes with him again. "What do *you* see?"

She had such pretty green eyes. Entirely different from the bright emerald color of Nadia's. They were darker and deeper, with sparks of brighter green and blue woven throughout. It probably would've been distracting to stare into them like this if not for those lingering emotional contradictions still churning deep inside his head. "Wrongness," he replied.

She narrowed those lovely eyes, confused. "What does *that* mean?"

But he could only shrug. "Just what I said." He looked down into that darkness once more. "It's just...*wrong* down there."

"Good enough for me," she decided, stepping back from the edge and pulling him with her.

Wrongness... The word seemed to linger in his throat. No matter how curious he became, he needed to make sure he steered clear of those things.

Fortunately, they were all way down there, well out of reach.

Violet lifted her flashlight and shined it across the emptiness of the space around them. "So which way do we go to get out of here?"

It was a good question. He turned and scanned their surroundings, but nothing stood out. There was only the plunging chasms, the towering pillars and the staircase from which they emerged. But of course, there was plenty he couldn't see in this limited light.

From here, the floor they were standing on stretched away from them in three directions, each path twisting and winding with the knotted and gnarled layout of the labyrinth below so that it was impossible to guess where any of them might lead. But then again, he had no idea where it was they were *supposed* to go. So could he really choose wrong?

He picked a direction and started walking. It wasn't entirely at random. That weird psychic sense told him there were fewer of those shadowy things lurking in the depths in this direction than the other two. But that was all he knew for certain.

Violet didn't ask him why he chose this way. She simply started walking with him, their arms still linked, their eyes open for anything unexpected.

It was still kind of weird, the feel of her body so close to him. He simply wasn't used to physical contact. For all his mother's overprotective insanity, she never liked touching. She hardly ever hugged him. Looking back now, it seemed like she never touched him more than was absolutely necessary. He looked down at Violet's hand, at the rings on her fingers, the scraps of polish on her uneven nails. Even if he'd had a *normal* childhood with a loving family, he was fairly sure he'd find this distracting. This woman was a complete stranger until just a few short hours ago.

Or was it considerably less than that?

Or was it *more*?

It was impossible to be sure. But it was probably too soon to be walking around, arm-in-arm like a couple. It felt kind of weird. He had to keep reminding himself that she believed this was necessary to keep them from getting separated, and she was probably right about that, given that they'd both lost literally everyone else they'd traveled with.

Ahead of them, the path split into two. Again, he had no way to know which was the right way, so he just chose left at random and kept walking.

But as they drew closer to it, Violet tugged him to a stop.

"What's up?" he asked.

She was staring down the other path, a distant sort of look on her face, almost dreamy.

"Something over there?" he wondered, shining his light in that direction.

"I feel like…" she began, "…maybe…we should go that way?"

He glanced up at her, surprised. "You think so?"

She nodded.

"Okay then." He wasn't going to argue. He certainly had no idea which way was which.

Again, they walked on, still arm-in-arm in this weirdly intimate way. He *liked* the feeling. But he couldn't make himself stop feeling guilty, like he was somehow taking advantage of her. (Not that he could, he was sure. He was fairly sure if he tried something truly ungentlemanly with her that she'd simply and quite easily kick his butt.)

"Tell me something," said Violet, still sounding distracted.

"Sure," he replied. He had no secrets. He was an open book.

"Do you think you're going to make it home?"

He blinked at her, surprised. He wasn't sure what he thought she was going to ask, but it wasn't that. "Where'd *that* come from?"

"Albert and Brandy said that two of us won't be going home."

"They said that?" This was news to him.

"They did. And I haven't been able to stop thinking about that."

He watched her for a moment, his thoughts churning with this new data. Two of them were supposed to die here? Was that really a thing? Nadia didn't tell them anything like that on the train. Nor did Maeve back in her fairy circle. It seemed like the sort of thing that should've come up. Or was it more like one of those things that was hidden away in the fine print?

He supposed it didn't matter. It wasn't as if they could back out now.

He turned his light toward the shadowy chasm next to them. "I'll bet that's the things down there," he decided. "They must be getting inside your head. Making you worry about stuff. I felt it when I looked down at them. Weird emotional stuff. Subliminal, probably."

But she shook her head. "I don't think so. I think it's something I was told in the dream I had. Before you and Andrea found me."

"Oh…"

"It's scary."

He wasn't sure what to say. It *was* scary, for certain. He didn't want to think about anyone dying on this trip. But if that sort of thing was already going to happen, then worrying about it wasn't going to make it any better.

Worrying about something that hasn't happened yet just means you'll suffer over it twice, he thought. The words belonged to the nice woman who took him in after he was separated from his mother. She used to say a lot of things like that. He remembered how strange it felt listening to someone say it was okay to be brave and hopeful and look forward to things. She was the one who nurtured his new mindset, who encouraged him to be brave and adventurous and not afraid all the time. He was trying to figure out what wise words she'd have for Violet if she were here right now when something new emerged from the darkness.

A single, upright rectangular block of stone jutted upward from the floor ahead of them, featureless except for a single, oval-shaped indention on one side.

"I've seen that before," she whispered.

"You have?"

She didn't stop when she saw it. In fact, she picked up her pace, as if she were excited to see it. "It was one of these that brought me here. I'm sure of it."

It looked like an ordinary block of stone. He wasn't sure how it could *do* anything. But then again, that was the kind of thinking that lost its meaning outside of the physics of the so-called "real" world.

Maybe it was another puzzle box of some kind?

Violet let go of his arm as they drew near and then reached out and touched the stone with both hands. "I can't explain how it works, but the one from my dreams used it to communicate with me."

"Cool," was all he could think to say. And it *was* cool. His curiosity was piqued. He wanted to know more. But she didn't say anything more about it. She leaned forward and stared into the indention. From this angle, it almost looked like it was made for her face, a perfect fit, as if it was built specifically for her.

He walked around and glanced at the other side, wondering if perhaps there was a hole for him to sick *his* face in as well, but there were no other distinguishable features on the stone.

When he looked back, however, something was wrong.

Violet's expression had gone blank. Her eyes were distant. She looked strangely lost.

"Hey… What's going on? What's wrong?"

But she didn't seem to notice him.

Worried, he grabbed her arm to pull her away from the stone, but before he could do anything, he found himself frozen in place.

Something was happening. Those strange, shadowy things below them had suddenly gathered close around them.

He didn't even feel them moving! How did they all get here so fast?

A dreadful feeling was creeping through him, wriggling like the tentacles of some grotesque Lovecraftian abomination through his mind. He turned and looked out over the darkness as something unthinkable reached up out of the chasm and descended on him, closing around him like a devilish hand.

Then everything went dreadfully dark.

Chapter 63

Those endless rows of teeth opened and unraveled, wider and wider, an impossible, endless, spiraling abyss of shadowy death and unspeakable agony, tearing and ripping at her body until nothing was left to swallow but her screaming soul.

Andrea could only wait for it to happen.

The worst part was knowing she'd failed everyone. She wished she could tell them all how sorry she was. Because now none of them were going to ever make it home. All because of her. Because she was too weak.

From somewhere in that suffocating darkness in front of her came a great, resounding crash that startled her so badly that it sent a jolt through her entire body and wrenched a terrified squeak from her throat before she could stop it. A death sentence, for sure. At this distance, the slightest sound could make it strike.

But the monstrous chasm of teeth in front of her snapped shut and twisted itself toward the much louder noise, instead.

She stood there, trembling, tears streaming down her face and dripping from her chin, her nose running, her heart practically bursting from her chest.

What happened? How was she still alive?

"Go now," whispered Erin, her voice so close to her ear that she could feel her ghostly breath upon her cheek.

She blinked back her tears and dared to lift her eyes. The monstrous glob of darkness was oozing away from her now, moving toward the source of the crash.

Had Erin toppled one of the sentinel statues in order to save her? That seemed like quite a feat for a dead woman, but she could imagine nothing else that could make a noise like that.

She took a shaky breath and slowly began to back away from the monster, careful not to draw its attention again.

It had approached her from that direction. Given that it was behind her when she first heard it moving, then the way out should be roughly this way. Assuming there was a way out at all…

No. That was no way to think. Erin said to go. Why would she bother if there weren't a way out?

She reminded herself that she wasn't alone. She never was. Erin was watching over her, even with that other presence continually pushing her away.

Slowly, step-by-step, she retreated from the thing on the ceiling, her gaze locked on it as it disappeared into the gloom. Her heart was still pounding. Her body was still trembling. Her nose was still running. And she might've peed herself a little. She wasn't entirely sure. But she was still alive. And that was all that mattered right now.

No sudden movements. No noises. She kept her teeth clenched tight, determined not to scream or squeal or even whimper, not even if another of those awful things grabbed her leg again. That was how she screwed up the first time, letting those things frighten her.

She just needed to keep moving. That was all. She could do this.

Then her heel struck something solid, startling her.

Her heart leaped, but somehow she managed not to cry out. And she immediately realized that the solid thing was merely stone. She'd backed into another column of murk. Another sentinel, most likely.

Reaching behind her, she confirmed it immediately. Those obscenely enormous penises… (Seriously, why did they have to be right at *that* height? It was like they were *trying* to make her touch them there! Gross!)

But what were these statues even doing here? Back in the first temple, the sentinels usually served as clues or warnings, but a lot of good that did when they were wrapped in literal darkness. She couldn't even see them!

But then again, maybe they still had their uses.

One hand pressed to the stone thigh of the statue, she crept behind it, placing it between herself and the squelchy magic bag of endless teeth slowly making its way to the far side of the ceiling. Then she continued backing away.

You're only delaying the inevitable, sighed Stella's voice in her head.

Go jump off a cliff, she snapped back at her, also in her head.

This was fantastic. She had voices in her head, she was talking to a ghost and she was trying to escape a scary shadow. How many more boxes did she need to check off before she was officially a lunatic? Was there just going to be a padded cell waiting for her when she got home or was she going to have to reserve one?

She could no longer see the oozing glob of darkness and those gross noises it made had grown fainter with distance, so she dared to retreat faster. She turned around and hurried onward, hoping to find an end to this awful darkness sooner than later.

What was she doing here? Where did all these murk-infested spaces lead? And would she even know when she arrived there in all this black?

She realized that she could hear the creepy mutterings of those ghostly voices again, faint, but audible. Did that mean it was safer here? Did those voices fall silent when the squelchy things were near? Could she use them as a sort of early warning system?

Ahead of her, the darkness seemed to suddenly jump out at her. She stumbled to a stop, barely stifling another scream.

Just another statue?

No… This was much wider.

Carefully, she reached into it with her left hand, deeper and deeper, until she found cool stone. Smooth and flat.

The wall! She'd finally reached the far end of the room!

But…where was the way out? She turned and walked to the right, her left hand still reaching into the blackness, dragging her fingertips along the wall. Was she even on the correct side of the room? What if she'd passed the exit already? She didn't want to go back. She couldn't!

She turned around, swapping the light to her left hand and reaching into the darkness with her right, then tried the other way.

What if she couldn't find it? How long before that monstrous glob of shadows squelched back this way?

She shined the light out into the open chamber she'd just crossed, her thoughts returning to those lone sentinel statues. She couldn't see them, so she wouldn't have known if one or both of them were different in any way. What if they were pointing the way out of this room and she never even checked? That *was* what they did, wasn't it? They helped? They gave Albert clues and warnings that aided him in navigating the first temple?

But wouldn't the Keeper, in all his apparent wisdom, have known that she wouldn't be able to see those statues in this darkness?

Keeper of Lies…

"Shut up," she grumbled. Around her, those whispering voices mocked her again. Shushing and hushing and demanding silence in their haunted tones, but she ignored them. She was thinking. She didn't have time to put up with Not-Stella's nonsense. Much less waste time wrestling with the concept that the Keeper was something other than everyone claimed he was.

Ada knew everything about everyone. That was why Gina called her a goddess. "The Great Beholder," she said. Wouldn't *she* know if the Keeper had been lying about things?

It's different this time.

It was true that Ada said she could only read humans. She didn't know the mind of the Keeper. She said no one did. But she knew so many *other* things. Didn't she?

The child goddess knows what the Keeper allows her to know.

You're as bad as the real Stella when it comes to not shutting up, aren't you? she thought.

Rude, said a perfect mockery of Real Stella's voice inside her head. So real, in fact, that she wasn't sure it was the evil thing haunting her or her own memories telling her exactly how Stella would've responded.

Her fingers slipped off the stone and into a void.

A doorway! At last!

She withdrew her hand from the darkness and stepped back to shine her light over it. There was a sort of indention in the black fog, visible when she looked for it, but it would've been virtually impossible to notice just wandering around. That slight depression in the darkness was all there was. Within a few inches, the murk completely enveloped the space within the next passage. She'd be continuing completely blind. But what choice did she have? The longer she lingered in this room, the more likely she was to attract the squelchy shadow thing and its impossible, spiraling abyss of teeth.

With a quiet whimper, she braced herself and stepped into the black void.

Chapter 64

Albert stepped up to the wailing face framing the entrance to the sorrow room. He'd forgotten how intense these doorways were. It was only cold, hard stone, utterly lifeless, utterly *colorless*, even, and yet at the same time it was so incredibly *lifelike* that he couldn't help but expect it to move. It had eyebrows and eyelashes. It had the rough texture of a shadow of a beard. It had a mole. It even had a scar on the right side of its chin. It was difficult to process these dual perceptions of it at the same time, both stone and flesh, both dead and alive. It confused his mind and baffled his senses. And yet in the end it was only a doorway. The stretched, chapped lips of its howling mouth and perfectly imperfect teeth framed a shadowy opening leading into the space beyond.

But there was more to it than mere realism. The moment it came into view, he felt tears welling up in his eyes. Brandy, too. And poor Gina was able to feel it even *before* she saw it with her eyes. The emotional trauma of that dangerous room was bleeding into this one, sinking its teeth into them even without laying eyes on whatever heartbreaking statues waited within.

That had never happened before. Was it their heightened psychic awareness? Something to do with the dirty shaman's training? Or was this room just that much more potent than the ones they faced five years ago?

"No fucking way!" sobbed Brandy. "I can't! Not again! There has to be another way!"

He was inclined to agree. The last time they entered one of these, the terror contained inside became so palpable that he actually *experienced* a violent, bloody death at the hands of something depicted in those nightmare statues. It turned out to only be some kind of intense hallucination, but it was more than real enough to make him believe it was happening. And he clearly remembered every agonizing second of it to this day.

He picked up the flashlight he slid across the floor and shined it back the way they came, trying to remember how far back the last viable intersection was. (Certainly not the last one they passed. That was where Gina felt screaming and pain and lots of blood.)

"I don't know," said Gina, wiping at her streaming eyes. "Like I said, I can't shake this feeling that we're supposed to go this way."

Albert blinked back his own tears as he stared into the great, open mouth of the grief-stricken man, pondering it. "Remember what Shanzer said about the sex room? About us being there somehow unlocking the way forward?"

"That creep can burn in hell," Brandy snapped. She meant to sound angry, he knew, but her voice cracked, betraying her, revealing the emotions building up inside her. "I *hate* that fucking pervert."

"I know. But if he was telling the truth, then maybe that's what these rooms are for. Maybe they don't just induce the emotions in us when we enter them, but also utilize the emotional energy we give off to activate something."

(*That first night in those tunnels, when you let yourselves be overwhelmed by those emotions...when you acted on those emotions...you fed your own energy back into that chamber, which activated its programming to unlock the way forward.*)

Shanzer told them they were the first key that opened the way up that mountain. All because that insane sex room took over their minds and turned them into crazed, sexual beasts.

It still sounded ridiculous, and yet they'd seen for themselves that sexual emotions were capable of unlocking their psychic abilities. Why, then, couldn't you use it to activate an actual magical lock?

But Brandy wasn't having it. She was shaking her head and backing away from the saddest door either of them had ever seen. And he could hardly blame her. He really didn't want to go in there. It was already toying with his head, making his eyes well up. What was it going to do to him if he tried going inside?

He needed to think more clearly.

He took Brandy's hand and led her back the way they came, past the rows of miserable sentinels slowly uncurling themselves and rising to their feet. He left the warning chamber, making sure that Gina was following them, and didn't stop until he was at least twenty or thirty yards back down the passageway. Then he seated himself on the tunnel floor with his back propped against the wall.

For the first time in hours, he reached for the shaman's spellbook. He'd completely forgotten he had it until he started thinking about Shanzer's magic lessons again. And it wasn't like they'd had a lot of time to stop and read. But somehow he found himself thinking that it might be helpful.

It was only as he withdrew it from his pocket that he realized it had been in there the whole time he was in the river. It was going to be soaked. He hoped he hadn't ruined it.

But when he looked at it, it wasn't even slightly damp.

Magic, he thought, a giddy, almost childlike awe washing over him. He still couldn't wrap his head around the idea that it could be real.

He opened the book and shined his light onto it as he flipped through the pages. He frowned. Not only had most of the gibberish that was scribbled inside it vanished, but he was fairly sure there were a number of pages in it now that he'd never seen before. He stopped on one of these pages and skimmed over it.

Emotional magic has been utilized for ages as a deterrent for trespassing. It was much more effective in the past, when fear of the unknown, belief in the supernatural and rampant superstition were more prevalent in daily life, but it's still common to this day. Whenever people speak of an area in the woods or a particular mountain or even a house that the locals claim is cursed and refuse to enter. That is almost always some form of emotional magic at work. Fear is the most common for this purpose. But any emotion can be effective. To those who don't understand what is happening to them, there is nothing more terrifying than losing control of oneself for no clear reason.

He knew all too well that this was true. Shanzer had just perfectly described what it felt like on the other side of the sex room that first night. It was terrifying. It felt as if some alien presence had invaded their minds and taken over, forcing them to do those things.

He closed his eyes and rubbed at his temples for a moment. This was weird. Did he just *happen* to turn to this particular page? Or would a real magic book just know what he was looking for?

This was all so utterly bizarre.

He opened his eyes and read on.

There is no simple way to confront emotional magic used in this way. There is no counter spell, no defense. Sometimes, when the spell is based primarily on visual cues, it can be fooled simply by closing one's eyes and proceeding blind.

That was exactly how they beat the hate room last time. Brandy, with her poor eyesight, simply removed her glasses and continued on mostly blind. The darkness and the fact that every surface was the exact same gloomy color helped. Without being able to see it all clearly, she was able to walk right through it without incident. Wayne was later able to do the same thing, even though his eyes weren't quite as bad as hers.

But some emotions will always seep through, especially for those who happen to be particularly swayed by that specific emotion. A cowardly man will cave under fear more quickly than a brave one. And a man quick to anger will be swept away by that kind of energy far more quickly than a man who rarely loses his temper at all. But anyone can be taken by any kind of emotional energy. And one's tendency to show anger doesn't always reflect their natural proficiency for that kind of emotional magic.

Yes… No matter what they did, they couldn't pass through the sex room simply by blurring Brandy's vision. It always affected her. They'd had to give her glasses to Nicole and hinder *her* eyesight instead. They thought it was simply that she'd already seen what was in there, that she remembered what those blurry shapes looked like, and he supposed that probably had something to do with it. But Shanzer also told them that they were proficient with sexual energy, just like this book was describing.

And then there was the fear room. That had affected all of them, no matter how poor their eyesight… Because they were all afraid.

He glanced back toward the warning chamber of the sorrow room, recalling the way tears had sprung to all their eyes just standing there. Everyone knew fear. And everyone knew sadness. Did that mean there would be no passing through this room without being reduced to sobbing wails?

Brandy was crouched beside him, reading over his shoulder. Now she reached out and pointed at the bottom of the page. "Look at this."

Depending on the individual and the situation, it may not be possible to avoid being affected by a particular emotional energy, but for those who possess the proper understanding of emotional magic, it is always possible to override one emotion with another.

He went over the passage again, making sure he'd read it right.

"Overriding one emotion with another," pondered Brandy. "So, like, our sexual energy might be able to counter the sad energy in that room?"

"Looks like it." He looked up and met her eyes. "Time to take our clothes off."

278

Chapter 65

"What's that sound?" Keith stopped walking and listened. It was fairly distant yet, little more than a muffled buzzing. Was there some sort of insect hive up ahead? And yet it also sounded strangely mechanical.

But when he glanced back at Nicole, she'd gone suddenly pale. Her eyes were wide open, her lips pressed tightly together, her teeth clenched. She looked as if she'd seen a ghost.

Or…heard one?

"What is it?" he pressed.

"Hounds," she whispered.

He stared at her for a moment, letting this process. He knew that word. Andrea had used it while talking about her first journey into this kind of weird nightmare. Those were what they called things that lived down there. *Dangerous* things. Four-legged horrors covered in slashing scales, like some kind of murderous walking food processor from hell.

He shined his light forward again, suddenly very nervous. Was that really what that noise was? How far away were they? Did they need to retreat?

Nicole turned her cell phone's flashlight on again and knelt down, studying the floor around her.

He glanced back at her, confused. What was she doing? Did she drop something? She hadn't started wearing contacts since they broke up, had she? He wanted to ask her, but he also still didn't want to talk to her. She'd just snap at him anyway.

But he didn't have to ask. "Albert figured out last time that hounds left signs in the passages they roamed," she explained.

He frowned and looked down at his shoes. "What, like they shit all over the place?"

"Sometimes," she replied. "Sometimes they drop scales. Sometimes you find splintered bones. But mostly it's their claws. They leave scratches." She stood up, her light still fixed on the floor. "No scratches, no worries."

He shined his own light down at the floor, too. He didn't see any scratches either. The stone was flawless. Perfectly flat and smooth and pristine, just like every other surface he'd seen since arriving here.

"They can't jump or climb or swim," she explained.

He nodded, remembering the offset passage they had to climb up to reach this area and that flooded area he fell into when he was separated from Olivia and Wayne. "So they'd be easy to keep corralled in a place like this," he deduced. He turned and continued onward. That was good information to have. Now he sort of hoped he was going to get to see one of them.

"They're aggressive as fuck," she warned him. "One of them chewed up Wayne's leg last time. He still has the scars. And he and Albert both watched a pack of them turn another monster into puree. They said it only took a few seconds."

Well *that* was a scary mental image. Maybe he *didn't* want to get close enough to see one in action. But it shouldn't be a problem if they were in separate areas of the labyrinth. Nicole wasn't his favorite person these days by any stretch of imagination, but he found that he didn't distrust her, exactly. If she said the things couldn't reach them, then he believed her.

He continued forward, his eyes peeled, following the strange sound. Even armed with the knowledge that those things couldn't get to them, he was still a little surprised to find himself more curious than frightened. After his encounter with that stubborn thing out in the forest, he wouldn't have thought he'd ever feel any desire to glimpse another monster.

"They have their own separate passages," said Nicole, "but there were plenty of times in that first temple where ours and theirs crossed."

"So it may not be possible to avoid them completely," he surmised.

"Right."

He nodded. "I'd like to say at least we can hear them coming, but I'm guessing they might not always be making that sound."

"Exactly. And they're fast. Also, they're apparently blind and deaf, but their sense of smell is fine. If we do find ourselves on the same level with them, we won't be able to run or hide. We have to stay out of reach."

"Sounds fun," he grumbled.

The noise was getting louder. They were getting closer to the source.

Two entirely separate areas, one filled with deadly creatures, the other safe for travelers, but intersecting. That was an entirely new level of difficulty. Depending on exactly where these "hounds" happened to be, it could randomly change which paths were accessible. He couldn't decide if that was clever or just plain sadistic.

But at least if they found their path blocked, they could always go back the way they came.

Well…maybe not *always*. Was it possible to find themselves trapped between monster-infested crossroads? That wasn't a pleasant thought.

He grimaced as he became aware of a foul odor on the air. It wasn't the kind of stink he'd ever encountered on a farm or at the zoo. It reeked like rotten flesh, swamp mud and sewage.

Nicole detected it, too. She groaned. "I forgot about the smell…"

Up ahead, the passage opened up. The walls and ceiling ended, but the floor continued on, much like back in that abyss where they ditched Hotdog Corpse. But when he reached the end of the passage and shined his light down, he saw that they were only about six feet above the ground. The path forward wasn't so much a bridge as a wall, separating the space and allowing them to walk safely out of reach.

Hopefully, anyway…

The floor down there appeared to be bare earth at first, but when he looked closer, he realized that it was the same stone he was standing on. It was still mostly intact near the walls, though scarred with deep scratches and gouges, sort of like how an old hardwood floor would be less scuffed and scratched along the baseboards and in the corners. The farther out into the room it went, the more the stone was worn and chewed, until it appeared to be little more than gravel and sand.

He turned and shined his light down on the other side, revealing the same. Then he cast it out into the greater darkness, scanning the space. The stench was almost overpowering. And the noise was quite loud now, like walking into a room with several power tools whirring away. From here, he could distinctly hear the sources of the noise moving around out there. But he still didn't see one.

What he *did* see, however, were bones. Lots of them. Dingy and yellowish, but still far brighter than the dark gray stone surrounding them. They were too broken and chewed to identify properly. And there were hundreds of thin little…flakes? Reddish-brown in color, sort of translucent, rectangular in shape. They looked almost plastic. Were those the scales Nicole mentioned? They really did look like razor blades, now that he was looking at one.

Nicole said something, but too softly for him to hear. He glanced back at her, an eyebrow raised. "What?"

"I said I fucking hate those things."

"Yeah… I don't think I'm gonna be a big fan of Satan's Petting Zoo, either." He started forward, making his way along the path. It was just as wide as it was back in the passage, but somehow it suddenly felt far too narrow. He couldn't help but imagine himself stumbling and falling down into the deathtrap below.

Then he caught sight of something. It was little more than a reddish-brown flash of movement in the dark, far too quick for him to see clearly, but more than startling enough to stop him in his tracks.

Nicole gave him an impatient nudge. "Move it," she shouted over the noise. "I'd rather not still be in here when those fucking things catch our scent."

As much as he wanted to tell her to stuff a sock in it, he really couldn't argue that logic. He continued forward, his light sliding back and forth between the two halves of the bone-littered chamber.

There was something going on somewhere ahead of them and to the right. Much of the noise was concentrated there. And as he drew closer, he found that he could make out movement just out of sight. The ground there was stained darker than the surrounding area. Blood?

He almost turned and went back the other way, convinced that his light was about to reveal someone Nicole knew being devoured by a pack of hounds. It was the only thing that made any sense at first. He hadn't seen any other kind of prey down here. But then he reminded himself that he also hadn't seen any hounds before now. If there was a sizeable pack of carnivores down here, then it only stood to reason that there must be prey species as well. Otherwise, these things would've starved off long before he showed up.

And indeed, he'd barely processed this thought when a bloody chunk of something furry bounced into view, accompanied by a sudden increase in noise from that area. A second later, two hounds appeared, chasing it, snarling and snapping at each other. He couldn't quite wrap his head around the sight of them. Those were like no breed of dog he'd ever seen. Strangely wide for their height, with short, stout legs, their flesh a bizarre, rippling blur of motion. His light illuminated the bright red gleam of blood spraying from a wide, toothy muzzle. The bigger of the two slammed itself against the other with a vicious roar and a violent spray of blood and broken scales, then snatched up the bloody prize and darted back into the darkness again with the smaller one right on its heels.

Did those things have *two tails*?

What manner of beast were they? They looked like something from an alien planet. (Which, he supposed, was exactly what they were…)

Shaken by what he'd seen, he reached back, offering Nicole his hand. When she didn't take it, he glanced over his shoulder and caught the annoyed look on her face. "Sorry," he said, withdrawing his hand. "Force of habit."

He continued forward, picking up his pace.

A hound darted into view on the left. He had enough time to take in the extra-wide back and the extra-short legs. And it did, indeed, seem to have two tails. But they seemed to jut out from each side of its hind-quarters, parallel to each other, rather than branching out from the middle.

The thing did a hard, gravel throwing turn and disappeared from sight somewhere below them. A second later, it was speeding out of sight on the other side, those stiff, slashing tails trailing after it. The two halves of the room were connected, he realized. There were openings in the wall beneath their feet, allowing the creatures to pass back and forth. That meant that those monstrosities could, at any given moment, be just beneath their feet. Suddenly, it was entirely too easy to imagine some kind of trapdoor waiting to drop unsuspecting travelers down into those violent, waiting jaws. It wouldn't be all that different from whatever mechanism dropped him into that underground lake, after all.

He was still processing this frightful thought when another hound burst into view and charged the wall directly below where they were standing. He could hear it down there, snarling, its claws and scales clashing against the stone. It sounded like a lawnmower blade grinding against a concrete curb.

Nicole let out a startled cry and cringed.

Keith decided that was his cue to pick up his pace and get them both out of this chamber before one of these things spontaneously learned how to fly. (Because that was just the kind of luck he was having.) He continued forward, focusing on the path at his feet, wary of anything that didn't look quite right, just in case.

Nothing would surprise him at this point.

Or so he thought. But as he hurried on, he was *very much* surprised by the feel of Nicole grabbing his hand and holding on.

He glanced at her, but she was making a point of not looking back at him, so he took the hint and just pressed on.

Chapter 66

"You're not gushing blood," Olivia assured him. "It's like you said about them being too small to cause much damage. But I can't count how many times they cut you! It looks awful. Does it hurt?"

"Not too bad," Wayne lied. The truth was that his entire back was burning. That was where he'd taken the brunt of that undead swarm while trying to shield her. But he wasn't going to give her any more reasons to worry about him. She had enough to deal with already. That was no small ordeal she just went through back there. And it wasn't as if she came away unscathed. She, too, was covered in cuts and nicks from head to toe. "Are *you* going to be okay?" he asked instead.

"I'm fine," she insisted for the fourth or fifth time now. "Really. Thanks to you."

"I thought I was on the naughty list."

"You are." She was still prodding at his back, fussing over the worst of the cuts. "That was *not* what I meant when I said I trusted you."

"Sorry."

"I forgive you. You saw a way out for us and you took it. It's not your fault I have a thing about heights."

"On the plus, side, maybe it'll help. Facing your fears, you know?"

"No, I'm pretty sure I'm more terrified of heights than ever now."

"Yeah, I can see that."

"*And* water."

"My bad."

She gave him a tired huff of a laugh, then lowered his shirt and very gently laid her cheek against his tender shoulder.

He was relieved. He really wasn't sure for a while there if she'd be willing to forgive him for putting her through that, regardless of the reason. It must have been beyond terrifying to be wholly enveloped in one of your worst fears.

That she might someday learn to resent him was *his* greatest fear, after all…

He sat there in silence, feeling her breath on his shoulder, so hot against his burning skin, but also so comforting. He kept his gaze fixed on the darkness in front of him, his eyes peeled for danger.

They'd landed in some kind of drainage area that was considerably different from the clean, stone passages they'd been exploring. There was dirt and mud covering the ground here, some of it knee deep as they struggled through it in search of dry land. It was foul and grimy and reeked of decay, as if they'd landed in some kind of festering marsh. But they weren't outside. That wasn't the empty sky of the Wood hanging above them. It was barely visible in the reach of his measly flashlight, but he could clearly make out more of that smooth stone above them. There seemed to be another floor up there. Perhaps they were *under* the labyrinth. Was this the very bottom? Some kind of basement level, perhaps? Or maybe "dungeon" would be a better word. Was this where all the unwanted things washed away to?

When he first landed here, he spotted the flashlights. They landed next to each other, still glowing, about eight feet down in the murky water and was able to swim down to retrieve them without any difficulty. There wasn't any real current to indicate a river, but there had to be some mechanism for carrying water out as quickly as it was entering. Thousands of gallons were rushing into this room every second through the channel that deposited them here, but the water level remained constant.

After trudging through the mud and muck for a few minutes, they were able to find a slope leading up to a sort of natural stone pathway. It was there that they encountered the first of the walls enclosing this enormous space. It was all the same kind of stone that comprised every surface of the labyrinth up above, but for some reason it was a strange mix of those smooth, perfectly crafted surfaces and raw, natural-looking cavern walls.

They found a small, relatively secluded area tucked out of sight behind a large stone outcropping to stop and gather themselves, but he didn't trust to linger in one place too long. Something about this area was unsettling to him. It was so very different from the rest of the temple. And he didn't understand why. Was this somewhere they were never supposed to see?

And of course there was the other pressing issue weighing on their minds: "Why is he here?" asked Olivia.

He shook his head. He didn't have that answer. Back in Gutler's Weep, the scarecrow man claimed he was looking for something they had. The thorn. One of the Three Whispers, keys to the otherwise unreachable City Beyond Memory. But the thorn was gone. Vanished when they used it to open the gate. He couldn't have it now if they *wanted* to give it to him. But maybe he already got what he wanted. Somehow, he'd sneaked through the impassible wall. And now he was in here with them, stalking them through these dark passageways. Maybe the creepy freak was free to focus on his morbid fascination with him and his curious immunity to being dead.

"He's going to keep looking for us, isn't he?"

"Probably," he replied. And he was more dangerous than ever. A dead bear was nothing compared to the toys he could find here.

And yet, the monster didn't seem to have sent any of his new playthings into the swirling maelstrom at the bottom of that chamber to see where they went. If he had, Wayne was fairly sure they'd still be running for their lives. Instead, this place was eerily quiet. Nothing seemed to be moving down here at all.

But why? It was nagging at him. It just didn't seem like it should be this easy.

Maybe the scarecrow man thought they were dead, but somehow he doubted it. And it wasn't as if those taxidermy nightmares had to worry about drowning, so why didn't he just toss his dead toys in after them? He must have known they'd all end up in the same place.

Was he playing with them? Was this all a game to a monster like him?

With a pained grunt, he rose to his feet. "We can't stay here. Let's keep moving."

Olivia didn't want to, he knew. She wanted to stay here as long as possible, hidden away from any more scary stuff. But she didn't argue with him. She didn't say a word. She simply stood up and took hold of his arm.

Again, he was struck by the queerness of this area, how it was so unlike those clean, perfect passageways above. Nor was it anything like the sentinels' road that brought them here. There was no pathway to follow. The ground was rough and rocky, uneven. And as they walked, the raw stone beneath their feet gradually gave way to coarse, black earth, with no indication of which direction they should be going.

And then, to his surprise, he found *plants*.

There were strange, pale-gray weeds growing all over the place, as well as bright-red, stiff, stalk-like things that he was pretty sure were some kind of fungus.

Were these darkness-dwelling plants native to whatever ancient world the city was built in? Or were they somehow bred solely to thrive here in this sunless space?

He swept his light back and forth in front of him as he walked, his eyes peeled, and found what looked like a long, black root creeping along the ground with strange, stalk-like leaves growing out of it, the top of each one a curious, pale-blue fan of delicate, feather-like fronds.

"This is freaky…" whispered Olivia.

"Like an alien planet or something," he agreed. The more he saw, the stranger it became. There were huge, gray leaves the size of ship sails hanging down from the ceiling. And three-foot-diameter fungus-like formations made up of fine, white strands that sort of resembled giant spiderwebs lying flat on the ground.

It was fascinating to see, like walking through some giant terrarium filled with amazing, never-before-seen specimens. But at the same time, he found it terrifying. What were these things? And were they dangerous? Had they found themselves surrounded by toxic plants that could cause crippling pain with a single careless touch? Or something that could, at the slightest disturbance, pump deadly spores into the air that would rapidly devour them from the inside out?

It sounded like the paranoid thoughts of someone who'd watched far too many science-fiction horror movies, but once you'd seen a night tree's branches twisting and squirming and grasping at your skin like some kind of Lovecraftian abomination, one simply learned to be cautious around unfamiliar plants in unfamiliar worlds.

And then there was the fact that the last new plant species he came across literally killed him. Twice.

Olivia felt it, too, he could tell. She was clinging to his arm again, digging in with those pretty nails.

He swung his light to the left and saw something crooked and prickly jutting up from the earth like a diseased and deformed cactus. It was so very easy to imagine that each of those spines were loaded with some horrific toxin that could melt their flesh all the way to the bone.

Olivia swung her light the other way, anxious, and then froze as something appeared in the beam.

He felt those nails dig into him a little tighter and joined his light to hers, revealing a ravaged skeleton covered in slimy looking clumps of a strange, red fungus.

Chapter 67

Corey had been walking for a while now, following that mysterious energy that flowed through these strange passageways.

He kept thinking about the sentinels. Who were they? *What* were they? And how was it possible for them to build something like this? He could grasp the concept of an alien universe's physics being incomprehensible and, as such, appearing to work like magic. What was that old Arthur C. Clarke quote? "Any sufficiently advanced technology is indistinguishable from magic," was it? The same could certainly be true of any technology that was fundamentally *different* from one's own. If someone had no idea what electricity was or how it worked, then everything from a cell phone to a toaster would seem magical. This place was like that. It only *appeared* mystical and mysterious because he didn't have the ability to comprehend many of its basic elements. But none of that explained this ever-growing certainty that these particular passageways had been sitting here since a time unimaginable, waiting specifically for *him* to arrive.

Never mind bringing him here from his apartment in Tunipet. How many *billions* of tiny details must have been required to come together over the course of an untold number of *universal lifetimes* to ensure that he would even be *born*?

The very thought made his head hurt.

He needed something else to think about for a while.

Again, he wondered where Violet was and what she might be experiencing in her own mysterious passages, but then he recalled what Albert and Brandy said about two of them not surviving this journey and decided that wasn't a better train of thought after all.

Twelve of them to make the journey...

There was Gina and her two friends. Andrea, the talkative redhead with all the piercings. And Nicole, the really attractive brunette that bloodied his nose. There was Albert and Brandy who made the trip here in the carriage with them. Wayne and Olivia and Keith, with whom he entered the gate. He was worried about them all.

Not so much that Austin guy. He wasn't very friendly. But the rest of them had all seemed like nice people.

That was eleven of them. And he recalled Olivia asking if he'd seen someone named Everett. She seemed worried about him, so he was sure he wasn't like that Austin guy, either. He didn't want to think about anything happening to *any* of them.

Twelve arrived, but only ten would return...

He scowled into the darkness. He didn't like those odds. Not one bit. But for all he knew, Albert and Brandy were wrong about that. Maybe they were lied to. Or maybe they misunderstood the message somehow.

Either way, he wouldn't accept it if he could help it.

Ahead of him, the flow of energy abruptly turned and vanished into the wall.

This was it. He was back at the point that caught his attention earlier. And he could already tell this one was different. It looked the same. Anyone else walking through here wouldn't know there was anything special about this one little section of wall. But he could sense it. Something right in front of his face when he stopped. So subtle. So perfectly blended into the stone that a part of his brain was still trying to convince him he was imagining it.

It was strangely...*familiar*...

He frowned at it, confused. Where had he seen something like this before?

It's like a machine, he thought for some reason. *All connected together.*

It's a bunch of rocks, he heard Violet respond in a voice that felt strangely far away.

"It's not," he said aloud.

A conversation from a long time ago... He remembered a large, dark space...filled with stones...

Was it a dream he had once? Because he couldn't recall having a conversation like that with Violet.

How strange.

He pushed the misplaced memory aside and then reached out and ran his fingertips across the cool, smooth surface. The nerve endings in his skin told him there was nothing there. Not a crack. Not a crease. Not a bump. Nothing. His eyes told him the same. It was stone for as far as his light could reach, with not a single shadow out of place. But something inside him knew better.

This was where he was supposed to be.

It was like that other place. He was supposed to reach *into* the stone, as if sliding his fingers into the very spaces between the molecules, as if such a thing were possible. It wasn't something he knew how to do, exactly. It was only something that he did.

Without any kind of true understanding, he dipped his hand into the stone and watched it rearrange itself for him.

This would be different, he realized as he reached farther into the mysterious depths of the stone, although he didn't entirely know what that meant. Different how?

He supposed all that was left was to find out.

He stepped forward, sliding his body easily through an opening that shouldn't have been wide enough to allow him to pass. He could feel the very atmosphere change around him. This was the part where he was supposed to feel fear, he was sure. But all he felt was exhilaration.

What would he discover next?

Chapter 68

"We should go back." Something wasn't right about this. Violet could feel it.

"Jussamint," grunted Corey around a great mouthful of chips.

"No, not in 'just a minute.' *Now.*"

"Jussamint," he said again.

"Even if we go down there, we won't be able to see anything," she reasoned. "It's too dark." Already, what little light reached the back of the cave had faded until she could barely see his shadow in front of her. They didn't have a flashlight. Why would they? It was a bright, sunny day. They had no way of knowing they'd end up anywhere dark and spooky. But here they were. And for some reason, Corey was still trudging downward, deeper and deeper into the earth, following a mysterious stone staircase that shouldn't even be here. She couldn't think of a single explanation for there to be a perfectly formed set of steps leading down from the back of a small cave in the middle of her parents' vacation property.

"Walls're smooth," he observed. He was dragging his fingers along one of them to steady himself in the dark. She reached out and did the same. It definitely wasn't a natural cave wall. It didn't even feel like concrete. The texture was too smooth. It was perfectly flat and seamless, like a single block of granite.

Was there some kind of *building* hidden down here?

"There's a light," said Corey.

"What? *Where?*" She grabbed his shirt, tugging him to a stop, then stood up on her toes and peered over his shoulder. "Let me see."

There was, indeed, a light. A very faint one, softly illuminating the floor at the very bottom of the steps. Was someone there? The mysterious figure they glimpsed in the woods? Her stomach tightened into a warm knot at the thought. Who *was* that in the woods? And why were they here? Her imagination was running away with her. Maybe it was criminals trying to get at her father's wealth by tunneling under the house.

Except…that didn't make any sense. They were a long ways from the house. That was a *lot* of digging. And why go to the trouble of building a staircase? Plus, they would've already had to go through the fence to get this far, which made being sneaky kind of pointless. And then there was the fact that this was her father's vacation property. He didn't keep any valuables here.

Unless they were after a different kind of valuable... Something like two naughty, adventurous kids wandering around unsupervised, just begging to be kidnapped for a king's ransom?

That was a much scarier thought. If that was what was going on, they'd likely already fallen into the trap. But was that a realistic possibility? Did that actually happen in real life? Or was that just another Hollywood action trope?

But her mind wouldn't be satisfied until she was thoroughly terrified, because she began thinking of all sorts of horrible scenarios. A murderous satanic cult that would happily make sacrifices of them. A deranged serial killer living alone in the darkness, his sanity dwindling with each passing, sunless day. Or maybe they'd find themselves descending into the subterranean lair of a foul witch with a real-life taste for children's flesh.

She should probably stop staying up late, eating sweets and watching all those scary movies Corey was so fond of.

Meanwhile, Corey continued descending the steps. He was almost at the bottom.

"Be careful," she whispered.

The light was coming from somewhere beyond the far end of a narrow passage. But as soon as they reached the bottom, the light seemed to drift deeper into the darkness.

"Flashlight," he whispered. "Or lantern." He stepped onto the tunnel floor and tipped his round head to one side, thoughtful. "Candle, maybe?"

"Who uses candles these days?" she whispered back at him.

He shrugged. "Candle'd be cooler than a flashlight. Mysterious-like."

"I don't think anyone creeping around in a place like this would care anything about being *mysterious*."

He ignored her and set off after the receding glow.

"Careful!" she hissed. "They'll see you!"

"Can't lose the light," he reasoned.

She looked back the way they came. She could see no sign of the sunlight from above. If they lost the cagey light bearer, they'd be stranded in this darkness. But at least the way back wasn't all that complicated from here. That could change if they kept pushing forward so carelessly. They had no idea how big this place might be.

But Corey was plowing on, armed with nothing but his noisy bag of snacks. And she knew him well enough to be certain that he wouldn't turn back. This was like a game to him. He couldn't help himself.

And yet, was she really trying that hard to make him stop? They'd known each other all their lives, after all. He was practically her big brother. And a *good* big brother at that. If she really wanted him to turn around, all she'd have to do was start crying. That had never failed to work on him as far back as she could remember.

The truth was that she wanted to know why this was here, too. It wasn't natural. This tunnel wasn't wet and dank and wormy. It felt like marble but was a uniform sort of dark gray color.

At the end of the tunnel was a round room, about twenty feet across, with several other tunnels leading away from it in different directions. The light was just fading from view in one of them, leading the way forward.

Corey picked up his pace. Violet followed. The deeper into this darkness they ventured, the more wrong this all felt to her, and yet there was a certain exhilaration to it all that she found thrilling. Her heart was pounding. She wanted to know where the light was coming from. She wanted to know why these stone passageways existed. She wanted to know who the mysterious, towering figure could have been.

They crossed the length of the passage and into the next chamber. This one was much bigger than the last. It stretched into the darkness before them, a great, black abyss that could have gone on forever for all she could see of it. The only things visible were several concentric circles of large, rectangular stone blocks standing in the space ahead of them.

The light was coming from somewhere in the middle of it.

This time, it didn't retreat. It didn't appear to be moving at all. Whoever was holding it had stopped. And they were right there, inside that weird arrangement of blocks.

Corey set off into the great, open space before she could grab the tail of his shirt and pull him back. "No!" she whispered after him, useless as it was. He probably couldn't hear her and if he did, when did he ever really listen to her?

But what was he thinking? They were going to get caught!

She hurried after him again. Inside, she was screaming, but she couldn't bear the thought of being left alone in the darkness. That would be entirely too scary!

He stopped at the nearest of the stone blocks and peered around it, but by the time she caught up with him, he was already moving farther into the stones.

She grabbed his shirt and yanked at it. But there was no stopping. He was at the innermost circle now, peering around the last corner.

At the very center of the circle was a single slab of stone. It looked just like the others, but smaller, and lying on its side. It was about the size of her parents' dining room table but only half as high.

The lantern was just sitting there on top of it. It was an ordinary, modern propane model, no different than the ones in her dad's camping gear.

"Where'd they go?" she whispered. A hot dread was rapidly filling her belly. Was this a trap? She turned and looked behind her, expecting to find someone creeping up on them in the shadows of the larger stones.

She knew this was a bad idea! They were in so much trouble right now!

And that slab of stone… Was it only her imagination, or did it look like some kind of altar? Like the sort of place where they sacrificed virgins in creepy movies. The thought sent a hard shudder rushing through her small body.

But Corey didn't seem fazed in the least. He was still moving forward. He walked right up to the mysterious slab, his hand reaching noisily back into his chip bag as if he had every right to be here.

"What're you doing?" she hissed, still clinging to his shirt, still searching every shadow for the owner of the mystery lantern.

But he wasn't listening to her. He turned and scanned the stones surrounding them and stuffed another handful of chips into his mouth.

"Are you *trying* to get us caught?"

"S'fine," he said with his mouth full.

"No it's not!"

"Is," he insisted. "Safe here."

"How do you know that?"

"I remember this place."

"What?" She turned and looked around again. He'd been here before? "When?" she asked. "Where?" And *how*? She was quite sure *she'd* never seen this place in her life and they did practically everything together.

"Dunno. But I remember it. It's a safe place."

She squinted up at him, confused. "How do you know it's safe if you can't even remember when or where you know it from?"

"Just do." He never looked at her. His gaze was sliding from one upright stone to the next, all the way around them, studying each one.

"Who was carrying the lantern, then?" she pushed.

"Dunno."

"Where'd they go?"

"Dunno."

"Why is this here?"

"Dunno," he replied again. He walked away from the slab, out into the space between the two innermost rings of stones, his wondering eyes still sliding from one to the next. She tried holding onto his shirt, but he was too big and too strong and she was too small. Like always when she clung to him like that for any reason, her only choices were to let him go or keep up. And she didn't dare let go. Not yet.

"What *do* you know?"

He stopped and turned his attention fully onto the stone in front of him. "I know I can do this." As she stood watching him, he reached up and placed his hand onto the smooth surface of the stone. Then, incredibly, his fingers seemed to dig *into* the stone, as if it weren't stone at all, but merely fine sand.

"How'd you do that?" she breathed.

"Dunno."

She scrunched up her face and glared at him. She was getting *really* tired of that answer. He obviously knew *something*. How else could he do that with his fingers?

He withdrew his hand, leaving no proof on the surface of what he'd just done. It returned to the same flat, featureless state it was in when he first walked up to it. He stared at it for a second, his pudgy face seeming to ponder the impossibleness of it all, and then he simply turned his attention to the next stone and walked away.

This time, she let go of his shirt. She reached up to try putting her own hand in the stone but found that she couldn't. And what did she expect, really? It was only stone. Hard and cool and unyielding. "How'd you *do* that?" she wondered again.

At the next stone, he reached up and did it again. Was there a trick to it? She watched him and tried to mirror his movements, but it just wasn't possible to dip her fingers *into* the surface of a big rock.

Was he just too dumb to know he couldn't do it? Seriously, what was up with him? He was always so *weird*.

She knew, of course, that he was anything *but* dumb. And that weirdness was her favorite thing about him. But this was *really* weird. And kind of frustrating. This wasn't some little oddity he noticed in the woods and started spouting wild theories about. He was literally defying the laws of physics down here! She wanted to know how he was doing it!

"It's like a machine," he said as he rummaged around in the mysterious stone's insides. "All connected together."

"It's a bunch of rocks," she informed him.

"It's not."

She started to tell him that he didn't know anything. How could he? He was no expert on mysterious stones in creepy underground rooms. But before she could open her mouth, she was startled by a voice that seemed to be coming from the center of the circles.

She turned and peered around the stone, but there was no one there. "Who said that?" she whispered.

"Said what?"

She looked back at him, bewildered. He was still focused on the stone he was rummaging around in, completely unfazed by any voice. But how could he not have heard it? She couldn't understand what the voice said, but it was definitely real. It made her heart skip a beat and sent all the hair on her arms standing on end.

Was it the voice of the mysterious lantern bearer? Or could she really have just imagined it?

Cautiously, she stepped around the stone and scanned the area. Everything was just as it was a moment ago. Or, at least, the *lantern* hadn't moved...which was pretty well everything.

The time draws near...

She shrank back behind the stone, startled. That was strange. Those words just now came to her as if spoken, but she didn't think she heard them with her ears. She was fairly sure she thought them herself. Except, she couldn't figure out *why* she'd think such a thing. She didn't even understand it. The time for *what*? What did it mean?

For some reason, she found her gaze drawn to the slab on which the lantern was sitting.

When the stranger falls from the sky, your journey will begin...

She reached up and rubbed at her head. Where was this voice coming from? Was it even speaking English? She could understand what it was saying, but the words sounded funny, like she'd never heard them before.

Seek your future and we will meet again in the dreamy in-between...

Meet again? Meet *who* again? Who was speaking to her? This didn't make any sense. Was she going crazy?

She turned to ask if Corey still wasn't hearing this, but he was gone. His empty bag of chips was lying on the floor where he was just standing. Had he moved around the stones? Or was she suddenly alone in this creepy place with this voice that made no sense and spoke in words she shouldn't understand?

Our circle will soon be closed...

Again, she turned her attention to the slab at the center of the upright stones. The voice was definitely inside her head. It had no origin. It came from no direction. And yet she found herself convinced that it was coming from there. From *inside the stone.*

It wasn't just a random slab, she somehow realized. And it wasn't an altar, either.

It was a *tomb.*

The owner of this mysterious voice was inside, sealed away in a darkness that hadn't changed in a nightmarishly long amount of time.

On the other side of eternity...in the lonely darkness...find me...

Violet let out a great gasp and sat up.

The light was blinding. She covered her face, confused. Where was she? Why was she on the ground?

"That was weird," said Corey.

She blinked through the gap between her hands. He was lying on the forest floor beside her, squinting up through the summer branches swaying in the warm breeze overhead.

"What happened?" she asked. When did they leave the cave?

"It was a machine," he said. "An old one. Made of stuff that don't exist no more."

"What?" She turned and looked around. She could see the bluffs they'd followed to reach the cave, the ones that funneled them toward the opening. Except when she looked at where the bluffs met, there was no cave there. "How did...?"

"Knew how to work it," said Corey. "Could do all sortsa things."

Where did the cave go? She rose to her feet and felt a wave of vertigo wash over her, nearly toppling her over. "Whoa..."

Corey rolled over and pushed himself up onto his hands and knees. "Queasy," he observed.

She closed her eyes tightly. (*Our circle will soon be closed...*) Those words... She felt so confused. What was happening?

"Machines..." muttered Corey.

She opened her eyes and looked back at the place where the bluffs met. Was...something supposed to be there? Wasn't she just looking for something? Everything felt so weird. What was wrong with her?

Corey frowned. "What was I sayin'?"

"What?"

He looked up at her, frowning. "Huh?"

The two of them stared at each other, confused. They were playing in the woods... She'd climbed a tree... Corey was talking about vampires, of all things...

Why did it feel like she'd forgotten something?

(On the other side of eternity...in the lonely darkness...)

She squeezed her eyes shut. Why'd she feel so strange?

(...find me...)

Corey stood up and brushed the leaves out of his hair. "Hungry," he said.

"How're you hungry? Didn't you just eat a whole bag of chips?"

"Just am," he said again, although he looked down at his empty hand for a moment, frowning.

She stood there staring at him. What were they doing before this? It felt like they were inside somewhere. Her eyes even seemed to still be adjusting to the sunlight. But that didn't make any sense. She'd been outside all day.

"Hungry..." Corey said again, nodding.

"Me too," she decided, dismissing the weird feeling. That was probably it, after all. They'd been out here a while. They probably missed lunch. They should go back and eat, maybe cool off in the air conditioning for a while.

Chapter 69

Andrea slowly made her way through the black passageway, her arms out to her sides, her fingers sliding along the smooth walls, toeing the stone floor with each step for hidden stairs, tripping hazards or drop-offs. She was still clutching the flashlight in her left hand and it was still on, but it revealed nothing through the murk. The darkness was absolute. She might as well have been struck blind.

Had she taken a wrong turn somewhere? This didn't feel right. Shouldn't Erin have warned her if the murk was so thick that she couldn't see her flashlight in front of her face? Maybe she'd messed up.

Something grabbed her wrist, wrenching a terrified scream from her.

"So afraid..." mocked the voices.

"...scared...alone..."

"...won't make it far..."

"...too weak..."

"Oh, shut up!" she growled at them. She yanked at the thing gripping her wrist, but it was unyielding. God, she hated these things! That cold, clammy feeling that made her think of dead things was almost unbearable, but she couldn't break away from it.

And yet, they hadn't harmed her so far. They simply grabbed hold of her and wouldn't let go. Until they eventually just...*did* let go. Because she'd never really done anything to free herself. They just held on for a little bit, no matter what she did, and then let go.

She took a calming breath, her other hand gripped so tightly around her flashlight that her fingers ached.

"Poor child..." taunted the voices.

"...never escape..."

"...cry in the darkness forever..."

She needed to remain calm.

What were these things, anyway? The rest of this eerie, unnatural darkness didn't feel like anything. It was like it didn't even exist. But these things were solid enough to seize her and hold her. They possessed actual texture. They were gross and fleshy. Were they really just concentrated murk that was so dense it became tangible? Or was it something completely different from the rest of this black stuff?

It still felt kind of like a human hand. Except that the fingers were far too long, she thought, now that she was taking the time to notice. And she couldn't really feel a palm, either. They were just fingers…wrapped all the way around her wrist…without any noticeable joints… Were they fingers at all? It felt more like when something gross brushed past her foot when her dad used to take her swimming at the lake. (She'd always hated that feeling!)

Her entirely unhelpful imagination gave her an image of slimy tentacles wrapped around her wrist, sending a queasy, skin-crawling sensation all the way through her body.

Then, just as suddenly as it had grabbed her, the creepy not-hand thing let her go.

Exactly like those other times.

What was the point? Why did it grab her just to let go again? Was it only acting on some kind of primitive reflex? Did these things simply grasp blindly at anything that brushed too close to them?

"The difference between body and spirit," whispered Erin. "The spirit feels things the body can't. And when the body doesn't understand, it lies."

"*I* don't understand *anything*," she grumbled.

That's why you'll never save them, the counterfeit Stella taunted.

She was actually kind of glad this thing was some kind of superpowerful entity that was toying with her mind. It was a relief knowing that it wasn't some part of her own brain saying these things. She would've hated to think that any part of her was capable of being such a bitch.

Sticks and stones, the impostor chuckled inside her head.

She crept forward, circling around the area where the groping thing in the dark was, and then kept moving.

It seemed like there were more of these things back in the first of these murky passageways, when she could still see the floor through the strands of impossible darkness. She had to make an effort to avoid them all. Were there less of them in the deeper murk? Or was it that most of them simply didn't bother grabbing her?

She had so many questions. She understood so very little. And she didn't even know who to trust to tell her the truth.

Not me, teased the impostor. *I'm batshit crazy*.

Andrea ignored her. She needed to stay focused on where she was going, where she was placing her feet, not on the voices in her head. As long as she couldn't see, she couldn't be sure she wasn't walking straight toward a deadly drop-off. But at the same time, she needed something to keep her from freaking out. Thinking about how all this weirdness worked helped keep her fear in check.

Erin—if that was really her a moment ago—said something about spirit and body... It sort of made sense, she thought. Gina and Ada both told her she possessed the ability to interact with things from the spirit world and Erin told her that there were things the living couldn't comprehend about the dead. Was that what she meant about the body lying when it didn't understand things? When these murk things touched her, did her brain simply make something up to explain what none of her physical senses could detect?

Her thoughts turned to Albert. He was always thinking about the first temple, about the things they saw down there, about all the unanswered questions. The other girls didn't like to talk about it. That place scared them. Brandy, in particular, discouraged it. And so he rarely brought it up. But occasionally Wayne would discuss it with him. And unlike the others, she always listened in. Because the truth was that she was like Albert. She wanted to know what that place was. She wanted to know how it worked. She wanted to understand all the crazy things that went on down there five years ago. Like him, she'd hoped to someday have all those answers. But she never came out and said so. Partly because she didn't want to be the only girl who wanted to know. But more so because she never wanted to actually go back.

The Temple of the Blind was a fascinating place full of incredible wonder and mystery, but it was also terrifying beyond words. Time and time again, she found herself in some kind of peril, whether it was racing down the side of a collapsing tower or struggling to free herself from a man-eating tree or being shoved off a cliff to what she had no way of knowing wasn't certain doom or saying goodbye to a dying friend or being stranded all alone in a black tunnel filled with speeding spirits and knowing everyone's life was in her utterly unremarkable hands.

Better pay attention, whispered the impostor.

"What?" she asked aloud, distracted. But it was too late. Lost in thought, she forgot to be careful where she was stepping. Suddenly the floor disappeared beneath her foot and she fell with a terrified scream.

Her toe struck the floor only a second later, but her momentum was already thrown too far forward, she toppled over herself and ended up slamming against the canted floor on her belly, her weight carrying her down a steep slope, plummeting head-first through the darkness, still screaming.

She thrust her arms and legs out, but she couldn't stop herself. She was moving too quickly. And the stone was too smooth to offer enough resistance.

Where was she going to end up?

Then light began to flicker before her eyes.

Her flashlight. The murk was breaking apart. She was passing through cobweb-like curtains of it as it thinned, revealing more and more of the steep passage as her mind raced to piece together the trouble she was in. Had she triggered a trap of some sort? Was she about to be fed to monsters or something?

The murk thickened one last time, plunging her into blinding darkness. Then she burst from the other side and saw that the passage ahead of her ended in a gaping hole.

She was going to fall! She screamed as she watched it speeding toward her, unable to stop. In an instant she was already past the ledge, staring wide-eyed down into a bottomless darkness.

Then something grabbed her foot.

For a moment, she thought someone had saved her in just the nick of time. She came to a jarring halt with her upper half dangling over the ledge, staring down into a black emptiness below.

That was too close! Her heart was racing. She felt dizzy.

But who caught her?

No... Not who. That didn't feel like a hand gripping her. It felt more like something wrapped around her shoe.

Another of those shadowy not-hand things?

"Wait..." she gasped. That wasn't good! Those things didn't hold on for very long. She tried to straighten her body out, her arms flailing, trying to grasp the edge of the stone slope before the thing let go of her, but she was already too far over the edge to get a decent grip. "Hold on..." she grunted, trying with all her might to lean over and gain a grip.

She managed to appreciate the irony of finding herself praying that the creepy, shadow-tentacle-hand thing *wouldn't* let go of her for once...

Her fingertips slapped at the ledge. She couldn't quite reach it... Just a little farther...

Almost...

But the thing in the murk let go of her foot. And with another terrified scream, she fell.

Chapter 70

"Dumbass," grumbled Brandy.

"Oh come on," said Albert. "I was joking."

"It wasn't funny. You scared the shit out of poor Gina."

"I'm fine," Gina assured her.

"Telling her to get naked…" Brandy went on, ignoring her. "Pervert!"

"I said I was sorry."

"I'm fine," Gina said again. She wasn't scared or insulted. In fact, she didn't even have time to register what he'd said before he told them he was kidding.

They were standing at the entrance to the warning chamber, peering in at the ominous darkness behind which was hiding a giant, hyperrealistic statue of a face that made tears well up in her eyes for no reason at all, even before she saw it.

The energy here was like nothing she'd ever felt before. It was frightening to feel her body reacting to this stuff on its own. If she couldn't control her own tears from this far away, what would happen to her when she stepped inside that wailing mouth?

"It's kind of weird, though," said Albert as he stood pondering the same darkness. "Last time the blind man came forward and *demanded* our clothes, saying it was just the way it was done…"

"Old No-Eyes was probably on the pervert's payroll," grumbled Brandy. "Paid him off to say that just so he could use his magic to peep on all of us."

"I mean, if there was some actual reason for us to have to be naked, shouldn't someone have told us to leave our clothes behind when we got *here*, too?"

"Why are you complaining?" she challenged, shooting him a dirty look.

"I'm not," he replied. "I'm trying to understand it."

"Well stop it."

Gina wiped at her eyes. It was such an unusual feeling. An *alien* feeling. She was no stranger to tears and sadness, but this was something different. It wasn't like the sadness she felt growing up in that awful house with no love. And it was nothing like Gwilym Glum's emotional torture, either. It wasn't drawing out her fears and insecurities and forcing them back on her. This was just empty sadness, without any sustenance. "This is one of the rooms filled with statues, right?" She remembered Andrea talking about them. Intensely detailed depictions of people engaging in all manner of sexual activity that filled whoever looked upon them with overwhelming carnal desire. Or of terrifying monsters and people being torn apart or devoured that instilled crippling fear.

"That's right," replied Albert. "We know how to get past these things. Brandy has really poor eyesight. She takes off her glasses and she can't see any of the details. No details, no effect."

"It doesn't always work, though," Brandy interjected.

"No. Sometimes details still get through. And it doesn't work at all if she's already seen what's inside the room. And it sort of sounds like there might be other variables depending on what emotions an individual person is proficient with."

"Saying it like that makes you sound like a D&D nerd," said Brandy.

"It does, doesn't it? But that's what it says in the book." He turned and met Gina's gaze. "And being blind presents *other* challenges. There are so many statues that it's like a maze. Without being able to see, it's easy to end up going in circles, trapping you inside, exposing you to it a lot longer. Even worse, some of them are boobytrapped with stone spikes. If you panic and try to rush through it blind, you could end up impaled."

"I really don't want to do this again," whined Brandy.

Albert was still looking at Gina, a thoughtful expression on his face. "But if there was a safe way for us to navigate it entirely in the dark…" he pondered, "…it might not affect us at all."

She knew exactly what he was suggesting, and it was absolutely a sound hypothesis. After all, her most useful talent was her curious ability to instantly know her surroundings. "I don't need to be able to see," she agreed. "I should be able to lead the way through and avoid any traps. But these walls are still doing something to my head. There could be blind spots I'm not aware of."

"Understandable. And I absolutely don't want you putting yourself in any danger. I'm basically just throwing out ideas, trying to find the best way to proceed. Don't do anything you're not comfortable with. I'll lead the way myself if you don't feel like you can."

She turned her gaze toward the darkness ahead of them. She

could sense the face looming there, mournfully screaming back at them. Tears welled up in her eyes again as the psychic part of her mind focused on it. "The problem is that I'm not so sure it won't still overwhelm me. I can already feel it, just by being this close. It's possible that being psychic like this only means it's not possible for me to simply close my eyes in there."

"Oh my god..." sighed Brandy.

"Yeah, that sounds bad," agreed Albert, looking forward again. "Maybe we *should* try to look for another way."

But as she cast her psychic eye back the way they came, she glimpsed just a flicker of something deeply unpleasant, something that made her think of the first job the goddess gave her, of the horrible tower looming over the city of Cakwetak, hidden in plain sight by some unfathomable force, and the monstrous things that prowled those unseen floors. "No," she decided. "I think I should at least try."

"It's not worth it if there's any chance you'll be subjected to all of that emotion," said Albert. "Being exposed to the whole room can change you. You could be stuck suffering this kind of sadness for the rest of your life. All the time."

But she was already making her way across the room toward the imposing doorway. She wasn't sure that would make much of a difference, honestly. She'd spent most of her life feeling sad. But she didn't say so. She wasn't looking for sympathy. Leaving that past life far behind was her own responsibility. "I don't think we'll find a way that doesn't include facing a room like this. The more we try to avoid it, the more time we'll waste." And this was the truth. Regardless of whatever that darkness was that she kept feeling, she found herself convinced that this was where they were supposed to be. Trying to find another way would only delay the inevitable at best and at worst land them somewhere far more difficult.

"I don't like it," said Brandy.

"It's fine," she insisted, pretending she wasn't scared. But there was nothing easy about this. Her tears just kept welling up. The emotions flowing from that room were like nothing she'd ever felt before. The closest thing she could think of was Tristesse Lane, but even that place didn't feel like this. It was like these emotions were rushing out at her, like heat from a thermal vent, burning, suffocating.

"Don't force yourself," worried Albert as he hurried after her.

Brandy followed him, cursing under her breath.

Gina focused on the face's teeth, careful not to bump her head against the stone as she ducked under. It wasn't hard. She was almost small enough to walk right through.

Behind her, Brandy switched off her light. A moment later, she felt her hand fumbling for hers and she grabbed it, happy for the comforting feel of her grip.

"We never tried feeling our way through in total darkness," recalled Albert.

"It was too fucking dangerous," she reminded him.

"We were too scared. After the sex room, we knew we weren't alone down there. That was why we came up with the plan using your glasses to get through the hate room. And then we found that spike trap waiting on the other side..."

"Fucking..." grumbled Brandy. "Yeah. Watch out for shit like that."

"I will," promised Gina. Being skewered alive didn't sound like a fun way to end this journey.

She stood there a moment, taking in her surroundings. This room was filled with statues, just as they'd described. Dozens of them. Maybe hundreds. Most of them were of people, but not all. There were *things* too. If she tried to focus on any one shape, she immediately felt a crushing ache begin to take hold inside her chest, not unlike she remembered feeling on countless hopeless nights growing up in that loveless house, crying into her pillow.

She wiped at her streaming eyes and forced those emotions down. If anyone could push through this, it was her. She spent years suppressing her emotions, wearing masks to hide her pain.

She could do this.

The statues were more than they appeared to be. They weren't just three-dimensional depictions of sorrow. They were somehow tethered across space and time to actual *events* that were saturated with the emotion they were associated with. She had no idea how she understood this, but she did. It almost felt like something she once knew but had long forgotten. Something imbedded in her DNA perhaps? But one thing was certain: the statues were definitely the *source* of the emotion. If she attempted to focus her psychic eye on them, it would be no different than turning on the light and staring at them with her eyes.

But that was one advantage to using her psychic eye over her physical ones. In the physical world, one's eyes behaved like a camera, taking in all that the light revealed, whether you wanted to see it or not. But her psychic eye could be more choosy.

She focused not on the statues, but on the *negative space*, the gaps *between* the statues, the open floor at her feet, the doorway on the other side. She started walking, following that path. The statues were crowded close together, making it impossible to slip between most of them. Only certain spaces remained, leaving an intentional, winding path that could be followed, but with diversions and dead ends interwoven throughout. It was, indeed, a maze. One that would be easy to get lost in while fumbling around in the dark, trapping its unwitting victims within, forcing them to soak up more and more of these awful emotions until...

Well, she didn't exactly know what would happen. Albert said it could change a person. And from what Andrea told her and how Brandy talked about their experience with that creepy shaman guy, it sounded like their exposure to the sex room gave them some kind of supercharged sex drive...which sounded weird, but who was she to judge? Could being exposed to a room like this somehow *infect* her with this sadness? Could it leave her permanently depressed and incapable of feeling happiness?

Now it was starting to sound like Tristesse Lane. That place got into her head and dredged up all of her worst fears and insecurities. The people they found there had been robbed of all their positive emotions and left with nothing but misery.

But that was a different kind of sorrow. Tristesse Lane attacked her with her *own* sadness. This was someone else's. Here, there was only the psychic signatures connecting these statues to the original experiences they were modeled from. It was like radiation emanating from a nuclear reactor. It bombarded her, flooding her mind with miseries that belonged to other people in other times and places, slowly poisoning her mind. And somehow, that was a difference she found she could cling to.

These tears didn't belong to her. And she'd shed quite enough of her own.

She pushed forward, weaving between the statues, careful not only to watch for stone appendages that might leave a nasty bump on her head, but also for her two companions behind her, veering wide of a hand here and an elbow there while forcing back alien thoughts of hopelessness and despair.

And then there was Albert's frightful warning about deadly stone spikes. She didn't sense any of those. Not yet, anyway. But she had no doubt that they wouldn't lie about something like that. She reminded herself that there were things she couldn't feel, that her psychic mind was blind to. Especially out here in the Denselands, where so many of those mysterious ruins were ancient beyond imagining and strange beyond her understanding. What if this temple's stone spikes were one of the things she was blind to? She could walk right into one without ever seeing it. Or fall into a pit filled with them, like they described. The very thought made her shudder.

Carefully, she tested each step she took. She forced herself to move slowly enough to withdraw before anything sharp could penetrate too deeply for her to recover. And she kept her psychic eye focused on the stone path, well away from the sorrow-inducing statues.

But she could only shield herself so much. Her tears kept falling. Her chest kept aching.

There was a shape looming to her left, she realized. Just one of these many statues. But something about it seemed to reverberate inside her head. She couldn't see it, but she knew it was in the eerily perfect shape of a woman. She knew this woman had long hair and gaunt, sunken features. She wasn't sleeping. She wasn't eating. She could barely even find her breath. She was wasting away, slowly being consumed from the inside out by her suffocating loss.

She stopped and clenched her eyes closed, willing herself to block out the vision, but it seemed to force its way into her head. She could feel this woman's pain as if it were her own. It was unbearable. Insurmountable.

The tiny shoe she was clutching against her chest...

"You okay?" worried Brandy.

"I'm fine," she replied through clenched teeth as tears streamed down her face. "Don't turn on your light. You really don't want to see this stuff."

"If we need to turn back, just say so," promised Albert.

"I'm fine," she said again. She forced herself to keep walking. It felt like wading through quicksand. It seemed to require every ounce of her strength. But she managed to push past it. And once it was behind her, the crushing weight on her heart lifted a little.

The path. She needed to focus on the path. Not on the awful things she was passing.

And yet, they invaded her mind anyway. Little things, mostly. A book, its pages marked with a scrap of paper and never opened again. A suitcase filled with joyous expectations, but never unpacked. A jacket still hanging on its hook, hoary with dust, years after last being worn. A favorite candy bar untouched in a desk drawer. A dirty hat lying in a ditch. An abandoned doll. An empty stroller.

A running theme...

This room wasn't filled with just any sadness. This was a very specific kind of sorrow. This was *grief.* And the images it forced into her mind tore at her heart like the sharpest of blades.

She wasn't sure how long she could take this.

"You doing okay up there?" asked Albert. "Don't push yourself too hard. We can take turns if we need to."

"I'm fine," she replied. It was a lie. She wasn't feeling fine at all. But it wasn't like she could just trade places with one of them. It didn't work like that. She could let one of them take the lead, but it wouldn't stop these awful visions from filling her head. She would be making one of them suffer pointlessly. As much as she wanted to turn around right now and flee this suffocating room, that wouldn't do anyone any good. They needed to push forward. She had to be brave. She had to be strong. By herself.

Like always.

She reached out with her mind and found the doorway. It wasn't far. She could see the path. She focused on it, forced her attention onto that open space. To the right. Around the big shape that made her think of shattered birthday wishes and broken promises. Then around to the left again.

The path *between* the stone heartaches. A safe gap.

But as she sharpened her mind's eye onto that path, she became aware of something else. Something shadowy. Something *unnatural.*

She stopped and stood there, her eyes wide open in the darkness, tears still streaming down her face.

They weren't alone in here.

Chapter 71

By the time Keith made his way to the far end of the chamber of the hounds he was pretty sure they'd attracted the attention of every last one of the freaky beasts. But he did somehow manage not to fall through any trapdoors and end up on another monster's lunch menu, which, given his track record so far, wasn't half bad.

But these things were something else. The way they were built was one thing—those slashing scales, those sharp teeth and claws, those powerful frames—but what really stood out was just how *violent* they were. Nicole wasn't kidding when she said they were aggressive. They were snarling and snapping and banging and clawing at either side of the walkway, those slashing scales constantly making that awful racket. And he'd lost count of how many times the nasty things broke into fights, each time resulting in those dramatic sprays of blood. Those oscillating scales not only bit into each other's flesh, but then sent it flying. It seemed to him that a species evolved in such a way would learn to steer clear of each other, but these things just kept going at it.

He could certainly see why she looked so afraid when she first heard their telltale sound. In fact, she didn't let go of his hand until they were well into the next passageway and the machine-like droning noise of those alien guard dogs had faded to a distant roar.

It was such a strange feeling, holding her hand again after all this time, and after all they'd been through. But he refused to comment on it. And so did she. He had a feeling she was going to simply pretend it never happened. Just like she pretended there'd never been anything special between them, like those amazing few months they spent together meant nothing.

He clenched his teeth and pushed the thought from his head. Why was he even thinking about that? He needed a nice long break. He was clearly exhausted. And maybe all this darkness was starting to get to him. Or maybe the air was getting thin. That might explain it.

He wished someone else were here with them. He wanted to ask questions about those creatures back there. But he didn't want to talk to *her*. And she didn't want to talk to *him*, so they just wouldn't talk.

His mind kept circling back to those two tails… By the time they crossed the dog pound from hell, he'd managed to get a close enough look to see that those weird tails appeared to be the ends of two separate spines. How did that work? Did anything on earth have a physiology like that?

It sort of sounded like Albert was the guy to ask about this stuff. Both Nicole and Andrea mentioned him whenever they talked about the temple or its strange monsters. Wayne and Olivia mentioned him, too, he recalled. It sounded like he was the guy with all the theories, like the nerdy smart guy in the group with all the answers.

When this was all over, he'd have to sit down and have a conversation with him. Maybe he could help him make sense of some of this insanity.

The passage split into three up ahead. He opted to go left for no good reason except that he didn't want to stop and discuss it. The new passage curved farther to the left, and after a while it began to feel like they were going in a circle. A dead end? Or would it spiral down to a single point and then spiral back out again? That was a thing mazes did, too, sometimes.

But he noticed that his breathing had increased. He seemed to be using more energy. His legs were aching. He was even beginning to sweat a little. He had a brief moment where he began to worry if something was wrong with him before it suddenly occurred to him that he was simply walking *uphill*. They were spiraling upward on a gentle but long incline.

It didn't seem to bother Nicole. She was always in fantastic shape. He was going to have to step up his game if he intended to keep up with her. If not, she'd just use it as an excuse to yell at him. And she'd probably call him a pussy while she was at it. Vulgar *and* demeaning. That was her style.

"Olivia didn't have anything better to patch you up with than your shirt?"

He glanced back at her. This caught him off guard. He'd practically forgotten he was walking around with his shirt knotted around his arm. "I told you, we didn't have any first aid supplies. My shirt was already bloody, so I told her to use it. I think she did a great job. What's it matter?"

"It doesn't," she grumbled.

You brought it up, he thought, but decided against saying so. He kept his mouth shut and pushed onward.

"It doesn't look very comfortable," she said after a moment.

"It's fine. Sorry if my naked back offends you."

"I don't give a shit what you do."

"Good." Up ahead, he caught sight of another intersection. There were four directions to choose from this time, not including the way they came.

"It's just…"

"Just what?" he sighed. Maybe he'd pick the far right this time.

"You look thin."

He looked back at her this time, surprised. "What?"

"You've lost weight," she grumbled. "We spent a *lot* of time naked together. I think I remember what you looked like. You're thinner than you used to be."

"So what?"

"I don't know. Nothing I guess. It was just bothering me."

"Why would it bother you?"

"It makes me wonder if you've been eating well. That's all."

He rubbed at the back of his neck. This was awkward. Why was she suddenly talking like she'd ever cared one bit about him? "I'm fine," he insisted. He chose the first path on the right and pushed onward. "I mean, it's not like I eat as good as I used to. It's different when you're only cooking for one. But I'm hardly starving."

For a moment, she was quiet again. Then she said, "You were always such a good cook."

"Thanks…"

The truth, of course, was that she was right. Cooking used to be his thing. It was one of the ways he took care of his mother. It made him happy to learn new dishes from around the world and serve them to her. And it always made *her* happy to try new things, especially since her poor health made it impossible for her to travel, like she'd always wanted to do. And as a bonus, it never failed to be a hit with the ladies. It seemed like there was always something about a man who could cook. But after his mother was gone, the idea of cooking *anything* was…well it was *depressing*, to be blunt. He couldn't find the joy in it anymore. He ate cereal or Pop Tarts most mornings. Instant ramen and microwave burritos for lunch and dinner. The occasional drive-through burger and fries. And yeah, he supposed he'd lost a little weight.

But why would she care?

"I know what a bitch I've been, but I wouldn't want you to not take care of yourself."

Again, he looked back at her, squinting this time. "What happened to the zombies can eat me first?"

"Is that what you really think of me?" she snapped.

"It's literally what you said! Along with a *lot* of other mean things!"

He thought that would start a really good fight, but again she surprised him: "I said I was kidding."

He stared at her for a moment. Her voice wasn't edged with its usual bite. It was uncharacteristically soft. And she wasn't staring him down. She wasn't looking at him at all. She was staring at the wall, avoiding his gaze. She looked strangely meek like that. Almost vulnerable.

There were two versions of Nicole that he'd known. The perfectly confident, sexy, fun, knock-your-socks-off version and the perfectly confident, mean-ass, bitchy, "fuck you" version that the first version mutated into at some point. He still didn't understand how it happened. Maybe someone fed her after midnight or something. But this was neither of those two and he wasn't sure he liked it. It was weirdly worrying. Had that monster done something to her? Did she hit her head at some point?

He didn't dare press her on the matter. Instead, he simply turned away and continued onward.

They walked in silence for a while. He turned left at the next intersection, then chose straight when the path forked beyond that. Then right... Left again... Right...

Mazes were boring. Why did so many people do this for fun in the fall?

Finally, something new appeared. He stepped out of the passage into an open chamber. It wasn't huge. It was about ten feet wide by about twenty feet long. But it was *tall*. The ceiling was about twenty feet high. Whatever it was, it was better than just another passageway. Or, so he thought at first. On second thought, however, he found himself stopping and looking it over.

There was nothing here. It was just an empty room with no apparent purpose. Was it some sort of trap?

"I remember these rooms," said Nicole.

He glanced back at her. She was staring up at the ceiling. He quickly shined his light up there. Was it designed to drop down on them as they crossed or something? Indianna Jones style?

"In the first temple, Brandy, Albert and Olivia all felt something weird in rooms like this," she recalled. "Because they were the psychic ones."

"Psychic?"

"Albert and Olivia both talked about hearing chains rattle when they passed through those rooms."

Chains? There was a creepy mental image. But he couldn't hear anything. Nor could he *see* anything. It was just an empty room with an unusually high ceiling.

"The more psychic you are, the more aware you are of it. A woman with really powerful psychic powers followed us down there that night. Whatever *she* saw was so terrifying she fled the room and fell into a trap." She lowered her eyes and met his gaze. "She died down there."

He stared back at her for a moment. Someone actually died? Andrea omitted that part of the story when she was talking about it.

"We should be okay," she decided, looking up again. "But let's not stand around."

"Yeah..." He crossed the room ahead of her, his light fixed on that empty space above. *Was* it just an empty room? Or was there really something in here, tethered with chains only a psychic mind could hear rattling? It sounded ridiculous...and yet it sounded absolutely terrifying.

He reached the passage on the other side and looked back one last time.

He heard no chains. He saw nothing move in that empty space as they passed beneath it. If there were some kind of psychic guard dog hidden in here, neither of them possessed enough psychic power to even glimpse it.

And yet, somehow, something about the idea of such a trap sounded weirdly familiar. Had he seen something like that in one of his many strange dreams? Or was that only his imagination confusing him?

Whatever. It didn't matter, he supposed. They were fine.

He lowered his gaze and looked at Nicole. She turned and looked back at him. Then he watched her gaze shift to the passage behind him and her expression flashed to terror.

He twirled around and instinctively stepped in front of her.

Zombie Hotdog was staggering from that darkness. His body was twisted and knotted with broken bones. He looked like he'd been through some kind of machine. And yet still he was on his feet.

Before he could even fathom what to do next, Nicole grabbed his hand and ran back the way they came, dragging him along behind her.

Chapter 72

Olivia and Wayne hurried onward, both of them eager to be well away from those remains before whatever left them there came back.

They weren't human remains. That would have been immediately clear even without her training as a nurse. Even broken and scattered, those weren't like any bones that would ever be found inside a person. Or any other mammal for that matter. Most of them were long and thin, almost needle-like, reminding her more of the sort of bones you found in fish, but much larger. Even the fatter leg and hip bones appeared to have been made up of several of those thinner bones twisted and knotted together.

They appeared to have been there for some time. There was no rancid blood or rotting meat. There wasn't even any smell. And then there was that bizarre, red fungus that was clinging to much of it. It was impossible to know how quickly that stuff might grow, but it *looked* like it had been there and undisturbed for some time. Still, they weren't taking any chances.

The scene was barely out of sight, however, when her light fell on something small and bristly crawling across the ground. It was black and shiny and looked a lot like a sea urchin, but with an odd little stalk jutting out from one side like some kind of probing antennae.

"Albert talked about this," whispered Wayne as they gave the strange little creature a wide berth. "About the first temple and how it didn't make sense that all those hounds could survive locked up in a place like that. He said there had to be some kind of ecosystem to sustain a predator like that."

She nodded. She remembered them discussing that once or twice. Albert was convinced that such large creatures, especially in the numbers they saw in that tower room, couldn't have existed without a sizeable food source. And the only other creatures they encountered down there were some kind of hairy, octopus-like things that squirted a vile, reeking fluid that nearly incapacitated poor Brandy in one of the first temple's reservoirs.

She'd forgotten all about *those* things. And now that she'd remembered, she found herself glancing back, wondering if there'd been any of those lurking in the water near where the stone pipe spit them out. She really didn't think she wanted to run into one. They sounded gross.

"He had two theories," recalled Wayne. "One was that just like the first temple opened onto both the Wood and our world, it also opened onto a third world, where there was a pre-existing natural eco-system that the hounds were a natural part of and could feed and re-produce freely."

She swept her light farther out into the darkness and then froze as something white blossomed into view.

Wayne turned his light on it, as well. There was something sitting in a tall cluster of those pale weeds, a strange, pure-white lump of fur, about the size of a small dog. There were six long, very thin, tentacle-like appendages reaching up from it, about three feet long, waving gently in the gloom, each one with fine, feathery, frond-like fans spreading open at its end.

"The other," he went on whispering as he stared at the mysterious creature, "was that there was a stable, *artificial* ecosystem hidden some-where *inside* the temple, with an entire food chain to support them."

As she watched, the pale shape shifted and crept forward a step. Those tentacle things didn't look so tentacle-like now. Were they part of the thing's tail? More like long, specialized feathers, maybe? Although it didn't look like a bird. It looked furry. Could things other than birds have feathers?

A small head lifted and sniffed at the air. The thing had a tiny little pink nose and what appeared to be long, floppy ears that dragged the ground.

"So cute!" she whispered.

The thing turned and darted out of view, moving so quickly that it was little more than a white streak cutting through the gloom. It was surreal to see, as if her eyes were merely playing tricks on her.

"No eyes," observed Wayne. "Just like the hounds."

Her first thought was that she simply couldn't see its eyes. It looked quite fluffy, after all. But she supposed he was probably right. What good were eyes in a permanent darkness? The same thing happened in their own world, deep inside caves. There were spiders, fish and salamanders found without any eyes because eyes were useless in environments devoid of light. Evolution eventually took away what wasn't needed.

Wayne shined his light after the creature, curious. "This room might act like a watering hole," he realized. "Every animal needs water. Predator and prey alike. It's an ideal hunting ground."

She looked up at him, worried. "Hounds."

He nodded. "I'd say there's a good chance one or more will turn up sooner or later. We should try to find high ground. If there is any."

She made a "don't tell me stuff like that" face at him, but he didn't see it. He was already leading her away, moving toward the outer walls of the space. He was right, of course. If this really was some kind of shared ecosystem designed to maintain all these animals, then those bones they passed were likely a good indication that the hounds fed here. Or other, equally dangerous predators.

If they didn't want to end up on the menu, they needed to get to higher ground, and quickly.

But was there even any higher ground to be had? What if there was no way out of here? What would they do? They'd already established that they were no match for a hound.

They passed more of those sea urchin-looking things. And those pale weeds were growing thicker and thicker, covering more of the ground. Now there were tall, stiff-stemmed things with twisted, brownish-red leaves and little flowers with waxy, sickly yellow petals.

"Feels like one of those exploration-type video games," he observed. "Like I should be scanning all these things and adding them to the database or something."

It really was weird. It was a surreal kind of feeling, seeing all these alien things.

Somewhere far away, she heard the dreadful sound of a hound revving up those deadly scales. It was very faint, very distant, and yet she found herself freezing at the sound, terrified, as if it were right behind her.

Wayne urged her onward, eager to keep moving. And he was right, of course. They couldn't afford to linger here.

The sound faded away again, the hound either quieting back down or running off somewhere.

"The ground isn't disturbed," he observed. "If those things can scratch up the stone floors in their passageways, it seems like they'd really churn up bare earth like this." He swept his light back and forth, curious, and revealed a stray bone too big to have come from one of those cute white creatures.

Unless the one she saw was only an infant, she supposed…

"Then again, maybe other animals trample it back down out here," he muttered, pondering to himself as he kept walking. "Can't really do that on stone…"

Olivia didn't really want to think about those monsters right now.

She just wanted to get away from here as quickly as possible.

"In the labyrinth, the hounds are confined to their own passages," he went on. "There should be something similar down here. Unless this is somewhere we weren't ever meant to be, I guess. But that wouldn't make any sense. That room with all the narrow pathways... I mean, I really don't think it just *happened* to be positioned directly over that whirlpool. Looking back now, it kind of seems like bringing us here was intentional, doesn't it?"

"You sound like Albert," she informed him.

"Do I?"

"Just like him."

He frowned as he tried to decide if she was complaining or complimenting him. And even she wasn't entirely sure. Albert was smart. She was always impressed with how intelligent he was. He was so good at solving puzzles and riddles. He was great with computers. He could even solve a Rubik's Cube, which had always been completely beyond her. And he was just an all-around nice guy. But he was also a little obsessive, she'd found. Once he started trying to solve a problem, he'd be distracted until he finished it. And the temple was a *very* complex problem with no obtainable solution. Brandy told her once that he sometimes lost sleep because he couldn't stop thinking about it. She really didn't want her dear Wayne to go tumbling down that rabbit hole, too.

Something long and glittery scuttled across the ground in front of her feet. She cried out, startled, and jumped back, practically pulling Wayne over backward in the process.

"What was that?" she gasped, shining her light after it.

"Some kind of centipede?" he guessed. "I didn't get a good look at it."

She didn't either. At first she thought it was a snake. But it wasn't really slithering, she realized. It was moving in a straight line. It was too dark and too fast to see if it had legs. Either way, it sent a shiver of revulsion through her body.

"An entire ecosystem," he pondered, staring after the thing. "Plants and bugs. Predators and prey. And there's probably things out there in the dark with good enough senses to keep well away from us. We'll never see them."

She shuddered again and gripped his arm more tightly. "Can we just find the way out of here before something *hungry* shows up?"

"Right," he said, continuing onward. "Sorry."

Chapter 73

Corey climbed his way up the narrow, vertical shaft. This wasn't part of the labyrinth, he somehow knew. This was an area no one else was meant to go. But for some reason that strange flow of energy led him here. He wasn't even entirely sure how he found his way into it. It was difficult to explain. He kind of just *fell* into it. And he was increasingly sure it wouldn't have happened for anyone else. But the presence of the ladder-like grooves in the stone was proof enough that it was meant for *somebody* to find. He couldn't shake the feeling that he was here specifically because of his curious understanding of this mysterious technology.

The stone here was practically buzzing with that odd energy that he felt under his skin. It was building up now, almost like a static charge. He kept expecting to be shocked every time he reached for a handhold. Except this wasn't metal. And it wasn't electrical. It was some other kind of energy, something altogether different, something *alien.*

Somewhere, in a world that existed long, long ago, this was a perfectly normal phenomenon. As common as rain or snow. As common as lightning. And for some reason that he was never going to be able to fully understand, this massive stone machine somehow allowed for it to still work. It was as if the stone contained the very *memory* of those bygone universes.

The more he explored, the less it felt like some ancient stone city and the more it felt like a vast and complex machine. He wondered if there was some kind of engine running it all. Did it contain a fuel source? Was there some sort of massive reactor hidden deep in the stone depths? Or was it powered entirely by this strange energy?

These were things he simply wasn't capable of knowing for certain, he realized. He knew he would never be able to understand the hows of it, but he also understood that he didn't have to. He only needed to understand that it *worked.* And that this vertical shaft was some kind of main component in the greater machine. A sort of central processor, perhaps.

He propped himself up against the corner and took a break. He needed to make sure he didn't overdo it. The last thing he needed was to fall and break something. Violet would be so cross with him if he was injured when they finally met back up.

He closed his eyes and relaxed for a moment.

Again, he could feel the layout of the labyrinth around him. It was getting easier to picture it. He could even glimpse little bits and pieces of the surrounding areas.

He opened his eyes, distracted.

A little to the left… Down a few levels… A hundred yards… Or maybe two hundred…

There were *people*.

Three of them. They were in a strangely chaotic area of the labyrinth, unable to hurry. They were being forced to move at an agonizing pace. Were they sneaking past something scary? Were they surrounded by traps? And why did it feel for some reason as if they were all overcome with an intense and suffocating *sadness*?

Albert and Brandy said that two of them wouldn't make it home… Had something happened over there? Had someone died in these dark depths?

Again, his thoughts drifted to Violet.

No. He couldn't think like that. Violet was too strong and clever to be defeated by a place like this. He wouldn't give the idea power.

But that strange sadness lingered in him after just that one glimpse…

Not that it mattered. Whatever was happening down there didn't involve him. That was a different part of the labyrinth. He could worry about the others, but there was nothing he could do from here. His strange awareness of the energy flow told him that he couldn't reach them if he wanted to. Not from here.

If he wanted to see his friends again, he was going to have to keep moving forward. He needed to focus on the path ahead of him. Which, of course, was currently *upward*.

He pushed those other three from his head and continued climbing.

This was an awful lot of work for a big guy like him. He hoped there was something interesting waiting for him up there after all this.

Chapter 74

Violet sank to her knees and squeezed her eyes closed.

Seek your future and we will meet again in the dreamy in-between...

Could all that have been real? Did she and Corey actually find that place all those years ago? It was the same kind of stone, just like the tokkatok nest in Minnesota and the mysterious field in Arkansas. But it wasn't just one stone. Or twelve. That whole room, the tunnels leading there, the steps leading down... It was *all* made of that stone.

It looked just like *this* place.

Was the voice she heard in her head over that mysterious, ancient tomb the same voice that spoke to her in the dream about the world with the colorful sky? Was that a dream at all? Even after all this time, it still felt so strangely vivid.

She rubbed her eyes. Her legs still ached from the climb up those stairs. And her head was starting to hurt from all this thinking. She suddenly had the bizarre idea that some mysterious, atrophied part of her brain she'd never used before had just awakened and was suddenly working overtime to process all of this new information and make sense of the dreams.

No. None of those were dreams. She was sure of it. The voice was always the same. The messages were all connected.

"Are you okay?" asked Everett.

"Yeah. Sorry. I'm just..." She trailed off, unsure how to finish that sentence. Just *what*? Just remembering some dreams that she didn't remember and that weren't dreams? Just having a little mental breakdown? What a pain. "I'm fine," she said instead, her eyes still closed, waiting for the headache to ease up a little more.

"Take my hand," he offered.

"I'm good," she scoffed. She wasn't some helpless little girl. She was a grown woman, fully capable of picking herself up off the floor. "I'm just...still a little wore out from all those steps," she decided. That was the real issue. She was just tired. It had been a long journey.

"We need to stick close together," he reminded her. "Don't wanna end up alone here. Like you said."

That was true. She *did* say that. "Yeah..." She sighed. Then she nodded. "Okay," she relented, holding out her hand.

Don't let it trick you!

Her eyes flashed open, startled, and she snatched her hand back. Who said that? Why was her heart suddenly pounding? Had something happened? She turned and looked at Everett.

But that wasn't Everett.

The thing standing over her looked like Everett. It was wearing the same clothes as Everett. It had the same face as Everett. It had the same charming grin and the same messy hair. But all those things were nothing more than a mask stretched over something shadowy and broken and melty. It was reaching out for her with a hand that bubbled and dripped and exuded foul, black smoke.

She cried out, terrified, and scurried away from the thing on her hands and knees.

"Don't be afraid," said the thing that wasn't Everett. "It's only the labyrinth trying to scare you."

Even his voice was wrong, she realized. It sort of gurgled under the words. A terrible, inhuman sound hiding beneath the words it spoke.

"It fills your head with voices," the thing said.

Don't listen...

"Warps what you see until your mind can't comprehend it."

Voices in her head? Illusions? Could that be true? Had the stone done something to mess with her mind? Was she having some kind of psychotic episode while poor Everett tried his best to talk her down?

Carefully, she rose to her feet and took a step backward.

The thing stepped closer, that hideous, boiling hand reaching toward her. "Come on," it urged. "You don't want to be alone down here, do you?"

No. She didn't want that at all. But which was the reality and which was the lie? How could she be sure?

Careful... Trust your instincts.

Her instincts? Her instincts were telling her to run like hell. But she couldn't leave without Everett. The *real* Everett, not this monstrous, unconvincing doppelganger.

Where was he? Did something happen to him while she was caught in that weird memory? Was he safe?

Or was it possible that this *was* him? Had something terrible happened to him while she was caught in that old memory? Had he been possessed or poisoned somehow? Or had he simply been deceiving her this whole time and this was the real him all along?

She didn't know what to do!

He took another step toward her. She took another step back. But she was running out of real estate. She glanced behind her and found that she was dangerously close to the edge. A long drop was all that awaited her in that direction. A hard landing. A disappointing ending to this crazy adventure.

"Don't let it lie to you," gurgled the monster wearing Everett's face.

Her instincts were telling her that it was better to be safe than sorry.

She ran.

The thing that wasn't Everett called after her, but she never looked back, never gave it a second chance to fool her.

In the event that she was wrong, that the labyrinth itself somehow concocted such an elaborate illusion and she was fleeing her only companion, it was better to be alone than to remain together. If that was how she saw him, she might panic and hurt him.

But somehow, the farther she ran, the more convinced she became that the thing speaking to her back there was *not* the real Everett. It *couldn't* be Everett. She wouldn't believe it. She didn't know what happened to him, why there was only that perverse mockery of him, but if she wanted any chance of finding him, she needed to get away from that fake. So she ignored his cries and ran, making her way across the strange, winding path between the deep, dark chasms stretching down into the depths of the earth on either side of her.

Ahead, the path split apart. She could hear the Everett thing chasing after her. She didn't have time to stop and think. She needed to pick a direction. But a dead end could be the end of her. She couldn't afford to mess up.

Which way?

I'll take you... whispered that mysterious dream voice inside her head.

"What?" she gasped.

But everything was going hazy. She stumbled and wavered. She started to fall. Her heart leaped at the prospect of passing out at this most terrible of moments. But she didn't fall. She felt her legs moving on their own.

Then she was dreaming again.

She dreamed of running.

She dreamed of leaping across those bottomless chasms, fearless and daring. She dreamed of mysterious pathways woven through the stone beneath her feet. She dreamed of secrets long buried and long forgotten.

She dreamed of a city of stone beneath a sky of magnificent colors.

And she dreamed of people without faces, who saw without seeing, who spoke without speaking and who could reach across the endless expanse of time and connect with a little girl on the other side of eternity with ease.

Chapter 75

Andrea didn't fall very far. In just a few terrifying seconds, it was over. And the landing was considerably softer than she imagined it would be, fortunately. *Unfortunately*, it was because she landed face-down in a great expanse of foul, reeking mud.

She lay there, dazed, a rancid taste pervading her mouth and nose, her eyes burning, her senses drowned in a foul, black blanket of filth. Her outstretched arms, a desperate though likely futile attempt to shield herself from the ground she assumed was speeding toward her, were thrust deep into the cold, vile muck, forcing her to wrench them free before she could lift her face out of the festering sludge.

For a frightful moment, she wasn't sure she was going to be able to do it, that after everything she'd gone through to get this far, she was going to choke and drown in this unspeakable filth. A claustrophobic flash of panic washed over her, her chest aching for air…but then she managed to lift and turn her head, freeing her face enough to take a desperate gulp of putrid air that turned her stomach and made her gag.

Where did this stuff come from? It was *beyond* foul. It smelled like the sludge rotting at the bottom of a swamp. And it tasted even worse than it smelled! Her stomach clenched and lurched, but she couldn't let herself throw up! Then she'd be stuck face-down in reeking mud *and* her own sick. Spitting and coughing, fighting back the wave after wave of violent retches that assaulted her throat, she tried to focus on righting herself and freeing her arms.

Where was she? She couldn't see or hear anything. Her eyes and ears were both clogged. It had even oozed up her nose! She was afraid she'd find that there was no way out, that she'd only keep sinking, doomed to be swallowed one way or another into this wretched muck, but in her struggling, she found that it was only about waist deep.

In the end, she managed to simply stand up, pulling her arms free of the sludge and clawing at her face, still coughing and gasping for breath.

By the time she finally managed to open her eyes and scrape the goo from the flashlight's lens, she'd already realized that this wasn't the first time she encountered this putrid muck.

This texture… This smell… This *taste*…

This was just like the mud chamber back in the first temple, while traveling with Olivia and Wayne, the one she had to wade through before arriving in the Sentinel Queen's eerily silent City of the Blind. Only that time, they were all butt naked and the foul gunk got absolutely *everywhere*.

Still gagging and spitting, the hideous taste still making her gag, her eyes watering, she turned and shined her light around. There was only this foul, black mud for as far as she could see in every direction, with no indication of which way she should go next. She lifted the light and peered upward. She could see the hole she fell from up there, unreachable now, of course. Ribbons of foggy murk trickled down from the infested corridor above like oozing slime and crept across the crusty surface like spreading weeds.

Muck and murk, she thought as she raked at the reeking sludge still clinging to her face. Had she messed up? Did she fall into some kind of trap? Or was this somewhere she was supposed to be? It was so hard to tell.

But last time she did this, the mud was part of the path, so maybe she was still on course.

This place could use some signs, in her humble opinion.

She stood there a moment, listening to the silence around her, waiting for the impostor to make fun of her for ending up in this unsanitary situation, but that mocking voice had gone refreshingly silent for the moment.

Maybe she lost her when she fell down that hidden slide. That would be nice. But she doubted she'd ever be so lucky. She'd be back soon enough, taunting her, trying her best to make her feel like she could never succeed.

She was such a bully!

Again, she turned and shined her light around, trying to decide which way she should go.

"This way…" whispered Erin.

She turned her light to the left. The voice was very faint, almost imagined. But for some reason she was sure it was coming from this direction.

Another ghost thing?

She began trudging through the rancid sludge, still trying to spit away that foul taste it left in her mouth when she landed in it. That stench was overwhelming. It made her queasy. And she could even feel it in her ears!

326

So gross!

It was eerie how much she was reminded of last time. She hadn't lost her clothes, and she was alone in here, but if she closed her eyes, she could practically believe that it was five years ago and that Olivia and Wayne were right here with her again.

It was a surprisingly nice feeling, given how deeply unpleasant this situation was.

She was so tired of being alone. Erin told her that her friends escaped from Glum and made their way here to the city, so where was everybody? Nicole and Gina? Keith? Everett and Violet? Violet told her that Brandy and Albert were here somewhere. And of course Corey. And Everett said he came here with Olivia and Wayne. And some other guy she didn't know. That was *twelve* of them. So where were they? Shouldn't she have run into *someone* by now? Or was this place so enormous that the very idea of crossing paths with one of only eleven other living souls was utterly ridiculous?

Ada called this place a city, after all. It could be a hundred times larger than the Temple of the Blind. This mud stretched on for as far as she could see in every direction. Was there an entire *lake* of this awful stuff down here? It could stretch for *miles* for all she knew.

And she wasn't going to escape it by standing here…

She pushed onward, still spitting, still gagging.

"Ew…" she whimpered.

Chapter 76

"You okay?" asked Brandy. She gave Gina's hand a squeeze. For some reason she'd stopped moving. She was just standing there in the dark.

"I'm fine," she replied.

"You sure?" pressed Albert.

"Yes."

Brandy wasn't convinced. It was starting to sound like "I'm fine" was simply her default response. But then she started moving again. Maybe she just needed a quick rest. At the very least, these rooms could be exhausting.

"Not much farther now," Gina promised.

"Good." She couldn't wait to be out of here. Even in the pitch-black darkness, there was a crushing tightness in her chest and tears wouldn't stop streaming from her eyes. She didn't get it. How could the emotions get to her without any light? Didn't you have to *see* the statues to be affected? That was why it was the Temple of the Blind. The hate room didn't affect her like this. She barely felt anything from those statues when she entered it without her glasses the first time. Why would this be different?

"Any sign of those spikes?" asked Albert. "They can be hidden in the statues, stuck out at dangerous angles."

Brandy stiffened a little at the memory. She'd forgotten about those. Albert walked into one last time. In his weary state, he thought he'd suffered a grave injury. It scared the hell out of her. But luckily it was much shallower than he thought, hardly even worth fussing over. It was a frightfully easy trap to fall into. And potentially a very deadly one.

"No," she replied in her usual sleepy voice, as if this room were boring her.

"That's good."

"But there's some kind of dangerous drop-off on the other side of all these statues. It's deep. I can't feel the bottom."

Brandy cursed.

Gina led her forward a few more steps, then steered her to the right. Something cold and hard brushed past her shoulder. Probably an outstretched stone hand.

Was it only her imagination, or did that mere touch, brief as it was, send a jolt of heartache through her?

She hoped Gina was okay leading the way like this. She was push-ing onward again, seemingly unfazed. And yet it was clear by the way she gripped her hand that she was feeling something from this room. She was good at putting on a brave face, but that was all this was. The longer they were in here, the more apparent it became that she was anything but blind to these statues. Her psychic eye was letting the mis-ery seep in.

Why did they ask her to do this? She felt so guilty. And yet, what other choice did they have? It wasn't like she wouldn't feel all these things even if she *wasn't* leading the way, so wouldn't that just mean that *two* of them would suffer this unnatural sorrow? But that was no excuse for simply throwing her to the wolves. There had to have been *some* other way.

Gina stopped and let go of her hand.

"What's wrong?" she worried. Did something happen? Had she discovered a trap?

"Nothing. We're almost through. The exit is straight ahead of us. But I need to make sure of something. Stay here for a minute."

"What?"

"Make sure of *what?*" asked Albert.

"Just trust me. And don't turn on your light yet."

"We should really stay together," he pressed. But she was already gone, her footsteps fading into the darkness ahead of them.

She felt a wild urge to bolt after her, but fear kept her nailed in place. She said there was a drop-off ahead of them. She didn't dare risk falling. But even with Albert right behind her, she felt strangely alone, almost stranded in this unhappy place.

She could feel the lifeless statues staring back at her.

"What're you doing?" called Albert.

But she didn't answer.

Brandy stepped back, crowding closer to him. "I don't like this. Where'd she go? Why can't we just leave this fucking room?"

Albert's arms closed around her and he pressed his body against her. "Relax," he told her. "Remember what the book said. Focus on me, not the room."

She grabbed his hands and pulled them away. "She's been gone a whole second, hornball. Settle down."

"I didn't say, 'Screw me.' I said, '*Focus* on me.' What's with you?"

"What's with _you_?"

"I'm worried about my wife. You're trembling."

"I am not." But he was right. She _was_ trembling. She didn't want to be here. She didn't want to do this again. She wiped at her eyes, muttering curses under her breath. Why couldn't she stop crying? What was up with this room?

"Just focus on me," he said again. "Use the good feelings to push away the bad ones."

"Fine," she groaned, letting go of his hands. "The things I put up with for you, I swear to God."

He slipped his arms around her waist and pulled her close against him. His lips brushed the back of her neck.

She _had_ always liked it when he did that... But it was hard to feel lovey-dovey when there were tears streaming down her face. She didn't want to be touchy-feely. She wanted to crawl off into bed by herself and cry herself to sleep.

What was taking Gina so long? What was she doing?

He kissed the back of her neck again, then slowly moved to one side. She felt herself tipping her head out of the way almost automatically. It was such a familiar sensation. He did that so often when they were at home together.

She felt her unnatural tears slowing down. That alien sadness seemed to shrivel up and fade away. Was it really overriding the sorrow with sexuality? Or did it have more to do with the familiarity of his touch that was so filled with the comforts of their home? Because this wasn't really sexual. He wasn't caressing her breasts or anything. It was only kisses. It was just..._intimate_.

Whatever it was, it was a huge improvement over what she was feeling before.

She grasped his hand and lifted it to her lips, held it there, kissed his strong fingers. So familiar... So warm... So _happy_...

Memories of their honeymoon flowed through her head. Every kiss. Every touch. Every passionate sigh and moan. She wanted that again. Every second of it. She wanted to live that week over and over again. Forever.

He was right. Regardless of these statues, she could easily get lost in this much lovelier feeling. Gina could take all the time she wanted.

Gina...

She stiffened and snapped back to attention. "Where'd Gina go?"

"She said she'd be right back," Albert reminded her.

"No... Something's wrong." She pulled away from him and fumbled for the flashlight in her pocket. "I can't feel her anywhere."

"*What?*"

She wanted to be moving already, but she didn't dare take a step in this unbearable darkness. She called out for Gina, but she didn't answer. Where did she go?

She switched the flashlight on and squinted into its sudden, blinding glare. There was, indeed, a drop-off waiting to swallow them up if they'd been careless enough to venture forward blind. They were standing in a doorway, looking down into a black abyss. The path ran left to right, into passageways leading in opposite directions.

Gina could have gone either way, leaving no trace.

"We have to find her!" she gasped, fresh panic welling up inside her.

"We will," he agreed. But which way did they even start? "Could you hear which way she went?"

She shook her head. "I wasn't listening. I didn't expect her to just vanish!"

He squeezed her hand and stepped closer to the hole, peering down into it. "She couldn't have fallen. She knew it was there. *She* warned *us*."

Brandy glanced back the way they came, but immediately diverted her gaze when she glimpsed the tangled labyrinth of statues on the other side of the doorway. Surely she didn't go through all that just to turn and go right back in there. That wouldn't make sense. But then again, nothing about this made sense. Did something happen to her? Did something steal her away while they were waiting for her to return? Another psychic predator, perhaps?

She called out for her. Her voice echoed, but otherwise there was no answer.

"We'll just pick a direction," decided Albert. "She can't have gone too far."

But they both knew that wasn't true. Wasn't that what the Denselands did to people? Sent them far away from each other?

She couldn't understand what happened. But they weren't going to find her standing around here.

Albert chose left and Brandy followed.

Chapter 77

Gina sat alone in the dark, her knees drawn to her chest, her hands clasped over her mouth, struggling to hold back the sobs she felt boiling up inside her, tears still streaming freely down her face.

"We'll just pick a direction," decided Albert. "She can't have gone too far."

But they wouldn't find her. This passage was different from the others. She felt it as she neared the end of the horrible grief chamber. This was where the unnatural feeling was coming from, the one that reminded her of other dark places, the one the goddess told her was unique to her, that only she could feel. And she didn't think they could reach her anymore even if they *could* feel what she felt. Something about the layout of the labyrinth had changed. There were passages nearby that weren't there before. And others that had disappeared. Something about that queer emotional energy…

And with no need of a light to help her navigate, they'd be hard pressed to spot her, even if they *could* follow her. The darkness would always be her ally.

"I'm so sorry…" she whispered into her hands. She didn't want to leave them like that, without so much as a goodbye. But she knew they'd never just let her wander off on her own. They'd try to stop her. And it was far too dangerous for them to come along.

She could feel something terrible somewhere in these mysteriously unnatural passageways, something they'd never see coming. This was the reason the goddess sent her here. She was sure of it.

She wiped at her eyes and then stood up.

It was time to go.

Chapter 78

You can't run forever...

Nicole hurried back the way they came, pulling Keith along with her. Her heart was hammering in her chest. She could feel tears trying to well up in her eyes. It was getting harder and harder to push them back down. She was so tired of it. Was it really just going to go on and on like this until something finally killed her?

Hotdog's ghoulish corpse had found them again. How was that even possible? Was his god able to navigate this vast labyrinth? Did it have some ability to track her? She didn't understand.

Eventually I'll have you...

The thing shouldn't have even been able to walk. Its legs looked like broken accordions. Its face was partially caved in. Its chest was broken open. There were things *hanging out of it!*

She needed to get away from that thing. But this was a terrible place to have to run away from something. A dead end would be bad. She couldn't risk being cornered again. She tried to go back the way they came, but it was difficult to remember all the turns Keith made. She wasn't paying attention. She was...distracted...

It is inevitable...

She squeezed her eyes shut and clenched her teeth together. "Oh my god!" she grunted. "Get the fuck out of my head!"

"What?" gasped Keith.

"Nothing. Not talking to you!"

"Not... *What?*"

Did this passageway look familiar? Of course it did. They all looked the same!

Even now, her thoughts were divided. Half of her was trying desperately to put distance between herself and that crumpled mass of flesh and shattered bones that was once Hotdog Creep. But at the same time, a part of her was strangely fixated on clinging to Keith's hand. For all her bitterness, it suddenly seemed very important that she not let go.

She couldn't lose him...

She turned left, then right. Was this the wrong way? Should she have gone left again? She couldn't remember. She should've made

Keith lead the way. But by now she'd probably only become more lost.

You'll embrace the pain eventually...

What was that noise? It was hard to hear over their echoing foot-steps and her own panting breath, but it sounded like they were heading back toward the chamber with the hounds. That was a nice big room with space to sprint. Maybe they could put some distance between themselves and Goar's grisly action figure.

Everyone embraces it eventually...

Did this freak *ever* fucking shut up?

Ahead of her, the chamber opened up. By now she could clearly hear the hounds. But this wasn't where they were before. She rushed out of the passage to find that they were on a different walkway. This one was up against the wall of the chamber, with the entirety of the room spread out on their left.

She definitely took a wrong turn somewhere back there, but at least it wasn't a dead end.

Not yet, at least.

She continued, her eyes peeled. Keith's light washed over the lower floor of the chamber. There were bloody bones and a scattering of loose scales glinting in the darkness, but she could see no hounds from here. The noise they made was concentrated farther out in the chamber, beyond the reach of his light. Perhaps they were still distracted by their scent from earlier.

She looked back the way they came and he turned his light back that way for her. But there was no sign of their undead stalker.

She couldn't hear his creepy words invading her thoughts any-more, either. Had they put enough distance between them to breathe a little easier? Or had it gone silent just to make her think that?

God, she hated this.

Ahead of them, the walkway came to an abrupt end and another passage led back into the labyrinth to the right. She was simultaneously grateful for an exit from this reeking monster den and terrified of get-ting lost in that endless darkness again. But she picked up her pace and hurried toward it.

The monster was there when she turned the corner.

She screamed as a great, clammy hand closed around her face and shoved her against the wall. At the same instant, it thrust its other arm out and struck Keith in his stomach. She felt his hand yanked from hers. And as she grabbed the foul, broken wrist holding her, she saw him tumble over the edge and into the chamber of the hounds.

She tried to call out for him, but the thing that used to be Hotdog

Creep was mashing her against the wall with a hand that didn't feel remotely human. It shifted and twisted in strange ways, more like a leather sack full of stones than flesh and blood.

She thrust her foot outward, kicking the monstrosity, but if the thing was capable of still feeling any kind of pain, it didn't show it.

It leaned toward her. It was impossible to imagine that she'd once thought that face handsome. It was barely even human now. Swollen, bloated and discolored, oozing blood and that strange, bubbling black goo from its mouth, nose and ears, the entire left side misshapen from one of its many great falls.

This close, he smelled even worse than the hounds.

She strained against the thing's grip and glanced toward Keith's light. It was still glowing. But she could see no sign of him. Was he still there? Or had the hounds already finished him off?

No. He'd be okay. The Keeper had all of this planned. Right?

That awful face drew closer and closer. That hideous black goo boiled from its parted lips, oozing down its chin, dripping to the floor. She felt something cold and vile spatter on her bare leg. The feeling made her stomach turn, but she couldn't stop fighting. Not for a single instant.

With a great grunt, she lifted both her legs, curled herself up, and thrust her feet out at the thing's chest with all her strength. Somehow, it was enough to loosen the monster's grip and she dropped onto the passage floor.

Immediately, the thing snatched at her again, but she ducked and crawled away.

Except she was going the wrong way now! *Away* from the light. Away from Keith.

She scrambled to her feet and ran anyway, hoping to put some distance between herself and the monster so that she could circle back for him.

But already it was on her again.

She was knocked to the floor and a great, broken mass of dead flesh piled atop her.

All she could manage was to scream.

Chapter 79

Wayne wished Albert were here. He was the one who figured out that the scratches in the floor were an indication that the hounds were nearby. He was smart about things like that. He enjoyed murder mysteries and puzzles. He had that detective aura, which sort of made sense, given that he had some kind of psychic power in addition to his smarts. If he were here now, he might be able to tell them if they were in hound territory or if something else might be responsible for the bones scattered around here.

He turned and swept his light back the way they came, paranoid that something might be stalking them through this strange landscape.

For the past ten or fifteen minutes, they'd been wading through a field of chest-high, blazing orange grass that felt weirdly cold to the touch and gave off an odd, sweet smell that for some reason reminded him of the smell of Olivia's morning coffee.

He didn't drink coffee himself. He'd never been a fan of it. But the smell of coffee brewing in the morning in their apartment had become as familiar to him as her favorite shampoo and perfume. It had grown into a comfort, a daily reminder of the greatest blessing in his life.

Except…this wasn't that smell. It didn't smell like coffee. Or like anything else that he could put his finger on at the moment. Maybe it reminded him on some subconscious level of one of the flavors she sometimes chose. Or maybe one of her creamers. But for some reason, it simply and quite strongly reminded him of waking up to that comforting aroma.

And yet, strangely, he didn't feel particularly *comforted* by this smell. Although it reminded him of moments that were comforting to him, it contained none of that comfort itself…which of course made no sense to him. It was far too complex to quite wrap his head around.

"It's kind of pretty," said Olivia, although he noticed she still didn't dare speak above a whisper.

He couldn't argue with her. It *was* pretty. But he couldn't stop wondering what kinds of unthinkable terrors could be hiding in a place like this. He didn't like that it hampered his visibility so much. He kept expecting to cast his light out over it and see it parting ominously as something stalked them, a grassy equivalent of a giant shark fin cruising toward them, perhaps.

And speaking of limited visibility, was his flashlight getting dimmer? He hoped his battery wasn't going dead. That was just what he needed.

But it could just be his imagination. He hoped so, at least.

Something darted from their path, disturbing the blazing grass. The sudden motion startled a squeak of a cry from Olivia and made her to dig her nails into him again.

"Sorry."

"Don't worry about it." He didn't mind. He was getting used to it. And he'd much rather her dig those nails in than freak out and run away. The last thing they needed was to be separated again.

They pushed onward, their eyes and ears open, wondering which direction the next big scare would come from, and when.

"Do you think everyone else is doing okay?" she asked.

"I'm sure they're fine," he replied automatically. He didn't know, of course. And she knew that. But the question seemed to come out of nowhere. It surprised him. And he refused to give a voice to any of those unthinkable possibilities.

"I'm worried about them."

He was worried, too. But there was nothing they could do about it. All any of them could do was take care of themselves until they all met up again.

"I just wish I knew, was all."

"Yeah. Me too."

Somewhere far off to their right, the frightful clamor of another hound abruptly came alive.

Again, she dug those nails in.

"Still sounds pretty far away," he assured her. "Just keep moving."

She nodded and pushed onward.

This one didn't fade away as quickly as the last one. It went on and on. He hated that sound. But at least it didn't seem to be moving toward them.

Again, he wondered if they were actually on the same level. This grass they were walking through... Would it be this tall if those things regularly hunted here? They were practically living lawnmowers, after all.

But then again, maybe this stuff grew unnaturally fast in spite of the constant darkness. He knew nothing about any of the things they witnessed down here. These things might not even be plants, for all he knew. They might be an entirely new kind of life that fit into no known category.

A horrible howl somewhere in the darkness behind them scattered his thoughts. They both turned and shined their lights back that way. Was that something falling prey to a hound? Or some other unknown predator?

Or was it the scarecrow man again?

He definitely didn't care to think too much about that. The freak was able to make that horror show out of a single dead hound. What the hell might he be able to do with an entire pack of them?

He gave Olivia a gentle nudge and the two of them hurried on through the blazing field.

Chapter 80

Corey had always asked questions. He was curious by his very nature from the day he was born. His parents were good and patient people who always answered as many questions as they could for him, and to the best of their ability. And when he happened to ask one that they couldn't answer, that was perfectly fine, too. He didn't always need an answer. It was the questions that really mattered. The wondering. The imagining. The *discovering*. A question that didn't have an answer was nothing more than a mystery that still required solving. Far from discouraging, an unanswered question, from his point of view, was an invitation to *adventure*.

That was the kind of child he was. And it was the kind of adult he'd grown into. He still liked asking questions.

And he had *so many* questions about *this* place. For example, where was he supposed to go from here?

He again sat cross-legged on the floor, staring at the scene before him.

At the top of the vertical shaft was waiting *another* shaft. Or, more precisely, two of them, running horizontally, lying perpendicular to each other and crossing directly over the vertical one. There was a large, stone sphere where they all met, with just enough space left for him to barely maneuver his bulky body around. And from the domed ceiling directly above the strange sphere, dozens of very narrow cylinders of stone jutted down toward it like the bristles of some great brush, each one aimed directly at the center of the sphere. A much larger stone cylinder ran away from the sphere on the floor of each of the four shafts. The energy he'd been following flowed up the vertical shaft and then out in all four directions, seemingly through those large cylinders, as if they were cables.

The problem was that all four paths felt the same. He couldn't decide which way he was supposed to go from here.

He stared up at those stone bristles. He could feel that a different kind of energy—or, at least, "energy" was the best word he could think of to describe it—was flowing down into the sphere through those, combining with the other energy and causing...*something* to happen?

He didn't understand it well enough to describe it. It was the clos-est thing to machinery that he'd seen since arriving in this labyrinth, completely different from all the workings he'd sensed. And yet some-how he understood that this shaft had nothing to do with moving walls or sliding floors or shifting passageways. This was something altogether different, something closer to a modern-day computer, perhaps, than to any kind of mechanical device.

He frowned at the thought. Yes. That was what it reminded him of. A computer. But not in the way his at home worked. There was no electricity. There were no electronics. There was no *data*. What he sensed had nothing to do with computers as he knew them. All he sensed was *emotions*.

But what the hell did *that* mean?

He stared at the mysterious sphere. It looked like the exact same stone that everything else in here was made of, but it was unique. He still didn't understand how he could know such things, yet it was clear to him that this particular hunk of rock had distinctly different proper-ties and a very specific purpose within the greater structure. He just wasn't entirely sure what those properties or that purpose were... Or how understanding such things was supposed to help him figure out where to go next...

He shifted his weight and tipped his head to one side. He even squinted a little at it all, but it didn't help.

The idea of a computer was still circling in his mind. This was something closer to the digital world than the mechanical one, he was beginning to realize. But there was nothing in his world that he could compare this to. Was it some sort of huge and ancient processor? The equivalent of a battery? A hyper-complex hard drive? The literal *brain* of this massive, alien machine?

"Maybe it's the Wi-Fi?" he muttered, then chuckled at himself. Although, on second thought, why not? Maybe this sphere had unique properties that allowed it to receive and send that strange energy with-out the use of conductive materials, explaining how it could move through the stone as if through wires.

Maybe this whole thing was some kind of server and everything that happened within all these walls was passed in and out of this one space through some impossibly fast process that he couldn't even imag-ine.

Or maybe he was just making stuff up and if Violet were here she'd tell him he was full of shit. That happened sometimes. She was good at keeping him grounded.

He gave up on the sphere for a while and turned his attention to those bristles again, and that strange "energy" that was pouring down from them. It was drastically different from what was flowing from below. What did it mean?

The fact was that he knew he probably wasn't going to figure any of this out. It was too alien. And it was likely based on concepts that were no longer even theoretically possible, or even *conceivable*. But without knowing which way he should go, all he could do was contemplate the possibilities and hope that something at some point jumped out at him, like it did with that hidden, fourth-dimensional whatever-it-was that he eventually managed to see through in that other intersection.

Old physics that no longer worked... The idea fascinated him. He couldn't stop wondering about it. The differences in the laws of nature and science between a dying world and a brand new one... What might have once been possible, as well as what might *yet* be possible someday. And that was only a single world. How many universes ago was this place built? How much time had passed? How many cycles had come around? And how much had changed in all those rotations?

His gaze settled on those bristles. They looked like ordinary stone, but they were all so perfectly sized, like everything else in this structure. Designed and built with laser-like precision.

Who *were* the sentinels? Did they possess unimaginable advanced technology? Or some kind of real-life magic, like Albert and Brandy described? Or did their entire civilization revolve around this one kind of gray stone?

So many questions...

And he'd always asked questions.

Chapter 81

Keith struggled to catch his breath. The wind had been knocked out of him and he'd struck the back of his head when he landed, dazing him and sending stars dancing through his vision.

He needed to snap out of it. He needed to focus. That monster... Nicole... The hounds... Too much going on...

He grunted and tried to roll over. The ground was hard and rocky. His elbows were stinging. Probably skinned and bloodied on the broken stone beneath him.

It stank even worse down here. He didn't think that was possible.

Somewhere above him, Nicole cried out.

He had to get up. He had to help her. He wasn't entirely sure *why*. After all, she'd never *needed* his help. Not once in her life. All he ever did was piss her off.

(*I know what a bitch I've been, but I wouldn't want you to not take care of yourself.*)

He growled, frustrated, and managed to push himself up onto his hands and knees.

He blinked into the darkness as his head began to clear. Right. The hounds. This was a terrible place to be. He sat up on his knees, his body tensing. Those things were fast. He'd seen them move. They could be on him in an instant. Would the smell of blood attract them even faster? He needed to be back on the upper level where they couldn't reach him. *Now.*

But his gaze fell on his flashlight. The impact must've knocked it from his grip because it was lying twelve feet away, aimed back at him, blinding him to whatever was directly behind it.

That was the only light he had. Nicole still had her cell phone, but that wouldn't last long if they had to rely on it. And they couldn't take on that zombified thug without a light.

But it was so far away. It was too dangerous. He'd never be able to grab it and get back onto the platform in time. There was no helping it at this point. He should leave it.

(*In foulest air, protect what shadows fear.*)

Wait... Was that what Cat Lady meant? The atmosphere of this room was definitely a good contestant for "foulest air." It reeked like hell in here. Could "protect what shadows fear" mean "don't abandon your light"? Was she telling him he was going to need it?

What kind of terrible advice was that? She was going to get him killed!

So many things going on... Indecision locked his muscles. He found himself frozen. Each second that ticked by was a second closer to one or more of those razor-covered beasts turning him into a Keith smoothie, but he couldn't focus. Everything felt tilted and off-kilter.

Again, Nicole cried out. What was happening up there? What was that thing doing to her?

He had to move!

He stumbled to his feet, cursing, and rushed forward.

This was stupid! He was going to be sliced and diced like a ripe tomato!

He stooped down, snatched up the light and thrust its beam into the shadows in front of him as he skidded to a halt and threw his weight back to flee.

But again, he froze.

His light struck the broad, prickly face of a hound roughly the size of a prize-winning hog. It was right there, hidden in the darkness until his light struck it. It wasn't making noise. Its scales weren't moving. It was just lying there, its flank flexing and relaxing. He could see four distinct nostrils flaring with each breath it took.

The better to smell you with! he thought with a shudder.

Was it asleep? The thing didn't have any eyes or ears, just as Nicole described. What it did have was tons of scars painted across its bony muzzle.

He was no labyrinth hound expert, but this thing had "alpha" written all over it...

Behind him, Nicole screamed. The sound snapped him out of it a little and he began to back away from the monster.

It couldn't see him. It couldn't hear him. But it was only a matter of seconds before it caught his scent.

Maybe less.

The thing let out a great snort and stiffened. Its countless scales rippled into action. It started at the thing's head and moved backward along its body, raising a cloud of dust in the process.

He'd never cursed as much as Nicole did. It just didn't appeal to him. It seemed unnecessary. Vulgarity for vulgarity's sake. But he made an exception as he turned and fled back the way he came. He said a really bad word. And he said it a *lot* of times.

He could hear the hound behind him. It sounded like it was right on his heels. Any second now it would run him down. And it was going to hurt like hell. Like being buried under a mountain of screaming power saws, maybe. Or getting sucked into a woodchipper. His would be a death worthy of the bloodiest horror movies.

The platform was right in front of him, but it was already too late. He'd never reach the wall in time.

And yet, somehow he did.

He tossed his flashlight up onto the walkway and then grabbed the ledge and jumped, scrambling upward. His arm screamed in protest, but he forced his way through it.

He was going to make it. It was going to be okay.

But something grabbed his foot before he could finish pulling himself up.

He was yanked down and backward. There was a sharp pain. And then his shoe was gone and he slammed against the wall. He was still gripping the ledge, but his feet were back on the ground. He looked over his shoulder to see the monster whipping his shoe back and forth in its bristling muzzle, chewing it to shreds, buying him one more precious moment of time. But only a moment. Another hound was already rushing toward him out of that endless darkness.

Again, he jumped up. Again, he swung his leg up over it (the other one this time) and ignored the screaming pain in his arm as he hauled himself upward.

He lay there, his heart thundering, as the space beath him erupted into a frenzy of snarls and growls and clashing scales. He didn't care to think too much about how close that was.

Nicole screamed, her voice seeming to drift from farther than it should have. He jumped to his feet and grabbed the light, but there was no sign of her or the monster. He rushed into the passageway where the thing surprised them. There was blood and something black splattered on the floor here. A trail led deeper into the passage.

Somewhere ahead of him, he heard Nicole scream again.

He ran forward, stumbling a little in his one remaining shoe.

What was this monster's obsession with Nicole, anyway? Why was it so hell-bent on kidnapping her?

And why they hell did he have to be the one trying to get her back? Stupid irony…

The path split. The trail of gore told him they went to the right.

But as soon as he turned the corner, a giant, broken hand closed around his neck and lifted him into the air, banging his head hard against the ceiling.

"Keith!"

"Yep," he grunted, dazed. Nicole was on the floor, crawling under the monster's twisted bulk as it turned its attention to him. "Still here…"

"Be careful!" she snapped.

Seriously? Did she think he was just dicking around here? Did it look to her like he was having fun?

He grabbed the monster's wrist and curled his body up, then thrust his foot into its crushed abdomen. He felt his remaining shoe sink much farther than it should have been able to. There was a *gut-wrenching* sound of cracking and squelching. And something black and vile spurted from another wound on the thing's chest. (That was just plain disgusting!) And yet the monster didn't even flinch!

"Aw, fuck," he coughed.

Then it slammed him against the wall and everything went dark.

Chapter 82

Everett was floating.

At least, it *felt* like floating. He couldn't feel anything beneath him. In fact, he couldn't feel anything at all. He seemed to be adrift in a strange, numbing void. Everything was darkness and silence and inexplicable emptiness. Even *he* felt somehow empty.

Was he even alive? Was his heart still beating? Did he still *have* a heart?

The last thing he remembered was Violet standing in front of that strange stone, looking unsettlingly lost and out of place. Was it some kind of trap? Did something bad happen to her? He wanted to get her away from there, but he never had the chance. The things below… They gathered so quickly…rose upward…reached out for him…

Then everything went fuzzy. How much time had passed since then?

It was hard to focus. Something wasn't right. His memory was growing hazy, as if even his *mind* were going numb.

This was bad. He couldn't forget everything. He needed to get back to Violet. He needed to make sure she was okay. They needed to stick together. Otherwise, she'd be left all alone up there. She didn't want that. She told him as much. She needed him to help her find Andrea. And her friend… What was his name again? Coby? Connor? And then there was… What were their names again?

It was getting harder and harder to remember things…

Where was he? Why was this place so big? And how was he going to find his way back if he couldn't even remember where "back" was?

I'm not afraid of dying, he thought. *Not anymore.* And it was the truth. He'd conquered that fear. His mother's poisonous words couldn't hold him back any longer. But he *was* afraid of letting his friends down. He needed to wake up. He needed to clear his head. He needed to get back to them!

Somehow, he managed to open his eyes.

But that was a mistake.

What he saw in that hopeless void was far more than he expected. It was like looking directly into the burning core of the sun, blinding and burning and all-encompassing. Except that it wasn't brightness that he saw. It was *darkness*. The kind of darkness that only existed in the deepest, emptiest holes in the maddeningly vast, farthest reaches of the true universe.

Chapter 83

Where was it?

Andrea felt her chest hitch as she plunged her hands into the reeking muck, rummaging through the filth.

It had to be down there somewhere!

She'd been struggling through the mud for what felt like hours but was probably mere minutes. It was painfully slow progress, after all, dragging herself through the thick, grimy sludge. Her legs and back ached from the effort of it. Three times, she lost her balance and fell. Twice she'd ended up with her face below the putrid surface and come up spitting and gagging.

But the third time she fell, the sucking goop held tight to her sneaker and she pulled her foot out of it. Now she couldn't find it.

It didn't make sense. Even in this perpetual darkness, the hard layer of crust dried over the top of the mud showed her exactly where she'd been, yet she didn't feel it down there when she tried slowly retracing her steps. Was it buried all the way down at the bottom? Or had she somehow pushed it to one side, out of reach?

It should be *right here*. But even resting her flashlight on the crusty surface and plunging her arms into the stagnant muck until her cheek was pressed against the foul surface didn't help. It was as if something snatched it away as soon as her foot slipped out of it...but that was an idea she definitely didn't want to dwell on. She didn't think she could handle the thought of something *living* down there.

She stood up, her weary body aching, wincing at the putrid stench enveloping her, and let out a frustrated cry as she tried to shake the filth off her hands. She didn't care what heard her. It didn't seem to matter anymore. She was completely over this awful place!

And yet she noticed that those eerie voices were no longer mocking her whenever she spoke. That was an improvement, at least.

A small one.

She waded forward another step and reached down into the cold, grimy mud again, groaning at the awful stench as she sank deeper into it, all the way to her chest, right up to her grimacing face. She hated this, but she wasn't leaving here without her shoe.

And it wasn't as if she weren't already covered from head to toe in this nasty stuff...

Where was it?

Wait... She frowned. Was that it? Her fingertips brushed against something, briefly but certainly. There was something there! Only a little deeper...

She squeezed her eyes closed and turned her head, probing a little farther with one hand. She felt her left ear sink into the cold sludge and shuddered at the feel of it, both gritty and slimy.

It was *right there*. She was touching it. She closed her hand around it...

But that was no shoe.

Something cold and slick squirmed against her closed fingers.

She screamed and tried to yank her hand away, but the mud sucked at her, holding onto her, forcing her to fight it.

She staggered backward, yanking her arm out with a grotesque squelching and belching of rancid muck, only to fall over backward the second it finally let her go, forcing her to struggle back to her feet again.

Why did it have to be so hard to move? She couldn't get away fast enough! What if the thing she touched was slithering toward her right now, angry about being disturbed? She tried to turn around, but again, the sucking mud gripped her feet.

She snatched up her flashlight and battled against it, retreating in maddening slow motion, tripping and clawing, her heart pounding in her chest, her breath escaping in short, ragged gasps, desperate to escape whatever fresh horror was lurking at the bottom of this foul pit, fighting it with each and every step. But it was a losing battle. The mud resisted her every movement, sucking at her legs, threatening to pull her under. Her feet felt like lead weights. Every step required all of her strength. Again, she stumbled and fell. Again, the filthy quagmire tried to swallow her. Again she fought her way back to her feet, aware of every agonizing second that she wasted battling the oppressive mire.

She couldn't even see! The flashlight was again covered in goop. It was little more than a dull, brownish glow in her hand. At this rate, she could be *swarmed* by foul, slimy, slithery things before she even knew they were coming!

She raked the lens clean, vaguely aware that she was practically sobbing with each exhausted breath she released, then turned and shined the grimy beam behind her, convinced that some wriggling, writhing abomination must be rising up from the black and odorous depths.

But there was nothing. The same crusty surface stretched out as far as the light reached in every direction, broken only by the pungent path she was leaving in her wake.

She was sure she hadn't imagined it. Something moved down there. She could still feel the grotesque sensation of it against her unsuspecting fingers. Her skin was still crawling. It was like closing her hand around a fat, squirming eel.

Her heart was still racing. She felt lightheaded, as if she might soon faint if she couldn't get herself under control. But it was so hard to calm her nerves. She was so deeply afraid. Tears were streaming down her face again and she couldn't even wipe them away without smearing this festering goop into her eyes.

"Get a grip," she whispered to herself. Nothing was back there. Nothing was moving. Everything was silent. Whatever it was she touched under all that mud, it wasn't coming to get her.

But she was still on her own. No one was coming to rescue her. That stupid Stella impostor had probably made sure of that. And even if someone *did* happen to stumble across this room, who in their right mind would try to cross it? The best she could hope for was someone to catch a glimpse of her light and call out to her, but she didn't even know how big this stinking, oversized mudhole was. She could be standing in the middle of an *ocean* of it, for all she knew.

She blinked hard. She sniffed back the tears. She tried again to spit away the foul taste in her mouth, but it was as stubborn as the darkness and the stench.

At least she could tell which way she came from. That was something. Her best bet was to keep pushing on in a straight line and just keep hoping it couldn't possibly go on forever.

She stumbled and fell again as she tried to turn around. A wave of weary frustration rolled over her and a great, frustrated sob escaped her.

She didn't want to do this anymore.

She didn't want to be here.

She didn't ask for any of this.

Again, she righted herself and pushed onward, forcing her way through the stagnant muck, wondering how much longer she was going to have to endure this torture.

Chapter 84

Nicole was able to crawl out from under the monster thanks to Keith's distraction, but at what cost? Even over the racket of the hounds in the nearby chamber, she heard the sound of his head striking the stone. From the corner of her eye, she saw him fall to the floor in a heap, saw his flashlight roll away...

That was all the distraction she was going to get.

She jumped to her feet and fled.

It pained her to leave him like that. He could be badly hurt, but Hotdog's repulsive god was clearly after her, not him. She was sure it would forget about him in order to pursue her. She was counting on it. *I'll be back!* she thought at him, as if she could simply will the message to reach him.

He's already dead, Goar Nangup taunted her in her own head with her own voice.

Blow it out your ancient ass! she fired back at the creep. It was no wonder the only follower this so-called god had was a psycho pervert with an unfortunate name.

She withdrew her cell phone and turned the flashlight back on.

The chamber of the hounds loomed ahead of her. There were now several snarling beasts fighting just beyond the walkway. And as she stepped into the room, they immediately grew more agitated.

Keith had managed to get out of there before those things turned him into mincemeat, but it seemed his scent had stirred them up. If she were to fall down there, she wouldn't last twenty seconds.

(God only knew how they could smell *anything* in this reeking chamber, though.)

Keeping close to the wall, as far from those beasts as possible, she made her way back along the walkway.

She had no idea what she was going to do. She was clearly no match for that monster. All she *could* do was keep moving and hope to stay ahead of it. But how far could she go and still realistically find her way back to help Keith? She needed to think of something soon.

But when she looked back, the mangled corpse was already chasing her. Worse, it wasn't bothering to run or even walk. It was crawling on the wall like something out of her worst nightmares. And it was moving with startling speed. It was already almost on her.

You can't escape!

She screamed and tried to run faster, but that foul, sack-of-sticks-and-rocks hand closed around the back of her shirt and yanked her off her feet. She fell backward, her butt slamming against the stone, a terrified shriek escaping her.

Her cell phone clattered across the floor and landed out of reach, its light cast upward, leaving the monster attacking her in stark shadow.

Then the thing was right in her face again, that horrible, bloated mouth stretched open and oozing black and bloody gore down its discolored chin. She could feel it dripping on her legs, cold and foul, making her skin crawl.

But far worse was the bloated and discolored tongue that seemed to unroll itself from between its filthy teeth and dangle in front of her face.

"Ugh!" She scrambled backward, away from it, but it crawled after her, that awful, broken hand groping at her, yanking at her shirt. What did it mean to do to her? She didn't understand why it hadn't just killed her. It was more than capable. For all she knew it might have already killed Keith.

No. She couldn't think like that. She *wouldn't*. He'd be fine. She lured it away from him before it could hurt him any worse. She had to have. She couldn't bear the thought of any other outcome.

Dead! the foul corpse puppet screamed into her head. *Skull crushed! Brain dashed!*

"*Fucking liar!*" she screamed back at it. Like she'd believe anything this monster said.

It was forcing itself closer to her, that oozing, gaping mouth descending on her. That awful, blotchy tongue dangling.

She thrust one arm against the thing's bloody chest and continued to use the other to keep scooting backward. There was nowhere left to go. All she could do was back herself against the wall and keep fighting it as long as possible. Maybe Keith would wake up and come to her rescue again. Or maybe one of the others would show up. Albert or Wayne or Corey could still rush in to be her hero. That was how this stuff worked, right? Everything was according to the Keeper's plan, right down to the last second?

Except, maybe she wasn't a part of the Keeper's plan. She was just the tagalong, after all. Maybe she wasn't meant to be here. Maybe that's why this stuff kept happening to her. Ada said the little creep didn't make mistakes, that there must be a reason she was involved. But what if she was wrong? What if she was the Keeper's *one mistake*? One he intended to fix?

She felt her shoulders strike the wall and drew her legs up.

Fuck the Keeper and his plans. She wasn't going to let that gross little freak write her future for her. If this pile of rancid flesh wanted her, it was going to have the fight of its life!

She felt the monster yanking at her shirt. She could hear the seams ripping. Was it only holding her by it, or did it mean to rip it off of her? Did this abomination intend to *rape* her?

"In your dreams you repulsive fuck!"

She shoved back at the thing with all her strength. Step by step she moved her feet upward, planting the soles of her sneakers higher and higher against the monster's crumpled chest, wedging herself between it and the wall, trying to make it impossible for it to do whatever the fuck it was trying to do with that awful, swollen tongue.

Her right foot pressed against the thing's chest and she felt the flesh give where its ribs were broken. It felt horridly spongy. And it made the thing make a terrible gurgling sound in its dead throat. Droplets of blood and black goo began flying out at her face. She could feel it on her skin, cold and repulsive. It made her want to puke.

She didn't think there was enough disinfecting soap in the whole world to make her feel clean again once this was over.

She grunted and pushed the thing back again, moving her foot a little higher. It was firmer there. The bones there were still intact.

The monster twisted its neck to one side, far more than it should have been able to, far enough to kill a human being, and made a hideous cracking sound. Then that horrid face and oozing tongue were moving toward her again, the flesh seeming to stretch like rubber.

It was now or never.

With all her strength, she thrust her legs outward. She had strong legs, after all. She jogged. She worked out. She was in great shape. Using the wall for leverage, she shoved the thing off her.

She watched the undead monstrosity topple backward, that awful, oozing face staring back at her with that one dead eye.

Then it disappeared over the edge of the walkway and dropped to the floor below where she could still hear the agitated hounds scuffling.

Hotdog's corpse made no sound, nor did his fucked-up god scream anything into her mind, which she found surprisingly unsatisfying. She sort of wanted to hear the murderous pervert wail in terror, she realized. She kind of deserved that much after all they'd put her through, didn't she? But there *was* sound. Wet. Violent. With tearing and ripping and squelching and splattering. A great spray of blood and that grotesque black goo spewed up and rained down around her.

And then there was nothing but the snarling and droning of the feasting hounds below.

She closed her eyes and leaned back against the wall, exhausted. It was finally over. Hotdog and his so-called god were gone. They couldn't hurt her or her friends anymore.

She might even have an appetite again in a week or so...

Gross.

But she couldn't just lie here. Slowly, she rose to her feet. She needed to check on Keith. *Please, let him be okay.* She couldn't stand the thought of walking back there and finding him dead like the ancient creep claimed.

He simply *couldn't* be dead. She had too much to apologize for.

But as she stepped toward her dropped phone, she had to stop. The room was spinning. She felt lightheaded.

Had she stood up too fast? Did she expend too much energy?

She stumbled and her heart leapt at the thought of falling into that awful monster den with Hotdog's filthy remains. She leaned against the wall and closed her eyes.

What was happening? What was wrong with her? She rubbed at her forehead, willing her head to clear, then opened her eyes and stared at her hand. Hotdog Creep's blood dotted her skin. Along with that horrid black goo.

Was it...bubbling?

Anun amum ut mu...

Her heart was racing again. "No..." She tried to wipe the foul gore onto her shorts, but everything was tilting. She stumbled. She swooned.

Hotdog was gone for good now, but of course his filthy god was still out there. This black stuff was some kind of extension of him. She didn't understand how she knew this, but she did. Without his faithful servant, his connection was dying, but not before he could get his ancient claws into her...

She turned and stumbled toward the passageway where Keith was lying. She needed him. She needed *someone*.

But she stumbled and fell.

Everything faded to darkness.

Anun amum Goar Nangup...

Chapter 85

Again, Corey managed to find his way. With the three intersecting shafts and the strange sphere at his back, he continued onward.

It wasn't anything he could really describe. There was no great sign to point the way, no "ah-ha" realization that he was missing the forest for the trees. Instead, as he sat there, he simply and very slowly came to the realization that he understood where the energy that was flowing up through the vertical shaft was going.

There were four specific components hidden within the enormous stone structure. Terminals, not unlike the control panels he located outside the city wall. Three of them required some form of interaction before the fourth could be activated. That fourth terminal, he somehow knew without a doubt, was the doorway Albert and Brandy said they were all here to open.

This was why they kept getting split up. There was more than one destination they were supposed to find. Not everyone was going to reach the door. Some of them, like him, were supposed to locate these terminals and likely other destinations scattered throughout the labyrinth.

The only question remaining was which terminal was *his* destination.

The answer didn't come in any easily describable manner. It wasn't as if he found some subtle arrow pointing this way. It was something in the flow of the energy itself. Something about *this* direction. It felt *incomplete* somehow. Like it was lacking something. Almost like it *needed* him...

It was an odd way to think of it, he thought, but that was the best way he could describe it. Something about this direction simply felt like it required his attention. It was probably something to do with the way his brain was struggling to process the unfamiliar input, he assumed. But the fact remained that there was something that needed done *this way*.

Something *he* needed to do.

After following the horizontal shaft for about two hundred feet, it abruptly narrowed, forcing him to continue on his hands and knees.

Here, the walls of the shaft changed from smooth, uniform stone to an odd pattern of rounded, squiggly grooves. There were no more structures in here like those stone bristles, which was good because he wasn't sure he could have crawled through a space any smaller than this one. He was barely able to navigate his formidable bulk through here as it was. But the strange shape of the shaft walls looked oddly and unsettlingly *anatomical*, as if he were crawling through some stone giant's guts. It reminded him of the yawning stone man they passed through when they entered the Denselands and how he teased Violet about there being an exit to match the entrance.

Suddenly, it didn't seem quite as amusing anymore...

But this wasn't something anatomical. The City Beyond Memory wasn't *alive*. He could sense that energy flowing around him as well as that uncanny sensation of it flowing under his skin. The shapes in the stone here acted like cables, he realized, carrying and directing that energy along distinct pathways, breaking it apart, directing it, applying it to whatever was waiting for him at the end. More like a circuit board...

He was almost there.

As the suffocating jaws of claustrophobia began to close around him, he distracted himself by focusing on the energy itself. He wondered if that really was some lingering remnant of a long-dead universe or if it might simply be something no one understood yet. Could it be at all possible, if only he could make himself understand it better, that he might be able to learn to utilize it in his own world? What kinds of possibilities would something like that allow? What impossible dreams could be transformed into reality? It could be the key to turning science fiction into reality, catapulting the world to the next level of technology.

But of course, even if he understood how it worked, he had a feeling this gray stone was a crucial element in the process. And there could be precious little of it in his own world, far too little to utilize, much less manufacture.

The end of the shaft came into view up ahead. Except it wasn't really the end. Instead, it turned ninety degrees upward. He was going to have to climb. And the vertical portion was just as small as this one.

It was a tight squeeze, making the turn. He wasn't able to fit into it upright. He had to roll himself over onto his back and wriggle into it, his big belly fighting his every move.

Fortunately, it wasn't a very tall shaft. Once he managed to get up onto his feet, he could reach up and grab the top of it. From there it was a simple matter of climbing into the roomier space above.

The energy was different now, he realized. Before, it had reminded him of a flowing stream, coursing through the passageway around him, but now it reminded him more of a waterfall. That same energy seemed to be breaking apart in a great, open spray, for lack of a better explanation. In his head he imagined a breaker box in a basement with the main power line running into it and dozens of smaller wires reaching out from it.

Whatever he was looking for was right in front of him. He was almost there.

He stepped up to the wall waiting there without hesitating. It wasn't a dead end. He'd already dealt with something like this before. He just had to remember how to open it. Something about reaching *into* the stone...

He couldn't remember exactly how he did it, of course. He didn't even understand it while he was doing it. But somehow his fingers recalled the trick for him. It was like muscle memory. There was another of those weird, lurching sensations in his gut and then the stone rearranged itself. He was looking into a small chamber filled with dozens of oddly shaped protrusions of the same gray stone, each one textured with those curious, curled carvings, making them look a little like protruding *brains*. There were other boxy shapes jutting from the walls as well, each one covered in small, round holes. There was a sort of hourglass-shaped column in the center, surrounded by thin, stone cylinders of various lengths descending from the ceiling. And there were several triangular columns reaching from the floor to the ceiling around those.

He knew in an instant that it was one of the terminals. He'd arrived where he was supposed to be. But that didn't seem to matter very much in the moment. He was far too distracted by the grisly scene at his feet.

There was blood everywhere. Strange strands of what looked like fine, gore-soaked strings were strewn about the space. And lying in the middle of it was a dead body, ripped entirely in half.

The wall disappeared so quickly that he wasn't given a moment's warning. He was shown every gruesome detail with no chance to brace himself. But on the other hand he also wasn't given a single moment to wonder if the body lying before him might belong to Violet or Gina or anyone else he cared about.

It was only Austin.

He felt kind of bad being relieved to know it was him and not anyone else, but the guy was a jerk. He *chose* to go off on his own and leave them all behind, after all. This was what he got.

Violet would call it karma.

He shined his light around the room, looking for whatever could have done this, acutely aware that it could still be here somewhere, waiting to pounce and do the same to him. But everything was silent. And there weren't many places for something to hide.

Austin's murderer seemed to have moved on.

Cautiously, he crept forward, surveying the scene. This must be the reason he felt that he was needed here. Austin didn't finish his job. Maybe that was his role in all this. Maybe he was the backup in case things went south for any of the others.

But he couldn't really think about that right now. There was something bothering him about this scene.

Austin was torn completely in half, but where were his entrails? There was nothing here but blood and those strange coils of gory strings.

He shined his light onto Austin's face, looking him in his dead eyes, feeling as if the man were staring right back at him in spite of the fact that he was clearly dead.

Why were they still so clear? They weren't glazed over at all. How recently did this happen?

Then, bizarrely enough, those eyes *blinked*.

"Don't just stand there," huffed Austin. "Assist me, please."

About the author

Brian Harmon is an independent author of horror fiction, suspense and dark adventure. He grew up in rural Missouri and now lives in Southern Wisconsin with his wife, Guinevere, and their three children.

For more about Brian Harmon and his work, visit
www.BrianHarmonBooks.com